LUNA GLOBAL MEDIA

Suncrest Dv. Melbourne, FL

+1 312 212 3899 U.S.

https://lunaglobalmedia.com/

Starseed

The opinions expressed by the author are not necessarily those of LUNA GLOBAL MEDIA the publishers of this book.

ISBN (Paperback): 979-8-9909829-0-1

Printed in the United States of America

Starseed

Jack Brown

Table of Contents

Chapter 1
<1>
1985

Jamarcus Bridge lay on the living room floor in front of his brothers and sister, absorbed in his mother's college textbook on cosmology. From a young age, Jamarcus had been fascinated with space. His soul held a quiet bliss while he read as his siblings watched music videos on the television set. He didn't know why, but thinking about space always gave him pure joy. His favorite television shows and movies were science fiction: *Battlestar Galactica*, *Star Wars*, and *Star Trek*. The imagery of those epics held him—not just the technology but the different worlds and alien species he saw in them. It always made him happy.

Science had become a passion now that he was eight years old. At the time, his mother was in college, pursuing a degree in psychology. Jamarcus had been able to read by the time he was two. By the time he was five, he had already moved past the childhood storybooks his parents had given him and started reading novels. When he got to age eight, he got bored with his books and stole his mother's schoolbooks. Her book on cosmology drew him in. He read about different types of stars and the planets surrounding them, galaxies, comets, black holes, and asteroids. To Jamarcus, those objects didn't feel like faraway things up in the night sky. They were normal things—things he saw outside his window.

"Jamarcus, why are you so skinny?" his sister asked, causing his brothers to laugh. Jamarcus ignored her and continued reading. "Why aren't you watching the video?" she added in an angry voice. "Why are you always reading? You act so white."

Jamarcus continued to ignore his sister and retreated into his mother's book, as he usually did when his siblings picked on him. Reading about science made him feel whole, feeding his natural curiosity. When Jamarcus began reading about the planets in the solar system, his curiosity turned into a passion.

Venus was the first planet he focused on, mainly because his family was religious, and Venus represented Lucifer in Christianity. However, Jamarcus felt he was pushing past his religion and focusing more on science. When he first saw pictures of Venus's atmosphere, his mind went wild with curiosity about what could have caused its cloudy appearance. He learned that Earth's atmosphere was a combination of the chemicals raised from its surface when it was still forming and the water that came down from repeated meteor strikes.

Perhaps Venus's climate was similar to Earth's, except warmer because it was closer to the sun. Maybe there was life on Venus, he thought—microbial, if not more. But no, that wasn't the case, Jamarcus soon learned, because Venus's atmosphere was caused by severe greenhouse gases, and the temperatures on Venus were too high to support life as it was known on Earth. The surface of Venus was nothing but a barren wasteland. Jamarcus imagined that an ancient civilization similar to humanity had lived on Venus long ago. Perhaps chemicals produced by their industry had caused the temperature to rise on their planet, killing all life in their world.

Jamarcus flipped through the book until he came to another planet: Mars. His excitement grew as he read to see if life could be found in that world. His hope soon faded as he read more about it. The temperatures on Mars were cooler than those on Earth but not by much. That was an encouraging thing. But Jamarcus learned that Mars's atmosphere was thinner than Earth's and did not give much protection from the sun's radiation. Furthermore, what little oxygen was in Mars's atmosphere wasn't enough to allow humans to live there. Disappointed, Jamarcus went about looking at pictures of Mars's surface. Suddenly, there it was: a massive stone face looking up into the sky.

That's it, Jamarcus thought as he searched for more information on the formation: the Face of Cydonia. From what Jamarcus read, NASA believed the face was just a trick on the eyes—that the image taken by the orbiter sent there had caught a natural formation at the right angle as the sun cast a shadow to make the formation look like a face. That might have been the case, but to Jamarcus, it still looked man-made.

Maybe it's a group of structures that were built on a raised surface, Jamarcus guessed, and he looked for more pictures of the area around the face. That was when he saw the mountains. They looked like pyramids. As soon as Jamarcus saw those structures, he walked to his mother's bookshelf and grabbed a book on ancient civilizations.

"Why are you walking on your toes?" His sister started in on him again.

Jamarcus barely listened to her as he returned and sat back down. He opened the book and found the section focusing on Egypt. He learned that the name for the capital of Egypt, Cairo, stood for the planet Mars. From that moment, Jamarcus shifted his attention to mythology since Mars was the Roman god of war. He went back to the bookshelf and retrieved his mother's book on mythology. She didn't have many books on Egyptian mythology, but she did have one on Greek mythos that he could read.

Soon Jamarcus realized that not only were the names for the planets based on the Greek gods and titans, but there were constellations of other Greek figures. *Clash of the Titans* was still showing on television, so Jamarcus began studying the constellations of Pegasus and Andromeda. Next were Hercules, Leo, and Orion. Having learned everything, he could about the mythical figures as well as where those stars were in space, Jamarcus gathered up his mother's sky charts and went outside to lie down in his backyard. He looked up at the night sky and watched the stars slowly march across the horizon over the Chesapeake Bay.

It didn't take long for Jamarcus to find his first constellation. Orion stood large over him, with the three stars at his waist shining like a diamond belt. With more searching, he found Gemini and, close to it, Pegasus. Looking around, he saw the M-shaped constellation of Cassiopeia. From there, he looked over to the Big Dipper. Jamarcus knew the Big Dipper was part of the Big Bear, and with little help, he found the Little Bear and the Fisher.

Jamarcus's mother and father had begun to think a while ago that his studying mythical European stories was weird for a black child. Since they had been unable to find any books on any African gods and they both had Native American ancestry, they had given Jamarcus a book on Native American legends. It hadn't taken long for him to devour the book, and of all the stories he read, the one that stood out to him most was the tale of the Fisher and the Bears.

According to the legend, a long time ago, a Great Bear stole the warm winds of summer and kept them for herself and her cub, retreating into the dream world above the night sky. As winter grew long, a group of animals, led by the Fisher, gathered together and decided to use all their skills to get into the night sky and bring back summer. After cutting a hole into the heavens, the animals managed to sneak by Mother Bear and steal the summer winds back. However, as they tried to go back through the hole they'd made, the Great Bear gave chase to them, followed by her cub. All the animals managed to escape through the hole except for the Fisher, as the Great Bear shot an arrow through his tail just as the hole closed. Ever since then, the Great Bear and the Little Bear had given chase to the Fisher among the stars.

Because of that story, Jamarcus would stare at the constellation of the Fisher at night, which he now learned was also called the Pleiades. As Jamarcus lay in the grass, looking at those stars, something stirred in his soul, something akin to how he felt when someone spoke of Jesus at church.

"Boy, get your butt in the house!" his father yelled at him from the back door. "How long are you going to lie out here?"

"I was only outside for a couple of minutes," Jamarcus told his dad as he got off the grass and picked up his mother's sky charts.

"You've been out here for over an hour." His father scowled at him as he came inside. "Get your butt into bed. Damn, you're so absentminded."

Jamarcus rushed to his room to go to sleep. He didn't have much joy in life outside of reading about science, but he did like going to sleep so he could dream. Jamarcus experienced vivid dreams so immersive that he could remember minute details from them. He'd told his mother about them before, but she just said that individuals couldn't remember their dreams and that he was probably making them up, so Jamarcus had stopped telling her about the dreams altogether.

Later that night, as Jamarcus slept, he found himself in another crystal-clear dream. He was in a dark room that seemed to be underground. As he walked about, he saw tree-root pillars coming down from the ceiling and piercing the floor, which was covered with thick earth. After a few moments of walking, he noticed a light like the sun behind a pillar, and when he approached it, he was surprised to find a little boy producing the light. He had blond hair the color of the light that shone from within his chest. He wore a white full-body suit that showed his chubby physique, with only his face and hands showing. His skin tone was pale white with pink freckles. This confused Jamarcus. He didn't know many white people, so he was surprised he'd be able to come up with such detailed features for one in a dream. Jamarcus and the toddler began walking toward each other at the same pace.

"Hello?" Jamarcus said.

"Hello," the boy responded, and he reached out and grabbed Jamarcus's hand.

Now closer to him, Jamarcus noticed his face was a little odd. Either his eyes were a bit bigger than normal, or his lips and nose were a bit smaller. His eyes were a fierce shade of blue and looked as if they glowed. There also seemed to be a bubble surrounding him that caused everything Jamarcus saw beside and behind the boy to curve, as if he were looking through a drop of water.

At that moment, Jamarcus noticed they were not alone. Behind the little boy were tall dark-colored beings that appeared to be locust people. Their eyes were large and black, and their arms and legs were long and skinny. Their hands had three fingers and a thumb. Their feet had four toes, and they stood on them like cats or dogs. From all the science-fiction movies he had seen, Jamarcus assumed the locust people were bad. Still thinking he was in a dream, Jamarcus drew the little boy close to him.

"Stay close. I'll protect you," Jamarcus said.

"You don't have to do that," the little boy replied.

Jamarcus ignored him and took the boy away from the locust men. He led him through the darkness and root pillars until he came to a door with blinding light shining through it.

"Go through. I'll stand guard," Jamarcus said.

"We don't have to leave," the little boy said, but Jamarcus shooed him into the light before entering himself.

For a moment, Jamarcus was surrounded by light—and then he heard the shrill beeping of his alarm clock. He opened his eyes and realized he was in his bed. However, there was light shining from the mirror above his dresser. As he stepped out of bed and walked to the mirror, he saw the little boy from his dream standing in it. When he reached out to touch the mirror, the little boy reached out also, and their hands met at the same spot. For a moment, they stood that way, staring into each other's eyes.

"Boy, turn your alarm off!" Jamarcus's mother yelled, and he woke up back in his bed.

Who was that? Jamarcus thought to himself, staring at the ceiling. But fear of his mother got him to get out of bed and turn off his alarm clock so he could get ready for school.

<2>

While lying in his bed, Jamarcus read a book on ancient Egypt. Seeing the structures on the surface of Mars, he imagined that people in the past, like the Egyptians, had been part of an advanced civilization similar to the people in the movie *Dune* and that they somehow had learned to fly through space and go to Mars. He was intrigued when he learned that the Great Pyramids of Giza represented the stars on the belt of Orion.

Read about the Mayans, a female voice said in his head, and without thinking, Jamarcus retrieved another book, one about the people of Central and South America. He was amazed to find out that there were also pyramids on the Yucatan Peninsula, at a place called Teotihuacan. The pyramids there were aligned with Orion's belt, and the buildings represented the sun and the planets in the solar system.

Jamarcus wondered about the odds of two civilizations parted by an ocean, with no known means of contacting one another, somehow deciding to build pyramids based on Orion's belt. And where had that voice come from? He'd heard the voice multiple times ever since he'd had the dream. Jamarcus's family went to church often, and he was very religious. Jamarcus thought the voice was of a guardian angel watching him while he read. But what if there was another explanation?

Jamarcus grabbed one of his mother's textbooks on psychology and read through it until he came to the topic of schizophrenia, a men-

8

tal disorder in which individuals heard or saw things that seemed real to them but were only in their heads. From then on, Jamarcus decided not to tell anyone about the voices and visions he heard and saw.

The one time he was tempted to tell was when his grandfather and grandmother decided to come for a visit. Jamarcus's mother cooked a meal for the occasion, and the whole family sat around the dinner table, talking to each other. Jamarcus sat staring at his father and grandfather when he saw a man step between them.

It looked as if the man stepped out from behind a cloak that showed what was directly behind it to whoever looked straight at it. He was a white man dressed in brown slacks, a white dress shirt, and a red suit jacket. When Jamarcus saw him, his eyes went wide with shock, but he didn't say anything. The man turned to Jamarcus when he noticed that Jamarcus could see him. With a smile, the man turned around and walked toward the wall behind him, fading away with each step like smoke.

"What are you looking at?" Jamarcus's father asked him, but Jamarcus only shook his head in response. He didn't want anyone to think he was crazy.

He talked to his parents about his idea that all the ancient civilizations were connected somehow in the past. He told them of his idea that Ezekiel's wheel probably had been an aircraft, which also could explain the Aztec god Quetzalcoatl. He also told them that maybe the gods in ancient Greece hadn't been gods but had been the stories they'd used to explain technology they couldn't understand. Maybe God in the Bible, and maybe even Jesus himself, could have been an alien. Soon afterward, Jamarcus's parents handed him a book written by Zecharia Sitchin: *The Chariots of the Gods*. In it, the author proposed the same questions he had, with the summary that mankind had been in contact with aliens in the far past.

As Jamarcus read about the Mayans, a vision came to him like a waking dream. He saw a land that appeared to be a city in ancient Egypt, in all its glory. The land was green and fertile, and the large pyramids and other structures were decorated with blue hieroglyphics and pictures. Above the city were craft that didn't have rockets or jet engines propelling them. They were either large, dome-shaped ships that seemed to float in the air or craft that looked like the Star Destroyers in *Star Wars*. The people in the land were ruddy, with a skin color that appeared more red than brown. He saw a group of them speaking to three tall white figures; two had long black hair, and one was blond.

"Jamarcus!" a female voice called out.

Jamarcus instinctively went to his mother in her bedroom, as he thought she'd summoned him. "Yes, ma'am?"

"I didn't call you," his mother said.

Jamarcus went back to his room and read more about other ancient civilizations. He started reading about India and how the gods in their mythology came down from the heavens in flying cities. The gods went to war with one another, either using the cities or flying through the air themselves. They used weapons that sounded like modern devices, such as heat-seeking missiles or laser beams. In one battle, a weapon was used that resembled the description of an atomic bomb, from its initial destruction to its radioactive aftermath.

"Jamarcus!" the female voice called out again, and again, he went to his mother.

"The next time you hear that voice, say, 'Yes, God?'" his mother suggested after he explained what was going on.

He returned to his room and his book. After reading some more, he heard the voice call his name once again.

"Yes, God?" Jamarcus said, but he didn't get an answer.

It would be a long time before Jamarcus heard that voice again.

Chapter 2
<1>
1989

The vivid dreams still came to Jamarcus regularly, and they were all connected. The dreams were based on the same environment and persons, and where one dream ended the next one would begin. One set of dreams began in or around a large chateau. It was located on an island that had many sandy and grassy knolls, with beaches composed of both sand and stone. There were other homes on the island, many of which were mansions.

The chateau Jamarcus dreamed about was set on a large hill, with several acres surrounded by a low stone wall. The building was both redwood and gray stone. The central base of it was a mansion itself, with a wooden tower above the entrance. One wing of the chateau was a regular house that had a stone gazebo with red wooden pillars. Behind the chateau was a forest with a dirt path that led to the back exit of the stone wall, where a beach was located. After walking through the grass that separated the wall from the beach, he saw a large, flat rock that stuck out of the sand at a low angle. At high tide, individuals could sit on that rock surface, have the waves wash over their feet, stay dry, and have no sand in their clothes. Jamarcus had many dreams in which he ran up and down that hill, or he would run along the stone wall. He also ran down the path and climbed up and down the rock as the waves washed over it.

Jamarcus wasn't alone when he played by the chateau. A girl he called the Bug Girl always accompanied him. Jamarcus knew the being was a girl because he could hear and feel her voice in his mind. She wore no clothes; was white all over; and had a skinny torso, legs, and arms. Her eyes were insect-like: they looked like black surfaces where eye sockets normally would have been, and they had swirling patterns in them. Her nose and mouth were small, and she didn't have any ears. She seemed like the locust people from the dream he'd had years ago, but they had been more like insects walking on two feet. Bug Girl seemed to be both an insect and a human. Jamarcus was fierce friends with the being, and they played roughly with each other, always laughing uncontrollably.

If the two of them weren't running up and down hills or through the forest in the back, they were causing a riot in the chateau. As one entered the front door, there was a clock by a wall on the left. It was a tall grandfather clock, but most of its body was missing. It looked like a polished rectangular wooden box that floated in the air. It housed a large pendulum that swung below a clock face, but no string or material attached it. When Jamarcus peered inside the clock, he could see cogs of different sizes and makes, all spinning along each other in mid-air, and he could feel the mechanisms vibrate as the gears worked on a part of the clock that was invisible.

Right by the clock was a hidden door that, if one didn't know it was there, was all but invisible. The door was small but tall enough for Bug Girl and Jamarcus to enter. The door led to a corridor connected to passageways and stairs that went to every room in the chateau. There were many types of rooms Jamarcus explored. One was a large library that was three stories tall. Texts filled bookshelves that lined the walls of the room, which were shaped like an even cross with round edges. Jamarcus would climb up and down the stairs of the library, grabbing any book he wanted, and if he couldn't reach one, he was able to float up to where the book was. The books used a language that Jamarcus couldn't read. The text looked like glyphs but not like any Jamarcus remembered reading about. The glyphs somehow placed information in his mind as he read them.

One book Jamarcus read was a history of a people who lived in a galaxy far from the Milky Way. It dealt mostly with the politics and ethnic groups of the people, which Jamarcus found boring, so he stopped reading after a few moments. Another book Jamarcus found, which scared Bug Girl, was one that described all types of life that existed in a plane between the third and fourth dimensions. The animals would appear as shadows if one could see them. One beast that frightened Jamarcus and Bug Girl was the shadow wolf.

The book projected an image in Jamarcus's mind of a large creature that was a cross between a giant horse and the creature from the movie *Alien*. It was completely black with smoke rising from its skin. It would roam all around, fearing nothing. One could stand next to someone, and the person couldn't tell unless he or she had the means to feel it. It fed on the strong dark emotions of individuals and, through the process of feeding, created more of the emotions via the psionic link it created with the prey. The process did not hurt the person, because the creature did not have the dimensional means to touch its victim, but that did not mean the beast could not cause the person to do something bad with the extra motivation created by the feeding. If one somehow found him- or herself in that thin world between the third and fourth dimensions, the creatures were powerful beasts, and unless a person was fifth dimensional or higher, they could make his or her day a bad one.

Another room Jamarcus loved to play in with Bug Girl was the Tree Room, which had a large tree growing in an open area in the center of the chateau. The tree was planted on a hill with its roots protruding out of the soil, which kept them clean from dirt. The trunk of the tree grew in one looped spiral in the circular room for four stories until the top branches sprang out across the open ceiling in a large, flat spread of green leaves. The tree was large enough that a little room had been made in the base of the trunk, filled with pillows, books, and toys Jamarcus and Bug Girl could play with. They could walk up the trunk into the open air via steps that were molded into the tree, and the branches provided enough stability for the two to monkey around among them. It felt like a natural gymnasium to Jamarcus.

The other portion of Jamarcus's dreams in the chateau took place in the normal house that the family lived in. The house was plain compared to the rest of the chateau, yet it still was a home that looked fit for a rich family to live in. The family had a father, a white man who looked to be in his mid-twenties. He shone like the little boy, and he had a bubble that curved everything around him. He was muscular and tall and had long blond hair and sky-blue eyes. Father was always kind to Jamarcus, yet Jamarcus felt cold to him. He didn't like a white man pretending that Jamarcus was his child, yet Jamarcus said nothing of that when they were together.

There was also Mother, who Jamarcus believed was an angel. Mother looked Oriental, was as tall as a normal human, and had normal arms and legs. Mother had four fingers and toes, her feet seemed a bit longer than normal, and she always stood on her toes. Her skin was almost pure-white light, with just a small tinge of blue. She had no hair, her eyes were dark, and she had a small nose and mouth. She was always stern with Jamarcus, but Jamarcus felt love behind it. He believed the love she showed him was the purest meaning of tough love. Jamarcus also believed she was the mother of the little boy he had seen years ago.

There was also Sister, who looked like any other white girl, with black hair and brown eyes. Sister would steal Jamarcus aside so they could talk alone with one another. She would sometimes hug and kiss Jamarcus, which made both of them laugh. Jamarcus could feel that Sister was always concerned about him and wanted to watch over him when he was with them.

Finally, there was Baby Brother, a small, glowing blue bundle of squirms and giggles. He was usually found in his room, lying in his crib, or being cared for by Mother. Baby Brother looked just like Mother, with wild black hair and the same type of hands and feet. Baby Brother loved when Jamarcus picked him up, and he always projected in Jamarcus's mind to do so. Jamarcus and Bug Girl always carried Baby Brother around when they could, except when Mother screamed into their heads that they were playing too roughly with him.

The dreams were fun for Jamarcus, but they seemed odd. There was no problem for Jamarcus in dreaming about Bug Girl, Baby Brother, and Mother. They were alien and could be explained as the products of the hyperactive imagination of a child who loved science fiction. But what of Father and Sister? It made no sense that Jamarcus would dream of white individuals when he hardly knew any white people at all. And why did they treat him like family? Despite that, Jamarcus loved the dreams he had of the chateau and the family. They were part of the only joy he had as a child growing up.

<2>

If Jamarcus didn't have a vivid dream of the chateau, then he had one of the city. The city was a group of large islands located in a bay or gulf. Three bridges connected the larger ones, while the smaller ones could only be accessed by boat or by flight. The chateau was located on one of the smaller islands. The largest island was the one Jamarcus called Metropolis. At the center of the Metropolis was a giant skyscraper the height of a small mountain, with four large cables that ran in four cardinal directions. Around the tower were massive buildings of different designs and heights. Roads in Metropolis ran either on the ground or raised structures hundreds of feet in the air. The cars in the city either drove on the roads or flew in designated flight patterns between the buildings. It looked to Jamarcus like a city built on top of another. Jamarcus knew that Metropolis served as a business or political center, but he didn't know how he knew.

The people in Metropolis and throughout the city almost all looked like Mother; many had black hair, and some had none. The ones who looked like Mother walked on their toes. The other type of people in the city were very tall humans of different ethnicities. The majority were white and had black hair, while others had blond, brown, or red hair. Other tall humans looked Asian and black. They all wore slacks and button-up shirts. The women never wore dresses, or at least Jamarcus never saw a woman wear a dress in the city. Almost all the buildings were white, and the city seemed to glow. The glow caused a bubble in the air, like the one around the little boy.

Another island Jamarcus called Hawaii. It was the residential area for the working folks of the city. That island looked like a massive

17

tropical island resort, with hundreds of buildings that looked like the hotels in Waikiki. There were shops and grocery stores in the central part of the island, and along the coast were a few small towns with bars and tourist attractions. Jamarcus had a couple of dreams in which he was riding a bicycle along a wooden path on a wharf in one of the small towns. There was a stretch in that town where Jamarcus knew many of the shop owners and the people who lived there, and the shop owners would invite Jamarcus in to look at their goods. Most of the shops sold works of art, such as paintings or sculptures.

No one went to the beach in Hawaii. There was an island he called the Beach. It was located at the end of the major bridge road, and it was, for the most part, a massive sand island. At the center of the Beach was a mall amid a forest, which mostly sold goods for people to use on the beach. The white sands of the Beach ran for a few miles, and the water was crystal clear, not like the gray Chesapeake Bay Jamarcus lived near. The north side of the island had calm waters, while the south side had waves breaking on the shoreline. When Jamarcus dreamed of the Beach, there were always thousands of people playing along the water line and in the surf or relaxing in the sun.

The only other island Jamarcus dreamed of was the one he called Suburbia. It was a mountain of rolling hills, with the top being a large dome covered in thick grass. The houses on the hill looked like ones a person might find in the rich part of a city but not where one would find the mansions. Father had a house there. It was smaller than the normal part of the chateau, and the design of it was unique. Some of the walls appeared to be missing, yet they were there as if the rooms had invisible glass walls that protected the people inside from the elements. The living room fit that description; one could sit on the couch, looking at the floating television screen, and then could simply walk out to the backyard enclosed by a bush fence, which had a single tree in it.

Jamarcus was never alone when he dreamed of the city. He was mostly accompanied by two beings, Thor and Athena. They were part of the family, but it seemed to Jamarcus that they had grown up and moved out. Thor was taller than Father, was far more muscular, and had black hair and a beard. Jamarcus loved Thor with all his heart because it felt like having Superman as a big brother. He was like Superman in every way. Thor was incredibly strong and fast and could fly. Many times, he took Jamarcus on his own to the different islands in the city. He mostly wore a skin-tight dark blue suit, just as Athena did, and many times, when he took Jamarcus in his dreams, he was with a group of friends of all types. They would goof around, as all the guys did when they got together.

Athena was slender and as tall as Father, and her skin glowed white like Mother's. She had long black hair and a long, slender neck. She looked like a Chinese goddess to Jamarcus, yet every time Jamarcus told her how beautiful she was, she would recoil in mild disgust. Jamarcus could also tell that she was lonely, and when he dreamed of her, she would carry him like a baby or hold him close to her body.

Athena and Thor took Jamarcus all over the city and let him wander where he pleased. Jamarcus always minded what he was doing and where he was going, though, trying to be a good little brother, which he knew made Thor and Athena happy. The main reason Jamarcus loved dreaming about Athena and Thor was because he knew how to make them happy, which he felt in his soul, which made him happy.

In a way, the family became more of a family to Jamarcus than his own. Jamarcus's family members were as different to him as he was to them. His sister told him that he didn't even look like them and that maybe he was adopted, which stung him. His brothers and sister always made fun of him because he was into science, while they were into music and trying to be popular. When Jamarcus heard what his sister said, her words drove a wedge between him and his family, and he never again felt a part of them. Yet in his dreams, he felt safe and loved with the family, especially with Thor and Athena.

One night, when Jamarcus began dreaming, he found himself on a sidewalk next to a large pier beside a blue-green ocean. Athena was carrying him, and Thor walked just ahead of them. On the land side were industrial buildings that manufactured parts for ships, or that was what Jamarcus felt he knew. The sides of the buildings that faced them were large open bay doors with craft flying in and out of them in all directions. The craft was too small to be driven by humans, so Jamarcus guessed they were remote-controlled. They all had large, flat sections on which all different parts, small and large, were strapped down. The majority of the craft flew in the direction Athena, Thor, and Jamarcus were walking. Jamarcus turned his head to try to see where the parts craft were going, but Athena kissed him on the neck, making him wiggle in her arms. Athena hugged him tightly to her, so he turned his face and placed his head on her shoulder to look at the water.

On and above the water were many different designs of ships: massive cargo ships, mass transportation ships, small cruise ships, and ships that were more like boats and yachts. The ships in the air ranged from disk-shaped ones to spheres to ones that looked like the pyramid ships Jamarcus had visions of to ones that looked like aircraft carriers Jamarcus's father had been stationed on. Jamarcus couldn't find any engine funnels or sails for the ships in the water, and he saw no thrusters or rockets for the ones in the sky. He couldn't understand what could cause the large ships in the sky to float as if they were as light as feathers or what propelled the ones in the water.

"Where are we going?" Jamarcus asked as he stared at the ships.

"We're going to the ships we made," Thor answered.

"What type of ships?" Jamarcus asked.

"Cargo ships," Athena said, patting Jamarcus's back. "Thor and I are going into business together."

"Cool," Jamarcus said.

"Do you want to see them?" Thor asked.

"Yes," Jamarcus answered, and Athena shifted him in her arms to face in front of them.

"Look," Athena whispered, and Jamarcus saw something that took him a while to comprehend. They were walking toward an enormous hangar over the water that looked to be miles long at least a mile wide and half a mile high. Two massive gray-surfaced tube-shaped ships were floating next to each other near the entrance of the hangar, with more than a dozen smaller tube ships docked next to each of them. Dozens of the parts craft constantly flew over their heads to and from the two large ships, filled with parts while flying toward them and empty when coming back.

"Do you want to see the ship we'll be living on?" Athena asked.

"Sure," Jamarcus said.

Athena and Thor leaped up into the air and flew into the hangar. Jamarcus felt a little dizzy in Athena's arms, but he was used to flying on Thor's shoulders, so it didn't bother him that much. Jamarcus always expected to hear the wind rushing over his ears when he flew with Thor, but he never did, as he didn't hear any now.

After a few moments, the three arrived at what seemed like a floating luxury cruise liner like the ones on the show *Lifestyles of the Rich and Famous*. Jamarcus could see floating blue robots that looked almost human bobbing about the deck. Their faces looked feminine, and their legs were cut off midthigh, with a rippled metallic surface that caused a curved bubble below them. Thor, Athena, and Jamarcus landed on the bow of the cruiser, which he knew because his father had taught him nautical terms. They stood in front of the helm of the ship, which was double-decked and covered with tall sheets of dark-tinted glass. When Jamarcus looked toward the water, he saw Metropolis far away, sitting on top of the highest point of the forested island, which swept from left to right as far as Jamarcus could see. The white tower at the center of Metropolis stood like a white monolith piercing the sky. On the sidewalk by the water, a large crowd began to form with people coming from the direction of the city. Cars either floated or parked on the paved concrete area in front of the industrial buildings, and more flew or drove in at a constant rate.

"Hello, Lord Thor, Lady Athena," a voice said to them from behind, and as they turned to face it, they saw an elderly man who looked like Mother and was just as tall, dressed in a black version of the skintight suits Athena and Thor wore. Next to him was a floating polished gray ball that had a bronze ring around it.

"Hello, Kukulkan," Thor responded, and Athena put Jamarcus

down and pushed him toward the visitor.

"Say hello," Athena said.

"Hello," Jamarcus said as he reached out to shake Kukulkan's hand.

"Hello, Your Highness," Kukulkan said as he shook Jamarcus's hand, which made Jamarcus squint in confusion.

"I'm not royalty," Jamarcus told Kukulkan.

"Yes, you are," Kukulkan said, patting him on his head, and Jamarcus felt the sincerity in his soul when Kukulkan said that.

"All of your ships are in order and ready for departure," Kukulkan told Thor and Athena. "The warp fields are primed and ready for entanglement, and we're just about done putting all of the supplies on the ships. Your androids have all been programmed with their jobs, with enough in storage to last you for about twenty orbit cycles in case of any breakdown. The androids are all programmed to replace themselves if they do break down, but your ships' computers have the program stored just in case you need to do so yourselves."

"Thanks," Thor said.

"Here is your logistics permit," Kukulkan said, handing Thor a small rectangular black block the size of Jamarcus's index finger. "This allows you to conduct business in this section of the galaxy for the next ten cycles. Just so you know, the loan you took needs to have its first payment by the beginning of the next cycle."

"That's no problem," Athena said. "We already have contracts set up for shipping resources between ten worlds, and we're hoping to gather up enough to build two more fleets just from those contracts in five cycles. We should be able to pay to pack the storage in about two cycles.”

“Just as a reminder,” Kukulkan said, “your father said you can’t conduct any logistical or trade business in the family’s solar cluster sector. It would be a conflict of interest.”

“Yes, we understand,” Thor answered in a peeved voice.

“Well, now that we’ve gotten that out of the way, you can entangle with the ships’ engines,” Kukulkan said, and the floating ball floated toward Thor and Athena. The two placed their hands on the ball, and for a moment, they stood there with their eyes closed and heads slightly bowed. A glow began to build inside them as Jamarcus felt air slowly rush past him at a steady rate. The wind then slowed down and stopped, and Thor’s and Athena’s chests shone like suns, both with curved lens bubbles about them.

“You’re now ready to go,” Kukulkan said. “Good luck, my lords.”

“Thank you for all your help,” Athena said, reaching down and hugging Kukulkan.

“Are you guys leaving?” Jamarcus asked, and with a start, Thor and Athena faced each other and then faced him. Jamarcus could feel their uneasiness, and he also felt they were mad at him.

“We kind of have to,” Thor said. “It’s about time for us to go out and make a name for ourselves.”

“You’re mad at me. Did I do something wrong?” Jamarcus asked, which made Athena sweep down and pick him up.

"You didn't do anything wrong. We just need to leave. For us, it's for the best."

"Will I see you again?" Jamarcus asked.

"Not for a while," Thor answered, which frightened Jamarcus. He knew it was a dream, but it scared him not to be able to dream about them. He couldn't help but feel incredibly lonely when he heard those words.

"Okay," Jamarcus said as he began to cry. When they saw that, Thor and Athena gave Jamarcus a big hug, and soon they began to cry as well. They stood like that for a while, trying to cover themselves with the love they felt for each other.

"The last of the supplies have been stored," Kukulkan said. "The people are waiting."

Thor turned, looked at Kukulkan, and then stepped back, wiping the tears from Jamarcus's eyes. He then closed his eyes and took a breath, and the ships began to move out from the hangar. Slowly, the craft moved into the open air, casting massive shadows onto the water, and it felt as if both of the large tube ships and their side vessels were connected to the cruise ship because they moved at the same rate. After a few minutes, the ships were above the large crowd, who cheered in adoration of the two lords. Then the cruise ship they were on floated down and landed in the water next to the sidewalk without causing any waves. Thor and Athena, with Jamarcus in their arms, flew off the ship and landed amid the crowd, who made a circle for them to land. They both kissed Jamarcus on his cheeks before putting him down.

"You know we love you, right?" Thor asked, and Jamarcus responded by nodding.

"The rest of the family love you too," Athena added.

"I know," Jamarcus said.

"Goodbye, Your Highness," Thor said, after which he and Athena flew back to their cruise ship. The crowd erupted in a swoon as they yelled wishes of good luck after the lady and lord. The cruise vessel rose into the sky until it was parallel to the tube-shaped craft. They all began to shine with a bright light that made them look flat and not real. Then, in a silent flash, the ships were gone.

For a moment, Jamarcus stood among the cheering crowd, but he couldn't understand why he was so sad. It was only a dream. Why did it hurt so much? He thought *They're not real; it shouldn't hurt that they're gone.* But loneliness filled his soul until all he could do was cry. He wept so hard that he woke up in his bed in his dark room. Not wanting to get his parents mad, he kept as quiet as he could until he fell back into a dark and empty sleep.

Chapter 3
October 1995
<1>

Jamarcus walked into his bedroom, closed the door behind him, and rested his back against the door. He stood there looking into the mostly empty room with no thoughts in his head. He wanted to go over to the house of a friend who was hosting a *Dungeons and Dragons* campaign, but when he'd asked his mother, she suddenly got mad at him. His sister was to perform at a dance recital that night at Georgetown, and several talent agents were to attend. It was a big deal for the family, and Jamarcus and his brothers wanted to go, but their mother didn't want to be bothered with them while she focused on Jamarcus's sister. Jamarcus had assumed it was okay to go out that night, yet she still had freaked out at the question.

"You should be focused on your sister!" she'd screamed after Jamarcus asked, which had confused him. But he hadn't bothered to argue. Jamarcus never questioned his mother when she was in that mood, so he just went to his room and did what he always did to make himself feel better: he looked out his window to his backyard. Besides, when she said, "Focus on your sister," she meant, "Focus on me."

He loved the look of the forest in fall, especially in October, when all the leaves changed to red and orange. The sun shone its last light onto the leaves of the trees and the Chesapeake Bay behind them, making everything look as if it were on fire. Jamarcus didn't know why it gave him butterflies in his stomach when he looked at that scene. He always loved nature, including the smell of the forest and grass. He loved looking at the sunrise over the bay in the mornings. Even when he closed his eyes, he still saw the sun rising in his window.

Jamarcus turned toward his dresser and looked at his *Dungeons and Dragons* books and dice bag. He had an itch to work on his character but decided not to, knowing it would just make him mad. After opening the window to let some cool air in, Jamarcus began doing push-ups to keep himself occupied. He long ago had decided to go into the military like his father once he'd realized his parents had decided to put all their efforts into helping his sister's dance career.

He wanted to be an astronaut—an astronautic biological paleontologist. Because of the visions and dreams he had, he had hopes of becoming an astronaut and going to the moon or Mars if NASA ever decided to go. He wanted to be one of the first human beings to find evidence of bacterial life on another world, or even something more advanced. If that discovery was made, then there had to be other life throughout the universe, which could explain all of his dreams. His parents had promised to send him to Space Camp at Hampton if he made straight As in elementary school, which he had. When he'd shown them his final report card after graduating from the fifth grade, his parents had just congratulated him.

"Don't you remember what you promised?" Jamarcus had asked, and his parents had looks on their faces that showed they had no idea what he was talking about. "You said that if I got straight As in school, you would send me to Space Camp once I got out of elementary school."

"Jamarcus, we can't afford that. We've got to focus on your sister," his father had said, and Jamarcus had shut down after he heard that answer. He hadn't waited for his parents to finish explaining; he'd walked away to his room and lay down on his bed.

He was angry, but he wasn't mad at his sister. His sister had legitimate talent and had been enrolled in Julliard's School of Dance since she was in elementary school herself. By the night of her recital at Georgetown, she already had been in a music video and even had been cast in a movie. She was on the verge of becoming a star. It was a wise investment for his parents to put all their attention on her since it was going to pay off soon.

He wasn't particularly mad at his parents either. He just assumed they didn't know how to develop a child interested in science. But it hurt Jamarcus to his core that he'd put in all that hard work in and that it had amounted to nothing. It had had such a profound effect on him that he'd completely stopped dreaming about the family, and by that night, he all but had forgotten about them. He knew that if he wasn't going to get any help from his parents in academics, he wasn't going to get into a good college just based on grades. Jamarcus knew the limitations that young black men had in trying to get into certain academic fields. He decided to focus on the military instead, wanting to have a career choice after he graduated from high school.

"Jamarcus, Jason is on the phone!" one of his brothers yelled, so he got up off the floor, wiped his sweat off, and went to the kitchen to grab the phone from his brother.

"Sup, Jay?"

"You coming over tonight?" Jason asked.

"Nah, I asked my mom, and she said no."

"Why not? You going to Vanessa's dance at Georgetown?"

"No," Jamarcus said. "My mom doesn't want to be bothered with me and my brothers."

"The fuck is that shit, dude? It doesn't make any sense."

"I know. My mom's in one of her moods."

"I swear your mom is bipolar, man," Jason said. "I know it."

"Whatever."

"God, you've got to come. I've got five guys coming up. The new dude in class, Kyle, is into *Dungeons and Dragons* too. He's got this wicked bard that's level eighteen."

"Ah, that's sick," Jamarcus said.

"Right? It fucking rules!"

"I always wanted to play in a group with a bard and a cleric." Jamarcus stopped short when he overheard his mother complaining about his talking on the phone.

"I know," Jason said. "Bards are so awesome. They may be weak when they're lower level, but when they get higher, they're so dope. Dude, I know your cleric and his bard are going to make our group unstoppable."

"Hey, Jason, I've got to get off now," Jamarcus said.

"Your mom?"

"Yeah, man, she's wigging out."

"Okay, man. I'll check you later," Jason said.

"Right," Jamarcus said, and he hung up the phone just as his mother walked by, ranting about everything that was an inconvenience to her at the moment.

"Vanessa, have you found your leggings yet?" Jamarcus's mother yelled.

"No!" she answered from somewhere in the house.

"Hurry up!" their mother shrieked as she happened to walk past Jamarcus. "Why is your friend calling at this time of night?" she asked.

"He was still wondering if I was going over to his place tonight," Jamarcus answered.

"Why do you need to play that with them? People don't play *Dungeons and Dragons* anyway. That's for Satan worshippers. How do you go to church and play that game?"

Jamarcus didn't answer the question, mainly because it would have been impossible to give his mother a proper answer that she would have liked anyway.

"I found them," Jamarcus's sister said as she walked up next to their mother, holding her bag of dance gear.

"Wish Vanessa good luck!" his mother said.

"Good luck," Jamarcus said.

"Thank you," Vanessa responded with a small smile.

With that, Jamarcus's mother walked through the front door with his sister following close behind and closed it behind her. Jamarcus went back to his room and lay down in his bed. The sun had already set, and he could see stars out his open window. Jamarcus wished he was up in the stars, somewhere in a world found in a fantasy novel, a place that had both magic and advanced science. That was the main reason he played *Dungeons and Dragons*—because it felt almost like home.

It was then that Jamarcus noticed a lone bright orb of white light in the sky. It was too low to be a star or a planet. It was stationary and illuminated at a constant rate, as a plane or helicopter would have been. But it did not move from its position. Jamarcus got out of his bed and looked out his window to get a better look at the object. While he was viewing it, a smaller orb of white light zipped past the stationary one at an incredible speed. Jamarcus swung his head to try to follow the smaller orb, but it vanished from his sight.

Turning back to the stationary orb, he saw two more smaller lights flying around it. They slowly flew in all directions for a few minutes and then streaked through the entire night sky and out of sight in an instant. Then the orbs streaked back just as quickly to the primary one and slowly fluttered around it. Jamarcus stared at the lights for a good half hour before he decided to go tell someone what he was watching. He first went to his brothers' room, where they were playing on their gaming console.

"Hey, come here," Jamarcus said as he burst through their door. "I've got to show you something."

"What? We're busy," one of his brothers groaned.

"Come here!" Jamarcus said, and he ran to their parents' room. "Pops, come here," he said, slapping on the door as his father was watching TV.

"What's wrong?" his father asked, but Jamarcus was already gone and walking back to his room.

"Come on, guys!" Jamarcus yelled as he got to his window, stretching his neck out to make sure the lights were still there.

"What, man?" his other brother said, and as his brothers and father stared out the window, they went silent.

"Oh my God," their father said slowly after a few minutes of silence.

Jamarcus stepped out from in front of them and left the room, running outside into the backyard. From that view, he could tell the objects were high in the sky and must have been moving at miles per second as they streaked across the horizon. Soon afterward, his father and brothers joined him with their necks bent back and their eyes fixed on the moving lights. As they continued to look, more lights gradually revealed themselves, until more than a dozen orbed lights were either flying around the primary orb or streaking in and out of their sight.

"Should we get a camera and record this?" Jamarcus asked his father.

"No," he answered quickly.

Jamarcus turned and looked at him and only then noticed that his father and brothers were frightened of what they were seeing. He didn't think about that, though, because he was too fascinated with the orbs. After a while, his father and brothers left him without a word and went back inside the house.

Jamarcus stood alone, looking into the sky as the orbs flew about. The lights then gathered together in a loose group around the primary orb, and one flew off to Jamarcus's left. The light flew to a point in the sky where a person could have drawn a straight line between it and the primary orb, parallel to the horizon. The orb then moved toward the primary orb in that straight line at a slow rate. When it got close, it increased its speed and drew a perfect sine wave in the sky, intersecting with the primary orb as it crossed the invisible line. When it finished, it flew back to Jamarcus's left, at the position it had been in before it had made the sine wave.

"My God, that's mechanical," Jamarcus said after he pondered what he saw. It had too perfect a flight pattern to be an animal or lantern in the sky, and no aircraft or helicopter could have moved at that high rate of speed and those angles without experiencing extreme g's, at least as far as Jamarcus knew. The light then slowly approached the primary orb again and performed the same sine wave.

"That has to be in some electromagnetic field that can repel gravity, or it makes its gravity," Jamarcus said. He imagined the craft was controlled by a set of relay switches and specifically controlled knobs. When the light completed the same sine wave again, he then knew what it was doing: it was creating a two-dimensional plane with four quadrants, with the primary orb being where the X-axis and Y-axis intersected. It next made a square sine wave, with one square going up on the left and down on the right.

"They're reading my mind," Jamarcus said after the craft changed its pattern. The small orb then flew the same square sine wave, this time putting a regular sine wave at the top and bottom of the squares. The orb then flew off away from the quadrant, and other ones flew in, flying in a pattern plotted by a math equation. One orb would draw a line that flowed in a cosine wave. Another orb would join it, drawing the cotangent of that wave. An orb flew in different nonlinear patterns for some time. Jamarcus guessed they were trying to tell him math equations, but he had given up on math after trigonometry. He was pretty sure any college student seeing that could have written down the equations with no problem. Afterward, the orbs began flying in algebraic paths, all different from each other. This went on for some time until all the orbs came to a stop.

An orb then flew to the primary orb and disappeared into it. The orb appeared after a moment and flew in a gradual outward path shaped in a golden-ratio circle, a continuous circular line that increased its trajectory by a specific set of increasing degrees. The lights kept doing this repetitively, sometimes two or three at a time at specific angles from each other. Jamarcus couldn't understand the meaning behind that formation or what the lights were trying to communicate to him if they were communicating to him at all. The formation had to mean something. He wished he'd stayed in math and science courses. Perhaps he would have known the answer.

It began to get chilly, so Jamarcus decided to go back to his room to look at the lights through his bedroom window. When he went back inside the house, he saw his father and brothers watching television in the living room as he walked toward his bedroom.

"Hey, you were still outside?" one of his brothers asked.

"I was only out there for about thirty minutes," Jamarcus said.

"Man, you were out there for over two hours."

"I only went out back at six o'clock," Jamarcus said.

"It's past eight-thirty," his brother said. "You were out there on your own the whole time too. That's crazy."

"You guys came out there with me for a couple of minutes," Jamarcus said as he walked toward his bedroom.

"No, we didn't."

"Yes, you did," Jamarcus said over his shoulder just as he went into his room. He rushed through the door and went to his window, searching for the lights. The primary orb was there, but the number of smaller ones had decreased. Steadily, the smaller lights kept disappearing, until only the primary orb was left. The primary orb then began to flicker and dim until it too disappeared. Jamarcus stood by his window, trying to understand what had happened. What were those lights? Were they trying to communicate with him? Why did they keep repeating the golden ratio pattern? As Jamarcus looked across the bay, his mind and stomach buzzed with adrenaline. He had to know more. But how?

"I'm back!" Jamarcus heard his mother yell as she entered the front door. "Vanessa blew everyone's mind at the college. Everyone loved her!"

The buzz of excitement Jamarcus had gone away, and he stood there with a blank mind, with all thoughts of the lights gone. He closed his window and went to greet his mother before she got mad.

<2>

June 1996

Jamarcus stood behind the cash register at a shoe store, watching an elderly woman muse over walking shoes. It was a summer job for him so he could have some money in his pocket before he went to army boot camp. He hesitated to go help the woman, tapping his finger on the counter in front of him. The store was empty except for the customer and himself. His eyes darted all over the walls as he tried to focus his thoughts. He looked at the shoes on the display shelves. He looked outside at the cars on the street. His chest felt as if someone had poked a hole through him right below his heart. He wasn't able to focus because his mind was obsessed with the phone call he'd gotten from his girlfriend the week prior. She had decided to break up with him because he was joining the military, which Jamarcus had known was going to happen sooner or later. But she had already gotten over him and wanted to go out with another person. That was why she'd called.

"I want to go out with Samuel," she'd said over the phone. Samuel was the brother of one of Jamarcus's friends, Douglas. He hadn't spent enough time with him to know him well, but he was an all-right kid. The family was well off. Their father was a representative for their district in DC. Because of that, he was popular at school, although he was shy at times.

"I mean, you're friends with him, right? He's a nice guy—don't you think?"

"Yeah, he is. He's great."

"And he likes me. He didn't want to say anything to you about it because he thought you'd get mad."

"It's okay," Jamarcus had said, switching the phone to his other hand.

"I like him too. And he's going to stay here after graduating from school."

"Yeah, that makes sense."

"And I like him too," his girlfriend had said. "It's just that I didn't know if we were going to see each other again. I just don't want to be alone."

"It's okay, Susan. I completely understand."

"You do?" his girlfriend had asked.

"Excuse me, sir," the lady called out to him. "Could you help me pick out a pair of shoes?"

"Yes, ma'am," Jamarcus answered, shaking his head to clear his thoughts. He walked over to the woman, who was in the sports section of the store.

"I'm trying to find a good pair of walking shoes. What pair should I buy?"

"Well, what type of walking shoes are we talking about?"

"I don't want anything fancy," the old lady said. "I just need a pair of shoes to replace these old ones."

"Well, these right in front of us are the best walking shoes we have in the store," Jamarcus said, pointing to a small section on the wall. "These are made for serious walking and are supposed to be comfortable."

"Okay."

"But they're also expensive, ma'am. I mean, these right here cost about one hundred dollars, and they're the least expensive of the group."

"I don't want to spend that much money," the lady said.

"We have a bunch of shoes over here for the, uh, for the—"

"Old lady shoes?" the lady said, which made Jamarcus laugh.

"Yes, that group of shoes is over here," Jamarcus said, leading the woman to the simpler walking shoes.

"These are fine," the lady said, and as she bent over to take a closer look at them, Jamarcus's mind went back to his girlfriend. That call had destroyed him, even though his parents and his recruiter had told him it was going to happen. When she'd wanted to break up, it had blown a hole in his heart, and he couldn't feel anything in his soul up to that day.

"Are you mad at me?" Jamarcus's girlfriend had asked.

"I love you, Susan," Jamarcus had said into the phone, looking at the kitchen wall. "I'm not going to be selfish here. I just want you to be happy."

"Are you sure?"

"Yes, Susan, I'm sure."

"Jamarcus?"

"Yeah?"

"Why aren't you calling me Sue?" she'd asked.

Jamarcus didn't know how to answer her. He'd just stood there rubbing his chest.

"You can still call me Sue."

"Yeah, I know," Jamarcus had answered.

"Why don't you?"

"Look, Susan, everything's fine. This was going to happen anyway. It's a part of growing up. I've accepted it. I'm at peace."

"But you're mad at me," his girlfriend had said.

"Of course I am. But I'm not going to take it out on you."

"Okay."

"Look, I've got to go. I'll talk to you later, okay?"

"We're still friends, right?" she'd asked.

"Yes," Jamarcus had answered.

"I'm still Sue, right?"

"What about these shoes right here?" the lady asked, picking up a pair of black shoes and showing them to Jamarcus.

"Those are pretty decent," Jamarcus said. "And they're not as expensive as the other shoes over there."

"Yes, you're right."

"But there is a pair of shoes that are just the same as the ones you're wearing right here. Do you want to get these?"

"No," the lady said. "I want something different to change things up. When you get to my age, a new pair of shoes is like moving into a new house."

"Yes, ma'am."

"Oh, you're so courteous. And you're handsome too."

"Thanks, ma'am," Jamarcus replied with a laugh.

"God, to be as young as you are now. And you're so in shape. You probably have four girlfriends, don't you?"

"No, ma'am, I do not."

"You don't have a girlfriend?" the lady said in disbelief. "Well, a young man like you needs to have a sweetie to settle down with. If I was younger, I'd make a proper man out of you."

"Wow," Jamarcus whispered, putting his hand over his eyes.

"You think you have this shoe in a size seven?"

"Hmm, I think so," Jamarcus said as he looked through the pile of shoeboxes beneath the display. "I'm confident there is a pair in the storage. I'll go get it."

"Thank you," the lady said, and she grabbed his arm as he walked toward the shoe storage. "Now, you listen," the lady said as Jamarcus turned back to her. "You find yourself a good young girl. Settle down, and have some kids. It's what God wants. You hear me?"

"Yes, ma'am," Jamarcus said with an awkward smile, and he walked into the shoe storage. It didn't take him long to find the shoes for the woman, yet Jamarcus stood there looking straight at the boxes ahead of him. He kept thinking about the phone call. He never answered his ex-girlfriend's question. He'd just said goodbye and hung up. Why had he done that? Jamarcus already had graduated from high school, so he couldn't talk to her again unless he went to her house.

Samuel was rich and white; plus, he was a good-looking guy. Any girl would have wanted to go out with him. *Did she break up with me because I'm black? Am I not good enough for her? Why am I not good enough for her? Why doesn't anyone like me? My family doesn't care about me. My girlfriend just dumped me. Why am I not good enough for anyone? What's wrong with me?* Jamarcus couldn't stop those thoughts from going around in his head and causing the hole in his chest to grow in size and pain.

"Let her go." A female voice buzzed in his head. He felt the voice in an area in his frontal lobe. Jamarcus recognized the voice as soon as he heard it. It was the voice he'd heard as a child growing up: his guardian angel. A calm blanket of warmth covered him, quieting his anxiety. He still had the hole in his heart, but the thoughts running in his mind stopped.

The voice is right, Jamarcus thought. He had to let her go. He wasn't a child anymore. He had to man up and move forward.

Jamarcus grabbed the shoebox he was looking for and returned it to his customer in the shoe store.

Chapter 4
<1>
February 3, 2003

Jamarcus stood under the shower faucet, letting the water run over his head and down his body in the shower room. His squad had just completed combat drills on the training grounds of Schofield Army Base on the island of Oahu, and they were pounded into the ground. Since four o'clock that mourning, they and many other platoons had practiced closed urban combat training at the makeshift town built within the last year. For months, they'd performed the same exercises over and over again: clearing out a building with suspected combatants inside, more often than not with civilians in proximity. Drills were dealing with unruly civilians interfering with a patrol out of protest, sometimes with combatants within the ranks of the protesters. They had fire practice at the range, movements with Humvees and Abram tanks, and practice with calling in artillery and air strikes. The officers spent hours each day getting the soldiers to have the movements become second nature. Once they got to the point that they believed they knew what they were doing, the instructors would throw something else into the scenario, making Jamarcus feel as if he'd just gotten out of boot camp. Murphy's law got embedded in his head as a sort of mental comfort zone. Once a person knew that anything could happen, he did not panic when it did.

The drills and exercises made for long days out in the Hawaiian sun; his BDUs—battle dress uniforms—were drenched with sweat, and his platoon complained jokingly about each new exercise. Living in Virginia, he was used to being in ninety-degree weather, but that didn't make the weather on the island, which was in the mid-eighties, any more tolerable. However, it was February, and the weather was all but perfect—which meant the NCOs could find more excuses to pound them even harder.

Jamarcus turned off the shower, wrapped himself in a towel, and went back to his room. He was alone as he left the shower room. He did everything he could to make sure he showered alone. It wasn't that he minded showering with anyone; he just didn't want anyone to see him. He looked at himself in the mirror as he dried himself off in his room. Jamarcus wished he were bigger. He was five foot ten, but he only weighed 160 pounds. He looked skinny. He always had been picked on in school for being thin, and no matter how hard he'd tried to put on weight after he joined the army, that never had changed. Most of the guys in his platoon said they were jealous of his metabolism, but Jamarcus found no comfort in that.

After getting dressed, he heard a breaking news broadcast announcing Secretary of State Colin Powell being introduced to the UN Security Council. He stood and watched as the secretary made a case that Iraq refused to give up weapons of mass destruction while still holding chemical and biological material to use as weapon payloads, along with the equipment to do so. The secretary at one point held up a glass valve containing a yellow substance, saying it was an example of a chemical agent Iraq might possess to use against the United States.

Jamarcus heard yelling in the hallway outside his door, and he walked toward the ruckus, arriving at the recreation room of the barracks. More than a dozen men and women were either seated or standing in front of a television, watching the UN broadcast. There were arguments all around about the speech, both in favor of and against Powell's presentation.

"I'm telling y'all—we're going to war," a man sitting in front of the television said in excitement.

"Why the hell are we going into Iraq?" another person asked. "I thought we were supposed to be fighting al-Qaeda. Al-Qaeda is in Afghanistan."

"Dude, we're going in there to get those WMDs," the frontman said, turning around to face the skeptic, and then he smiled when he saw Jamarcus. "How you doing, Staff?" the man called out.

"Sup, Jesse?" Jamarcus responded.

"This is pathetic," the skeptic said. "There is no reason to go into Iraq. The US is in a kill-Muslim mindset. We went into Afghanistan and beat up those Muslims. Who's the next bad Arab we can find? Oh, look—there's Saddam. Let's go kill him."

"It ain't like that, man," Jesse said. "We're just trying to keep those chemicals and stuff away from al-Qaeda."

"The hell it is!" another man shouted. "We can go in there and kick those camel jockeys' asses!" That statement made everyone in the room erupt in disapproval.

"What the fuck, man?" one of the soldiers asked in disgust.

"What? You know I'm right. We can go in there and get those guys who hit the Twin Towers!"

"No one in Iraq was even part of the 9/11 attacks, you racist fuck," the skeptic said. "It was Saudis who did the attacks."

"What's the difference?" the man asked.

"Hey," Jamarcus said calmly to the man, who turned to face him. "Cut that shit out."

"Fuck this shit," the man said, walking out of the recreation room. "You know I'm right!" he shouted as he walked back to the living quarters.

"Hey, Abdul, not everyone is as racist as that guy," Jesse said to the skeptic.

"That's the thing I'm talking about, though," Abdul said as Jamarcus walked through the group and sat on a couch, watching news analysts debate the speech. "I get that we were attacked. Al-Qaeda did it. Fine—let's go after Bin Laden. But now everyone is in a kill-all-Muslim mentality. No one else sees that as a little bit racist?"

"What about the chemical and biological agents in Iraq?" Jesse asked. "What if Saddam sells some of it to al-Qaeda?"

"Saddam hates al-Qaeda as much as we do," Abdul said. "Why would Saddam give weapons materials to a group who would use the weapons on him?"

"Saddam tried to buy missiles from North Korea. He could have used those and put WMDs on them to attack Israel or us."

"Oh, here we go again about Israel. Americans worried about Israel. You're not worried about them; you think you are them. You guys couldn't care less about Jewish people. Christianity is the greatest cultural appropriation in human history. You guys aren't Jewish; they are. And all this bullshit about Jews controlling the world? It's Americans controlling and using Israel that's the problem. And all of you fall for it because as soon as someone says, 'Israel is under threat,' you hear, 'The US is under attack.'"

"I don't know about all that," Jesse said. "You're thinking too much."

"But I'm thinking, right?" Abdul asked. "Hey, Jamarcus?"

"Sup?" Jamarcus answered.

"You seem like a pretty intelligent guy."

"Yeah, you're the only one here who thinks that," Jamarcus said, causing some of the people in the room to giggle.

"Hey, I'm being serious here," Abdul said. "Look, everyone in my platoon knows I'm Muslim. I don't hide that. But like I said, I'm not going to say that the hijackers were right and that America is evil. I'm as patriotic to this country as that redneck fuck back there. But you got to see that we're going into this country for the wrong reasons, right?"

Jamarcus watched the television a bit more, watching a group of pundits argue about the same discussion as the one in the room, before facing the skeptic. "Straight up—you want to know what I think?" Jamarcus asked.

"Yeah?"

"You're right," Jamarcus said. "This has nothing to do with al-Qaeda. This has nothing to do with weapons of mass destruction. I don't even think Iraq has any now. They did back in the eighties, and that's part of the reason why the world is going along with this. You're right, man. The US is in a kill-Muslim mentality right now, and they are looking for any country that fits that bill for them. We're not used to fighting an ideology. Ideologies don't have borders or ethnic groups to easily target. But a country does. And, man, Iraq, and Saddam fit the bill real nicely."

"So you think that because Saddam is an asshole, that's justification for going into Iraq and killing innocent people who had nothing to do with 9/11?" Abdul asked.

"Hell no," Jamarcus said. "You have to think that Daddy's little boy up in Washington has been itching for a chance to go into Iraq and finish the job Senior didn't. And you know what? I agree."

"Why?"

"I don't know if any of you guys remember the Iraq–Iran war in the eighties. Iraq and Iran got into an oil dispute—because no matter what, all of this is about oil, right?"

"Right," Abdul said.

"There are ethnic Kurds in the north of Iraq who have been disenfranchised by Saddam's regime for not being the right shade of Islam or not being Arab at all."

"This has nothing to do with Islam," Abdul said.

"And Saddam's persecution of the Kurds didn't either," Jamarcus said. "It was just an excuse for Saddam to get the rest of his people to go along with his ideas. In the war, we supported the Kurds; we gave them equipment, guns, and high-powered munitions to fight Iraq, but

Iraq still massacred them. But once Iraq and Iran signed a peace treaty, Iraq slaughtered over one hundred thousand of those people. And Iraq used poison gas, a WMD, against them. And it was our fault. We abandoned them to get slaughtered. Saddam is a madman—we can agree on that, right?"

"Right," Abdul said.

"And we can agree that his sons are worse, right?" Jamarcus said. "We see news reports every other day about Saddam's son Uday. That man's a certified maniac. Once Saddam's gone, who knows what he will do?"

"What does that have to do with al-Qaeda?" Abdul asked.

"Nothing," Jamarcus answered. "It's only about getting to Saddam and taking him out—something we should have done years ago. Now we're caught up in the spirit of the times and have an excuse to do it. We can go in, take him out, and set up a free democratic nation for the people there, especially for the Kurds. If we can do that—set up a stable democracy in that region—maybe we can have it springboard to other regions. Maybe Iran. Look, I'm Christian. I'm not going to blast Islam here, and I haven't so far. But I truly believe that God gave us a chance to do good by these people we screwed over. We've got to do good by the Kurds this time."

"It just so happens that the region most likely to accept a US presence in Iraq has a decent-sized oil reserve and two cities with refineries, right?" Abdul said.

"You know, I can't say anything against that," Jamarcus said.

"That's what I'm talking about," Abdul said. "You just made a speech talking on how Saddam probably used Islam—and we both know Saddam is not Islamic—as a tool to get his people to commit genocide against the Kurds. You have to know some of these politicians aren't Christian like they say—or the right shade of Christian, as you say. What makes you think the politicians in DC aren't using that same tactic on the American people and you?"

Jamarcus thought about that for a moment and couldn't come up with a logical response. "I don't know," he said.

"And what makes you think we are going in there to help the Iraqi people and not to grab the oil reserves?"

"I don't know. I just believe we're going in there for the right reasons."

"Well, take away the fact that you are Christian. Take away the fact that I'm Muslim. Take religion out of this, and is there still a good enough reason for us to go into Iraq?"

"I rely on my belief, man," Jamarcus said.

"And that's what I'm talking about," Abdul said. "Nobody thinks."

"Well, I think you wore me out, man," Jamarcus said, getting up from his seat. "I'm going to my room to lie down and contemplate my existence. You guys take it easy. Have a good afternoon, Abdul."

"You too, Staff," Abdul said.

"Jesse, you remember what that guy's name is?" Jamarcus asked.

"His name is Darrel Wilkens, Staff," another person in the recreation room said.

"Cool," Jamarcus said as he exited the room. "See you tomorrow, Jesse."

"Later, Staff!" Jesse yelled after Jamarcus as he walked back to his room.

Once Jamarcus arrived and closed his door behind him, he rubbed his face as he thought about the skeptic's words. *If you take religion away, would going into Iraq still be a good idea?* The question kept ringing in his mind like a bell. Jamarcus lay down on his bed and looked up at the ceiling. Just hearing that question had struck something deep inside him.

Jamarcus never really recovered from his girlfriend dumping him, and he was bad at connecting with people. He just never saw anyone. If he never had to interact with anyone, Jamarcus would just be fine being alone. He assumed he suffered from depression because of the negative reinforcement he'd gotten from his family and classmates growing up. His only memories of his family were of them saying something bad about him. If there were any others, either he had forgotten them, or he felt they were irrelevant. He didn't remember any of his family's faces or look at most people's faces at all. His mind told him that any new person he met would make fun of him. It was classic paranoia, but he couldn't help but think that way. He had never made the necessary healthy connections he'd needed while growing up.

He still remembered the faces of his best friends in high school, however, especially Jason. Jason was his brother, a friend he could open up to without being afraid of being judged or ridiculed. He often thought about calling Jason or any of his friends from high school, but Jamarcus felt he was just not that important. Why would anyone care about talking to him? When his ex-girlfriend dumped him, it made everything worse. He had truly loved her, and a lot of his self-confidence had come from the fact that he believed she loved him, so when she'd broken up with him, there had been no one Jamarcus could put his faith in.

That was when he'd dived into his Christian faith. He went to church just to feel he was socially part of a group, even though he could never connect with anyone. His mind wouldn't allow him to. But somehow, he felt that if he was righteous, God would give him someone in his life who would love him. He clung to that hope like a man clinging to a small bush when getting sucked in by a whirlpool. Every night, he prayed to God for a loved one, and every night, when he could, he looked up to the sky to find the Pleiades and get a little hope from them.

But the skeptic's question kept nagging him. The skeptic hadn't asked him if, with no religion, they would be going into Iraq. He'd asked Jamarcus if, with no religion, he had a reason for being. Frankly, Jamarcus hadn't had much hope in a God up to that point. If he didn't have that desperate hope, he would be all alone. That terrified Jamarcus. He lay in his bed, thinking about going into Iraq, terrified of his existence.

"I will protect you," the voice said in his head, and a familiar feeling from his childhood came back inside him as if he'd swallowed a drink of nostalgia. He became calm, and the fear subsided in him, but not all of it. He didn't overthink the message in his head, nor did he question it. It could have been an angel, or it could have been a voice in his head. He accepted the message as truth, and after rubbing his head from the buzzing, he flipped onto his side and went to sleep.

April 12, 2003

It was just after three o'clock in the afternoon as Jamarcus sat in the lead Humvee of his platoon and watched the buildings on the outskirts of Baghdad being bombarded by artillery and air strikes. His Humvee and three others in his platoon were parked along the highway leading into the city as the Abram tank they were escorting fired shot after shot into a group of residential buildings a quarter of a mile in front of them. Blackhawk helicopters hovered in the air a mile into the city, directing air strikes. Every so often, an Apache helicopter would fly overhead into the city, unload a payload into a building, and return to where it had come from. Jamarcus looked out the door window next to him and examined the buildings near them. A few of the structures were destroyed, with fire still burning in the ruins of a store to Jamarcus's right. When Jamarcus looked into his Humvee, he watched Jesse in the driver's seat and his squad in the back, who looked to be in awe of the destruction that was happening in front of them. Concerned, he reached for his radio.

"Bridge to First Platoon," Jamarcus said into his mic. "Make sure you keep your eyes on a swivel. We could still have bozos in the buildings next to us."

"Roger that, Staff," one of the soldiers said in the backseat.

Jamarcus returned to looking out his door window, contemplating how the invasion had gone so far. It was a blur from when his battalion had left Hawaii and arrived in Kuwait from the carrier. The next day, the company tried to find out which tank platoon they were assigned to escort, along with everyone's call signs, formations, and locations they were assigned to reach in the next few days. Jamarcus simply wrote everything he could down on a notepad, knowing he was never going to remember all of it. If anything, the last months had taught him not to panic when things seemed to go over his head. It was just Murphy's law.

Once everything got organized and the army began to invade Iraq, it was day after day of watching the tanks and artillery destroying every suspected structure in front of them. Jamarcus's formation was lucky with their travel to Baghdad, as they rarely encountered any intense close combat. What little they faced the gunners on the .50-calibers on the Humvees were able to repel. It was like that for more than a week, with little sleep, the shitty food of the MREs, and strategic targets being blown to smithereens. But that day, they reached Baghdad, and no matter how lucky they had been beforehand, Jamarcus knew they would have to do door-to-door close combat from then on. He kept wondering if he was going to be ready for it, but he realized the only way to learn was to get dirty. He was going to get mud on him the first time he went through the jungle anyway, so he might as well jump in.

"There are going to be two in the room when you go in," Jamarcus's guardian angel said in his mind. "One will be right in front of the door."

Jamarcus rubbed his forehead as the buzzing began to wear off. When the voice spoke, he saw a two-story house at a corner of a block, with a sandy field on the side of it. Jamarcus pushed the voice to the back of his thoughts when he heard a transmission over the radio.

"Oversight to Charlie One. Oversight to Charlie One. Over," the radio squawked.

"Oversight, this is Charlie One. Over," their lieutenant responded.

"Charlie One, we believe we have enemy combatants in a house with civilians. We can't direct a strike at the target. We need your platoon to clear that building out. The house is about a mile from where you're at right now. We will provide directions. Over."

"Understood, Oversight," the lieutenant answered. "Sergeant Bridge, did you read that last transmission? Over."

"Bridge to Charlie One. Roger that, LT," Jamarcus answered. "We're Oscar Mike to the target. Over." Staring at the city in front of him, Jamarcus took a deep breath, rubbed his forehead, and let out a long sigh. "Let's go, Jesse. Time to get fucked. You know where to go, right?"

"Hell no, Staff!" Jesse said with a laugh. "When do we ever know where we're going?"

"I know, right?" Jamarcus chuckled.

It didn't take long for Jesse to get his Humvee moving, and one after the other, each vehicle drove back onto the road and sped toward the city. As the outskirts got closer, Jamarcus's heart kept pounding harder and harder. Soon they were in the shadows of empty or destroyed buildings, and Jamarcus's mind completely focused on the house he saw in his mind.

"Oversight to Sergeant Bridge. You're going to make a left at the intersection ahead of you and head west. You'll see a house with graffiti on the side of it at the corner of a block. It has a dirt field on the south side of it. Over."

"Bridge to Oversight. Understood. Over," Jamarcus said into his mic. "Look at that, Jesse; they gave us directions."

"Miracles do happen, Staff," Jesse said as he turned left at the intersection, as instructed. As soon as he did, Jamarcus saw the building that was in his mind a block away from the vehicle. Just as the ops command had said in the overhead Blackhawk, it was at a corner of a block, right at an intersection of roads on its south and east sides. It was part of a row of houses that it connected to on its north side.

"Slow down, Jesse," Jamarcus said, thinking of where he was going to stage his men.

"Roger that, Staff," Jesse said, slowing the Humvee down to a crawl and halting the entire column.

"All right, Charlie squad, stage yourself a bit past the house on the road on the south side," Jamarcus said into his mic. "Delta squad, do the same on the road to the east. Don't let anyone near this area without giving them hell. Charlie, make sure no leaves out the back of that house. Both squads, make sure you keep your eyes peeled for anything inside the buildings, especially the upper floors. Alpha and Bravo will park right at the corner of the intersection. Don't step in the dirt. Alpha and Bravo are going in." After Jamarcus gave his command, the soldiers in the back gave out a holler, getting themselves ready to raid the house.

"Let's go, Jesse," Jamarcus said, and after a hoot, Jesse sped his way to the intersection and parked. Jamarcus stepped out of the Humvee and positioned himself on the side away from the house just as Charlie's squad's Humvee drove past him and parked twenty feet away from them. After the Bravo squad parked their vehicle on the east corner of the intersection and got out, Jamarcus banged his helmet on the roof of his Humvee to pump himself up.

"All right, guys, follow me!" Jamarcus yelled, and he walked slowly toward the front entrance of the house with his rifle trained at the windows in front of him. The soldiers in the Alpha squad followed right behind, with Bravo making a row behind them. Soon the two squads lined themselves on both sides of the front door.

"Should we go in the front door?" Jesse asked behind him.

"Does it make a difference?" Jamarcus said, and then he lowered his rifle when the lieutenant came up to him. "Wanted to have some fun, LT?" Jamarcus asked him.

"Hell yeah, Sergeant," the lieutenant answered.

"Do we know how many civilians are in the building?" Jamarcus asked.

"Hold on," the officer said. "Charlie One to Oversight. Charlie One to Oversight. Over."

"Charlie One, this is Oversight. Over."

"Oversight, do we know the number of civilians or soldiers in the house? Over."

"Unknown on the civilians. We saw two Iraqi soldiers enter the house behind a family who ran in front of them, we believe. Over."

"They could be a family," Jesse said. "It could be their house."

"Doesn't matter," Jamarcus said. "We're wasting time. Get ready to breach. I've got a point!" Jamarcus raised his rifle and pressed the hilt tightly against his shoulder. He then pointed to one of the Bravo squad members, who had a shotgun. "Shoot the door," Jamarcus ordered.

The soldier approached the door and shot the knob twice, leaving a hole, and the door slightly opened. The soldier then kicked the door open and stepped back to his squad as Jamarcus stepped through the entrance, feeling the most scared he had ever been in his life. He slowly walked to the staircase in front of him as the rest of the squad went to all the corners of the room before each yelled, "Clear!"

"Mind the top of the stairs," Jamarcus said as the Bravo squad came in behind them and searched the hall connecting the front room they'd entered to an area in the back of the house, as well as the rooms along the hall.

"We have a kitchen back here," the lieutenant said.

"On it!" Jamarcus answered, and he slowly walked toward the kitchen, training his rifle up the stairs as he walked by it. When he entered the kitchen, he went to the corner to his right as Jesse came in behind him to the left, and the rest of the squad cleared the room.

"Charlie squad, did you see anybody leave the house?" Jamarcus asked into the radio.

"Negative, Staff," a soldier responded.

"Shit," Jamarcus grunted, looking back at the stairs. "All right, fellas, let's get these bozos." He walked back to the stairs and climbed up slowly, followed by the two squads.

"There are two of them in the room to the left," the voice in his head said. "One is right behind the door."

Jamarcus saw two men in desert fatigues, one in a corner of the room right in front of a door and the other to his left. A family was lying in the middle of the room—a mother lying on top of her kids. Once Jamarcus got to the top of the stairs, he slowed to a crawl until he got to a door on his left. Nodding, he pumped himself up to enter the room.

With stomach and anus clenched, Jamarcus reached forward and opened the door, lunging back just in time to dodge bullets piercing the wall to his right. Screams erupted inside the room, and Jamarcus leaned on the wall opposite the door and fired through the wall of the room until the shooting stopped. Jamarcus then walked into the room, and as soon as he saw the Iraqi soldier in the corner in front of him, he fired three more shots into the man's chest before the man fell to his side. The man to his left turned his gun at Jamarcus and managed to fire a shot that struck the wall behind him before Jesse came in and shot the man multiple times. The man fell face-forward to the floor. The family continued to scream as the rest of the squad entered the room. Bravo squad walked past the door behind them to clear out the next room as Jamarcus looked about to make sure no one else was in it.

"Watch these guys," Jamarcus said to two of his squad members as he left the room with Jesse and another soldier behind. With the Bravo squad, they quickly cleared the second floor. All the while, Jamarcus could hear his heart pounding in his ears.

"Thank you," Jamarcus said to his voice after they cleared the last room.

"What's up, Staff?" Jesse asked.

"Nothing," Jamarcus said, and then he paused after he heard yelling in the room with the family. He rushed back to see the two squad members desperately trying to keep the family away from the two bodies.

"Yo, Jay, what do we do?" one of them asked.

"Grab their weapons, and make sure there aren't any on the bodies," Jamarcus ordered. His squad quickly grabbed the two AK-47s and searched the dead soldiers while the two previous squad members held the family back.

"They're clear, Staff," one of his soldiers said.

"Let them go," Jamarcus said. The two soldiers let the family go, and the mother dove onto the man in front of the door, with a scream erupting from her that hit Jamarcus deep in his gut. The children sat in the middle of the room, holding each other and crying with despair on their faces. Jamarcus's mind was able to clear enough for him to see that the man in front of the door was older, probably in his early forties, and the one to the left was just a kid, not even seventeen.

"Jesus, Jesse, you were right," one of the squad members said.

"We're clear, LT," Jamarcus said after he cleared his thoughts.

"Roger that, Sergeant Bridge," the lieutenant said. "Charlie One to Oversight. Charlie One to Oversight. Over."

"Charlie One, this is Oversight. Over!" the radio yelled back.

"House is clear. Two combatants down. The family's still here. Over."

"Understood, Charlie One. Good job. We have another building two miles north of where you are. Same situation. Can't call in an air strike if civilians are in there with targets. We need you to clear it out. Over."

"Fucking Christ," someone behind Jamarcus said.

"Acknowledge, Oversight," the lieutenant said. "We're Oscar Mike. Sergeant Bridge, let's move."

"Yeah, LT," Jamarcus answered. He descended back down the stairs and out of the house with the two squads behind him.

"What happened in there?" one of the guys from the Delta squad Humvee asked, but Jamarcus ignored the question as he got back into the Alpha vehicle.

"Sergeant Bridge to Oversight. Sergeant Bridge to Oversight. What are the directions? Over," Jamarcus said into the mic after the rest of the squad entered the Humvee.

"Oversight to Bridge. It's back up the road you enter the city on, about two miles north and on the southeast side of a rotary. It'll be on your right as you hit the junction; you can't miss it. Be advised some civilians left the building after the soldiers entered, so we are unsure of the number of people in it. We need that building cleared to allow armored divisions to enter Baghdad on that highway. Over."

"Roger that," Jamarcus answered. "All right, Jesse. Let's move."

Jesse silently got the vehicle running and spun it back toward the road they'd entered. After a moment, the other Humvees formed a column behind them, and soon they were speeding through the city toward the target. The soldiers in the back were soberly quiet, and Jamarcus's stomach was clenched so hard it was beginning to hurt. He took a deep breath and forced his stomach to relax.

"You saved my life back there, Jesse," Jamarcus said, trying to get his mind not to focus on his shaking legs.

"Fuck, Staff, that was badass the way you handled that door, man. Shooting through the wall. Where did you come up with that?"

"A voice in my head," Jamarcus answered, and then he leaned forward as he saw the junction to the rotary ahead. "Slow down, man," he said, and Jesse brought the column to a halt on the road. "Bridge to Oversight. Bridge to Oversight. Is that the rotary ahead? Over."

"Affirmative, Sergeant Bridge. The three-story office building to the right of the junction in front of you. Over."

"Understood," Jamarcus said into the mic. He took in two quick breaths before he spoke on the radio again. "Alpha and Bravo, park your Humvees just east of the junction. Charlie and Delta, park on the right just before the junction. Alpha and Delta, watch the roads. Delta, you should be able to see the rear of the building. Make sure no one leaves out back. Bravo and Charlie are going in." Jamarcus took the clip out of his rifle and replaced it with another. "Let's go," he said, and Jesse drove the vehicle past the junction and parked on the southeast part of the rotary.

Jamarcus stepped out of the Humvee and moved around to place it between himself and the building. When the other vehicles came to a stop, Jamarcus took one last look at the office windows, watching for any movement inside.

"Bravo, Charlie, let's go," Jamarcus said on the radio, and he, the two squads, and the lieutenant all walked slowly to the front entrance.

Once each squad was lined up on each side of the glass door, Jamarcus slowly walked toward it with his stomach clenched in pain and opened it. He calmly walked in, followed by the other squads, and they proceeded to systematically clear all the rooms. It took them only five minutes to clear the place, and when they'd finished, they'd found only empty cubicles, desert fatigues, and small arms on the ground.

"This place is empty, LT," Jamarcus said to the lieutenant after they were done.

"Okay," the lieutenant responded. "Charlie One to Oversight. Charlie One to Oversight. Over."

"Charlie One, this is Oversight. Over."

"The building is clear. Over."

"Good job, Charlie One. Set up a perimeter on the rotary so we can have the convoy come in. Over."

"Understood," the lieutenant said. "We're Oscar Mike, guys," he said to the group, and they quickly walked back to the Humvees.

"Set up the perimeter, Sergeant," the lieutenant commanded.

"On it, LT," Jamarcus said, and he gripped his radio before giving directions. "All right, guys, we're going to stage on each of the junctions here. Delta, stay at this junction. Charlie, take the junction on the east. Bravo to the north, and Alpha to the west. Don't block the roads, so the convoys can come through. Let's move."

Jamarcus ran over to Alpha Squad as quickly as he could and jumped into the vehicle. "You know what I'm trying to do, Jesse?"

"Roger that, Staff," Jesse said, and he quickly got the Humvee moving around the rotary and parked in front of the junction to the west. After the vehicles stopped, they all stepped out and took positions around the vehicles. They stood there quietly for a few minutes before they heard the rumble of the armored convoys. Soon column after column of tanks, Humvees, and construction vehicles came rushing through the junctions, all going in different directions. Minutes later, civilians, mostly men, came out first in the dozens and then in the hundreds, cheering the vehicles as they drove by.

"We did it," Jesse said as he took off his helmet, with his red hair blazing from the afternoon sun and a wide grin spreading over his freckled face. "We took Baghdad, man."

"I guess so," Jamarcus said. Then he looked at one of his soldiers, who looked distressed. "Salters, you okay?"

"We destroyed that family, man," the soldier said with tears streaming down his cheeks.

Jamarcus wasn't sure what he was doing when he put his rifle down in the vehicle, walked over to the soldier, and embraced him. The man cried, holding on to Jamarcus, as armored vehicles rushed past them, and Jamarcus didn't know how to feel at that moment. He felt the same as when his ex-girlfriend had dumped him. He felt empty.

Chapter 5
<1>
July 2003

Jamarcus stood in the company commander's second-floor office with his lieutenant in the early morning hours as the captain spoke on the phone with the ops command. The company had commandeered the office building that Jamarcus's platoon had cleared months before and was using it as a base of operation and living quarters. Most other battalions took over mansions or abandoned forts, but since the company had done so many operations around the junction, they had taken the office building out of familiarity. There wasn't much space in the building, just enough to stow their gear and cots to sleep on, and the building didn't provide much physical protection in case there was an attack; the front of the first floor was all glass. But someone had to hold that junction so the United States could enter and out of Baghdad from the southeast part of the city, and most of the other buildings in the immediate area were residential homes. There was nowhere else they could stay except in that building.

"Sorry, guys," the captain said after he got off the phone with a troubled sigh. "That was ops, and they're pretty pissed about the past IED bombings the last few days. They're blaming us for the ones happening near the rotary, and they want us to crack down on any cells that could be making them. So, I have to make some changes to the patrols and increase the hours and areas that each squad will have."

"Is that possible?" Jamarcus asked with a troubled voice.

"You know what, Jamarcus?" the captain groaned, rubbing his face. "I'm not in the mood to get chewed out by you after I just got chewed out by ops. Okay?"

"Hear me out, Cap," Jamarcus said. "I'm just saying that we don't have enough men to patrol this entire area. The command is asking us to hold practically the whole southeast part of the city by ourselves."

"Don't exaggerate, Jay."

"Cap, I know that we have other companies who perform operations around here, but our company is the only one patrolling the area at a constant rate. You're asking one squad to patrol ten square blocks all by themselves for twenty-four hours straight. We need another company out here."

"You don't think I just finished telling ops that, Jay?" the captain asked.

"Bobby, if you're mad at my platoon, it's my choice to keep my squads together," the lieutenant said. "I don't want to put any of my men in a compromising position."

"It's not that, Bubba. I agree with you. Considering we're living right next door to the entire Iraqi army; I'd do the same. But ops are telling us that we can't anymore. We're going to have to eat it."

"Murphy's law." Jamarcus sighed. The sound of the phrase was therapeutic to his mind.

"Damn right, Jay," the captain said. "But I've got another urgent issue. We just got a tip from a civilian that an IED may have been planted on the highway about five miles west of the Rotary. Bubba, I know your platoon just came back from patrol, but I need you to take your men set a perimeter around the site, and wait for EOD to show up.”

Jamarcus took in a short breath and looked at the wall to his left silently.

“Murphy’s law,” the captain said.

“Murphy’s law,” Jamarcus replied. “Do we know when EOD will show?”

“They’re en route,” the captain said.

“Do we know what we’re looking for?” the lieutenant asked.

“The tip says that it may be in a broken part of the highway heading westbound next to a light post. You’ll have to find it, Bubba.”

“Roger that,” Jamarcus said, and he walked out of the office with the lieutenant close behind. He took a few steps toward the stairs and stopped, trying to convince his body to keep the fatigue shaking away.

“All right, Jay?” the lieutenant asked.

“I’m good, LT,” Jamarcus answered, and then he descended the stairs with the lieutenant following behind, and they walked over to the platoon as they took off their gear.

“Don’t take off your stuff, guys; we’re heading back out,” Jamarcus said, and then he stood quietly as his men lamented the news. They went on for a while until they noticed that Jamarcus and the lieutenant stayed silent, and gradually, they stopped complaining.

"Everybody got that out of their system?" Jamarcus asked, and he waited until he knew everyone was ready.

"Captain Hill just let us know that there is a possible IED on the highway west of the junction, and we've got to set up a perimeter around it," the lieutenant said.

"LT, it's morning," one of the soldiers said. "We've got morning traffic going through that road. A lot of people are going to be pissed."

"Which means there are a lot of people we're trying to save," Jamarcus said, and the platoon went silent.

"Sergeant, you got a formation set up?" the lieutenant asked.

"Yeah," Jamarcus said before taking in and letting out a deep breath. "Delta squad, we need you to block all outbound traffic heading west from the west junction. You'll have to direct traffic somewhere else." He waited until the squad stopped grumbling and then continued. "The rest of the squads will go westbound and find this IED for bomb disposal. Hopefully, we can locate it before anyone gets killed."

"Do we know where it is?" another soldier asked.

"That's our job to find out," the lieutenant said.

"Everybody set?" Jamarcus asked the platoon.

"Yo, Jay, why are you always leaving us out of all the action?" someone from the Delta squad asked. "Why can't we go to the IED?"

"If you guys want to switch with any other squad, be my guests."

"We'll switch with ya, man," one of Charlie's squad responded.

"Let it be known that you're only switching because you don't want to deal with the locals."

"Now that we've gotten that out of the way," Jamarcus said, waiting for the platoon to stop laughing, "let's get ready to go. Drink some coffee, and put something in your stomach. I don't want someone passing out from hunger." Jamarcus himself went over to the food table and grabbed two doughnuts and a large plastic cup of sugar mixed with coffee.

"Hey, Staff, I call bullshit that they dropped this on us now," Jesse said next to him, grabbing a bowl of sliced apples and shoving them into his mouth.

"Yeah," Jamarcus said, noticing Jesse's new haircut for the first time. He'd gotten a crew cut, with stylish parts cut along one side of his head. "New hairdo?" Jamarcus asked after stuffing down half of the first doughnut.

"Yeah, the guys in the squad said I had to get a tight cut if I was to ride with them," Jesse said after downing a water bottle.

Jamarcus could only laugh as he finished the first doughnut. After taking a small sip of the scalding coffee, he grabbed his rifle in one hand and the coffee and last doughnut in the other.

"Let's go, gentlemen!" Jamarcus said as he walked out the entrance.

The lieutenant and a couple of other guys were outside waiting for the rest of the platoon. Jamarcus reached his Humvee and finished the second doughnut. He just managed to swallow the last of his coffee before the rest of the Alpha squad piled into the vehicle.

"Everybody ready?" Jamarcus asked the guys in the vehicle, and when they said they were, Jamarcus got on the radio. "Bridge to First Platoon. Bridge to First Platoon. Is everybody ready to go? Over."

"Hold up, Staff. We're still waiting for one more person," someone called out on the radio, and as Jamarcus looked at the office building, the last soldier came running out, trying to drink a cup of coffee before jumping into a Humvee.

"Bridge to Charlie One. All present, LT. Over," Jamarcus said.

"Roger that. Charlie One to Valhalla. Charlie One to Valhalla. We're Oscar Mike to the IED. Over."

"Valhalla to Charlie One. Understood. Stay safe out there. We'll let you know when EOD is heading your way. Over."

"Understood. Bridge, let's go," the lieutenant said.

"Roger, LT," Jamarcus answered, and he looked out at traffic going around the rotary. It was getting busy, with dozens of cars rushing by their column. "Ready to go, Jesse?" Jamarcus asked.

"Moving," Jesse answered, and he slowly drove into the turnabout, pausing long enough so that the rest of the column could get in behind them. Once on the road, Jesse directed the column around to the west junction and slowed down once again on the westbound road.

"Stop here," Jamarcus said, and Jesse brought the Humvee to a halt. Jamarcus stepped outside the vehicle and watched Charlie's squad behind them park their Humvee in front of the road. The squad got out and stopped all traffic as quickly as they could. The local people were not happy about it, and soon there was a good-sized group of them complaining to Charlie's squad. Once Jamarcus was satisfied that the road was clogged, he got back into the vehicle.

"Let's go, Jesse. Take it slow."

"Roger that, Staff," Jesse said as he slowly began moving the column westbound.

Along the way, cars and trucks zoomed past them on the eastbound highway. Jamarcus couldn't help thinking that any second, he was going to hear a large boom either under him or on the other side of the road. They drove like that for a couple of minutes, until Jamarcus saw a broken part of asphalt next to a light post in the median between the eastbound and westbound highways. On the south side of the road, on their left, was a grassy hill that had apartment buildings at the top. On the north side of the eastbound road was a field separating the highway from a large number of houses.

"Slow down, Jesse. I think this is it," Jamarcus said.

"How do we know?" Jesse asked as he brought the Humvee to a halt about a hundred feet from the light post.

"We don't; we have to wait for EOD to show up," Jamarcus said before the squad got out of the vehicle. Jamarcus looked up at the apartment buildings to the south, searching for anyone who might be staring at them out of any windows.

"Bravo, squad. Drive over the median, and block traffic going eastbound," Jamarcus said into the mic. "Don't get close to the light post right in front of us."

"Roger that, Staff," someone said over the radio, and Bravo's Humvee carefully drove over the median and across incoming traffic. Once they got to the north side of the road, they traveled eastward until they were about a hundred feet away from the light post and drove in front of traffic again. A couple of times, Jamarcus was sure someone would be unable to stop and would slam right into Bravo's Humvee, but they managed to get onto the highway and stop traffic going past the light post.

"Bridge to Charlie One. I think we found it," Jamarcus said into the radio.

"Roger that. Moving to your location," the lieutenant answered.

Jamarcus saw him get out of Delta Squad's vehicle and walk over to him. *The bomb is going to blow. The bomb was going to blow*, and Jamarcus's mind kept repeating until the lieutenant arrived.

"What do we have?" the lieutenant asked.

"Do you see that hole in the asphalt right by that light post ahead of us?" Jamarcus asked, pointing at it.

"Yeah. Do you think that's it?"

"I don't know. But it fits the description Cap gave us. Call it in?"

"Okay," the lieutenant said.

As he called in the location of the possible IED, Jamarcus looked across the street at Bravo dealing with the crowd. One man was getting in the face of one of the soldiers, which got Jamarcus's blood hot.

"Hey, what's up with that guy over there, Bravo?" Jamarcus asked over the radio.

"These guys are pissed off, Staff," one of them responded. "I think they're cursing us out in at least two different languages."

"Don't let them get up on you like that," Jamarcus responded. "Fuck, man, we're only trying to do our job."

"They don't know that, Jamarcus," the lieutenant said. "We've got to cut them some slack."

Jamarcus didn't respond; he only looked at the light post, expecting it to blow up at any moment. They waited for more than half an hour in the increasingly hot sun with the civilians screaming at the Bravo squad, and as Jamarcus looked at the apartment buildings above them, he saw a good number of people looking down at the commotion. Slowly, the hole in Jamarcus's chest began to fill with cold anxiety and anger.

"Do we have word of when EOD is coming?" Jamarcus asked.

"Bobby said they are en route, but no ETA yet," the lieutenant said.

"Crap," Jamarcus said. His body froze, and the hole in his heart thrust open in pain as he saw a boy running down the hill toward the highway. It seemed the child was using the stopped traffic to try to get quickly across the highway. Jamarcus was running toward the kid before he knew what he was doing. He could hear the lieutenant and Jesse yelling from behind him, but he was trying to get to the kid before he got to the highway. The whole time, Jamarcus kept expecting the light post to blow right in his face.

"Hey!" Jamarcus yelled at the child, waving at the boy to come to him, but when the kid saw Jamarcus, his eyes went wide with fright, and he ran away from Jamarcus toward the light post. When it was clear he wasn't going to stop the boy in time, Jamarcus turned around and ran back to the Humvee, almost running into Jesse. Running back,

Jamarcus began to feel a little better since no explosion had occurred.

"I think I'm wrong!" Jamarcus said as they ran back. "I don't think that's—"

That was all Jamarcus was able to say before an incredible force slammed into him, and he heard the loudest noise he'd ever heard in his life. He had known some guys in the band while he was in high school, and during some football games he'd attended, they had joked around and placed their ears on the large bass drum while someone hit it as hard as he could. The sound he now heard was that sound times ten; it hurt every part of Jamarcus's body inside and out. When he fell to the ground, his perspective was as if he were still standing up. He looked at himself rolling on the ground as if in slow motion. It was a peculiar sensation, and somehow, the curiosity he'd had as a child came back to him. *What is this? What am I doing? Is this an out-of-body experience? What's causing this?* More questions would have kept coming, but he saw Jesse run to him and try to pick him up.

"Staff, you okay?" Jesse asked when Jamarcus got up.

"Yeah," Jamarcus said, looking at Jesse as they ran back to the Humvee. Jamarcus looked back at the light post, trying to find the boy, but he didn't see anything except dust in the air and a large hole in the ground. He looked up at one of the apartment buildings just in time to see two lone men looking down at the explosion from the third floor, one with a video camera.

"Right there!" Jamarcus screamed, pointing, and the rest of the men by the Humvee looked up just in time to see the two voyeurs spot them and turn back into the apartment. "LT, call it in! Alpha squad on me!" Jamarcus said, and he didn't wait for anyone to respond as he raced up the hill toward the apartment.

When he got to the east side wall of the building, he slammed against it to stop himself and then slowly moved along it until he reached the road on the south side. His stomach clenched in pain when he heard the footsteps of Jesse and the rest of the squad catch up with him.

"Don't shoot," the guardian angel buzzed in his head.

Jamarcus almost ignored it as he slowly looked out from around the corner to the front of the apartment. When he saw the entrance of the building, which was open, he stepped toward it, but he stopped when he heard screaming above. When he looked, he saw the two voyeurs three stories above him on a balcony, contemplating trying to climb onto the balcony of the building next to them.

"Stop!" Jamarcus yelled, causing the men to look down with fear filling their eyes. One of the men began climbing the balcony, causing Jamarcus to raise his weapon.

"Don't shoot. Don't shoot," the voice buzzed, but Jamarcus instinctively ran out onto the road and began to fire at the men and into the apartment behind them. Both men fell immediately; one was dead, while the other screamed from his wounds in agony.

"Fuck yeah, Staff!" one of the squad screamed as they came around the corner.

They couldn't stay down there for long, Jamarcus thought. They had to go get the two men.

"You two stay down here and watch him," Jamarcus said. "Salter, Jesse, let's go."

Jamarcus then slowly entered the apartment building. As they climbed up the stairs, they could hear people screaming through the walls. Once they got to the third floor and walked toward the apartment, Jamarcus saw a woman in a black dress, multicolored blouse, and beige head scarf looking at him in distress. She ran back into her home before Jamarcus could say anything. The door was already open, and with a quick breath, Jamarcus walked in.

They could hear the man on the balcony crying in pain as they slowly cleared all the rooms in the apartment. Jamarcus walked into the living room area next to the balcony. In front of the man writhing in pain were broken glass and two bodies: a woman and a baby with its head blown out. Jamarcus stood there watching the bodies of the woman and child as his heart filled with grief and guilt. Jesse walked past Jamarcus and approached the two men on the balcony. He searched the dead man and found a cell phone and some change in his pocket. He grabbed the camera from the crying man and began to look through the footage on it.

"Staff, they recorded the whole thing," Jesse said, his eyes wide with excitement. "There's even footage of them making bombs. We got them, man."

Jamarcus stood and looked at Jesse before collecting his thoughts and grabbing his radio. "Bridge to Charlie One. Bridge to Charlie One."

"This is Charlie One, Sergeant. You guys all right?"

"We got the bombers. One is dead; the other is wounded," Jamarcus said. "We got evidence that it's them. We have a dead family here too."

"Roger that, Sergeant," the lieutenant responded. "Backup is on the way. Stand by. Over."

Jamarcus sat on the couch across from the woman and the child. *Why didn't I wait? There was no reason to shoot. They didn't have any weapons. Why did I shoot? Why didn't I listen to the guardian angel's voice?* He kept looking at the dead child, and before he knew it, he was crying uncontrollably. Salter walked over to Jamarcus and held his head against his chest, and Jamarcus wept into his hands.

<2>

December 2003

Jamarcus and the Alpha squad were on foot patrol one cold, bright day northeast of the office. The cold weather had been a shock to Jamarcus when late November hit, and when it had rained, he had been floored. His only knowledge of that region was from what he had seen on television, which he had to admit was lacking in facts and mostly filled with prejudice or sometimes flat-out lies. It amazed Jamarcus that on bright, clear days, the city looked like it was hot. It still looked like a desert out the window. But when he stepped outside and the cold hit him, it put Jamarcus's mind in a dissonance. It just didn't feel right. Jamarcus just assumed it was because, in the United States, there was a clear difference in the environment when the season changed. But in Iraq, the city looked the same year-round. The only difference was that the hills around the city turned green from the winter rain—not a lot, but when they did, Jamarcus couldn't help but think they were beautiful.

That day, it wasn't that cold, and walking the streets warmed Jamarcus up. The low humidity made it that much more comfortable. There was still a bit of tension between the local people and the US soldiers, but that day, the local Iraqis seemed to ignore them to a point. Ever since the incident at the apartment, the bombings in the immediate area had stopped, and the operations command had listened and brought in another company to bolster the mission. Together the companies provided a constant presence on the ground to give bozos the impression that the United States was monitoring any suspicious activities in the area.

The street Jamarcus found himself on that day was busy. It was a shopping area, and the side of the street his squad was on was lined with restaurants, with the smell of midday lunch rolling out the doors and windows. Crowds were already forming in and around many of them, with people on lunch break trying to get their meals before the US troops made another vehicle movement through the rotary that would clog up traffic. It felt like walking through DC during lunch hour to Jamarcus.

"Hey, you guys want to get something to eat from that restaurant?" Salter asked.

"I do," Jamarcus said.

"Man, let's go," Jesse said, and as the squad walked a few more yards down the street, they detoured into a small hole-in-the-wall restaurant. The place was an anomaly in that part of the city because besides serving quick Iraqi meals, the husband and wife in it also served Western-type food. One of the guys from their company said their squad had come across it while on patrol. Since then, a lot of the men had frequented it, even though they had been instructed not to patrol in the same patterns. Going there often would put their lives and the people there in danger. But there weren't many places that made excellent hamburgers and french fries like that restaurant did.

Perhaps the couple wanted to take advantage of the influx of soldiers to make more money, Jamarcus thought. Either way, Jamarcus believed that if he was going to die in Iraq, it would be over a good cheeseburger.

"What do you guys want? I'm buying," Salter said.

"I want their fried chicken wings," Jesse said.

"I'll get my usual," Jamarcus said, and after the other squad member gave their orders, Salter went into the restaurant while the rest stood by the road.

Ever vigilant, Jamarcus surveyed the street, admiring the Iraqi people as they went about their lives. Everything was different there, from how individuals interacted with each other based on different situations to the language they spoke. If Jamarcus hadn't been there because of the war, he would have loved to learn more about the culture there. It felt like being on an alien planet in one of the sci-fi movies he used to watch as a kid.

"Did anybody watch the Patriots game last Sunday?" one of the guys asked.

"Yeah, you see how they blanked the Bills, man?" Jesse responded. "Thirty-one to nothing."

"Especially since the Bills blanked them with the same score the first week of the season."

"That's because Lawyer Milloy went to Buffalo and gave them

the entire Patriots playbook," Jesse said. "But I'm telling you, man: Patriots are going to the Super Bowl this season. We just need to stay alive for the next week, and we're home, and I'm going to the game."

"Dog, do you have to say it like that?" someone asked.

"My bad." Jesse laughed.

"Think they're going to win?" Jamarcus asked, still scanning the street.

"Hey, Staff, with that defense, nobody's going to beat them."

"Man, they had one good game last week, and everybody's already giving them the trophy," Jamarcus said. "And besides, you have to admit they cheated in that game."

"What? Because the Patriots blanked the Bills? The Bills cheated when they blanked the Patriots. Every team in the NFL steals each other's plays, man. If you ain't cheating, you ain't trying."

"Hey, I got the food," Salter said as he rejoined the group.

"Sweet," Jesse said as the guys grabbed their lunch from him.

"Hey, man, this is Sprite. No Coke?" Jesse asked.

"Nobody said what drink they wanted," Salter said in defense.

"Hey, Jesse, what else are you going to do when you get home?" Jamarcus asked as the squad continued on their patrol.

"Probably go home to visit my family back in Texas. Hang out with my boys and watch some football. Go to Mexico and raise some hell. You know, the typical good ole boy stuff. What about you, Staff? You going to visit family?"

"No, I'm not that close to my family. Probably hang out around Oahu."

"Yo, that reminds me," Salter said. "Guess who I found out is Staff's sister? Goddamn Vanessa." The rest of the squad was stunned and quiet for a moment before they erupted with screams.

"Yo, Staff, your sister's Vanessa?" one of them asked. "She's the next Janet Jackson! What the hell?"

"Yeah," Jamarcus said grudgingly.

"You don't talk to her?"

"I don't talk to anyone from my family really," Jamarcus said. "I was never close to them. I just don't get close to people."

"Yeah, we kind of noticed. You do just ignore us sometimes back at the office. I figured you were just an introvert."

"Is that what I am?" Jamarcus asked himself.

"Shit, I forgot to give them a tip," Salter said.

"I'll do it," Jamarcus said, giving his food to Salter and turning back to the restaurant to get away from the scrutiny. "I've got some change to give."

"You're sure?" Salter asked.

"Yeah. You guys stay here; I'll be back." Jamarcus was already on his way toward the shop, not giving anyone from the squad a chance to argue. Jamarcus didn't want to talk about his sister.

On the way back, he walked around a bunch of teenage boys sitting by the side of a store, acting like typical boys, up to no good. He walked into the restaurant, made his way past the line, and came up to the wife, who was working the cash register.

"Ma'am?" Jamarcus called out with a few American dollars in his hands.

"Oh, thank you," the lady said with a smile as she took the bills.

"Bye," Jamarcus said as he quickly walked out of the restaurant and back toward his squad. The teenage boys he had seen earlier were laughing hard about something as Jamarcus approached them, and when one of them saw Jamarcus, the boy flashed a cocky smile at him.

"Wassup, my nigga?" he said as Jamarcus walked past them.

"Hey, watch that!" Jamarcus said, walking backward to face them. "I don't know you that well. I don't even use that word, punk." He then turned back in the direction he was going, smiling at how arrogant those kids were. He was caught off guard when the boy ran in front of him and slammed his chest against his.

"What you say, man?" the boy asked, but Jamarcus barely heard him. His stomach clenched, and his heart blocked up with fright, and he instinctively pushed the boy away from him, sending the teenager sprawling onto the sidewalk. The boy quickly recovered and, out of nowhere, pulled a knife, lunging at Jamarcus.

"Stop!" Jamarcus shouted, bringing his rifle up and aiming it at the kid.

The boy stopped dead in his tracks, staring at the rifle. He then began yelling in Farsi at the teenagers behind Jamarcus. Jamarcus looked around, trying to assess the situation. The rest of the boys huddled together, their eyes wide with shock and confusion. People on the street came to a stop, and others ran away. All the while, the boy with the knife kept screaming at his friends.

"Drop the knife!" Jamarcus screamed at the boy, trying to intimidate him. Jamarcus's finger was pressed against his trigger, and every fiber in his body was screaming at him to fire. But every time he was about to, he saw the body of the baby he'd shot, with the head completely blown away. For a moment, Jamarcus stood there, not sure what to do.

"Staff!" someone yelled, and Jamarcus looked past the boy and saw the rest of his squad running as fast as they could toward the confrontation. The boy with the knife turned to see the approaching soldiers and then ran across the street away from them, followed closely by the rest of the teenagers.

"Don't shoot!" Jamarcus screamed at the squad when he saw that their weapons were trained at the boys. Soon the squad arrives by Jamarcus, panting and confused.

"What the hell happened?" Jesse asked.

"Nothing. Just some punk kids trying to be tough."

"Why didn't you shoot?"

"I didn't hear a voice telling me to," Jamarcus answered. "Hey, you guys got my food?"

"What the fuck, Jay? We dropped all the food trying to get to you," Salter said, which made Jamarcus laugh. The stress seeped out of him with each chuckle.

"We'd better go clean that up," Jamarcus said as he walked past them. "You know how these people get with every mistake we make."

"Shit, I'm not picking anything up! You do it!" someone shouted at him from behind.

"All right!" Jamarcus yelled back as he faced away from them, not wanting the rest of the squad to see that he was on the verge of tears.

Chapter 6
<1>
July 2004

Jamarcus entered a grocery store in Kalihi, a suburb of downtown Honolulu, looking for some snacks to eat while he binged on playing video games. He'd gotten an apartment off base as soon as he got back from Iraq, so he didn't have to interact with anyone. He knew that it was a stress-coping mechanism and that it was wrong to distance himself from other people, but he wanted to get as far as possible away from the military as much as he could. On base, everything had changed between the soldiers who'd served in the initial push into Iraq and those who hadn't. It was all everyone talked about. Recruits asked the vets what the fighting was like, and the vets hazed the recruits because they'd gotten some salt behind their ears from combat. Jamarcus just wanted to forget about Iraq for a few months, so he'd gotten an apartment, and he spent hours off duty playing games on his Xbox to relieve his anxiety.

Jamarcus had been in the supermarket a few times before, so he knew exactly where the snacks aisle was and went straight there. Command on base had told him to be wary of the local people for their dislike of anyone from the mainland. It wasn't hard to see why from Jamarcus's point of view. He only had noticed after being in Hawaii for a few years, but mainland Americans were loud and needed to be the center of attention.

Jamarcus walked straight to where he was going and stood in front of the chips section, trying to figure out which ones he was going to buy. Down the aisle, a female employee stocking shelves smiled at Jamarcus as he walked close to her.

"Hi," she said as Jamarcus stood looking at the chips.

"Hey," Jamarcus responded.

Jamarcus was expecting to spend a good forty-eight hours straight playing *Halo 2* with the crew he regularly played with to get as high on the leaderboards as possible. The leaderboards could change just minutes after one changed a rank. That year, the game had created a new ranking system that took into account how well you played and whom you beat based on ranks, which meant that if you were ranked high and lost to a lower-ranked group, your ranking could drop significantly, and it could take forever to get back to where you were. That weekend, Jamarcus was going to stick with a group he knew was good and marathon *Halo 2* until his controller fell apart. Besides, it was a great stress reliever from all the tension he'd built up in Iraq. He could spend hours having fun.

Jamarcus was getting himself hyped up so much that he barely noticed the store employee still looking at him. When he turned to her, she gave him another smile.

"Hi," she said again.

"Hi," Jamarcus replied.

"Here by yourself?"

"Hmm, yeah," Jamarcus answered. "I was going to buy some snacks to munch on while I do a video game binge this weekend."

"You going to play video games all weekend? What's your girl-friend going to say about that?"

"I don't have a girlfriend. I'm too pathetic."

"How do you not have a girlfriend? You're so sexy."

"Yeah, I think you're the only one in this store who thinks that," Jamarcus mumbled.

"My name's Kathrine with a *K*," she said as she walked over, holding out her hand.

"Jamarcus," he replied, shaking her hand.

"Are you in the military?" Kathrine asked.

"Yeah. Army."

"How long have you been in?"

"Over six years now."

"Have you dated any local girls here?"

"I haven't been off the base much when I'm off duty. I usually stay in my room playing games or go to the movies."

"Well, at least you go out to see a movie," Kathrine said snidely. "What movies do you go see?"

"Mostly sci-fi," Jamarcus answered. "I'm a huge *Star Wars* fan, so I've watched *The Phantom Menace* and *Attack of the Clones* count-less times."

"I don't like the new *Star Wars* movies. I'm still a fan of the old ones."

"Yeah, I hear that a lot. What about you? What movies do you watch?"

"Well, I watch a lot of cartoons," Kathrine said. "I mostly watch anime. I love Studio Ghibli."

"Oh yeah, *Spirited Away. Kiki's Delivery Service.* Those are beautiful movies."

"You watch anime too?" Kathrine asked.

"Yeah, all the time," Jamarcus answered, grabbing a couple of tube packs. "I'm a huge nerd, so I've watched all the typical classics. *Akira* and *Ghost in the Shell* about fifty times. Huge *Dragon Ball Z* fan too."

"What about *Sailor Moon*? I love *Sailor Moon*."

"You know what?" Jamarcus said. "The friends I used to hang out with in high school were such otakus that we used to make fun of people who proclaimed they were otakus but never watched *Sailor Moon*."

"Oh my God, you said *otaku*." Kathrine laughed, putting her hands on her round cheeks.

"Well, yeah," Jamarcus said. "Back in the late eighties and early nineties, the only anime you could watch on television was *Sailor Moon*, so it became sort of a badge of honor for us nerds. I mean, it wasn't an anime that was targeted toward guys—well, straight guys. But I love *Sailor Moon*. Some of those episodes broke my heart."

"What was your favorite episode?"

"Shin-Chan," Jamarcus said plainly, causing Kathrine to giggle.

"Shin-Chan is my hero."

"What anime are you watching now?" Kathrine asked.

"Well, right now, I've been buying a lot of *Inuyasha* to watch. Other than that, mostly *Dragon Ball*."

"Oh, I want to go over to your place and watch *Inuyasha*. Sesshomaru is so hot. Can I come on base with you?"

"I've got an apartment close by here. You can come over if you want."

"Oh, but wait," Kathrine said while she pushed her shoulder-length black hair past her face. "You said you were going to play video games tonight."

"Yeah, well, I have a woman who's willing to come over to my place," Jamarcus said. "I think that takes precedence."

"I get off soon if you want to wait for me. And you can meet my friends too."

"Okay."

"Is that all you're going to get?" Kathrine asked, looking at the tubes of chips. "I want some too. Get me the barbecue-flavored ones."

"All right," Jamarcus said.

"You want anything to drink? I'll buy that."

"Hmm, I was going to get a sports drink."

"I'll get one too," Kathrine said. "I don't need to drink any more soda anyway. I'm already big enough as it is. But black guys like big girls, right?"

"I'm just happy to be talking to one." Jamarcus laughed.

"What is wrong with you?" Kathrine asked. "You need to stop talking down on yourself. Look, I'll meet you out front in about thirty minutes, okay?"

"Okay," Jamarcus agreed, and Kathrine walked down the aisle, waving goodbye.

Jamarcus grabbed the tubes of chips and brought them to a cash register to buy them. Afterward, he stepped out of the grocery store and sat on one of the benches out front. It was late afternoon, and even though the temperature was in the mideighties, central Honolulu made the climate feel hotter. Watching a few of the locals walk by, he noticed that a lot of the men wore swimming trunks. That seemed like a smart idea to Jamarcus, so he decided one day he was going to get out of his apartment and buy a pair.

It wasn't long before Kathrine showed up with three other women, two her age and one Jamarcus guessed was his age. As soon as the other women saw him, one of them let out a huge laugh and covered her eyes.

"Kathrine, what is up with you and *papolos*?" the woman said. "What—you no like local boys?"

"Girlfriend, I'm tired of Asian men now," Kathrine said. "And *holes* too. My last two husbands were either-or."

"Never you mind her," one of the other women said as she walked up and hugged Jamarcus. "My name is Mary."

"Hey, Mary," Jamarcus said.

"This is my girlfriend, Sam," Mary said as she pointed out the younger one in the group.

"Sup?" Sam said as she offered Jamarcus a dab.

"And my name is Tasi," the third woman said, holding her hand out to Jamarcus like a debutante. "Hawaiians say *aloha* when they greet each other, but we Samoans say *talofa*."

"Hey, Tasi, take it easy there," Kathrine said, sitting down next to Jamarcus.

"What? I can't talk to him?" Tasi asked, sitting on the other side of Jamarcus. "Have you ever dated an older woman before, Jamarcus?"

"No," Jamarcus said while looking at Kathrine. "But it seems like only older women are interested in me."

"You're so young, though," Mary said as she and Sam sat across from him. "How old are you?"

"I'm twenty-four."

"You know Kathrine is forty-four, right?"

"What, girl? You're older than me," Kathrine said. "And Sam's just as old as Jamarcus."

"I'm thirty, yeah?" Sam said. "So there's only a sixteen-year difference between me and Mary."

"Oh, Sam, guess what?" Kathrine said. "Jamarcus is into anime too."

"What? Yo!" Sam yelled, giving Jamarcus another dab. "I'm

Japanese, yeah? So I watch a lot of anime, period."

"I'm going over to Jamarcus's apartment today to watch some *Inuyasha*," Kathrine said.

"What, sista? You just met him." Tasi laughed. "You already going home with him?"

"Sista, I get it," Kathrine said. "Sex is important to me. And Jamarcus is hot, right?"

"I didn't know we were going to have sex," Jamarcus said.

"Wait—a *wahine* says she going to your place, and you don't think she like smash?" Sam asked. "What type of man are you?"

"I mean, I didn't know," Jamarcus said bashfully. "It's not always the case."

"Brah, if you were white right now, you'd be blushing," Tasi said, making all of them laugh.

"You don't like big girls then?" Tasi asked.

"I never dated a big girl," Jamarcus said. "I don't care what a woman looks like. I don't see people. Although I have to say I'm a tits-and-ass guy myself."

"Word, but," Sam said. "That's why I love Mary. She doesn't have the boobs, yeah? But she has that ass."

"Polynesian girls don't have big boobs!" Mary shouted. "And you're Japanese! What about you?"

"Oriental girls don't have any boobs either," Sam said.

"Speak for yourself, honey," Kathrine said as she puffed up her chest.

"That's because you're thick," Sam said. "And you're Filipino. You got all that fat in the right places."

"Wow!" Kathrine yelled, trying to hit Sam.

"Look at Jamarcus sitting here," Tasi said. "Just being quiet as girls randomly talk about tits."

"I'm not complaining," Jamarcus said.

"Kathrine, you got to go out on a proper date with him," Tasi said. "How about you guys come out to Laie? Jamarcus, have you ever been to the Polynesian Culture Center?"

"I've seen some pamphlets for it on base," Jamarcus said.

"My brother is part of the performance of *Ha: Breath of Life.* You should come to watch it with Kathrine."

"Go to the show," the guardian angel voice buzzed in Jamarcus's head.

"Hmm, yeah, I'll go," Jamarcus said, rubbing his head. "Do you want to go, Kathrine?"

"Yeah, I'll go on a date with you," Kathrine said with a big smile on her face, and then she stood up from her seat, and her expression changed as if she remembered something. "Wait a minute—we should go. You said you were going to play games with your friends tonight."

"Yeah, that's right," Jamarcus said.

"You game?" Sam asked. "What system?"

"Xbox."

"What's your gamer tag?"

"Moriaen. It was the name of a *Dungeons and Dragons* character I played with in high school."

"I'll send you a friend invite when I can."

"Okay," Jamarcus said as Kathrine dragged him up from his seat.

"Damn, girl, you can't wait?" Mary laughed at Kathrine.

"I want to see him play," Kathrine said. "I'll see you girls later."

"Talofa," Tasi said to Jamarcus.

"Watch it, girl," Kathrine said as she and Jamarcus walked away.

"Bye, ladies," Jamarcus said as he led Kathrine to his car.

"What type of apartment do you have?" Kathrine asked.

"Just a small, cheap one-bedroom. There's not much in it. Just a bed, a clothes drawer, and a desk and chair for gaming."

"I'm going to have to spruce that place up."

"You're already laying claim to me?" Jamarcus asked as he opened the car door for her.

"Is this going to be a one-night stand?" Kathrine asked.

"I hope not," Jamarcus said after he got in the driver's seat. "But I haven't had sex in a while. Just with my right hand."

"Don't worry, honey; I'll show you what to do. Sex is important to me, yeah?"

"Okay."

<2>

"You don't like talking about Iraq, do you?" Kathrine asked, looking at Jamarcus as he drove his car.

"Not really," Jamarcus answered.

"You know, it might be good to talk about it, honey."

"Yes, I know that it might help with my depression if I talk," Jamarcus responded.

"Have you talked to anyone on base about Iraq?"

"That's the main reason I moved off base."

"Have you talked to a doctor?"

"We have to go through a type of decompression program when we get back. We talk about how we're not in Iraq, and we have to leave the fight there on base and not bring it home. That helps. But I haven't gone to see a doctor."

"You should go see one," Kathrine said.

Jamarcus looked over at her and then looked past her out the window. They were on a highway that wound up the windward coast of Oahu. The sun was just setting over the mountains to his left, but there was still an orange blaze over the blue-green waters. Every once in a while, they drove past a few houses built close to the shoreline,

95

and on some of the open beaches, there was a mix of locals fishing and tourists sunbathing or playing in the ocean.

"Look, the main reason I don't want to talk about it is because it hurts," Jamarcus said. "And not just mentally. It physically hurts to think about it. My stomach clenches up so much that it feels strained. And my heart seems to block up when I'm surprised."

"That doesn't sound good," Kathrine said.

"Look, Kat, I just don't want to think about it. I'm good at leaving what I do at work. I separate it. So right now, I just don't want to put on the on-the-job face. What about you? Let's talk about you."

"What do you want to know?"

"You said you were married twice, right?" Jamarcus said, looking out his driver's window at the green mountain ranges. The tips of the peaks just blocked the sun, making shadow fingers float in the air toward the ocean. "What types of guys were your husbands?"

"Drunk idiots," Kathrine said with a laugh. "I can't believe it happened to me twice in a row, yeah? You don't drink, do you?"

"No, never liked the taste of beer," Jamarcus answered.

"Good. God, I'm tired of drunk idiots. They were fun at first, especially my first husband. None of the guys I would have loved to date would go out with me because I'm fat, and my last two husbands said they liked big girls."

"I think you're sexy," Jamarcus said. "Maybe I do like big girls. All the tits and ass I want."

"Or maybe you just like bending me over so you can see my ass and not my face."

"That is not what I'm saying." Jamarcus laughed.

"Yeah, well, I didn't have that much confidence in myself, so I guess that's why I dated any man who showed any interest."

"Well, it's not fair to dismiss every white and Asian guy because of two bad dicks."

"No, you're just trying to be nice," Kathrine said. "I know local boys here in Hawaii. They can be a little full of themselves."

"Every man is full of himself when he's young," Jamarcus said.

"You're not."

"I just don't think I'm important."

"There you go again, putting yourself down. Don't do that."

"Sorry," Jamarcus said.

"I only started dating black guys recently," Kathrine said. "Only two before you. Both didn't last long, because one was in the military like you, and the other was a traveling businessman."

"I guess I should be happy for that?" Jamarcus asked with a smile.

"You'd better be." Kathrine giggled. "What about you? You have any girlfriends before you came to Oahu?"

"Last girlfriend I had dumped my butt just as I was going into the army."

"Bitch," Kathrine sneered.

"I'm not mad. She was younger, and there was no guarantee I'd see her again. You can't expect to keep a teenager devoted to you and not go their path."

"Well, she didn't have to dump you like that."

"And what's the best way to break up with someone?" Jamarcus asked. "We were kids. That's what happens when you're kids."

"Did you love her?" Kathrine asked.

"With all of my heart. It's part of the reason I don't think I'm that important."

"I think you're important," Kathrine said.

"Okay," Jamarcus replied.

"I know you're just saying that."

"Okay."

"Hey, we're coming up on the culture center," Kathrine said, pointing in front of her. "It's on your left."

Jamarcus was driving past a public park when Kathrine spoke up, and he soon came to a large parking lot on his left, filled with tourist cars, with many of the passengers walking to and from a large complex. It didn't take long for Jamarcus to park, and soon he and Kathrine were walking toward the building.

"I hope I don't look like a tourist."

"You're mainland, honey. Most mainland people are either military or tourists."

"Good God," Jamarcus groaned. He looked over to a potbellied man in an Aloha shirt, khaki shorts, and socks pulled up to his knees. "At least I don't look like that guy," he said, causing Kathrine to laugh hysterically.

"He looks like my second husband," Kathrine said.

"Ha!" Jamarcus snorted.

"I see Tasi over there with her brother," Kathrine said, and she led Jamarcus through the parking lot until they reached Tasi and a large man with the same tattoos next to her.

"How's it, sista?" Tasi greeted Kathrine, bending over to hug her.

"How's it, girl?"

"Jamarcus, this is my brother, Nathan," Tasi said, pointing at her brother.

"Hey, man," Jamarcus said.

"How's it, brah?" Nathan said, giving Jamarcus a handshake. "You're in the army, yeah? I served in the Marines for ten years. I retired back in ninety-six."

"That's when I joined," Jamarcus said. "What was service like back then? I hear stories that serving abroad in the nineties was a blast."

"Man, you don't even know." Nathan laughed. "Back then, we didn't have al-Qaeda, right? And when the Berlin Wall came down, the whole world was at a party. I was stationed at Pine Gap in Australia. Man, brah, I still don't know why I'm here."

"'Cause you a loser," Tasi said with a disgusted look on her face.

"You're just a hater," Nathan snapped. "Jamarcus, don't let these girls keep you down, yeah? Stay a playa."

"Don't put that in his mind, Nathan," Kathrine said, slapping his arm. "We just started dating. I want to hold on to him."

"Anyway, I got you guys good seats for the show," Tasi said, interrupting.

"Girl, you giving us the VIP treatment?" Kathrine asked.

"You know it, sista. I got the connections."

"You mean you're using my connections," Nathan said.

"Don't you need to get ready for the show?" Tasi said.

"Bye, hater," Nathan said as he walked away from them. "I'll talk to you after the show, Jamarcus."

"Okay," Jamarcus answered. "Your brother is awesome, Tasi."

"No, he's not," Tasi said. "Let's go in already and get our seats. The last thing I want is to tell a hole to move."

With that, they walked inside the center and gradually to the large auditorium, where they took their seats in the front row. It took another thirty minutes or so for the rest of the patrons to take their seats, and when the lights lowered, everyone focused on the stage.

It was a great show, mostly about the rise of a village chief from infancy to manhood, with different dances from many Polynesian cultures. The crowd was really into it, especially all the local people. Jamarcus smiled when all the local guys cheered on the men onstage as they performed a haka. The part that struck him the most was in the beginning. A man appeared on the dark stage with a torch, and as soon as he did, a buzzing started on Jamarcus's forehead.

"Pay attention to this," the guardian angel's voice said, so Jamarcus listened to the man explain that the fire was Ha, the breath of life that was in all living people. When he heard the explanation, his mind flashed back to the boy in the mirror he'd seen as a child, whose chest had shone like a sun, the same type of light as the torch.

I don't understand. What are you trying to tell me? Jamarcus asked the voice to himself, but he got no response. The memory was a good feeling in his soul, but Jamarcus soon forgot about the girl and watched the rest of the show, tightly holding Kathrine's hand.

Chapter 7
<1>
April 2005

Jamarcus stood at a makeshift guard station near an entrance to a small hospital in a suburb near Mosul. He and two other private first classes right out of Ranger school stood guard in the early morning hours, screening all the workers coming into a construction site. There had been a lot of IED attacks that year throughout Iraq, and Mosul wasn't immune.

There were dozens of suicide attacks in the northern region of Iraq, with insurgents trying to keep the northern Kurds from gaining their independent nation-state. The hospital Jamarcus was guarding had been attacked earlier that year by a suicide bomber, who'd killed about a dozen Iraqi policemen and injured dozens more. There had been a major offensive operation in Tal Afar and Mosul earlier that year by Iraqi and US forces to try to root out as many of the insurgents as they could, but all it had done was either scatter whatever insurgents were there into dozens of smaller cells in small towns in the region or make more insurgents out of their neighbors. There was no clear solution on how to end the violence. For the months Jamarcus had been in the region, the operation had felt less like the United States ensuring the safety of the Iraqi people and more like the Crips and the Bloods guarding whatever territory they had.

Because of that, Jamarcus wanted to be at the guard station at the hospital as much as possible. The company commander didn't want him there as much to help out with the other new men on their first tour, but Jamarcus wanted to be sure the men at the hospital didn't fall into complacency.

"Yo, Sergeant Bridge," one of the privates called out as he searched a local worker's tool bag. "You're stationed out of Hawaii, right?"

"Yes," Jamarcus answered as he finished his screening.

"What's it like, man? I'm stuck at Fort Bragg. Hawaii must be the shit, right?"

"Well, the state is beautiful," Jamarcus said as he started screening another worker. "I always wanted to live there since I was a kid. I live in Oahu, so there are a bunch of tourist activities to do. But after a couple of months, there's not much left. It can get boring quickly."

"Yeah, but that weather. It must be great to wake up to perfect weather all the time."

"You can get spoiled—I'll give you that," Jamarcus said. "But hey, Fort Bragg is all right. The local population supports the military. And there is always some type of huge festival for the servicemen going on every month. Kamaaina in Hawaii doesn't like the military at all."

"But the weather sucks in the winter, Sergeant," the private said as he began a new screening. "I lived in San Diego all my life, man. I can't stand the cold."

"Holy shit, man. San Diego is a dope-ass place to live." Jamarcus laughed. "I'd have rather gotten stationed in San Diego than Hawaii.

Too bad there are no army bases there. There's a block party in that city every week, right?"

"Yeah, Sergeant. But the city is always crowded. And it's so damn expensive to live there. I hope one day I can move back there, but then I heard about Schofield in Hawaii, so I figured I'd try getting stationed there."

"No luck there either, man. It's just as expensive, and they raise the rent in Hawaii every quarter when the military allotment goes up. It's a goddamn racket."

"Well, that's shitty," the private said.

"Yeah, I know," Jamarcus said before facing an incoming worker. "Morning, Faruk. How's it going, man?"

"It is good, Jay," Faruk said as he handed Jamarcus his tool bag. "It is still too early in the morning, but I need a job."

"Yeah, tell me about it," Jamarcus said as he put down the tool bag and began patting him down. "How's your family doing, dog? Your brother still in school?"

"Yes. He is good. He will move up in grade soon. He plays a lot of football now. Too much football. He wants to be the next David Beckham."

"What about your mom? How's she doing?" Jamarcus asked after he was done, handing him his tool bag.

"Why do you always ask about my mom?" Faruk asked in an annoyed voice. "We don't need to talk about her all the time."

"My bad, man," Jamarcus said. "I won't talk about your mom

again. What about you? You still in college?"

"Yes, I'm still in school."

"You should think about what I told you earlier, man. Get a student visa and go to school in Europe. Heck, why not in the US? You speak English well enough. Get yourself a bachelor's degree, and get a job as an interpreter. There's got to be a high demand for people who speak Farsi in the West now. You can get a good job to provide for your family."

"It's hard, you know," Faruk said with a stutter, looking at the hospital. "I don't know. It's hard. I have my family."

"Yeah, man, I get it," Jamarcus said, seeing Faruk's unease. "Let me not hold you up, dog. See you later, okay?"

"Yeah, man," Faruk said with a smile, and he walked toward the construction area.

"That guy was nervous," the private said after Faruk was a good distance away.

"What? Faruk? Nah, man, he's a good kid. He's really smart too."

"He seemed a bit twitchy, Sergeant."

"It's probably because you two guys are new," Jamarcus said as he began to pat down another worker. "I swear every new guy we get out here acts like a moron when he first goes on a guard watch. Especially when we have to screen people going through a checkpoint. I swear you guys think it's all right to beat the crap out of the locals."

"We have to make sure they don't have anything on them, right?"

the private asked as he finished screening another worker.

"But we don't have to be a dicks about it," Jamarcus said. "You just got here, so I know you still have all the training you learned on how to deal with the people here. How and when to be hard or soft. Just don't forget they are humans. We've been at this site for a month and a half now, and there have barely been any workers brave enough to come out here to rebuild the hospital. And I see some of the same guys in here, okay? I tell you, I was part of a raid a couple of weeks back a few blocks from here. I swear one of the guys we killed during the raid was a worker who got treated like shit when he came through the checkpoint last month. I'm not certain, but it fucked me up when I saw him."

"Jesus," the private said.

"I'm not trying to say let's be all 'Kumbaya, my Lord' or any-thing, but there is one thing about this culture I've noticed: they are particular about courtesy. And Americans aren't the most courteous bunch. I swear half the bombings would probably stop in Iraq if we learned how to say please. Or I could be full of shit."

"Yeah, Sergeant. I think you're full of shit."

"Watch it, Private," Jamarcus said with a laugh. "I just try to treat the workers here fairly. Most are afraid of us, and then they have to be afraid of their neighbors when they go home. I just want to make this place as safe as possible for everybody. That means we do our job completely but while being respectful. So I talk to workers to make them feel at ease.

"But Faruk was cool. The first time he showed up, he was asking all these questions about the US. About music and the NBA—all different types of topics. He knew a lot about the US already, so I asked if he was going to college. He opened up about his school and his mom and brother. He's the man of the house. There aren't many opportunities for kids your age coming out of high school in the US to get a job to provide for themselves. Faruk is providing for his family and going to school. That's legit."

"Seems you're hard up on him, Staff," the private said.

"Fuck yeah I am," Jamarcus said. "He's a great kid. I just don't want to see a young man's life wasted out here. That's all suicide bombings do: destroy young men. As a black man, I can't help but feel for that."

"Excuse me," a voice said from behind, and they turned to see Faruk approaching them from the hospital. "I left my lunch in my car," Faruk said. "I just need to go get it."

"Yeah, man, go for it," Jamarcus said, letting Faruk past the checkpoint.

"Thank you," Faruk said as he walked by.

"Besides, he motivates me too," Jamarcus said while he kept an eye on Faruk as he walked to his car. "I've been in the army for almost ten years, and I haven't taken any opportunity to go to school. If Faruk can get his butt in gear and go to college with everything he does, there's no excuse for me, right?"

"Yeah, I know what you mean," the private said. "I've been thinking about taking advantage of the college fund for serving."

"You should," Jamarcus said as he watched Faruk go to the rear of his car. A feeling of tension rose in Jamarcus's chest as Faruk opened the hatch door, reached in, and pulled out a small red-and-white cooler. It only slightly eased once Faruk closed the hatch and began walking back to the checkpoint.

"Be careful," his guardian angel buzzed on his forehead.

"How long is your service stint?" Jamarcus asked the private as he checked another worker's bag.

"Only three years," the private said as he did the same.

"You got the GI Bill, right?" Jamarcus asked as he began to pat down the worker.

"I'm not that stupid, Staff," the private said as he began his pat-down.

"And you're serving in Iraq. Just do your three years, and you'll get a free ride at a college, right?"

"Yeah, Staff."

"There you go," Jamarcus said while turning his head to watch Faruk walk through the checkpoint.

"Hey, Faruk, we've got to check the cooler, man," Jamarcus called after him.

"It's okay; it's just my food," Faruk answered as he continued walking.

"Be careful," the voice buzzed again.

"I know it's your food, man. We've still got to check it."

"It's okay," Faruk said as he turned to face Jamarcus. "You know me. We're friends. I come here all the time."

"And I've still got to check my friend's lunch." Jamarcus laughed while his stomach began to clench, and his heart blocked up. "You might have some food I want to steal."

"It's okay," Faruk said as he turned back toward the hospital.

"Stop right now!" Jamarcus screamed as he pulled out his sidearm and aimed it at Faruk. The two privates almost fell over themselves as they got their rifles and raised them at the young man. The workers froze where they were with their hands up, and a couple fell to the ground. Faruk stopped and turned around; his eyes were glazed over and confused, not looking at Jamarcus.

"Drop the fucking cooler!" the private shouted at Faruk.

"Shut up, Private!" Jamarcus ordered, and the private flashed him a stunned look. "Hey, Faruk, I need you to put the cooler down carefully," Jamarcus said as he slowly made his way toward him.

Faruk continued to look away from him, his face showing an internal struggle.

"Hey, man, everything is going to be okay," Jamarcus said. "I just need you to put the cooler down."

Faruk put his gaze on Jamarcus and was about to speak, when three more soldiers from Jamarcus's watch approached from the hospital, screaming at Faruk.

"Everyone calm down!" Jamarcus yelled at the men.

"What are you doing, Staff?" one of the soldiers yelled at Jamarcus.

"Just chill the fuck out!" Jamarcus shouted, and he noticed Faruk's face trembling as he saw the three soldiers behind him. With teeth clenched, Faruk tried to open his cooler. "Stop!" Jamarcus yelled.

Faruk looked back at Jamarcus with his face drenched with sweat and his hands trembling on the cover of the cooler.

"Faruk, please put the cooler down," Jamarcus said, watching Faruk stare at him.

"You don't understand," Faruk said to Jamarcus. "My family. You don't understand."

"I know I don't understand. That's why I need you to tell me. Just put the cooler down."

"Staff!" one of the soldiers shouted, and a panicked look came upon Faruk's face. Faruk turned toward the voice with his hands on the cooler's cover.

"Don't!" Jamarcus yelled at him, but Faruk pulled the cover off the cooler to reach into it. Jamarcus fired five times at Faruk, and three of the shots hit him in the chest. The cooler dropped to the ground, and the lid flew to the side as Faruk fell onto his back.

"Everyone stay back!" Jamarcus ordered when he saw his soldiers trying to approach Faruk. Jamarcus made his way to the cooler, seeing Faruk gasping for air. Jamarcus looked inside the cooler to see a clay-colored block of a malleable substance with a metal tube sticking in it. A digital watch was attached to a metal tube with a wire. When Jamarcus looked back at Faruk, he was dead.

"I need someone to call base to have EOD come out here," Jamarcus said. "Do not use your radios; use a landline. Two of you guys go to the workers and search them again. Make sure no one has anything." When the three squad members went back to the hospital, he turned back to the privates. "Make sure nobody goes past this check-point," Jamarcus ordered.

"Roger that, Staff," one of them answered.

As the two privates ordered the workers away from the hospital, Jamarcus walked to the checkpoint entrance, looking back at Faruk with the hole in his heart filling with guilt. He'd just thrown another life away. His mind wouldn't allow any other thought in. The only thing he felt outside of his guilt was the buzzing in his head.

"Thank you," Jamarcus whispered as he rubbed his forehead.

<2>

July 4, 2005

It was just past noon as Jamarcus rode in Nathan's fishing boat by the windward shores in Kaneohe Bay. Hawaiian reggae was blasting on a radio next to Jamarcus on the bow of the craft, a mixture of Jamaican reggae and jazz with some Hawaiian flavor. Sam and Mary were sitting at the aft of the boat with Kathrine. Tasi was by her brother, who was at the helm of the boat, while Jamarcus sat next to Sunny, a Chinese guy Tasi was dating, who was Jamarcus's age. When Tasi had started dating Sunny, Jamarcus had realized Kathrine and her friends were a bunch of preying cougars trying to date whatever young person they could feast on. Jamarcus had started calling Kathrine, Mary, and Tasi Cougar Town whenever he met up with them, which never failed to piss off one of them.

"Man, I'm so pissed off about last night," Sunny said as Jamarcus looked into the waters of the bay.

"Camping is a legitimate strategy," Jamarcus said. "You can't get mad at teams who learn the spawn points of the map. We do the same thing."

"But we had just gotten our ranks over twenty-five on *Halo 2*, brah," Sunny said. "That loss just put me back at twenty. God, Bungie needs to do something about that."

"What can they do? They already put in rotating spawn points. Nothing else can be done. That team was legit, though. I just don't understand how we dropped that many ranks from a team that was practically the same as us."

"They were playing with the one guy who was ranked eighteen. That's the problem. He's the reason our rank dropped so much."

"Yeah, that sucked," Jamarcus said. "I'm just waiting for any other good first-person shooter we can play. I love *Halo 2*, but that game is going to give me a heart attack."

"You should get *God of War*, brah," Sunny said. "That game is so good."

"Don't have a PlayStation, man. Xbox guy."

"You can't afford a PlayStation?" Sunny asked.

"I can, but I'm cheap. My other console is the GameCube. And I've got to have my Mario."

"Yeah, I hear that," Sunny said. "Isn't it weird? You can have an Xbox and a GameCube. You can have a PS3 and a GameCube. But you can't have a PlayStation or Xbox."

"They're both so expensive," Jamarcus said. "Nintendo just does the right thing and keeps their consoles affordable. You've got to respect them for that. Oh, but check this out. Kathrine still has her Super Nintendo, and it works."

"Holy shit, that's got to be so much fun."

"Wait. She has *Castlevania, Star Fox*—"

"*Star Fox*!" Sunny yelped. "That game is so fun!"

"And she has *Mortal Kombat 2*. Oh my God, playing against Kathrine all night long has been a blast. We just do the craziest things when we play."

"Hey, Jamarcus!" Nathan called out. "How close are we to the sandbar?"

Jamarcus looked out to the bars that were north of the marine base in Kaneohe. There were already more than a dozen boats anchored on top of them for the holiday.

"We're about half a mile away," Jamarcus said.

"You guys let me know when we're near, yeah?"

"Sure," Jamarcus answered.

It didn't take long for the boat to approach the sandbar, and when Jamarcus and Sunny signaled Nathan, he stopped the motors and raised the blades. They glided just over the sand, and Jamarcus jumped out of the boat to help guide it to an open spot on the bar. The other boats around them were filled with either marine from the base or local people, with music from all different genres playing and people cheering or drinking beer.

"Let's stop here," Nathan said once they got to a good spot. Jamarcus slowed the boat to a stop, almost going under the water with the weight, which made Sunny laugh at him.

"You want to do this?" Jamarcus laughed up at Sunny.

"That's why I'm up here," Sunny said. "So I can laugh at you."

"Ha."

"Hey, Brotha Jay, grab the anchor," Nathan said as he handed the anchor to Jamarcus. Jamarcus went to the aft of the ship and plunged the anchor into the sand, making sure it was secure.

"Hey, Cougar Town!" Jamarcus yelled at the ladies in front of him.

"What?" Mary yelled back.

"We're here," Jamarcus said with a smile.

"Why do you have to keep calling us that?" Tasi said with an annoyed look.

"Cougar Town," Sam sang to the music from the radio, receiving a prompt slap on the arm from Mary.

"Don't you start," Mary warned, but that only made Sam stand up and start shaking her hips and twirling her tattooed arms around.

"Cougar Town," Sam said again, and when Mary slapped her butt, she just bent over so Mary could continue hitting her.

"Oh no," Jamarcus grunted, making his body slightly convulse.

"Don't do it!" Tasi shouted.

"It's coming," Jamarcus groaned with his head slightly twitching.

"Brah, don't do it!" Mary yelled.

"Get it, honey!" Kathrine shouted, and with a grimace across his face, Jamarcus struck a pose with his legs spread out with right knee bent, and his left leg straight. Jamarcus pointed his right hand up to the sky and his left hand to the sandbar and held his pose as the people from the other boats cheered, and Mary and Tasi screamed in horror.

"Get it, brotha!" Nathan yelled.

"No, please stop!" Sunny said with his face reflecting mock terror.

"It's the greatest dance move ever," Jamarcus said, still holding the pose.

"No, it's not," Tasi said.

"I'm standing still," Jamarcus said. "Yet I look like I'm boogying down like there's no tomorrow."

"Yeah, honey!" Kathrine shouted, which made Jamarcus shake his hips and move his arms like Sam.

"That reminds me," Tasi said. "I'm pissed off at you, Jamarcus."

"What'd I do now?" Jamarcus laughed.

"Kathrine said you stopped going to church."

"Here we go," Jamarcus said with a sigh.

"Hey, if he stopped going to church, it's his choice," Nathan said. "Just like it's his choice to go."

"How can someone believe in God?" Sunny asked.

"It's called faith, Sunny," Tasi said. "I'm not going to argue with you on that."

"Okay," Sunny said, holding his hands up.

"With all the things going on in the war, this is the time you're supposed to hold on to your faith," Tasi said to Jamarcus.

"You see, that's the thing," Jamarcus said. "If there is a God and if he is aware of the war going on and knows that part of the basis of the war is mankind's misinterpretation of his will for us and he chooses not to act, then it doesn't even matter if God exists or not. I don't want any part of such a God."

"What if God is using you to help spread the right message? How can you stop believing in God?"

"Oh, I'll tell you right when I stopped caring," Jamarcus said, looking down at the water. "It was right before I came back from my tour. There was this kid I knew who got tricked into doing a suicide bombing over there. He was a smart boy who was going to college and taking care of his family. But a bunch of idiots got a hold of him and convinced him that we're straight evil and that he needed to blow up the hospital we were trying to rebuild. We found out they promised him thirty thousand American dollars for his family if he did it, which is a good chunk of money over there. He couldn't say no because of his family. And we're sure he didn't even know the bomb he was going to use would go off when he activated it. I had to kill this kid when he went through our checkpoint.

"Now, if the God of Ishmael is the same as the God of Isaac, and if the God of Isaac is used to convince me to kill Muslims, and if the God of Ishmael is used to convince Muslims to kill Christians, then what's the difference between them and me? And who's to blame for all of this? Christians, Muslims, or God? It was then that I said, 'Fuck it. There can't be a God if we're killing each other over this nonsense.' And if there is one, then I don't care. I sure as hell don't want to go to heaven if he's there. I'd rather go to hell and be next to someone I care about than go to heaven and be next to someone I hate. At least I can ask for forgiveness when I'm down there."

When Jamarcus looked back up at Tasi, he noticed that everyone on the boat was looking at him quietly with a solemn look in his or her eyes.

"Besides, we're out here on the Fourth, Tasi," Jamarcus said to change the mood. "I don't want to think about all of that. Let's get this party started."

"Fuck yeah," Nathan said, flinging his arm in the air. "Yo, Sunny, turn the radio on to something different, yeah? I want to get my jam on."

Sunny went to the radio and turned it to a hip-hop station, and when a song came on, Nathan began an incredibly awkward dance with his shoulders lunged back, swaying from side to side. Everyone on the boat broke out in laughter at the sight of it. Jamarcus started doing the same thing, and Sam jumped into the water next to him, performing the same dance.

"Why can't there be any good dancers here?" Mary complained.

"Don't hate. Don't hate," Jamarcus sang as he and Sam began breaking out terrible robot dance moves.

"I'm hungry," Tasi said. "Get the ahi out; I'm going to make some poke."

Nathan and Tasi took out different bowls and coolers, and they mixed chopped ahi with sea salt, sesame oil, chopped seaweed, and soy sauce. Tasi passed paper bowls of the dish to everyone after they were done preparing the food, and they grabbed beers to wash it down.

"Honey, do you want wasabi sauce in yours?" Kathrine asked as she prepared Jamarcus's plate.

"Yes, please," Jamarcus answered.

"How can you eat poke with wasabi?" Sam asked as she walked toward the boat to get a beer from Mary.

"Have you tried it?"

"I hate wasabi. It's too hot for me."

"I love it," Jamarcus said. "And Kathrine loves spicy food anyway. She's always putting something spicy in our food when she cooks."

"Here, honey," Kathrine said as she leaned over the boat to give Jamarcus a bowl and a sports drink.

"Thanks, Kathrine."

"You okay?" Kathrine asked.

"Yeah, I'm good," Jamarcus said, and he devoured his plate.

For the first hour, they ate and drank, laughing and listening to the radio. Afterward, everyone got off the boat to walk on the sandbar. The group got a laugh when Kathrine, Mary, and Tasi tried getting into the water without falling.

"Honey, don't laugh!" Kathrine cried after she clumsily got down.

"I'm sorry," Jamarcus said as he went to give her a big hug. She grabbed Jamarcus by his testicles and reached around to grab his ass as she looked up and kissed Jamarcus.

"You have to make up for it when we get home," Kathrine said as she looked up at him with her dark eyes.

"I can do that," Jamarcus said.

For the next few hours, they spent their time telling embarrassing stories about each other or dancing when a good song came on the radio. Jamarcus and Kathrine spent a good amount of time walking the sandbar, trying to find shells or a small octopus. She insisted Jamarcus catch one but would squeal when Jamarcus tried to touch her with it. Hours flew by, and the sun moved past the mountains to the west, when the group decided to go back to the boat and eat some more. They stood in the ocean water, eating and laughing, when fireworks began popping in the sky above the base. As they watched the display, no one noticed a group of local men walking by with too much liquor in their stomachs and causing problems wherever they went.

"Wassup, brotha?" one of them said as they saw Jamarcus, and the man walked up to him, trying to give him a handshake. "Sup, my nigga? What's popping?" the man slurred drunkenly as he put his arm around Jamarcus.

"Take it easy there, man," Jamarcus said, moving out of the person's arm. "I don't know you that well."

"Ah, don't be like that, brotha," the man groaned.

"Easy, tiger," Nathan said as he stepped between Jamarcus and the drunken group. "We've got no beef with you. Just take it easy."

"Why you got to be like that?" the man said, and Jamarcus shut down inside, walking back to the boat.

"What the fuck's wrong with you?" Kathrine screamed at the group, getting in the face of one of the men.

"Back the fuck up, bitch!" the man said, pushing Kathrine back.

Something physically unhinged inside Jamarcus's soul, and before he knew it, he flew at the man, pushing him flat on his chest and sending him crashing into the water. When the Iraqi teenager from the restaurant stood up out of the water, Jamarcus stood ready for him. When the boy threw a punch at Jamarcus, he ducked it and came up throwing a haymaker at the boy's chin. Once the teenager was stunned, Jamarcus grabbed him, slipped his leg behind the boy, flipped him into the water, and sat on top of the boy's head, twisting the kid's arm. Jamarcus didn't hear everyone's screams around him. His mind was fixed on his target.

Nathan grabbed Jamarcus and yanked him out of the water, shoving him toward the boat. "Get on the boat," Nathan said, and Jamarcus silently climbed up and sat down on the bow. Once the man got out of the water, the drunken group began throwing insults and slurs at Jamarcus.

"Go home, nigger!" one of them screamed, throwing a beer bottle at Jamarcus and missing terribly.

"Get the fuck out of here!" Mary screamed at the group, and after a few more minutes of yelling at each other, the drunken men walked off. Nathan and Kathrine climbed onto the boat and sat down next to Jamarcus, who sat staring straight ahead, still seeing the Iraqi teenager in front of the restaurant.

"Honey, you were so fast," Kathrine said.

"Hey, Jay," Nathan said, grabbing Jamarcus's shoulder. "You're not in Iraq."

"Yeah," Jamarcus said.

"You're not in Iraq, man."

"Yeah. I know."

"Say it," Nathan said.

"I'm not in Iraq. I'm not in Iraq," Jamarcus repeated, and the punk kid faded in his mind. "I'm not in Iraq. Jesus, I tried to kill that guy."

"Honey, I'm so sorry," Kathrine said.

"It's not your fault. Jesus. It's not your fault. I … God." Jamarcus sat holding his head in his hands as Kathrine held him in her arms.

Chapter 8
<1>
May 2006

"Honey, I think I should go to the hospital," Kathrine said as she sat on their bed and she talked on her cell phone.

"Okay!" Jamarcus yelled back to Kathrine as he sat on the living room couch and played a fantasy RPG on his console.

"How does it feel?" Mary asked from the other end of the line.

"I get a sharp pain in my back every once in a while."

"You have gotten bigger. Maybe you're pregnant."

"That's what Jamarcus says," Kathrine said.

"You could be!" Jamarcus shouted.

"You don't think you're pregnant?" Mary asked.

"I didn't miss my period last month. And I've been regular on my period the last few months."

"When did the pain start?" Mary asked.

"A couple of weeks ago."

"I think you're pregnant."

"Girlfriend, I wish." Kathrine sighed as she watched Jamarcus playing. "I would love to have a little Jamarcus Mini-Me running around the apartment."

"What if she's a girl?" Mary asked.

"Oh God, Jamarcus would have a heart attack. She would be a chili pepper fiend like me. Jamarcus can handle some spicy food. If two girls like me were here, his asshole would be on fire all the time."

"That almost sounds horrible." Mary laughed.

"Anyway, girl, I want to play this game Jamarcus just bought," Kathrine said. "He made a character that looks just like me, and he's going to teach me how to play."

"Oh my God, he's got you playing?"

"I like watching him play. It's fun, especially when I tell him what to do. The craziest shit happens when I tell him what to do."

"Whatever, girl," Mary moaned.

"I'll see you at work tomorrow," Kathrine said. "Bye. Love you, girl."

"Bye, girl," Mary said before she hung up.

Kathrine put her cell phone down and walked into the living room to sit next to Jamarcus. "I think I should go to the hospital," she said as she sat down.

"Anytime you want, sweetheart."

"Honey, don't play too much!" Kathrine yelled as she watched the television. "I want to do something."

"Okay," Jamarcus said as he handed the controls to Kathrine.

"Where am I supposed to go?" she asked.

"Do you see the compass at the top of the screen?"

"Yes."

"You have to go in the direction of the star."

"Okay," Kathrine said as she changed the direction her character was going. Jamarcus had made the character look as close as possible to her, except the character was skinnier, which Jamarcus laughed about.

Jamarcus sat quietly and watched as Kathrine walked through a forest toward her goal.

"How long do I have to go this way?" Kathrine asked. "This is boring."

"I'm not sure. You can't fast-travel to where you're going. It may take a few minutes."

"Oh." Kathrine sighed as she pressed on in the game. After a few moments, she noticed that the music changed to a tenser theme, and she grew a bit concerned. "Honey, the music changed," she told Jamarcus.

"I think something is chasing you," he said, and when Kathrine turned her character around, she saw a giant bear racing toward her. She let out a huge scream, making Jamarcus laugh hysterically.

"What do I do?" Kathrine asked as the bear attacked her.

"Put your shield up," Jamarcus said, and Kathrine made her character do just that. When the bear attacked her, it slammed into the shield and recoiled back, stunned. "You have to time it, but after the bear attacks, you have to hit it with your sword," Jamarcus said.

"Okay," Kathrine said, and when the bear attacked and recoiled, she slashed at the bear a few times. The bear quickly recovered and hit Kathrine again. "He's not dead!" she yelled.

"Bears are tough in this game," Jamarcus said. "Keep fighting, and you'll kill it."

It took a few more moments for Kathrine to put the beardown, and when she did, she let out a war cry while pumping a fist.

"Good job," Jamarcus laughed.

"But I'm hurt," Kathrine said.

"Just stay there for a few seconds, and your health will come back," Jamarcus said, and after she did, Kathrine continued toward the star on the screen. While she was traveling, the sky in the game turned dark and overcast, while the music became more sinister in tone. Soon a huge arc of fire appeared in a field in front of her character.

"What is that?" Kathrine asked.

"I think that's a gate to the game's hell," Jamarcus said, and as soon as he finished speaking, an imp-like creature walked across the screen, followed by a lightning strike and thunder. Both Kathrine and Jamarcus let out shouts and leaped a good foot off the couch.

"Holy shit, that was so cool," Jamarcus said.

"I don't want to play anymore, honey," Kathrine whimpered. "That scared me."

"You want me to play?"

"No. Just save the game. I'll play it later. I think we should go to the hospital."

"All right," Jamarcus said as he saved the game and turned off the console. "Where does it hurt anyway?"

"In my upper back," Kathrine said, and Jamarcus spun her around and began massaging the area that Kathrine pointed out. "That feels good, honey," Kathrine moaned.

"Does your back feel better?"

"It hurts on the inside," she said.

"Okay, we should get going," Jamarcus said, and after grabbing a few things, they made their way to the door to the apartment.

"Wait a minute," Jamarcus said, keeping the door closed when Kathrine tried to open it. He reached into her blouse and grabbed a breast with one hand while he reached down into the crotch of Kathrine's pants with the other.

"Quick dip?" Kathrine giggled.

"Quick dip," Jamarcus said as he leaned over to kiss her. He pulled her pants down in front of him, and after he did the same to his, he went at her with passion. They stood there kissing and thrusting at one another. Jamarcus then squeezed Kathrine tightly as he released inside of her with Kathrine kissing him all the while.

"Did you go inside me?" Kathrine asked with a smile.

"You're pregnant. Can't get you pregnant again."

"What if I'm not?" Kathrine asked, pulling up her pants.

"What's the difference?" Jamarcus said as he zipped himself up.

"You're so bad; you're going to leave me sloppy for the nurses to find," Kathrine said as they walked out the door.

"Just use some wipes in the room you get," Jamarcus said, and Kathrine laughed in response. Jamarcus locked the door behind them, and they made their way to the car and were soon on the road to the hospital.

"The only problem is that if you are pregnant, I won't be here when you give birth since I'm leaving next week," Jamarcus said.

"Maybe you can ask command to give you an early end of your tour to be here," Kathrine said.

"That's a good idea, but it doesn't work all the time."

"It was an idea."

"I'll tell you one thing," Jamarcus said. "Our kid will be a nut-case."

"I was just telling Mary that." Kathrine laughed. "If he's a boy, he'll probably be born with a video game controller in his hand."

"Oh God, the doc and the nurses will freak out," Jamarcus said. "The doctor will pick him up to slap him to breathe, but the baby will slap him with the controller. Then he will call me over to pick him up and slap me in the face when I do. 'Take me home, Dad. Got to play games.'"

Kathrine laughed until tears ran down her cheeks. "I'll still be on the bed, heartbroken as he's leaving," she said. "I'll just lie there crying. 'Baby, don't go.' He'll turn around and say, 'Shut up, Mom. Got to play video games,' and then drag you out the door."

"He'll drive the car home with me screaming in the passenger seat." Jamarcus chuckled. "He will lead a bunch of cop cars in a chase: 'Ah, be advised we've got a sedan speeding down the highway with an unseen driver. The only thing seen is a controller on the steering wheel and a black guy screaming bloody murder in the passenger seat.'"

"Oh, what if she's a girl? I told Mary she would be a chili pepper addict like me."

"God, then she would be born with a chili pepper in her hand. That's got to burn."

"I would scream at the doctor, 'My vagina's burning!'" Kathrine said. "The doctor would look down and see a chili pepper burst out in her hand and say, 'Well, there's your problem.'"

"When she comes out, she'll probably be chucking chili peppers at my mouth," Jamarcus said as he parked the car at the visitor section of the hospital. "She'll be a ninja chili pepper baby."

Jamarcus and Kathrine got out of the car and laughed as they walked to the emergency room. A nurse checked Kathrine in at the nurses' station, and after a short wait, a nurse escorted Kathrine to a room. Jamarcus waited in the lobby, watching the television to keep up with the latest sports scores. After an hour, a nurse arrived to escort Jamarcus to Kathrine's room, where she waved at him from a bed when he entered.

"Did you wipe?" Jamarcus asked after the nurse left, making

Kathrine shush him.

"They didn't even check that," Kathrine said as she slapped Jamarcus when he sat next to her. "They took x-rays of my chest and belly. Then they had me wait here."

"Did anyone tell you what they found?" Jamarcus asked.

"No," Kathrine said, and then a smile spread across her face. "Think we've got time for another quick dip?"

"Oh yeah, that's all the patients need to hear right now in the emergency room—bodies slapping and loud grunts. The nurses would probably think you're having a heart attack."

"Yeah," Kathrine agreed, and then she cut short her laughter as the ER doctor entered the room. The doctor stood there for a moment and watched Kathrine and Jamarcus stifle their laughter.

"Hello, Kathrine. I'm Dr. Carr," she said.

"Hi, Dr. Carr. This is my boyfriend, Jamarcus."

"Hi," Jamarcus said as he reached out and shook Dr. Carr's hand.

"So, Kathrine, we took an x-ray of your chest and abdomen. We found a lot of fluid in your chest cavity. That's what is causing the pain. So we're going to have to get that out, okay?"

"Okay."

"We also found a mass in your abdomen. Now, since you're over the age of forty, we took a few tests from your blood work," Dr. Carr said. "You were in the hospital a few years back due to a growth in your uterus, correct?"

"Yes," Kathrine answered.

"We found a number count for proteins associated with ovarian cancer," the doctor said, and Kathrine sucked in a sharp gasp.

Jamarcus sat next to her, stunned, not sure how to process the news. His body was telling him that he needed to do something physically. He'd been trained to react to all types of emergencies in his service. Murphy's law was his motto. He didn't know what to do now. He sat there confused; his body wanted to take action, but his mind was empty.

"Do you know what stage it is?" Kathrine asked.

"We have an appointment for you to meet with an oncologist. That person can tell you everything you need to know. A nurse is going to arrive with a device we use to drain liquid from inside patients' cavities. I'll talk to you after he's done."

When the doctor left the room, Kathrine grabbed Jamarcus's hand and brought it to her bosom. "Honey," she whimpered with tears rolling down her cheeks.

Jamarcus enveloped her in his arms, doing his best not to cry himself. Military service had taught him not to cry in times of crisis.

"I'm scared." Kathrine cried into his chest.

"It's okay to be scared," Jamarcus said. It was the only thing he could come up with to say.

<2>

August 2006

Jamarcus stood with a squad of soldiers looking over a large congregation of Afghani villagers who were protesting a recent missile strike that had killed close to a dozen civilians near the Pakistani border. The soldiers were next to a white-and-red bar gate that was a vehicle entrance to their base. Although the base Jamarcus was stationed at, Bagram Air Base, was hundreds of miles away from the strike, it was the closest US military institution the local population could voice their frustration.

"This is bullshit, Staff," one of the soldiers grunted in Jamarcus's direction. "Why do we have to deal with this?"

"Part of the job, Summers," Jamarcus answered absently.

"Hey, Brent, didn't that strike kill an al-Qaeda leader?" Summers asked one of the other soldiers.

"Every missile strike kills an al-Qaeda leader," Brent answered. "Makes you wonder how many al-Qaeda leaders there are."

"It's not our fault those people got killed," Summers grumbled. "They shouldn't have been hanging out next to a terrorist."

"Fucking hell, Summers," Jamarcus said as he turned to face him. "Want to keep that to yourself and not piss off the more than one hundred protesters in front of us?"

"Fuck these guys, Staff," Summers responded. "Why the hell do we have to deal with these idiots?"

"I swear, Summers," Jamarcus growled. "If you don't cut that shit out, I'll have you doing latrine duty so much your skin color will be the same shade as the shit we burn out back. Do you follow?"

Summers went quiet after that reprimand, turning his eyes back to the crowd.

The people were protesting relatively peacefully. There were women and children in the group, and some carried signs with the typical "Go Home, US" or "George Bush is a …," with the blanks filled in with expletives. A number of them spoke English.

"Don't they know we're trying to bring them a better life?" Summers said.

"Oh, we're not here to bring them a better life," Jamarcus said. "We're here to make money."

"Oh, come on, Staff. Don't give me any conspiracy-theory bullshit."

"What, man?" Brent jumped in. "We found billions of tons of mineral ore in the southern part of the country. It's probably worth hundreds of billions of dollars."

"And there is a major offensive going on in that region," Jamarcus added.

"What? We're here to dig all of that up?" Summers asked.

"The poppy fields too," Jamarcus said. "Don't forget those things."

"Yeah, how can we forget the fields we have to patrol every other day?" Brent said.

"Yeah, why are we patrolling that anyway?" Summers asked. "Isn't most of the world's opium made here?"

"As far as news outlets and research show, yeah," Jamarcus answered.

"We should burn that shit then," Summers said, walking along the bar gate. "That would probably get rid of the world's heroin problem."

"That's not all you can make from opium," Jamarcus said. "Oxycontin. Oxycodone."

"What are those?"

"Painkillers," Brent answered. "You could probably get that now if you went to the medic complaining about your back."

"Wait—America makes painkillers from those poppy fields?" Summers asked.

"America can make painkillers from the poppies here," Jamarcus said, correcting him.

"Where do we get them from?"

"China. Well, most of it we get from China."

"What? Wait. I don't understand. So the US gets opium from China?" Summers said.

"We get the ingredients to make Oxycontin and the like from China," Jamarcus said.

"And China gets their ingredients from Afghanistan?"

"No," Jamarcus answered with a smile.

"Then what does China have to do with the opium here?" Summers asked.

"Some of the opium flowers growing here are Chinese."

"So the Chinese are growing poppy fields here?" Summers said.

"I'm not saying that at all," Jamarcus said. "I'm saying that the US gets some of the ingredients to make opioids from China and that Chinese poppy flowers are growing in Afghanistan. Ones we may be guarding. You're the one connecting the dots."

"How do you know all of this shit?" Summers asked.

"My girlfriend takes Percocet to help deal with her chemo," Jamarcus said as he watched the growing crowd. "She hates it, so I did my research."

The crowd began to worry Jamarcus as it grew. They were allowed a designated area in front of the base, but they had already outgrown that. Sooner or later, Jamarcus and his men would have to inform the protesters to stay in their allowed area, which he knew would get testy. In the front of the group was an old man who could speak English and every so often bade them to walk over to them.

"What does that guy want?" Summers asked, speaking to himself, his face growing agitated.

"Don't know," Jamarcus answered as he watched the crowd come ever closer to the entrance of the base. A young man with a sign walked in front of the protesters, showing a poster with George Bush wearing a dunce hat to them. That made the large front portion of the protesters surge forward.

"These guys need to back up," Summers grumbled angrily. Jamarcus was beginning to get pissed off at Summers, but he had to agree with him that things were getting uncomfortable. He was just unsure how to approach the locals.

"You're not in danger," the voice buzzed in his head.

Jamarcus rubbed his forehead, trying to convince himself to move forward.

"We've got to do something, Staff," Brent said nervously as the rest of the squad huddled together with their weapons clasped tightly in their hands.

"You're not in danger," the voice said, and after a sigh, Jamarcus slung his rifle to his side and walked toward the crowd.

"Stay right here, guys," he said as he directed himself to the man who'd asked the squad to approach. When Jamarcus got close to him, the crowd parted to give him space.

"Sir, can you speak English?" Jamarcus asked as he got next to the man.

"Yes, I can speak English," the man answered.

"My name is Jamarcus," he said, putting his hand forward.

"My name is Rumi," the man responded as he shook it.

"Rumi, I need you guys to move back to the designated area," Jamarcus said, pointing his hand in that direction with his palm open. Rumi nodded and spoke out to the crowd in their language. The pro-testers moved back to the area, with Jamarcus accompanying them.

"You will talk?" Rumi asked.

"Yes, I can talk," Jamarcus answered.

"The missile strike that happened earlier this month. You know about this?”

“Yes, I know about the strike.”

“Why did this happen?”

“You know as much as I do. The strike was directed at an alleged al-Qaeda leader.”

“They were not al-Qaeda. They were Taliban,” Rumi told Jamarcus.

“I did not know that, sir.”

“You don’t know who was attacked?”

“No, sir,” Jamarcus responded. “It was most likely a special ops strike. I don’t know what is going on with the missile strikes. I’m just a grunt.”

“Why did they have to kill women and children?” Rumi asked in a harsh tone.

“Are you in support of the Taliban?” Jamarcus asked snidely.

“Sir, I am a human being. I don’t like the Taliban, but I don’t want innocent people dying.”

“I completely agree with you, sir,” Jamarcus said. “But I don’t have any control over that.”

“This should stop,” Rumi said hotly.

“Unfortunately, there is little I can do about this,” Jamarcus said as he looked at the protesters around him. “Is that your only concern?”

“No, your convoys,” Rumi said, making Jamarcus regret his

question. "Why do you block off the roads to areas around the town during your convoys?"

"It's to ensure the safety of the military personnel and civilians from attacks from terrorists," Jamarcus answered in a practiced cadence.

"But you prevent people from going where we need to go," Rumi argued.

"We're sorry for the inconvenience, sir, but we are only doing our job."

"But I'm not a bad person. I work hard for my family. Why do you keep me from going to where I need to go?"

"Sir, I'm not saying you are a bad person," Jamarcus said, growing more pestered by the constant bombardment of criticism. "We're just doing our duty. It's our job. It's independent of who you are."

"I live here," Rumi said madly. "People know me here. Why must we be treated this way?"

"Look, sir, there is nothing I can do about these things. We can't change the way procedures are done. But they are done with everyone's safety in mind."

"You need to stop treating us this way. This should stop."

"Look, sir, there's nothing more I can say," Jamarcus said as he turned from the man and walked back toward the base entrance. "I'm pretty sure you don't want to keep talking to an American any longer." He paused. "Especially a nigger one," he said to himself.

"Why did you use that word?" Rumi shouted at Jamarcus, walking after him. "I did not say that word!"

"I was only talking to myself," Jamarcus answered, stunned by Rumi's anger.

"I am not racist!" Rumi said, slapping Jamarcus's arm. "I did not use that word! I am not racist!"

"I'm sorry, sir," Jamarcus said.

"Staff!" Summers shouted as he and the rest of the squad rushed to his side. "Back the fuck up!" Summers slammed his rifle into Rumi, sending him tumbling back. That enraged the protesters, causing them to rush forward to help Rumi and to yell at the soldiers.

"Calm down, Summers!" Jamarcus yelled.

"They need to back up, Staff. We—"

That was all he was able to say, as Jamarcus lost his cool, grabbing Summers by his collar and flinging him back with the rest of the squad.

"Everyone shut the fuck up!" Jamarcus roared at the top of his lungs, which made his throat sting. He was shocked for a moment when everyone became quiet. "Get back to the gate now!" he said to the squad, who walked back in silence.

Jamarcus then walked through the protesters and stood at the spot where they were allowed to assemble. "Stand here, please!" he said as he pointed his open hand toward the ground, and the crowd walked back to that spot. Barely able to keep his composure, Jamarcus began his way back to the base.

"Why did you use that word?" Rumi asked as Jamarcus walked

by him.

"I'm sorry!" Jamarcus shouted as he turned back to Rumi. "I fucked up! I was wrong. I'm sorry!" Not sure what else to say, Jamarcus walked back to the squad.

"Why do you hate us so much?" Rumi asked behind Jamarcus, but Jamarcus didn't answer. If he had, it would have been to say that it wasn't them he hated.

<3>

Jamarcus stood beside the battalion commander's office later that day, leaning against the wall and staring holes into the wall across from him. The pressure over his heart was like a brick wall, and his stomach stung with fury. His mind kept going back to when he'd left Kathrine in the hospital after her surgery. He'd stayed as long as he could with her before he was deployed. Kathrine had been in her bed, not able to speak coherently, every so often pressing a button to allow a morphine drip to take the pain away or pressing it anyway even when it didn't allow it. His guilt was suffocating him, drowning out any other emotion he might have had. If he smiled or laughed, those emotions were only surface deep; he truly didn't feel any happiness anymore.

Jamarcus snapped back to attention as a head popped out the door and looked at him.

"Come on in, Staff," the man said.

"Sure thing, Cap," Jamarcus responded before entering the room. It was small, with only a few chairs and a desk with a computer.

Jamarcus's commanding officer stood behind the desk. Jamarcus stood at attention in front of the desk and saluted the colonel.

"Take a seat, Staff," the colonel said as he returned the salute. After everyone was seated, the colonel took a good look at Jamarcus.

"It seems that things got heated with the protesters earlier today, didn't they?" the colonel asked.

"Sir, yes, sir," Jamarcus answered.

"And it was reported that you yanked at another soldier's uniform when things escalated."

"Yes, sir."

"I don't have to remind you that NCOs are not to abuse the men they are in charge of, no matter the circumstances. We don't tolerate that behavior in this army."

"I completely understand, Colonel," Jamarcus said. "It won't happen again."

"There was also an argument between you and some of the protesters?" the colonel asked.

"Yes, sir. One person."

"What happened?"

"It was all my fault. I was talking to an individual about the recent missile strike and traffic problems. I said he didn't want to talk to me while using a racial slur. He was rightfully upset. I shouldn't have tossed a racial epitaph out, and I was completely in the wrong. I apologized to the individual."

"That's good," the colonel said. "I don't need to tell you that I do not tolerate that language at all, and you will be reprimanded for that."

"Yes, sir."

"I have to commend you for trying to strike up a conversation with the group to try to calm things down. It did put you in a compromising position, but I trust that you knew there was no danger. Correct?"

"Sir, yes, sir."

"All right, Jamarcus, let's drop the rank act here. Let's just be friends, okay?"

"All right, Mike."

"Look, Bobby and I admire you. You're a smart young man. Not many twenty-eight-year-olds in the army are E6. The only thing keeping you from being promoted to first class is your age. You are a damn good Ranger. And I don't want to see any of my men lost here, especially if it could get them hurt or more. No matter what you may have thought, that type of thinking in a combat scenario could have gotten you and your men killed. Correct?"

"You're right," Jamarcus said. "I agree. I was completely in the wrong."

"You weren't completely in the wrong, Jay," Bobby said. "That was a pretty decent thing you did, talking to the crowd. If that scuffle never had happened, it would have looked great for us. Too bad Summers went all Rambo out there."

"He's young," Jamarcus said. "Guy's been trained for months

for combat, so he's probably itching to do something. He hasn't been taught that violence doesn't solve every situation."

"And that's the point," Mike said. "If there is one thing I've noticed about you, it is that you are calm. During raids, patrols, that ambush we had where you saved those men—calm as hell. You don't get flustered when shit hits the fan. I'm surprised you haven't decided to go Special Forces. You went to Fort Benning, right?"

"Yeah."

"So you've been trained to handle your shit. But you got pissed off out there. That's why we're talking. Now, no bullshit—tell me the truth. Why are you here?"

"No bullshit?" Jamarcus asked.

"No ranks. No military discipline," Bobby said. "Just speak the truth, Jay."

"Well, in that case, let's go deeper," Jamarcus said. "Let's take away that we're in the army. Take away that we're the United States. Take away patriotism and duty to God and the country. Let's take away God. No Jesus or Muhammad. Religion is taken out of the equation. Let's say you guys aren't white, and I'm not black. Let's say the people outside this base aren't Asian or Indo-European. We're all human beings. If you take all those things away, then I don't know why we're here. No one has given me an explanation based on pure logic. I know that we first came here to fight al-Qaeda. To hunt down Osama bin Laden. Al-Qaeda is a threat to the US. That's a logical reason. I might have done some raids to root out some cells, but I haven't seen much of them. And I'm pretty sure we keep creating cells every time we kill some innocent bystander who happens to have a brother with nothing to lose.

"The only thing I know is that what we are doing doesn't add up to the narrative that is being told at home, and I just want someone to tell me the truth. Just the simple goddamn truth. No bullshit. No propaganda. Just tell me the truth. I might go along with it then. But if I don't know what our goal is here, then I'm lost."

"Rooting out the Taliban and giving the people here a safe environment to live free aren't good reasons to be here?" Bobby asked.

"Hell no," Jamarcus answered. "That's not a logical explanation. If that is the case, then why aren't we in countries in Africa that are Christian, are more accepting of a US presence, and suffer from the same oppression that the people here face from the Taliban? If that was true, the US would be all over the world. But we're here. Still."

"Well, if you take away everything you detailed, then there is no logical reason we're here," Mike said. "Is that what you want to hear?"

"I don't know."

"I know you have a girlfriend who has cancer," Mike said. "Have you talked to her?" He watched Jamarcus, who did not answer. "I know the stress of a loved one who is sick can be distracting," he said. "But we need to know that you can still do your job."

"Jesus Christ," Jamarcus muttered, rubbing his face.

"There is nothing wrong with admitting that you need help, Jay," Bobby said. "We're trying to save your life."

"Are you going to send me home as a psych case?" Jamarcus asked.

"We can't," Mike answered. "You haven't shown any real behavior that has revealed you need any help other than today. You probably wouldn't, would you?"

"Fuck no," Jamarcus answered.

"Just make it through this tour, Jay," Bobby said, patting Jamarcus's shoulder. "You've served ten years for your country. Leave the army, and go to school. Make something of yourself. Don't throw your life away."

"Is that all?" Jamarcus asked.

"Well, yes," Mike answered.

Jamarcus stood up at attention and saluted Mike. "Permission to be dismissed?" he asked as he stood.

Mike got out of his chair, walked over to Jamarcus, and hugged him, surprising Jamarcus and making Bobby laugh.

"We do care about you, just to let you know," Mike said.

"Yes, Colonel."

"Permission granted," Mike said, and Jamarcus turned and left the room, closing the door behind him.

Chapter 9
<1>
June 2007

Jamarcus and Kathrine sat in a medical cubicle, watching a movie on Jamarcus's cell phone. Kathrine was taking her weekly chemotherapy, surrounded by other cubicles ordered in aisles with women taking their treatments. Many were sleeping in hospital beds, while a few had family members to keep them company. One woman had a spiritual practitioner performing a healing on her. Jamarcus and Kathrine were watching a comedy on Jamarcus' phone, sharing earplugs as they sat in each other's arms. Every once in a while, they would let out a laugh that made the other women next to them give them an evil eye.

"We have to keep quiet, honey," Kathrine whispered into his ear, doing everything she could to keep herself from laughing in hysterics.

"Don't blame me," Jamarcus said. "You laugh so loud."

"No, I don't." Kathrine giggled, keeping her eyes shut.

"God, remember when we went to the movies with Mary and Sam last week? That monster movie?" Jamarcus asked.

"They were so mad at us," Kathrine said. "They kept telling us to stop saying what was going to happen."

"What did they want us to do?" Jamarcus snickered. "Horror movies always follow the same damn clichés, right? It was just asking for somebody to predict what was going to happen.”

“Honey, remember when the black guy went into the dark room?”

“Oh, he dead,” Jamarcus said in a snarky voice, making Kathrine giggle while covering her mouth.

“Sam slapped you in the back of the head.” Kathrine broke out laughing.

When Jamarcus saw two women looking in their direction, all he could do was cover his eyes and laugh silently. “Holy shit,” he whispered. “She was like ‘Stop doing that.’ What? It’s the token black guy in a horror film. They always die.”

“Honey, stop,” Kathrine said, holding her stomach. “I think I’m going to pee.”

“That movie is so bad. I mean, horror movies have gone up a notch recently. How did they make that movie and think it was good?”

“Mary and Sam still think that movie was good.”

“How? Oh, wait. Let’s splash together a whole bunch of clichés from other horror movies. Dark haunted house in a secluded part of the woods—check. The evil monster we can’t see till the end—check. Group of beautiful college-age people ready to bone each other. Y’all goin’ die.”

“Y’all goin’ die,” Kathrine repeated, snickering as she covered her eyes.

“And they had the token black guy!” Jamarcus said. “My God, I knew he was dead as soon as the movie started.”

"Honey, stop. We have to watch the movie," Kathrine said as she watched the phone's screen.

"I'm sorry," Jamarcus said as he leaned close to her so she could see.

They sat and watched his phone for a good period, chuckling every so often. Jamarcus looked up from the phone and noticed a family go into a cubicle across from them—a mother and father with two daughters and a son. One of the daughters sat on the cubicle bed, talking to her parents.

"This movie is okay," Jamarcus said as he went back to watching his phone.

"I think it's great," Kathrine said, making Jamarcus grimace in response. "You're so elitist," she complained.

"I just don't like the actor in this film."

"You don't like chick flicks—that's all," Kathrine said.

"What? I don't," Jamarcus said defensively. "I am a guy. I don't understand chick flicks. There is nothing wrong with that."

"There is nothing wrong with that," Kathrine said in a mocking voice. Then she went back to the film as the actress decided to be silent to the main actor because of a misunderstanding.

"You see? Right there," Jamarcus snapped. "Why is there conflict here? Explain, writer."

"What?" Kathrine laughed. "It builds tension. All types of tension."

"There is no need for this to happen," Jamarcus spoke in a precise, robotic voice, making Kathrine laugh. "There is conflict. Why is there conflict? There is a misunderstanding. Answer to conflict: someone is a goddamn adult and mentions the misunderstanding. Conflict solved. We bang! Everyone's happy."

When the family across the aisle turned to face them, Kathrine put a hand over Jamarcus's mouth. "Honey, be quiet." She laughed silently.

"Sorry," Jamarcus said sheepishly as he bowed his head.

As they continued to watch the movie, a scene appeared in which the two main protagonists were introduced to another actress just to add more conflict. When Jamarcus rolled his eyes, Kathrine slapped him on his arm. When Jamarcus recoiled, he looked up to see the resident oncologist enter the cubicle across from them.

"Hello, everyone. I'm Dr. Hogi," he said to the sober group, who politely greeted him. "And you must be Sarah." The doctor extended his hand to the nervous young woman on the table.

At the same time, both actresses in the movie got angry at the main actor, which made both Jamarcus and Kathrine cover their giggles with their hands.

"To let you know, I'm an oncologist," Dr. Hogi said. "I specifically deal with ovarian cancer. I know you're young, Sarah, but the growth you have is a tumor. Cancer can develop in women your age."

On Jamarcus's phone, one of the women slapped the actor's chest, making him recoil awkwardly against a chair, which sent Jamarcus and Kathrine into a tizzy as they tried with all their might not to laugh.

"The tumor is large and has spread to other organs," the doctor said. "That means it is stage four. Now we have to perform surgery to remove the mass. If we don't, you will die in a month."

The other woman in the movie slapped the actor across the face so hard his hair barely had enough time to catch up with it. When the two women stormed away from the man, Jamarcus and Kathrine grabbed each other in their arms. Kathrine used her hands to cover their shaking faces as Jamarcus held on to her bald head. They pressed their faces against each other, doing everything they could to keep silent.

"Oh my God," Kathrine hissed, her body trembling.

"We're going to hell," Jamarcus whispered with tears rolling down his cheeks.

They sat like that, shaking as they suppressed their laughter. While they held each other, they didn't notice one of the nurses on the floor come into the cubicle and begin removing the IV from Kathrine's arm.

"All right, you two," the nurse said with a smile on her face. "That's enough troublemaking for you today. Your treatment is done, Kathrine."

"Thank you, dear," Kathrine said, breathing heavily, as the nurse placed a bandage where the needle had been in her arm.

As they got up and left, they held each other and kept their faces to the ground while they walked past the other cubicles, muffling every sound out of their mouths. As they left the office and walked toward the clinic's exit, they erupted in hoots and grunts, hanging on to each other so they wouldn't fall.

"Holy shit," Jamarcus said as he squeezed Kathrine. "I thought the father across from us was going to kick our ass."

"Honey, why did you have to say we're going to hell?" Kathrine cackled against his chest. "I can't stop laughing at that."

"I feel so bad," Jamarcus said as they left the clinic and went to his car in the parking lot. They continued to laugh all the while. They sat in the car, holding hands and breathing desperately for air. They kept laughing for a few more minutes until they looked into each other's eyes.

"Kat, you know how I said that I was going back to the mainland?" Jamarcus said.

"Yes," Kathrine said, and she went silent and still.

"You're sure you don't want to come with me?"

"I can't leave the islands, honey. I don't want to go."

"So I decided to stay. At least to stay to take care of you while you take your chemo. I figure that once you're better, you'll change your mind."

"Thank you," Kathrine said as she began to cry.

"Well, it was shitty that I was going to leave," Jamarcus said. "I'm just having a hard time living in Hawaii. The local people here are driving me insane. But that's no excuse to leave you."

"I'm sorry," Kathrine said as she squeezed Jamarcus's hand. "I do need you, honey. You're helping me so much."

"Yeah, well, I need you more than you think. If I didn't have you, I don't think I would be able to step outside the apartment. I know I'm going to school after I get out of the army soon. I don't know if I could if I'm not with you."

"I guess we're stuck with each other then," Kathrine said as she stared out the front window of the car.

"Sorry about that, Kat," Jamarcus joked as he started the car.

"Love you, honey," she said, still holding Jamarcus's hand.

"Love you more."

<2>

Jamarcus sat on the couch with Kathrine's legs over his lap as they watched the latest episode of a zombie survival show. He massaged her legs constantly as she moaned in pain, barely watching the television. It was late at night, and Jamarcus knew he wasn't going to get much sleep before he had to get up early the next morning to arrive at the base. The more he sat massaging her legs, the more he grew agitated and tired.

"Kat, you're not even looking at the show," Jamarcus said as he looked at Kathrine, who lay with her face in her pillow.

"It hurts, honey," Kathrine moaned as she looked at him with sad, sleepy eyes. "It feels like ants crawling through my legs, biting everything they touch."

"Kat, you've got to take your pain medication."

"I don't want to," she said. "I don't want to take anything with opioids in it."

"Sweetheart, I don't mind rubbing your legs as much as you need, but I'm tired. And I have to go to work early tomorrow. Plus, you're not watching your show."

Kathrine turned back into her pillow, covering her face. Soon Jamarcus heard her muffled crying, and his agitation became anger. He tried watching the show, but he didn't want to concentrate on anything else. Kathrine was in pain, and Jamarcus guessed the male part of his brain just wanted to do anything he could to make Kathrine's pain go away now. Maybe it was all his years in the army that made him want to act immediately, but he just wanted to act.

"Kat, you've got to take your pain medication," Jamarcus grunted at her in a strict voice.

Kathrine stared back at him with a concerned look. She got up slowly off the couch and walked to her purse. She took out a pill from her medication bottle went to the sink to drink a cup of water and she swallowed it. She sat away from Jamarcus when she went back to the couch.

Jamarcus sat next to her, not sure if he should move closer to her or give her space. When she began rubbing her thighs, he couldn't resist anymore and slid next to Kathrine. He wrapped her in his arms, massaging her whole body, and then moved one hand over her breasts and his other hand between her legs. He massaged those areas until Kathrine leaned against his body, softly crying.

"I'm sorry, honey," Kathrine whispered into his chest. "I don't want to be a burden to you."

"You're not a burden. You're just in pain. I don't want to see you in pain."

"That feels good," Kathrine said after she kissed him.

"Is the pain going away?" Jamarcus asked.

"A little bit."

"That's good."

"What did I miss?" she asked.

"Not much," Jamarcus said as he looked back at the show. "The group was walking through an abandoned town and found a lone survivor. Last I knew, they were contemplating if they should help him, leave him, or take his stuff."

"What would you do?"

"Me personally? I don't know. If I had enough supplies that I could help the guy, I would cautiously approach him. He could be a psycho, or he could have a valuable skill. If I didn't have enough supplies to help, I'd make sure he didn't know I was there."

"Fuck that guy," Kathrine said in a harsh voice as she placed a hand on Jamarcus's crotch.

"Wow," Jamarcus laughed. "I didn't know you would be that cruel."

"I'm not letting anyone risk our lives. I'd fucking kill him if he got near us."

"I guess I know who I want on my side during the zombie apocalypse," Jamarcus said.

"Don't be too sure, honey. If a horde of zombies is after us, I'm tripping you so I can get away."

"Holy shit," Jamarcus yelped as he erupted with laughter. "Goddamn, woman. You are cruel."

"What? My legs are bad because of chemo. Besides, you don't have to be the fastest one, just faster than the slowest person."

"Oh my God, end-of-the-world philosophy. I love it."

"Do you want to eat, honey?" Kathrine asked.

"I can order some pizza," Jamarcus said.

"That's too expensive," Kathrine said. "We already ate out this week. I should cook something for us. What do you want to eat?"

"Well, we had steak yesterday," Jamarcus said. "Do you want to eat corned beef and cabbage?"

"What do you want to eat, honey?" Kathrine asked as she stood up and made her way to the kitchen.

"Oh, I want to eat your mochiko chicken," Jamarcus said in an eager voice.

"Okay." Kathrine looked in the refrigerator. After taking some items out, she placed them on the kitchen counter and threw away some things in the trash. "Honey, can you throw the garbage out?" she asked when she noticed the trash can getting full.

"All right," Jamarcus said as he retrieved the trash bag and headed out of the apartment to throw it into the dumpster bin.

"You're going to get into a fight," the voice buzzed in Jamarcus's head as he threw the trash into the bin.

As he walked back, he saw two local men with beer bottles in their hands walking by the apartment.

"Go home, hauole!" one of the men shouted as Jamarcus walked away.

"Chill out with that shit," Jamarcus said as he turned to face them. "Why don't you get sober and stop fucking with people?"

"Fuck you, asshole," the other man said. "Why don't you stop coming over to Hawaii and stealing our jobs?"

"Bro, I'm black!" Jamarcus said as he stopped in front of the apartment building. "It's fucking hard for black men to get jobs. That's why I joined the military."

"So what?" one of them shouted in a slurred voice. "You still one mainland hauole taking our land from us. What? Now that you colonized Hawaii, you goin' to colonize more of Afghanistan?"

"What the fuck did you say?" Jamarcus said, his heart filling with rage.

One of the drunken men walked straight up to his face, so close that Jamarcus could smell the alcohol on his breath. "I said you're a colonizing fucka." The man spit in Jamarcus's face.

As the man sprawled backward away from him, Jamarcus realized he'd littered the man's face with a flurry of punches. The other man ran and tried to grab Jamarcus to keep him from continuing his assault, but Jamarcus was lost, with his anger controlling his actions. When one of the men grabbed his arms, Jamarcus jolted so hard that his perspective shifted to a view above the fight. He watched himself and the two men moving in slow motion. It took a while for Jamarcus to register what exactly was happening, and when it did register, his mind went from shock and confusion to curiosity.

"What is this?" Jamarcus asked himself, noticing that his voice buzzed inside himself. That struck him as odd, as he could see and feel his body being held below him, and the buzzing didn't happen in his physical form. He looked at himself: his face was full of rage, and one man was frightened as the other was barely able to hold on to him.

"Why am I so angry?" Jamarcus asked, his voice buzzing inside himself again, and then he began to question the nature of the buzzing. *What exactly is buzzing? What is this state? Is it my soul? Then how is my soul separate from my body right now? Is this safe? Am I in danger?*

"You're not in danger," the voice buzzed in Jamarcus's state, and somehow, Jamarcus knew the voice came from above and behind him. When he turned his view around, he saw a white light orb streaking down from the night sky above the city. It came to a halt and floated for a moment before it disappeared.

"What was that?" Jamarcus buzzed to himself, and then he changed his view as he heard people coming from the apartment to break up the fight. His perspective then shot back down into his body, and rage filled his mind again.

"Don't you call me a colonizer!" Jamarcus yelled as his neighbors pulled him away from the drunk men.

"Fuck you, hauole!" one of them shouted as they stood on the sidewalk.

"Honey!" Kathrine shouted from behind Jamarcus, and Jamarcus's anger disappeared instantly. He turned to see her. Her face reflected terror as she covered herself with a bathrobe.

"Come inside now!" she demanded, and Jamarcus immediately walked through the crowd, past Kathrine, and back into the apartment. He stood in the living room of the apartment, looking at the cut-up pieces of floured chicken on the kitchen counter, as his rage slowly turned to guilt.

"What happened?" Kathrine asked as she closed the door after she entered the apartment.

"Kat, I can't stay here in Hawaii," Jamarcus said. "I'm trying, but I'm so mad right now. I don't want to be angry anymore. I don't want to lash out at anyone. I have to go for my good. The last thing I want to do is hurt someone I love. I want you to come with me, but I will leave you here. I can't live here anymore."

"Honey," Kathrine said in despair behind him.

"I have to go," Jamarcus said as he turned to face her with tears streaming down his cheeks.

Chapter 10
<1>
November 2008

Jamarcus sat holding his cell phone to his face while looking at his apartment's wall. He was renting from a halfway home in Fort Walton, Florida. There wasn't much in the apartment except for the essentials. It was a studio with a bed, a desk for his gaming console and television, a chair, and a dresser for his clothes. It was the same as his apartment in Kalihi before Kathrine had moved in and brought in all the other house furniture most people felt they needed. Jamarcus couldn't afford much of those things now since separating from the military, and even if he could have, he would have brought in only items that Kathrine would have wanted. He didn't want that because it still hurt too much to be separated from her, and he didn't want to be reminded of that every day.

"You're sure you're doing okay, honey?" Kathrine asked on the other end of the phone.

"Yeah, I think so," Jamarcus answered as he lay down on his bed and looked out at the night sky out his window. It was late out enough to see the Andromeda constellation with his eyes.

"Were you able to find a job?"

"Yes. I stopped trying to apply for a job that had nothing to do with the military and ended up applying for a security firm. I swear all these companies around here say they support veterans, but they're full of shit."

"But you have a job?"

"Well, I got accepted with the firm I applied for and just finished their training. In Florida, you've got to go through security guard and first-aid training before you get on-site. They haven't placed me at a site yet but said that most likely, they'll place me at an industrial plant since I don't want to be at an armed site."

"You don't want to be at a place where you'll carry a gun?" Kathrine asked.

"I hope I'll never touch another gun again," Jamarcus said. "Every time I touch a gun, something horrible happens."

"Did you apply for school already?"

"Oh yeah, I applied at a college out here. There's this thing that you have to pay more if you are an out-of-state student, so I decided to go to a lesser-tier school instead of a full-on college. I'm in my first semester. I swear if I had known that, I probably would have stayed with you."

"Don't say that, honey," Kathrine said in a grim voice.

"I'm sorry," Jamarcus said as he rubbed his eyes. "That was pretty selfish of me."

"No, that's not it. I know you had to leave. You went through a lot during your time overseas. You don't want to talk about it, and that's fine. I just wish I could have helped you. Maybe I wouldn't have lost you."

"You haven't lost me. I'm still here. I still need you."

"Maybe I should have gone with you," Kathrine said.

"You know, there is a cancer center here close to where I live," Jamarcus said. "It's about half an hour away from here on the freeway. Once I get a place, you should think about it."

"I don't think my sister would want that," she said.

"Oh. Is she still mad at me?"

"A little bit."

"Yeah, she's mad at me."

"It's not that," Kathrine said. "She just wants to take care of me. She doesn't want me to leave."

"Which means she's mad at me," Jamarcus said.

"Well, she doesn't want me to talk to you."

"That makes sense."

"It's because she doesn't want you sending me money all the time. She's trying to control my diet, so she's stopping me from buying fast food."

"By the way, did you get the money I transferred to you?" Jamarcus asked.

"Yes. Thank you, honey."

"No problem."

"You sure you have enough for yourself?"

"I'm good," Jamarcus said. "I don't spend money on myself anyway. I might as well send some to you."

"Do you have the letter I sent you?" Kathrine asked.

"Yep. Right on my gaming table."

"Just make sure you're taking care of yourself."

"Anyway, did you go to see any movies lately?" Jamarcus asked.

"I went to see Wall-E a few weeks ago," Kathrine said. "I liked it. Wall-E was so cute."

"I loved that movie," Jamarcus said. "But then, anything that movie studio puts out is gold. Eva just made me laugh."

"Oh God, I loved it when she almost blew up Wall-E, and he was shaking because he was scared."

"That was cute. Did you go see it with your sister?"

"Yeah, but she didn't like it. She always gets mad at me for watching too many cartoons."

"Anime. There is a difference," Jamarcus said.

"Yeah, she doesn't see that. She just thinks I'm being dumb. Oh! Guess what I rewatched the other day when I was thinking of you? *Requiem*!"

"Get to da choppa!" Jamarcus grunted in his worst Arnold Schwarzenegger imitation. His heart swirled with joy and pain when he heard Kathrine laughing.

"Oh God, everyone dies in that movie. It is so good."

"Right. Man, first the Predator dies. Then the father and the son die! Man, no one was safe in that movie."

"Oh, honey, I miss laughing like this." Kathrine giggled before she became quiet on the phone.

"Kat?" Jamarcus called out.

"Honey?"

"Yeah?"

"I'm scared," Kathrine whimpered into the phone, causing Jamarcus's heart to fill back up with guilt and shame.

"It's okay to be afraid," he said. "You still have me. You can always call me when you're scared."

"I don't want to die." Kathrine wept, and Jamarcus lay silently as he listened to her cries. "I'm sorry, honey. I don't mean to get emotional."

"That's what the body does when it's trying to cope with trauma," Jamarcus said. "Otherwise, you'd explode like I always do."

"Honey, I've got to go," Kathrine said. "My sister's getting worried that I'm crying. I'll talk to you later."

"Okay. I love you."

"Love you too, honey," Kathrine said before she hung up.

Jamarcus put down the phone and got up to get dressed. He needed to step outside and look at the night sky to clear his head. After he stepped out of his room, he walked down the hallway, minding his neighbors, who were talking to one another. Many were out of jail, recovering from drug addiction, or getting off the streets from homelessness. Jamarcus was surprised at the number of veterans who were there, many of whom had served tours in Iraq or Afghanistan. It boggled his mind how much he heard on the radio that everyone supported the troops coming home from war, but it amounted to jack shit in practice. Jamarcus wondered when people were going to figure out that the best way to help a vet was to give him or her a job.

Just as Jamarcus reached the entrance to the halfway home, an older man he'd met when he first moved in came through with a big smile on his face.

"Hey, Jamarcus, how's it going?" he said with enthusiasm.

"Doing okay, Max," Jamarcus said after he shook his hand.

"Did you get a job at the security firm?" Max asked.

"Yes, I did. I just finished the training last month, and hopefully, they'll put me at a site soon."

"Did you get a job as a contractor?"

"You know what? They asked me if I wanted to do the same thing," Jamarcus said. "I didn't want that. I'm trying to forget the war, not relive it."

"But you can make a lot of money doing that," Max said. "You're still young. If you were to tough it out for a decade and save or invest your income, you'd be a millionaire."

"Max, man, I'm done with that life. I want to get as far away from that lifestyle as I can."

"Okay, I can respect that," Max said. "Guess what?"

"What's that?"

"I finally got a job myself," Max said with a little pride.

"All right!" Jamarcus cheered. "What job did you get?"

"Well, I kind of took a note from your book there. I stopped trying to get a job that was different from what I did in the military and applied to a trucking firm. They're going to help me get my license, and I'll be driving in a month."

"That's great, Max," Jamarcus said. "I'm happy for you."

"It's still bullshit, though. I tried applying for all these jobs at places that say they hire vets, but it's all a lie. I think they say it more for the advertisement than to help us out."

"I was just thinking that," Jamarcus said.

"I know what you mean too about not wanting to do what you did in the military. When I think of truck driving, I see myself driving into Baghdad for the first year of the war. I still have nightmares of IEDs going off."

"Yeah," Jamarcus said as he looked down at the ground.

"My bad, Jamarcus," Max said before he began walking away. "I don't want to keep you up too much. I'll talk to you later."

"Okay," Jamarcus responded with a wave as he walked out of the halfway home and into the parking lot.

It didn't take long for him to find Mama Bear and the Baby Bear above him. After a bit of a search, he found the Fisher. He watched those stars for a long time, trying to remember the fun he used to have as a kid trying to find all the constellations in the sky.

Jamarcus then remembered the dream he'd had of the boy of sunlight. He smiled, recalling his many dreams of aliens in other worlds with cities and different cultures. Soon he remembered the family and Bug Girl. Jamarcus couldn't help but laugh about the dreams he'd had about him and Bug Girl running through the chateau, making Mother yell at them. When he remembered Thor and Athena, his nostalgia became grief. The dream in which they'd left sent a spike into his stomach, and he began to cry. Not wanting anyone to see him, Jamarcus wiped the tears from his face and quickly forgot his dreams, walking back into the halfway home.

<2>

February 7, 2009

Jamarcus sped along a highway on his motorcycle on a cold, wet afternoon. He had his rain gear on, and it did its job of keeping him dry and warm, but somehow, the cold, moist air still froze his hands to the bone. He had on three layers of gloves, and his hands were still freezing. Yet he still did not want to buy a car. On his tour of Afghanistan, he had seen many men driving around on scooters or all-terrain bikes. Somehow, those guys could fit their entire lives onto their bikes. It was harsh when the weather was cold, but the financial payoff for it was great. It impressed Jamarcus that a motorcycle and all-weather gear had been the first major purchases he'd made when he got to the Panhandle. He'd thought the weather there was going to be comparable to that of Hawaii, but the first winter there woke Jamarcus up quickly.

Jamarcus soon arrived at the industrial site he was posted at, and it was as busy as he'd suspected. Trucks were already piling into the entrance, giving the guard there a hard time as he checked each vehicle and loaded in one by one. After Jamarcus got into the guard booth and his proper uniform, he checked into his shift and rushed out to relieve the guard, who was in an argument with one of the truckers.

"Get out of here, Kenny," Jamarcus said as he grabbed the hand-held logistics device out of his hand.

"Thanks, Jamarcus," Kenny said as he walked toward the booth. "There's nothing to pass down."

"Okay," Jamarcus said as he took paperwork from a truck driver to process.

"Oh, wait—I forgot," Kenny said as he turned back. "The plant wants us to make sure to process each truck correctly. We have to make sure their load matches what is on their work orders."

"Did something happen? Did I screw up on something?"

"Not you. We usually only match up the paperwork with what is in the system. On the morning shift, a trucker had a load that didn't match the paperwork, so now they want us to check everything."

"Oh, that's great," Jamarcus said as he waved goodbye to Kenny and turned back to the trucker. "Hey, man, I need to check the load."

"Go ahead!" the trucker shouted from his seat. "The info's on the machinery on the flatbed!"

"I need you to go up there and tell me the work order number. If you've been here before, you know you're supposed to do that if requested."

"Man, I've already wasted enough time dealing with this shit. You need to get you guys' act together!"

"Dude, I'm not in the mood to hear any bullshit from you!" Jamarcus yelled at the driver. "Now, I wasn't rude to you, so I expect the same courtesy! Just show me the damn work order, and you're out of here!"

The driver huffed as he got out of his cab and onto his flatbed to show Jamarcus the cargo's work order.

"You're done, man," Jamarcus said as soon as he scanned the paperwork.

"I'm gonna tell the plant exactly how you talked to me," the driver said as he got back in his cab. "Tell me your name."

"Jamarcus Bridge!" he yelled up to the driver. "You tell them exactly what I told you. And make sure you tell them that if any more drivers come in who don't do what they're supposed to do, I'm going to say the same thing!"

The driver looked down at Jamarcus, bewildered before he got his rig into gear and drove into the plant.

For the next few hours, Jamarcus went through his routine of checking the drivers' cargo to see if it matched their paperwork. Only a couple more drivers gave Jamarcus a hard time about the new process, and he resolved their issues just as abruptly.

After the last of the daily trucks had come onto the plant, Jamarcus went to the guard booth and pulled out his laptop, hoping to do some work on a few papers he had been assigned. The post he was in was a stationary one, so there was no need for him to go on patrol. All he had to do was monitor who came onto the plant, and since they were mostly workers who had badges they scanned to get onto the plant, the post was easy. Jamarcus got much of his homework done on that shift.

It was closing in on midnight, and most of the afternoon workers of the plant had already been replaced by the graveyard shift. A guard had already come on to relieve Jamarcus's other coworker who patrolled the plant. Jamarcus put his laptop away and got his bike ready to go home. He had classes first thing in the morning, and the first class was taught by a professor who was strict on attendance. If students were late or didn't show up, they got a zero for the class. Jamarcus was keen to get home and go to sleep so he could get up early.

When it got to a half hour past midnight, Jamarcus called his partner on the site. "Hey, did Sheila call to say she was coming in?" he asked when the guard answered.

"Nah, man. No one called. Maybe you should call the supervisor."

"Okay, thanks," Jamarcus said, and he hung up and called the area manager's phone. After he let her know what was going on, the manager said she was going to try to get in contact with his relief.

Another half hour went by, and anxiety began to fill up Jamarcus's chest. He knew he could miss a class, but the thought of having to work another shift was driving fear into him. The booth's phone rang, and Jamarcus answered after one ring.

"Hey, Beth," Jamarcus said.

"Sheila said she's sick and can't come in."

"That's twice in one week," Jamarcus said. "Can Kenny come in early to relieve me?"

"Kenny said he had to make sure his family got to school, and his wife needs the car to do that."

"Jesus, Beth. That's two sixteen-hour days I've done already this week. I can't keep this up."

"I'm sorry, Jamarcus. Sheila is on notice now. She can't miss another day, or she's gone. I need you to stay on-site for me, okay?"

"Yeah," Jamarcus said, pushing his anger down.

"Do you need anything?"

"Can I ask you something?"

"Sure," Beth answered.

"A person opens his or her eyes from sleep, goes to work, and goes through all the stress that he or she has to deal with at work, let alone being a security guard. That person goes home, falls asleep, wakes up, and is back at work. Nothing in between, just work and sleep. Tell me—how is that different from being in prison or slavery?"

"Jamarcus, I know you're stressed. Just … I need you to work that shift tonight. We have to have someone on site."

"Yeah," Jamarcus answered.

"Thanks a lot," Beth said.

"Yeah," Jamarcus responded before hanging up. A panic quickly rose in his heart, the same panic he'd felt when he had to do another patrol in Iraq after he already had done a twelve-hour one. Jamarcus knew he wasn't over there, but the same fear took hold of him.

For an hour, Jamarcus sat in a chair, breathing in and out slowly, trying to bring his fear down. He thought of everything that could bring him joy—a song he'd loved back in high school, a favorite anime show. Nothing was working.

Somehow, the fear subsided into a cold slat in his belly, resting there, not giving Jamarcus any relief. He decided to send an email to his teacher to at least let him know what his situation was. Afterward, Jamarcus sat looking at the street in front of the plant as the night hours slowly crept by, and the fatigue shakes took hold of him as the morning relief arrived just before dawn. Jamarcus got his gear on and waited for Kenny to come into the booth so they could go through the pass-down.

"Anything new?" Kenny asked as he checked in.

"Nothing," Jamarcus said before checking out. "I'll see you in a couple of days."

"Sorry I couldn't come in earlier," Bubba said.

"Don't worry about it," Jamarcus said as he left the booth.

He quickly got on his bike. He made sure to take his time going home while driving through the morning traffic. He once had to change lanes suddenly because a driver didn't see him or just didn't care to. As soon as he got home, he showered and changed, grabbed his schoolbooks, and was back out the door. After another fifteen minutes, he was at his school and in his classroom, where his teacher was going over a new set of math equations.

After the class ended, Jamarcus walked up to the teacher as the other students left the classroom. "Professor, did you get my email?" he asked as he knelt by his desk.

"Yes, I did," the professor answered before he sat down.

"I'm still getting a zero?"

"I can't make an exception. I have to treat you the same as everyone in the class."

"All right," Jamarcus said, shutting down and walking away from the desk.

"Don't worry about it, Jamarcus," the professor said as he walked away. "You're getting an A in the class. It's not a big deal."

"Okay," Jamarcus responded, but he simply walked out of the classroom, not caring about what the professor had said. He went through the motions of each class; his body had moved past fatigue to a realm of mental and physical pain that simply kept him awake. By midday, Jamarcus was done with his classes and riding on his motorcycle home. After he got into his room, he lay down on his bed, where he remained still for hours.

He had been in that state before: he'd worked so hard that as he lay there, his body was completely paralyzed, not able to move, while still wide awake with anger and stress. He made sure his head was positioned the right way, or he might have suffocated on his pillow.

When he felt his arms and legs again, he slowly got up and went to his laptop to work on his class assignments. Just as he turned it on, his cell phone rang, and his heart jumped when he saw Kathrine's number on it.

"Hi, Kat," Jamarcus said.

"Jamarcus," another woman's voice said on the other end, "this is Nancy, Kathrine's sister."

"Hi, Nancy," Jamarcus said, the hole in his heart filling with dread.

"I'm calling to let you know that Kathrine died an hour ago."

"Okay. Thanks."

"Thank you for taking care of her. Even after you left."

"Okay," Jamarcus said as he looked out his window at the night sky.

"Are you all right?" Nancy asked in a concerned voice.

"Yeah," Jamarcus said.

"Well, thanks a lot, Jamarcus. Goodbye."

"Goodbye," Jamarcus answered, and after ending the call, he curled up into a small ball.

His mind was on fire. His entire body—his skin, his bones, his insides—was full of pain. An aching cry erupted from the depths of his soul, and tears soaked his pillow. Kathrine, the only reason he was alive, was gone. He didn't have a reason to live anymore. He had no reason to step outside his room. He had no sense of who he was, no identity. He was broken. At that moment in time, Jamarcus felt that he was nothing.

"Everything's going to be okay," a male voice buzzed in his head.

Paranoia filled Jamarcus's mind. It always had been a female voice that spoke to him, and it always had been the same voice. He didn't know what the voice was—a guardian angel or part of his subconscious mind. But it had been the same voice always. Having a different voice buzzing in his head created a deep rage in his chest, and his belly clenched in pain and fear.

"Who is this?" Jamarcus whispered to himself in a harsh voice. "Who are you? What are you? I don't need to have voices in my head right now. I'm in pain, and I don't need this. You tell me who you are. You show me what you are. You do this, or don't ever talk to me again."

An energy shot through Jamarcus like a waterfall crashing from the top of his head, smashing through his throat and his body, leaving him paralyzed again. His perspective shot out of his physical form, and he watched himself lie still in his bed, shocked by what had just happened. Tentacles of white light that seemed to Jamarcus to be bending space-time wrapped around his soul, or whatever was out of his body, and he was whisked up out of the window and into the sky.

Startled, he flew up for only a few moments, but when he looked down, Fort Walton was only a patch of lights in the land. Jamarcus then felt a presences around him, and a ringing filled his consciousness. It was a chord that Jamarcus had never heard before, an almost angelic tone, ringing over and over again. His mind filled with curiosity, and white orbs that also bent space-time around them appeared above him. The white tentacles that held his consciousness came from the large orb directly in front of him. Soon the ringing subsided, and Jamarcus felt the large orb's thoughts enter his mind.

"My name is Ra," the orb said, now with no buzzing, and Jamarcus felt the love of the voice in his soul, like a soothing balm over his aching mind. "I am your father. Your mother, Ixchel, is here too. So are the rest of your family. I am what the people of this world call a Pleiadean. Your mother is an Andean from a galaxy you call Andromeda. You're our son, Scar Amun. Your soul was sent here to Earth to learn what it means to be a sentient being. To understand that your choices have consequences. Through your struggles, you can learn to be better than what you believe you can be or allow yourself to be. To learn how to join us again after this life. You're not alone. We're always here. You may have forgotten us, but we will never forget you. Do not despair."

Jamarcus floated silently, trying to take in all that he heard and felt. He reacted whenever instances of Murphy's law happened in his life by letting go and trying to control only what he could. Although he felt the love coming from the voice that called itself Ra, he pushed the message out of his head and thought in an analytical mindset. After a few moments of thought, Jamarcus went through confusion, calm, curiosity, skepticism, and then rage.

"You are not scared?" Ra asked him.

"No," Jamarcus answered.

"You are angry."

"Yes."

"Why are you mad?"

"Are you really from another world?" Jamarcus asked.

"From another universe and time, yes," Ra answered.

Jamarcus pondered those words, and the more he thought, the angrier he became until his grief and anguish exploded out of him. "Where the fuck are you?" he screamed with all his might, his entire state buzzing. "Can you not see us? We are confused and divided. Full of hate and anger. We wage war among ourselves. I've waged wars. I killed a baby! I killed a boy just on the cusp of being an adult! Why are you just watching us? You can help. You don't have to do anything. You just have to reveal yourselves to us. Then we would know there are other civilizations out there better than us. We would know that we have to be better and do better to join you. We are so full of bigotry, racism, and greed. All of this would end if you just show yourselves to us. Why do you just watch? Why?"

The last scream shook Jamarcus so hard that he woke in his bed with his body covered in sweat and his belly and chest burning from inside. He could feel the heat emanating from him as he held his hand over his chest. Amazement returned to Jamarcus as he thought about what had happened. Were those aliens? Was there a way for him to communicate with them again? Would they even want to talk to him after his outburst? Regret racked his soul, but the moment gave his mind a burning curiosity.

Jamarcus needed to tell someone, and he grabbed his cell phone, ready to call Kathrine to let her know what had just happened. Then he remembered the call he'd received from Kathrine's sister, and he put his phone down. Loneliness filled his heart again, and he placed his phone on the desk. He got under the covers of his bed and curled up into the fetal position. He lay there with his body and soul in pain until he fell into an empty black sleep.

Chapter 11
<1>
March 2009

Jamarcus sat in a circle of students in his public speaking class, listening as each one gave an impromptu speech about his or her favorite hobbies. He didn't look at any of the students' faces; he mostly looked at the walls or at the clock to see what time it was. All of the students were engaged with each other, laughing and commenting on each other's topics. The topics that came up weren't unique. One student said he loved collecting old comic books and not the most popular ones. Another student said he would draw for hours. Jamarcus was sure that most of the students' hobbies were interesting, but they were kids straight out of high school. In truth, a lot of their interests, he believed, were based on naivete. Or perhaps he was just being mean-spirited toward them.

"So I'm Sasha, and I love plays," a student said during her turn. "I have always liked plays. My mom would watch all these Broadway musicals when I was a kid."

"Which musicals did you watch?" a student asked.

"Oh, like *Cats* and *The Phantom of the Opera*—you know, the modern classics. So I wanted to get into acting at a young age. My mom would drive me to all of these acting and singing classes."

"Was it tough?" another student asked.

"It was. I wasn't good at singing, so that went out of the bag. But I stuck with acting. That's actually what I'm majoring in at school: performance arts."

"How many plays were you in?"

"I've been in quite a few," Sasha said. "Most plays that had kids in them were the most popular ones. You have to do *Death of a Salesman* and *Hamlet*. You know, my favorite one I did was *Twelve Angry Men*, because, if I was onstage, that meant there weren't twelve angry men."

"What was the weirdest play you performed in?"

"You know what?" Sasha said after a thought. "I was in a play based on *Scarface*. And I mean, we did all the lines in certain scenes in the movie. Some so many parents were pissed off that we did that play because we were swearing and talking about drugs and murder. I had fun, though. I still don't understand why my mom let me do that play. So yeah."

"Good job, Sasha," the professor said after the students clapped. "So who wants to go next?"

"I'll go," another student said. "My name is Chrissy. I love playing video games."

"You play video games?" one of the female students lamented, which made Jamarcus smile. "I hate when my boyfriend plays. I can never get him off."

"So I play a lot," Chrissy said as the group laughed. "I've only started recently. But I play all the time. It's actually kind of bad how much I play."

"What console do you play on?"

"I don't play on a console," Chrissy answered. "I have a gaming computer rig. I play MMOs. My favorite right now is *World of Warcraft*."

"That's my game!" A student cheered, making the group giggle.

"Oh, I'm hardcore into that game. I play a human paladin, and I mostly tank for the guild I'm in. I admit I will spend hours on that game. But you need to. It's coordinating with other people in the guild, and some live in different time zones. Sometimes in different countries. Then you have to do different types of raids that need a good number of people to complete. And let me tell you, trying to get twenty-five guys together to do a raid that can take up to an hour to complete is about the hardest thing a person can do. Trust me on this."

"Do you play any other types of games?"

"Mostly strategy games. Those are games in which you have to direct an army to search an area on any given map. You have to search for resources, make bases and weapons, or summon more troops for your side. The real reason I began playing *World of Warcraft* was because it's based on a strategy game made by the same developers. There are so many in the genre that I loved, but when *WoW* was made, I abandoned them. And that is my speech on gaming addiction."

"Okay, Chrissy, we enjoyed that," the professor said as he looked over the group. "I see that the only person we have left is Jamarcus. If you may, sir."

"Yeah, *Dungeons and Dragons*," Jamarcus said matter-of-factly, which made the whole group laugh.

"Oh my God, you would be the last person I would think would play *Dungeons and Dragons*," one of the students said. "That's a game a bunch of skinny nerds like me would play. You're like some fit, good-looking black guy."

"Well, I'm a bit of a nerd," Jamarcus said with an annoyed squint.

"Do you want to go into more detail, Jamarcus?" the professor asked when Jamarcus went silent.

"Yep. When I was in elementary school, I wanted to be an astronaut. I read a lot of science fiction and watched a lot of movies. When my parents didn't send me to Space Camp, I kind of gave up on academics, but I still loved reading fiction. I went from reading books like *Dune* to reading *The Hobbit*, and I fell in love with the worlds the authors described."

"Did you like the *Lord of the Rings* movies?"

"Of course, but before the movies came out, there was no way for anyone to get immersed in those worlds. That's what I wanted to do. Then I met a group of guys in the high school I went to who played *Dungeons and Dragons* during lunch. I joined them, and I got hooked."

"There was *World of Warcraft*," Chrissy said. "Why didn't you play that?"

"When I was in high school, we didn't have the internet yet."

"When did you graduate?" another student asked.

"Ninety-six."

"How old are you?"

"I'm thirty this month," Jamarcus answered, which was greeted with laughter.

"But you're only starting college now, man? What did you do for a job?"

"I served in the army," Jamarcus said while looking at the classroom door.

"Oh, did you serve over in Iraq?"

"I don't want to talk about that," Jamarcus said bluntly, and the group became silent.

"Thank you for that, Jamarcus," the professor said to end the quiet.

"Yep," Jamarcus responded.

When the teacher dismissed the class, Jamarcus quickly gathered his books and left the room to go to the school cafeteria. He had worked another long shift and had had no time to eat anything, so he wanted something in his stomach to at least get rid of his cranky mood.

After arriving and getting a meal, Jamarcus sat at a table alone and pulled out his laptop. He hadn't saved up enough money yet to move out of the halfway home, and it didn't have internet, so whenever he wanted to go online, he needed to use the school's Wi-Fi. The college was the only place where he could research UFO phenomena. The experience he'd had the previous month still captivated him. If that experience hadn't happened, Jamarcus wasn't sure if he would have been alive right then. The only thing keeping him going was learning all he could about UFO encounters.

Considering that *Close Encounters of the Third Kind* had been a favorite of his growing up, the first thing Jamarcus wanted to learn about was what types of encounters there were. The movie explained what the first three were. When an individual saw an unknown craft or phenomenon in the sky, that was an encounter of the first kind. The second kind occurred when an individual saw an unknown object that left physical evidence, such as scorched earth or material from the object. The third kind occurred when a craft sighting was accompanied by the sight of an alien entity.

"Why is he sitting by himself?" Jamarcus heard a female voice say behind him.

Ignoring it, he began reading about the other types. An encounter of the fourth kind occurred when an individual was abducted. The abductions could seem like dreams or hallucinations. Since Jamarcus's experience had felt like an out-of-body episode, he surmised that it fell under that category.

After taking a bite of his sandwich, he read about the fifth kind, which dealt with communications with foreign intelligence, sometimes through some type of telepathy or in dreams or altered states of mind. Jamarcus categorized the voice he'd heard in his mind for years as that type. An encounter that resulted in the death of a living being was the sixth type. When Jamarcus delved deeper into that type, he ended up going through a crash course on cattle mutilations, something he'd laughed at when he saw a report on television as a kid.

The seventh kind occurred when the encounter resulted in a hybrid of a human and another species. Jamarcus read stories of men and women who swore they'd had either sperm or eggs taken out of their bodies or had intercourse with an alien, willingly or not. There were stories of the people's children showing characteristics of both the parents.

"Why doesn't he want to sit with his kind?" another female asked.

Annoyed, Jamarcus got up from his seat and moved to a part of the eating area that was more secluded to focus. There were dozens of alien species that individuals testified they'd seen, surprising Jamarcus. He had figured aliens would all be the typical gray ones, with large almond-shaped black eyes and little noses and mouths. Come to find out there were many types of gray aliens.

The main ones, researchers said, were from Zeta Reticuli, a binary star system in the Reticulum constellation. There were Ebens, who was tan in skin color, which Jamarcus joked were the black aliens. There were also many more based on different types of species of animals on Earth. There were catlike types, birds, aquatic ones, and reptilians.

The one that caught Jamarcus's eye was the insectoid. When he read about mantis-type beings, he remembered the Bug Girl he used to play with in his dreams of the chateau. Perhaps the dreams of Bug Girl hadn't been dreams at all, Jamarcus thought. Maybe they had been encounters—dozens of encounters—he'd had as a child. That explained Bug Girl, but it didn't explain Ra or Ixchel, whom Ra had called his mother.

Jamarcus assumed it was a coincidence that the name Ra sounded similar to the Egyptian god, but when he researched the name Ixchel, he found out that the name was of a Mayan moon goddess. A being of light named Ra with a mother named Ixchel appeared too perfect, especially since Jamarcus had never heard the name Ixchel before. He remembered that Ra had said his mother was an Andean, but he wasn't able to find any information about aliens with that name. However, when he looked at information about Andromeda, what he saw stunned him: he saw pictures that looked like Mother from the chateau and the people from the city. They were beings with skin colors ranging from blue to white to tan. There were some with white hair and others with black hair. The pictures he saw online didn't make them look as Oriental as he remembered, but perhaps he was wrong.

When Jamarcus finally looked up Pleiadeans, he was a bit disappointed. There were mostly pictures of pretty blond-haired, blue-eyed beings. He remembered Father, the man of the chateau. He'd had long hair like most of the pictures Jamarcus saw, and he had been muscular from what Jamarcus could remember in his dreams. What of Thor and Athena? Were they children of Ra and Ixchel? They might have been Pleiadeans, but they looked more Asian than the normal Nordic depiction.

The information he read still didn't explain why Ra had called Jamarcus his son or any process of someone being sent down from another world to live on Earth to learn life lessons. With the battery life running low on his laptop, Jamarcus turned it off and packed all his things away, still not satisfied with what he'd learned as he headed home. He needed something more, something real. He just didn't know how to find it.

<2>

Jamarcus sat on his bed with his legs crossed and his hands folded in his lap late at night. From what he'd read, most individuals who had encounters—or experiences, as others called them—would pray to the aliens they wanted to communicate with. Jamarcus didn't want to pray like he did when he went to church, so he studied other types of spiritual practices. He came upon meditation practices used by yogis in the Hindu faith and decided to try them.

While he sat on his bed for a few minutes, breathing steadily, he tried to clear his mind. He began to feel a small trickle of energy flow from the top of his skull down his back. When he became excited about that, it stopped, and try as he might, he wasn't able to re-create the sensation. So, he sat on his bed, getting mad at himself, then at the woman who'd sat next to him in the cafeteria, and then at the nerd in his speaking class. Jamarcus then remembered the men he'd killed during his tours, and he stopped to keep a panic attack from happening.

Jamarcus decided to quit, and he lay down on his bed to watch an anime on his phone. After watching two and a half episodes, Jamarcus was in a half-asleep state, too lazy to get ready for bed and wanting to finish the show. He was barely watching his phone, but the light from the screen kept him awake when a crashing flow of energy shot through him again just like on the night of the orbs.

Jamarcus's phone slipped out of his hand, and he lay paralyzed. He was frightened this time from reading about so many horrible encounters with terrifying aliens. When a force tried to push what he guessed was his consciousness out of his body, he clenched up so much his anus hurt. Over and over again, the force tried to push him out of his body, until Jamarcus finally gave up. He knew that if he wanted to encounter another alien species, he'd have to go through this, no matter what happened. He didn't have anything else to live for anyway.

Jamarcus relaxed his body completely, and the force easily possessed his soul. He floated in his room until he once again flowed out of his window and into the sky. It wasn't long until he was high in the air next to a bright white orb. Jamarcus was close to the light now, but the brightness of the orb didn't hurt his sight, which made sense to him because he wasn't seeing with his physical eyes. The light dissipated until Mother from the chateau appeared in front of him, dressed in a tight-fitting black jumpsuit. Jamarcus could see that she'd closely trimmed her hair, leaving only fine black stubble showing. Her Oriental eyes were larger than the rest of her face, dark and piercing. She didn't have any physical features on her body that distinguished her as a female that Jamarcus was familiar with, such as breasts or rounder hips, but he felt her motherly spirit in his mind.

"Hello, Scar," Mother said in the same voice he'd heard in his head for years.

"Hello," Jamarcus responded after a pause.

"Are you still mad at us?"

"No, ma'am," Jamarcus answered in a guilty voice. "I'm glad I was able to talk to anyone from the group of lights. I wanted to apologize for how I acted. I just lost my girlfriend. She was everything to me, and I'm so angry now. I just lashed out at you for no good reason. I'm sorry."

"Are you all right now?"

"Besides the fact that my soul, I guess, is floating tens of miles in the air, yeah."

"You are not scared?" Mother asked.

"No. A little."

"It is important not to elevate the energies of your light in this state because it will end our communication," Mother said. "You will have to go on an all-living diet now to maintain this energy."

"Living?" Jamarcus asked.

"Eat only live plants and fruits."

"You want me to go vegan?" Jamarcus said in a lamenting tone.

"Are you prepared to do this now, or should we come back later when you are ready?"

"No, I'm prepared. I started this journey. I might as well go all the way out of the tunnel."

"You need to know that you are all right," Mother said, and Jamarcus felt a tough love in his soul from her words, a loving anger. "You cannot be so angry. It is not good for your light; it clouds it when it should shine like a star."

"My soul, you mean?" Jamarcus asked.

"Your light, yes," Mother said, and then she floated close to Jamarcus with a smile on her face. "We love you, Scar. You are not alone. You need to know this."

"I understand," Jamarcus said.

"Kathrine is in a much better place now also. Would you like to see her?"

"No!" Jamarcus spoke out sharply and then calmed himself, not wanting his sorrow to overcome him. "That's okay. I don't think I can see her now. Besides, it would defeat the purpose of me talking to you."

"You have many questions, do you?" Ixchel asked.

"Yes," Jamarcus answered in an eager tone.

"Go ahead."

"Your name is Ixchel, correct?"

"Yes. You are wondering how I have an Earth-bound name."

"Yes."

"The people from the continent south of us are connected to us through the light. We send many souls to them and others to learn to live in the lower dimensions of this universe, where actions carry more weight, as opposed to higher dimensions, where mistakes can be erased with meaningless thoughts. When they learn all they can, hopefully, these lights can rejoin us in our universe. In our communications long ago, we shared our language with them."

"So wait. I had a vision when I was a kid," Jamarcus said. "I was looking over a land that seemed like Egypt, and there were large spacecraft in the air. Was that you guys?"

"Yes," Ixchel said. "You must have looked through Aten Ka and into another person's soul at a time in your past, which is another universe to us with higher densities. We live in a world in another galaxy that is six million cycles in the future from your chronological one. That may be hard to understand, but it is easier to think that there is no past or future. There is only the now."

"Ra said you're from the Andromeda galaxy," Jamarcus said.

"That is what your father said," Ixchel responded.

"And that your species are called Andeans." Jamarcus felt and saw Ixchel flinch in mild annoyance when he said that.

"Your father lived on this world a long time ago—to you—and is accustomed to defining lights by the bodies they are in. I am your mother. Is that what you mean?"

"Yes, ma'am," Jamarcus said, almost laughing at the strict love coming from her. "But what is your civilization like? Your home world?"

"We are part of the Federation of Light, Scar," Ixchel answered. "It is a sort of governing body that handles the back-and-forth of many beings across many cultures across the waters of the universes. Our family is a leading house in the Federation. We provide travel, resources, and energy for many nations in our home galaxy cluster."

"Cluster?" Jamarcus asked.

"Yes," Ixchel said with a beam, her light growing brighter. "Your father and I bring light to many nations and provide travel across the waters."

"What type of technology do you use to accomplish this?"

"No, Scar Amun," Ixchel said, broadcasting a mild anger at Jamarcus. "We do this—your father and I. And so will you. That is why you chose to be here on Earth. That is why I want you to change your diet—so more of the light can flow and shine from within you."

"Okay," Jamarcus said, trying to keep up with the information. "We are a leading house in the Federation, correct?"

"Yes."

"Who is in this house?"

"It was once owned by my mother before she joined the light. At that time, it was my father; my mother; my sister, Chac'chel; our cousin Chab and his family; and me. My sister and I disagreed about how we should rule the house after my mother joined the light, so she decided it would pass on to one of our children whose light was enough to sustain our influence."

"It was a business decision?" Jamarcus asked.

"To be frank," Ixchel said. "It just so happens that I married your father, who was the same light density as your grandmother. But he could not hold the speaker of the house title due to xenophobic aspects of our home culture. Because those of our genetic lineage are the predominant people of our home civilization, they wanted someone like us to be the speaker of the Federation. Your brothers and sisters declined to go through the process of ascension, but you chose to."

"So there is still racism in advanced civilizations?" Jamarcus said.

"Unfortunately, yes."

"I have brothers and sisters. And a grandfather still with you?"

"Correct."

"Tell me about them. How about your father?"

"Your grandfather's name is Aapo. He is an old serviceman working for the military branch of the Federation. He has been in it for a few thousand of your planetary orbit cycles. He is one of the highest-ranking admirals of the Service Fleet. He is partly the reason I served in the fleet for over two hundred cycles. He loves that position so much that he has delayed going into the light with my mother. He has always been a prideful man. And he adores you. He is very proud that you served in the army of the country you lived in."

"Okay," Jamarcus said somberly.

"I hope you remember Bernini," Ixchel said. "You used to travel through the light when you first arrived on Earth to play with him. You would make me so mad when you and your fiancée ran all over our home with him in your arms. He is not that much older than you in our universe, but I believe he is ninety-nine cycles to you."

"He's that old?" Jamarcus said.

"He is still only a child, however. He is only eight cycles in our universe. He watches you all the time. He strongly wants to talk to you. You do not mind if he comes to visit you every so often, do you?"

"I would love that," Jamarcus answered. "His name is different. I believe it's an Italian name on Earth."

"Your father named you all," Ixchel said. "He wanted to name you based on gods or important people on Earth. Your sister Rhiannon, well …" Ixchel looked upward in a display of disappointment.

"Is it that bad?" he asked.

"Not at all. She is in university on our home planet. Her light density is well established. We have her prepared, after she graduates, to provide light for a world just entering the Federation. Most would be ecstatic with that prospect. It is just that—"

"Are you mad at her?"

"I know it is wrong to force someone to go through the ascension process," Ixchel said, and Jamarcus felt a parental regret in her mind. "It is a harrowing process. You know more than anyone about that. But it is such an important part of our culture. Our religion. You cannot join the light unless you ascend. Your siblings see the light as only an end, not a means. You have to see, Scar, that your brothers and sisters live in a universe where they are worshipped as deities for who and what they are. But the light can only shine brightly in someone based on what he or she does. That is what you need to learn on Earth, Scar Amun. I swear to Aten Ka if Thor and Athena had not had so much influence on Rhiannon—"

"Thor and Athena?" Jamarcus said, interrupting, and as soon as he said their names, he felt their souls enter his. He could almost see them in his vision of sight. The emotions of longing and love that flowed from them were overpowering.

"They're my brother and sister," Jamarcus said, and his heart burst with happiness and sorrow. His soul began to cry, and when he reached up to wipe his face, he saw that his hands were thin lines of faint yellow light with curved space-time around them. He ignored that, though, because he felt that Athena and Thor wanted to be there to hold him, just like in his dreams as a child.

"Scar, you need to be calm," Ixchel said, but a deep, aching joy swept up in Jamarcus, causing a sob to pour forth from him that jolted him from his state, and he rushed back in a flash of light into his body.

For a moment, he wept, still feeling echoes of Thor's and Athena's emotions. A driven desire appeared in his mind, replacing the loss of Kathrine. Jamarcus decided he would commit to joining those beings. He would be with Thor and Athena.

Jamarcus lay in his bed for a bit, waiting for his tears to go away, before he fell asleep.

Chapter 12
<1>
August 2009

"So how long were you in the military?" Jamarcus asked as he looked out of the guard booth at the street entrance to the industrial plant.

"I served for over twenty years," Terry answered as he sat on a chair beside him.

"What branch?"

"Navy. I was an ombudsman on a few cruisers."

"Okay, okay. Pussy on a boat. All right."

"Take it easy there, young man." Terry laughed.

"Where did you serve?"

"Well, I spent almost my entire time of service in Norfolk, Virginia, from the naval base there."

"My dad served there," Jamarcus said. "We lived in Virginia Beach, where my mom taught at a high school."

"Your dad was navy then. Outstanding. Do you talk to your dad about his time in?"

"No, never did. I'm not that close to my family. I haven't talked to them for over ten years.”

“Yeah, I hear ya,” Terry said as he adjusted himself on his chair. “My dad and I had a bad falling out after I joined the navy about my late wife. He thought I was too young to get married. And my brother just stayed under his umbrella of influence. But I have my son and his family now, so I’m happy. Can’t complain.”

“That’s great,” Jamarcus said. “What does your son do?”

“He’s a carpenter at a construction company. It pays well when there are projects, but when they have to wait for a new client, it’s rough.”

“I can believe that. Where did you go while you were in the Navy?”

“Oh, on my first tour, we went through the Mediterranean. My God, Spain, and Italy back then were so beautiful. I got a chance to go out to town at Rota Naval Station while I was on liberty once. I had too much fun for any young man to have.”

“That had to have been a blast,” Jamarcus said before sighting two trucks coming toward the booth. “Looks like we got some business. Grab the handheld, and I’ll show you how to process these.”

“All right,” Terry said as he slowly got up from his seat and grabbed the device.

As they left the booth into the late afternoon heat, Jamarcus directed him out to the first truck as the driver rolled down his window. “First thing we do is grab the work order sheet from the driver, which they should have,” Jamarcus said.

Terry took the paperwork from the driver and showed it to him. "What am I looking for?" he asked.

"We don't have to look for anything on the sheet. Do you see the number on the top of that paper?"

"Yes."

"That number can be seen on the handheld. Do you see it?"

"Yeah, it's right there," Terry said. "So we just scan this, right?"

"Yeah, but there's more," Jamarcus said. "We had an issue last winter, and a driver who had the wrong load was scanned in under the wrong work order. So now we have to have the driver tell us the model number on the cargo to see if it matches up on the paper."

"We still got to do that bullshit?" the driver said out his window.

"Yeah, man," Jamarcus said, and he stepped back as the driver got out of his cab and climbed onto his load. After the driver read off the model number to them, Terry scanned the paperwork and handed it back to the driver.

"I sure hope we don't have to keep doing this asinine crap," the driver said as he got back into his driver's seat.

"It's the new norm now," Jamarcus said. "You're going to have to do this from now on."

"Yeah, yeah," the driver said as he drove off.

"That guy was mad," Terry said as he and Jamarcus waited for the next truck to drive up.

"They all are. Most people don't like change. Especially when it requires effort from them."

"Tell me about it," Terry said as he took the work order from the next driver.

"Hey there, Jamarcus," the driver said.

"Hi, Sally," Jamarcus said. "Where's your husband? Is he falling behind?"

"He got caught up in a traffic jam about an hour ago," Sally said as she walked out onto the trailer. "Looks like you got yourself a new worker."

"Yeah. Sheila burned too many bridges these last few months, so our boss let her go."

"We'll let's hope you stay," Sally said to Terry after she read off the cargo's model number.

"I hope so too," Terry said.

"Did you go to the veterans' parade on the Fourth, Jamarcus?" Sally asked as she got back into her cab.

"No. I stayed at home and slept after work."

"You're a combat vet, Jamarcus," she said in a reprimanding voice. "You deserve to be honored. You've got to get out of that apartment and enjoy life."

"Okay, Sally," Jamarcus said.

"You're a good-looking boy," Sally said as she got her truck into gear. "Get out there, and find a girl who can make you happy. Have a family."

"All right," Jamarcus said as Sally drove to the plant. He turned to Terry. "Pretty simple process, right?"

"Yeah," Terry said as they walked back to the guard booth. "You served during the Iraq invasion?"

"Two tours in Iraq and one in Afghanistan," Jamarcus said after they stepped inside the booth. "I was part of the first push into Baghdad."

"God, that had to have been tough," Terry said as he sat down in his seat.

"The first push in, no," Jamarcus said, his heart pumping a little faster. "The first push was easy-peasy. We just sat back in the escort Humvees and watched the fireworks. After the IEDs started going off, that's when things got hectic."

"You don't mind talking about it?" Terry asked as he watched Jamarcus's anxious face.

"No, I don't mind," Jamarcus responded with a smile. "I need to anyway. The only way to get over the war is to talk about it, right?"

"Okay, man," Terry said with a nervous laugh. "What was Baghdad like after the push-in?"

"Stressful, to put it plainly," Jamarcus said. "It's hard to explain it in a way that makes sense because we here in the US have our own perceived vision of what war is. The best way to describe it was having war in the middle of downtown Norfolk during rush hour if that makes sense."

"Yeah, I see your point," Terry said with a smile. "That doesn't make sense."

"I know. 'Yeah, I know there was an IED attack, but I've got to get to work. Can the army stop fighting so I can get by?'"

"Did that happen?"

"All the time, man," Jamarcus said. "After a blast, everyone is scared and concerned. After an hour, it's normalized, and everyone wants to get back to their normal patterns. And it's always our fault."

"How many IEDs have you been through?" Terry asked.

"Only the one. I got lucky, and we were able to block off the area before it blew."

"Were you able to find the ones responsible?"

"Yeah," Jamarcus said as he rubbed his eyes.

"Yeah?"

"We did get the guys, yes," Jamarcus said as his stomach began to clench. "There are no clean operations, you know, right?"

"You are correct," Terry said. "How was the rest of your tour?"

"The first tour, mostly patrols. Our company and another had to make sure that a major freeway into Baghdad was clear. So we would patrol nonstop. That day of the bomb, we patrolled for twenty-four hours straight. That can be the norm too. God, it would make my whole body shake when that happened. On my second tour, I got assigned to a sort of strike group based on how well I handled a few fire missions. I had to do so many raids that I didn't want to remember. Some of the guys on those squads were goddamn hard-core mother-fucks. I didn't have to be in the action a lot of the time, but when I did, I was glad I was with them."

"Were you scared?" Terry asked.

"Every single time." Jamarcus laughed. "Scared shitless. But I never let it show. I was beside some Green Berets at times. There was no way I was going to act like some coward next to them."

"Did you have to put some guys down?"

"Yeah," Jamarcus said, looking out of the booth, and he sprang up as he saw another truck come toward them. "We've got another one," he said, and they grabbed the handheld and walked out to greet the new truck.

"Sir, I'm going to need your work order form," Terry said, and the driver handed it to him. "I'm going to need you to verify the cargo's model number to the paper, sir," he said after he matched the work order numbers.

"Why do we have to do that?" the driver asked in an exasperated voice.

"A truck got its cargo mixed up, and we have to make sure everything matches now," Jamarcus said as he wiped sweat from his brow.

"When did we start this?" the driver asked as he stared down at Jamarcus and Terry. "I've been coming here for years, and I never have to do this."

"We had to start doing this last winter, man," Jamarcus said with his stomach clenching harder and his chest blocking up.

"Let the plant know that it's Markdown here, man," the driver said. "The guys at the plant know who I am. I don't need to do any of this."

"Sir, we need to check the cargo model. It's our job."

"Why do I have to do any of this shit? I haven't done anything wrong."

"Nobody said you did anything wrong, sir," Jamarcus said, growing more frustrated. "We were instructed by the plant to have the drivers check the cargo models."

"Go fuck yourself!" the driver said as he sat firmly in his seat. "I ain't doing a goddamn thing!"

Rage exploded in Jamarcus's chest, but he held it in the best he could. "Sir, please don't curse at me; I didn't curse at you," he said to the driver.

"Fuck you!" the driver spat at Jamarcus as he pointed his finger at his face.

Jamarcus stood calmly in the late hot sun for a brief moment before a volcano of wrath spewed out of his soul. He yanked the door of the truck open, climbed up, and put his face inches away from the driver's, seeing the face of Rumi, the protestor from Afghanistan.

"I'm only doing my job, asshole!" Jamarcus roared. "I'm not saying you're a bad person! I don't even care who you are! I'm only doing my job! I didn't ask to do this, and I sure as fuck didn't ask to get cursed out by you for doing something I don't want to do! If you think I like pissing off every asshole who comes here, you're fucking mad! We're only trying to do our job!"

The last scream made Jamarcus's stomach clench so hard it felt as if a dagger were digging into his gut. Jamarcus jumped down from the truck and walked out into the street, grabbing at his belly.

"You all right, man?" Terry asked as he walked behind him.

"No," Jamarcus grunted as he tried to get his mind to cope with his pain. Murphy's law kicked in, and Jamarcus focused on what he could control. He was in pain. Where did the pain come from? It came from his anger. Why was Jamarcus angry? It wasn't because of the driver. It was because of the war. What about the war that made him angry? The fighting. The killing. The people. Why did that make him angry? Why would that have made anyone angry?

"Because I'm scared," Jamarcus muttered to himself, and slowly, the pain in his stomach began to go away as he relaxed his entire body. He began to cry irrepressibly, and he didn't care who saw him. In his crying, there was a relief that he had felt before only when he'd sensed Thor's and Athena's presence in his mind months ago. He stood there and bitterly wept.

"Are you all right, man?" the truck driver asked as he stood outside his cab, no longer looking like Rumi.

"We just need to check the model number," Jamarcus said as he turned to face the driver.

"Go into the booth. I've got this," Terry told Jamarcus, who then went into the guard booth and sat down in a chair. He calmed his nerves enough that the tears stopped just as Terry entered the room.

"Are you better now?" Terry asked.

"Yeah. Easy job, right?" Jamarcus said with a smile, which made

Terry laugh as he sat down.

<2>

It was just past midnight when Jamarcus arrived at the apartment he'd recently rented. He had finally saved up enough money to buy all the things he'd needed to move out of the halfway home. It had been a pain to find the time to rent a van, go to a donation shop that sold cheap furniture, and then move all of that furniture into his apartment by himself. Jamarcus didn't know anyone well enough to ask for help, but it hadn't been too difficult to get everything in place and return the van in one day. The center had asked Jamarcus why he only had his motorcycle, just as everyone else asked. He just smiled and said it was cheaper every time.

As soon as Jamarcus got home, he took his clothes off and got into bed. The summer semester had just convened, and he had a rare moment when he could go to sleep and not have to worry about waking up early in the mourning. He opened the windows next to his bed and turned on the fan by his head to full blast. He had done that many times while overseas, and it usually lulled him to sleep. It hadn't been as humid there as it was in Fort Walton, though, and Jamarcus was too cheap to turn on the air conditioner. He was also hungry due to the new diet Ixchel had made him go on. He ate fruits and a cup of nuts for lunch at work, and he mostly ate salads for breakfast. The sudden lack of protein from his meals hit him hard, and it seemed he could never eat his fill. He guessed he was just going to have to get used to it.

As he lay in bed, he kept thinking about the driver he'd screamed at earlier that afternoon. He felt regret and guilt that he'd yelled at the man. He knew his boss would hear about it. Fear built up inside him as he thought about what might happen. Would he get reprimanded? What would happen if he had to talk to that guy again? He realized that being on that job kept him in a constant state of fear. He was always worrying about the next event that might happen. Being in the military, he only knew one way of handling situations like that, and he had to start learning another way. His body was in too much pain to live like that.

While Jamarcus lay down, he started to feel an energy flowing from his head and down his back, as if a water faucet were turned on inside him. Jamarcus's body soon fell into a resting stillness that he never had experienced before. His eyes were closed, and his body was resting as if he were asleep, but he was wide awake. He was also able to see around his room while his body remained sleeping. He could feel the environment of his entire apartment to the point that he could see all of it and an area in a large diameter around it in his mind. Although it was dark, Jamarcus could see, as if a light illuminated from within the subject he concentrated on.

He thought about what could be causing that perception. Maybe with the new diet, Jamarcus hypothesized, he was able to channel the energy that flowed through him when Ixchel and the other lights appeared to him. Maybe it created an electromagnetic field around him that allowed extended sight as the field passed through any object.

His wonder turned to concern as he felt a figure walk into his soul field and toward his apartment. When Jamarcus focused on the entity, he felt that it was short, skinny, and cloaked in darkness. The black figure walked straight through Jamarcus's front door into his apartment and toward his bedroom. Jamarcus's heartbeat pulsed in fear as he looked at the figure climb onto his bed and crawl to his head. He felt the entity reach into his head and seemingly grip his consciousness. For a few moments, the figure pulled at Jamarcus's soul, and he heard the being grunt with a few tries. The entity would succeed a little, but when Jamarcus got scared, clenching his body, his soul sank right back into his physical form.

Determined to find out what the being wanted or at least who or what it was, Jamarcus relinquished and relaxed his mind and body so that with one final tug, the being yanked his soul out. When it did, the figure began to shine with a sky-blue light. He was a young boy, most likely an Andean. He wore a tight navy-colored suit that fit his thin frame. His black hair was wild, and he smiled with a childish glee, his dark eyes piercing Jamarcus's mind with a sharp joy.

"I got you out!" the child cheered as he stood Jamarcus up outside his body.

Jamarcus looked down at himself and noticed that what he guessed was his astral form was composed of translucent sun-yellow light. He was naked, but the form didn't have any anatomical features of a human male. The surface skin was curved space-time, and when he moved his body, it rolled like oil through water.

"Are you feeling all right?" the boy asked as he raised his hands to be picked up.

"Yes?" Jamarcus answered, confused, as he bent down to pick up the child. As he held him, the boy kissed Jamarcus's cheek and hugged him around his neck, and Jamarcus felt a concerned love shine from within him that melded into Jamarcus's worried consciousness.

It calmed all the concerns Jamarcus had from the previous day, and Jamarcus was crying before he knew it. He didn't know how or why he was crying outside his body, but feeling the boy's happiness was a comfort he never had experienced before.

"Are you still sad?" the boy said into his chest.

"No," Jamarcus answered, looking down at him.

"You have to be happy," the boy said, and his straightforward emotion poked right into Jamarcus. "You've got to smile. See?" The child grinned in a way that, as with most young children, made him look as if he were grimacing instead.

"Why are you angry?" Jamarcus jokingly asked.

"I'm not angry," the boy said with quick hotness in his soul sparking up, which made Jamarcus giggle. Feeling the child's pure, innocent emotions was exhilarating, like experiencing something new over and over again.

"Do you know who I am?" the boy asked.

"Tell me," Jamarcus said, not wanting his subconscious to dictate what was happening, which he knew could be a dream.

"My name is Bernini, and I'm one hundred years old," the boy said with a prideful smile and his light shining a bit brighter.

"He's ninety-nine." A voice from an older soul spoke from above them.

Jamarcus looked up at the ceiling of his apartment, trying to feel if anything was above them, but he didn't see anything. How he knew it was an older soul confused him, but he somehow just did.

"I'm ninety-nine," Bernini said with a conceding sigh. "In our universe, I'm your big brother."

"You are?" Jamarcus asked.

"Mhmm," Bernini said as he nodded. "But in this universe, you're my big brother."

"Cool," Jamarcus said, feeling the joy coming from him.

"I was sad when you left. I only have one big sister at home now, and Rhiannon thinks I'm dumb sometimes. And Thor and Athena are not allowed to come home that often."

"That's terrible," Jamarcus said, wondering what would make Ixchel and Ra make that decision.

"But Mommy said I can play with you now, so I can come over as much as I want," Bernini said. "Oh, do you want to share lights?"

"What's that?" Jamarcus asked, and Bernini lunged up and placed his forehead against Jamarcus's. Bernini's head then slipped into Jamarcus's, and a white tunnel of light shone in front of Jamarcus's vision. Once Bernini pulled his head away, the tunnel disappeared, but Jamarcus could feel everything Bernini felt—his breathing, his joy, his arms as they held one another. Jamarcus felt a giggle bubbling up from Bernini, and in unison, they both began to laugh.

"See? Now I'm always with you," Bernini said with confidence, and an excitement blossomed in his chest that made Jamarcus's heart skip a beat. "Do you want to go on my ship? Grandpa is with us. He can take us anywhere we like."

"Okay," Jamarcus said, and Bernini broke out of his arms and grabbed his hand. He flew through the apartment, tugging Jamarcus along behind him, and through the front door.

When Bernini flew up, Jamarcus saw a circular, disk-shaped object above them that had dozens of white, red, and green lights underneath it, with an antenna-like structure sticking out of it to one side, with a light at the end. Jamarcus wondered if the craft was there all the time but he just couldn't feel it.

Suddenly, he felt them shift upward, and they appeared in a large, circular room whose dimensions seemed larger than the craft appeared to be. A window revealing the outside arced in front of them, while along the white wall were some type of technology stations that glowed slightly, with space-time somewhat bending around them. A group of Andeans with black hair and skin ranging from pure white to tan worked around them, dressed in clothes that appeared similar to Earth fashions from the early twentieth century.

In the center of the room was a seat that had a helmet held by a curved pole above it. Standing next to the seat was an elderly Andean male dressed in a tight-fitting suit similar to Bernini's. He smiled at Jamarcus. From that distance, Jamarcus could feel the confidence in his soul. A joy bloomed in him as he walked to Jamarcus and hugged him with a strength that defied his skinny frame. When the old man held Jamarcus in his arms, he noticed a silver emblem that had four faces connected by a circle around a star. The four faces were a man's face, a face that appeared Andean, and the faces of an anthropomorphic lion and bird.

"Hello, Scar," the old man said, patting Jamarcus's back. "It's good to see you."

"And you are?" Jamarcus asked when they were released.

"I'm your grandpa Aapo," he answered with a joking smirk. "Why do you have to be so empirical?"

"I'm just trying to make sure I'm not making this up," Jamarcus said as he looked around the room.

"You can never be sure if anything is real," Aapo said. "That is the ultimate paradox of the light."

"Yeah," Jamarcus said, trying to control what he could. "Everything here seems to bend space-time. Your technology. Even you."

"This craft is entangled with your brother's light. Our light is dense enough to pierce through the waters of reality."

"Is that how you can hold this craft here and not be seen by people below us?" Jamarcus asked as he looked at the city lights out the window.

"They don't have the density perception to see us," Aapo said.

"How does this craft fly? Does it have an engine that warps space-time?"

"Bernini's ship has a microwave emitter as its main engine," Aapo said. "It is encased in a superconductive material that keeps all the particles inside of it but releases the loops connected to the particles, which pushes back the waters. But that is not enough to make a craft move swiftly through the waters. It needs a strong light to entangle with the loops to intensify them and push the waters back completely. That's what allows us to move faster than the speed of sound."

"The speed of sound?" Jamarcus said. "Don't you mean the speed of light?"

"Oh, I'm sorry," Aapo said with a laugh. "I forget that *light* means something different to you on Earth. In the density we are in, we move similarly to the particle you call light."

"You do?"

"Go look," Aapo said as he pointed to the window.

When Jamarcus walked to look out, he paused as he stumbled a bit. As he caught his balance, he looked down to see that his feet stood on their toes. Once he got his bearings and moved to the window, he didn't see anything wrong at first, but when he looked carefully at a car in the street next to his apartment, he noticed that everything was moving extremely slowly. The rear lights from the car stretched out like a time-exposed picture, and the red lights looked solid.

"Because in our density we are composed of matter that is almost pure, we naturally emit the particle of light to you," Aapo said. "To us, that particle moves as fast as sound."

"That is completely amazing," Jamarcus whispered.

"Do you want to fly the craft?" Aapo asked, and before Jamarcus could answer, he felt enthusiasm swell up in Bernini's soul.

"I'll help!" Bernini said as he grabbed Jamarcus's hand and led him to the chair. After he made Jamarcus sit, he climbed up onto his lap and grabbed the helmet to fit it on his head. "Are you ready?" Bernini asked as he moved close to Jamarcus's face. "I'm going to entangle you."

"Okay," Jamarcus responded.

A rush of energy like the time he'd talked to Ixchel rushed through his body like cool water from a stream. Jamarcus felt the field surrounding the ship and the fabric of space-time next to it, like a constant pressure that needed to collapse.

"Take us up into space," Bernini told Jamarcus, who laughed. Bernini sounded as if he were telling his brother to take him to the park.

"How do I move the ship?" Jamarcus asked.

"Breathe in the energy until it fills you up," Aapo said.

"All right," Jamarcus said, and he slowly began to breathe in and out, noticing that his body shone brighter with every intake. He took in a large breath and felt the water of the stream build up inside him until it was a significant pressure. He could also see outside the craft while looking at the interior at the same time

"Hold your breath there," Aapo said, and Jamarcus complied. "Can you feel the water inside you?" he asked, and Jamarcus nodded. "Hold on to it as you let your breath out," Aapo said, and when Jamarcus released, he could feel the water fill his soul like a balloon.

"Now you're able to control the water with your mind," Aapo said. "You should feel it in the frontal region."

Jamarcus imagined moving the field and felt it in the front part of his head, which was still in his bed in his apartment. Once Jamarcus got over the strangeness of that, he moved the field about like a ball. The ship slid along with the field, and after a moment, Jamarcus became confident in how the craft moved.

"Take us up," Bernini demanded with impatience growing inside.

"Okay, hold on," Jamarcus said as he carefully moved the field to roll upward into the sky. When he got excited, he felt a warmth inside his sleeping body, and remembering what Ixchel had said, he calmed himself. As his soul cooled, he moved the craft faster until he saw that they were well above Earth. Looking down at the planet with his outside vision, he saw Florida, with the northern and southern parts of the state covered in patches of light and the central section relatively dark. Around and above were so many stars and galaxies that he couldn't recognize any constellations.

"Can we go see the fires?" Bernini asked Aapo, who shrugged.

"If Scar wants to take us there."

"Which fires?" Jamarcus asked.

"There are these large fires on the western part of the continent you live on."

"Oh, I know what fires you're talking about," Jamarcus said, and the field began to move slightly before he intended it to. He saw North America scroll below him as if he were gliding inside a touch screen until the craft was above California, where large forest fires littered the central part of the state.

"Take us down," Bernini said as he curled up in Jamarcus's lap.

Jamarcus carefully scrolled the ship downward, surprised he didn't feel any resistance when he entered Earth's atmosphere, just like when he had flown with Thor in his childhood dreams. He gradually brought the ship to a stop above a city Jamarcus guessed was Los Angeles and saw large areas of fire threatening to engulf its buildings.

"Let's go out there," Bernini said as he rose in Jamarcus's lap.

When Jamarcus took off the helmet, his body dimmed, and the pressure inside him dissipated. Bernini pulled him out of the pilot's seat, and after a few steps, they shifted outside the craft, and Bernini guided Jamarcus down into a part of the forest that had already been torched. Jamarcus could feel wonder and worry inside Bernini as he walked through the ashes in front of a slowly encroaching flaming wall. Jamarcus looked at the flames dance in slow motion as they ate up the trees and grass.

"This is sad." Bernini sighed. "Why is the world like this?"

"There're a lot of reasons," Jamarcus said.

"Don't you know that you're causing the world to do this?"

"That's why there are a lot of reasons this is happening," Jamarcus said with a smile.

"But people can die. Aren't the people of this world worried about the climate?"

"I'll try to explain it the best way I can understand it," Jamarcus said as he walked over to Bernini and ran his sunlight fingers through his hair. "You probably understand it more than I do, but let me try. If you don't know, we burn a substance that is called petroleum for energy. The fumes produced by burning this material are what you are concerned about. Why can't we see that the gases are causing the weather that is making this fire, right? The problem is that we use a tool on Earth called money."

"Money?" Bernini said.

"Yeah, I figured as much. You see, we here on Earth agree to work for each other on special tasks in exchange for this money, which we exchange again for things we want. To keep us wanting to use this money, we created a way of thinking to justify this money. It's just that petroleum is completely tied to this money, and to stop using oil is to stop using money."

"Why can't you make anything by thinking?" Bernini asked innocently, which made Jamarcus giggle.

"I guess we aren't like you. We have to work harder to make things. And to do that requires energy, which requires oil. Some people know that the energy we use is part of the fault for these fires, but there are others whose way of thinking is so entrenched in their souls that they are incapable of thinking any other way. They are convinced that it is a sin to do that. They think the weather we cause is a sign that a savior is going to come down from the sky and save us all, instead of learning that we need to save ourselves."

"Can't you tell them that you need to change things, to make it better?" Bernini asked.

"No. I'm a young, intelligent black male in a society that doesn't listen to young, intelligent black males, especially in the black community. I got bullied in my own family for being too smart. My sister said I acted like a white person. I'm not tall enough and not strong enough. I don't play sports. I don't sing or listen to the only type of music black people allow themselves to listen to. I'm useless. I'm probably the most disenfranchised demographic in the nation I live in."

"Why do you say that about yourself?" Bernini asked when he felt the depression in Jamarcus's soul. "That makes you angry and cry."

"I know. It's just the truth. That's why I asked Ra and Ixchel—"

"Mommy and Daddy?"

"Yeah. I told them they needed to show themselves to us. You don't have to do anything. Just reveal yourselves to us—and for a significant amount of time—so we know you are real. We won't change ourselves, because we think we are alone and are the best living beings the universe ever created. If we know you exist, then it will force us to reevaluate ourselves. It will mean that not only are we not alone, but we're at the bottom of the universe's new order. We'll all have to change instead of convincing ourselves we don't need to. But change is hard. It's easier to tell someone else they need to change when you need to do it yourself."

"I think I know what you're talking about," Bernini said, and Jamarcus felt his soul trying to understand what he'd just rambled about.

"Don't worry, little bro," Jamarcus said.

"Can we go over there?" Bernini asked, pointing to another area of scorched Earth.

Jamarcus nodded and allowed Bernini to lead him through the slowly burning forest.

Chapter 13
<1>
September 2019

Jamarcus sat looking at his laptop in the college's cafeteria, sitting among some of his classmates. He'd started some of his main classes for his anthropology major and wanted to begin reading about the pantheons of some of the ancient cultures he was studying. One of his classes was on ancient Mesopotamia, and he was interested in the Anunnaki.

"Hey, Jamarcus, did you play the latest first-person shooter that came out?" Joe asked, leaning over him to look at his computer screen.

"Yeah, man," Jamarcus said as he pushed Joe's head back and turned his laptop away.

"Did you guys finish the main campaign yet?" Jamie asked from her seat across from them.

"Holy shit, the level in which the city got blown up," Jamarcus said with a shudder. "That made me cry. And I don't cry during stuff. I didn't cry when Sephiroth killed Aerith." He was not surprised when the table erupted in cries and laughter.

"How do you not cry when Aerith dies?" Robert asked in disbelief next to Jamie.

"I'm not into the whole pure and innocent Nippon girl trope. I think it's demeaning to hold women to that type of social standard. But maybe I'm overthinking it."

"No, I get you," Jamie said. "There are some skanks in anime that I just can't stand because they're nothing but doormats. Fuck that shit. I'm no one's doormat."

"Besides, I'm a Tifa fan," Jamarcus muttered.

"I fucking knew it!" Joe shouted in Jamarcus's ear, making him wince. "You just like her better because she has boobs."

"And there's nothing wrong with that," Jamarcus said, defending himself. "Besides, I'd have Tifa beat me up any day. She's my goddam waifu."

"Oh, please don't start the otaku language," Robert said.

"Anyway," Jamarcus said, "man, that level. That has to be the most horrifying thing I've seen in a game. The only other time I've cried during something was at the beginning of *Saving Private Ryan* and *Black Hawk Down*."

"Yeah, but you served during the war," Joe said. "You're going to be biased."

"So?"

"Were any of those movies like anything you've been through?" Jamie asked.

"Middle part of *Black Hawk Down*," Jamarcus said with a deep breath. "That part was too real."

"Yeah?" Joe said, and Jamarcus noticed that the group's eyes were focused on him.

"Yeah, but this game is legit. I've already finished that campaign on hard difficulty. I even beat the plane level twice."

"Twice? That's sick," Jamie said.

"Yeah, but I have no life, and I'm pretty sure I have PTSD, and video games are my only outlet, so it's not that impressive."

"I've only played multiplayer," Robert said. "I've been busting my ass trying to keep my ranking up on the scoreboards."

When Jamarcus saw that the group was firmly talking about the game, he went back to reading about the Anunnaki. It seemed that for every serious UFO enthusiast out there, learning about those gods was Aliens 101. However, the translation of the name was off. When UFO hunters referred to the Anunnaki, they said the name meant "Those from the heavens come." But from the language he was able to translate, it had the same meaning as the name Elohim in the Bible: "royal sons of the sky father God" or "sons of God."

From reading the Bible a hundred times when he was a kid, he knew that the Hebrew people had ended up occupying the land of Canaan, and the Canaanite gods were practically the same as the Anunnaki. Since it was written in the Bible that Abram had come from Ur, a city in ancient Babylon, the gods of Sumer might have been the same phenomena that Israel believed were angels from God.

Since his vision of Bernini and Aapo, he couldn't help but think about the emblem on Aapo's uniform. He wasn't sure, but the faces looked like the messengers from the book of Ezekiel. He also remembered the vision he'd had when he was young of a land like Egypt but in a fertile environment. He remembered the beings that had come from the ships in the sky. *Were they from the Federation? And did they interact with other civilizations, such as Sumer and Babylon? Maybe even Israel?* Answers seemed to be at his fingertips. Jamarcus hoped he could experience more visions.

"I'm not a vision," Bernini spoke in his mind, and Jamarcus felt anger in his voice at the thought of not being real. Jamarcus smiled at the emotion he felt from Bernini.

"Whatcha smiling at?" Joe asked.

"Nothing," Jamarcus said as he focused back on his classmates.

"You guys played on the map with the Black Hawk crashed on the ground?" Jamie asked.

"That was straight from the movie," Robert said. "The RPGs. The smoke."

"That was pretty dope," Joe said.

"That map is a camper's paradise," Jamarcus said. "A group I played with got on that map in a capture-the-flag mode. Since we knew all the spawn spots and where we needed to cover each other, we just lay down for days, killing the other team."

"God, I hate when that happens," Joe said. "It pisses me off that dudes just stay in one place with no actual skill to do anything."

"That's a legitimate strategy," Jamarcus said. "Hey, I survived an ambush by doing that."

"But that's real life. You shouldn't do that in a game," Joe said, and then a look of shock came over his face as he turned back to Jamarcus. "I'm sorry, man," he said with a look of shame.

"It's chill, bro." Jamarcus laughed as he tapped on the desk in front of Joe. "I get what you're saying. It's different rules if nobody dies and the purpose is to win a competition. Get out there and play. But dudes can get toxic when they play—camping, throwing Xbox racism at you."

"Yeah," Jamie said. "That, and guys need to stop treating female gamers like shit every time they meet one. I swear there are only two types of reactions I get when a guy meets a chick when he's playing. It's either 'Hey, you're a chick, you cunt' or 'Hey, you're a chick; you have a vagina, and I have a dick, so we should come together.'"

"I don't know what you're talking about," Jamarcus joked. "What is this rare female gamer species you speak of? I usually only encounter a boy who hasn't gone through puberty yet."

"I'm not a squeaker, God dammit," Jamie grunted, causing the group to laugh out loud.

"I hear that some guys at school are going to hold a tournament," Robert said. "We should form a team and try to compete."

"What should be the name of the team?" Jamie asked as Jamarcus went back to reading his laptop.

During his conversation with Ixchel, she briefly mentioned a phrase that seemed Egyptian: *Aten Ka*. Jamarcus knew from his childhood that Aten was a god from ancient Egypt. It was symbolized as the sun and was supposed to be the giver of light. Jamarcus remembered reading a passage in which a king died and joined Aten, a huge disk of life, who was the creator of all things. The word *Ka* was Egyptian for "soul." With the words combined, Jamarcus imagined the term meant the same thing as *Ha* in Polynesian culture: "this fire within us that is the source of life."

While reading online forums about UFO contacts, Jamarcus read that many believed aliens from the Pleiades and the Andromeda galaxy had influenced Egypt. That still didn't explain Bug Girl, the friend he'd played with in the chateau. He had been too awestruck to remember to ask about her and a lot of other things, so now Jamarcus mostly had been reading about other cultures that had insect mythology.

Ufologists seemed to refer to a Hopi legend about ants, so Jamarcus began reading about one of their creation myths. It was a story about how at first, the people on Earth of different ethnic groups lived in peace with each other, the animals, and the planet, but soon there came a period when people didn't live by that path and changed the vibrations of their souls to earthly pleasures. First came racism between humans and animals. Next came suspicion between everyone, and the war started to break out. A wind came to those who still wanted to live in harmony and told them to see with their soul vibrations and to look for a cloud in the daytime and a star at night and to follow it. When others saw them, they were ridiculed, because those humans didn't see anything. When the people gathered, they found out they were able to talk to each other with their soul vibrations. The wind came again and told the group to live underground with the ant people while the wind destroyed the world. While they were underground, the ant people taught the remaining humans how to live in harmony before they went back up to the new world.

When Jamarcus read that, the story didn't feel right. It explained the sensation he felt whenever he heard the voice from his guardian, but Bug Girl seemed to fit the descriptions of mantis-type encounters. The stories of some of the encounters were the stuff of nightmares, but Jamarcus believed that a bit of xenophobia might have played a role in that. He had to admit that when he first saw the locust people in his dream long ago, he had been racist toward them and should have listened to the little boy. He probably would have learned much from them.

Since he was in a class on African studies, he began to learn about a group of tribes in southern Africa called the Khoi. They had a culture and tradition that included a spiritual connection to certain stars. At a young age, children were lifted to the Pleiades and were taught to revere them. They also believed that through a process of ascension, they could become Sky People and be like gods. Their ancestors were considered Sky People and were worshipped. Of particular interest to Jamarcus was their reverence for the praying mantis, which they called the God of the Khoi. Another side branch of the Khoi, the San, said that the mantis had taught them how to speak and to use fire. Perhaps Bug Girl was part of a race of beings who had been in contact with those tribes long ago, and they and the Pleiadeans had sent souls down to them to learn to ascend. That could explain why he and Bug Girl were friends in his dreams.

"You're still researching for class?" Joe asked as he read Jamarcus's laptop screen.

"Yeah," Jamarcus responded as he turned it off. "My bad, guys. My laptop is dead anyway. I can do my homework when I get back from work."

"So you get off from work around midnight, right?" Robert asked.

"Yep," Jamarcus answered.

"And you come to school early in the morning, get off, and go straight back to work?"

"Yep."

"How do you find time to do all of your papers?" Jamie asked. "That would drive me insane."

"I've done worse schedules in Iraq," Jamarcus said with a shrug. "I think you guys are just lazy."

"Just tell it like it is, why don't you?" Robert said with sarcasm.

"Come on." Jamarcus laughed. "You guys are young. Either out of high school or just about. Are you working?"

"I am," Jamie said.

"Me too," Joe replied.

"Full-time?" Jamarcus asked.

"Me," Joe said, raising his hand.

"So you guys still use the rhythm of going to school, hanging out with your friends, and then doing your homework. I've spent years where I had to be on high alert for over twenty-four hours straight. I'm not knocking you guys, but if I want to go to school to get a degree, I have to be an adult and just do it. I can't complain."

"You say while you are knocking us," Robert said.

"How do you make time for gaming?" Jamie asked.

"I always make time for gaming," Jamarcus said in a serious tone as the table laughed. "Besides, I have a job where, for a good period, I have a lot of downtime. I get a lot of homework done in that booth."

"Hey, Jamarcus, whenever you want to play some games, you can always come over to my place," Joe said with a shy tone.

"Nah, man, I'm good," Jamarcus said with a grunt. "I'm terrible company anyway."

"Dude, stop trying to get into Jamarcus's pants," Robert said, jokingly scolding Joe.

"Having him come over isn't the same as trying to hook up," Joe said.

"Joe? Joe," Jamarcus said until Joe looked him in the eye. "I'm going to tell you something that a good friend told me. If someone wants you to go over to their place just to hang out alone and you think they don't want to smash, there's something wrong with you."

Joe looked down for a moment until he put his head in his arms on top of the table in shame.

"Oh my God," Jamie said as they all laughed. "I bet your face is so red."

"Shut up," Joe said in a muffled tone, which made them laugh even harder. Joe then looked up at Jamarcus and stared at him for a while. "You're just so hot," he said, which prompted Jamarcus to slap the table in mock anger.

"Why does this always happen to me?" Jamarcus said while the others looked at him in wide-eyed surprise.

"Guys always try to pick you up?" Robert asked.

"No. It's just that the only people who say they're attracted to me are people I can't get with. Usually, it's older women who are married or way too old for me." Jamarcus turned to Joe. "And you." He laughed.

"Ha-ha," Joe said snarkily.

"The only woman who said she liked me and I was able to go out with died on me. I just don't have any luck."

"Your girlfriend died, man?" Joe asked.

"Yeah, but don't get worked up about it. It happened." Jamarcus looked up at the cafeteria clock and noticed the time. "Hey, guys, I've got to go," he said as he gathered his stuff together. "I'll see you tomorrow."

"Why don't we go to a bar sometime?" Jamie said. "Maybe you just need to find a girl with the right amount of liquor in her."

"Not too much but just enough," Robert joked.

"We'll see," Jamarcus said while walking away. "Truth is, I'm in a weird spot in my life now, and I don't think I'm good for anybody. But I'll keep it in mind."

Jamarcus didn't wait for a response as he stepped out of the cafeteria and toward his motorcycle. The truth was that UFO research was the only real source of joy in his life. Reading up on new information was just as good as sex sometimes. He knew he enjoyed it too much, but it was a way for him to deal with his depression. All he wanted to do was stay home and learn as much as he could.

As Jamarcus got on his bike and rode off, he hoped another encounter would happen soon.

<2>

Half an hour after Jamarcus got home from work, he was in bed, half asleep. He had gotten good at allowing the energy to flow through him when he was in a rested state. Ever since he'd started on a vegan diet, he constantly felt energy pulsing in his head and down his back. When he went to sleep, it would increase in intensity, partially paralyzing him. It could also be attributed to the fact that he was mentally and physically stressed and exhausted sometimes after work, he thought.

That night, when Jamarcus entered the energy state, he became alert and awake, while his body was asleep, just as he had been when Ixchel, Aapo, and Bernini visited. He was slightly startled as his soul popped out of his body and floated above his bed. As he looked about the room, he saw that everything was lit up by an unknown light source. Not a single object in his bedroom had a shadow. He didn't see one on any surface. His soul body was brighter now than before, and it shone with more yellow light, like the sun hours before noon instead of at dusk or dawn.

Jamarcus steadied himself for a bit and tried to meditate. It seemed odd that the first thing he wanted to do was try to meditate, but he began doing it instinctively. Instead of trying to quiet his mind, he began to search the environment inside and outside his apartment. He noticed that when he looked about, his vision began to walk away from him, first out of his bedroom and then through his home. While he moved his vision, he felt energy rolling in the forward part of his head in his body, which lay on the bed. It was the same area that buzzed when he heard the guardian's voice.

Jamarcus wanted to go outside and see what he could, so he walked his vision toward the door. He reached out to open it and realized that he was moving his sunlight arm and his physical arm slightly in his bed. With a bit of hesitation, he walked through the door, just as Bernini had before, and felt himself slip right through. He moved his vision above his apartment and looked all around his complex. It was dark outside, but Jamarcus could see well, as if everywhere he looked, there was a flashlight shining in that direction, illuminating everything it touched from within.

Jamarcus could see cars rushing by the apartment complex on the highway. Above him, he could see commercial and private aircraft flying by. Whenever he concentrated on a vehicle he was interested in, he could hear the people inside the car or plane. He could also see a wavelength in front of him that vibrated as a person talked. The wavelength abruptly fluctuated as he heard a car horn blare next to his apartment. He looked in that direction and saw a car almost merge into a passing van. Just as the two vehicles were about to collide, Jamarcus braced himself, preparing for a crash. The world slowed to a crawl when he did that, and the car gradually corrected its course and returned to its lane. When everything seemed fine, Jamarcus relaxed, and time sped up back to its normal pace.

Jamarcus suddenly saw a light above him, and he looked up to see a hole in the night sky. From the hole, a wave of disturbance came toward him until it washed over his vision like a wave on a beach. A massive V-shaped object of lights flew out of the hole, and once it was completely out, the hole naturally collapsed on itself to form the normal sky. Hesitantly, Jamarcus moved his vision into the air to get a closer look at the object. The V-shaped lights slowly moved through the air until they were directly above Jamarcus. He could see that the lights were part of a large pyramid-shaped craft that must have been a mile long.

Jamarcus felt a presence appear below him, and when he looked down, he saw a short, skinny dark-brown-skinned figure walk up to and through his apartment door. He extended his vision to follow the being, realizing he could see inside his apartment as if he had x-ray eyes. The alien walked toward his bedroom and stopped in front of his bed.

"Come here," the being clicked at Jamarcus, commanding him just as Bernini had when he'd visited him a while ago.

Jamarcus pulled his vision back to his light body and looked at a young insect-like being. The alien was not clothed, so Jamarcus saw that its brown skin was leathery, and he could see its skeletal frame under the skin. The being had small features for a face, except for its eyes, which were large and almond-shaped and had a shiny black surface. Three nodes on the being's forehead had a little light coming from within them.

"Come here," the being said again, and Jamarcus could feel butterflies in the creature's belly as it anticipated Jamarcus's approach— not the fearful kind but the waiting-for-something-good-to-happen kind.

Jamarcus floated off the bed and walked over to the alien, and when he got close, he was able to see the light of the being's soul. It was that of a human girl with dark brown hair and brown eyes. The girl's face smiled as she reached up to hug Jamarcus, and as he knelt and held her, he felt happiness light up inside her mind. The being then sat on the floor and patted the ground, indicating for Jamarcus to sit as well.

"I wanted to come see you," the alien clicked. "I haven't been able to play with you since you stopped going to Nima. You didn't want to play with me?"

"I think at that time, I didn't believe you were real," Jamarcus said.

"He still doesn't," Bernini boomed from within Jamarcus.

Before Jamarcus could react, he saw the alien's female light face turn to anger.

"You don't believe in us?"

"I don't know what is going on," Jamarcus said. "I'm confused right now."

"But you remember me, right?" the being asked.

"Yes, I think so. What's your name?" Jamarcus felt a small bit of shame as the alien looked up at him.

"My name is Sneeze," it said, and Jamarcus knew the translation it had meant to say was something else.

"Your name is Achoo." Jamarcus laughed, realizing that a name in the alien's language was a sound and the emotion connected to the sound.

"Don't laugh. My name is Sneeze," the alien said.

"I'm sorry," Jamarcus said. "I think it's cute."

"Do you?" Sneeze asked, instantly cheering up.

"Yes. Do you know why we played together?"

"We're going to get married," Sneeze said as a smile spread on the female light's face. "Our parents wanted us to play together so we could be friends growing up."

"We have a prearranged marriage?"

"Yeah," Sneeze chirped.

"The ship above us—did you come here on it?"

"That's my daddy's ship. He said I could come here to play with you. He said you were ready for that."

After the answer, Jamarcus thought for a bit. "Are you a human?" he asked, and he felt a confused state in Sneeze's soul.

"Yes, stupid. My mother is human."

"Oh. That's interesting."

"Scar?" Sneeze said.

"Yeah?" Jamarcus answered.

"Do you like Kaggen people?"

"I don't know," Jamarcus said, thinking hard about the situation. He chose to remain neutral in the matter, still not sure if any of this was real.

"Is it because of the way we look? Are you scared of us?"

"I'm not scared of you. I remember playing with you at the chateau."

"Do you like me?" Sneeze asked in fear.

"Yes, as a friend," Jamarcus answered, and he felt Sneeze grow a little melancholy. "I think it's okay," he said. "I don't think our parents would have set us up if we weren't able to be together."

"Okay." Sneeze sighed, and then instantly cheered up. "Do you want to play a game?" she asked in excitement.

"Okay," Jamarcus said.

"Do you remember how to make figures of light?" Sneeze asked as she made a small figure between them. It was a hologram of an adult woman with dark skin and long brown hair, wearing a brown-and-white dress. The woman's eyes were black, but still made expressions with her eyebrows.

"You do it," Sneeze said.

"How do I?" Jamarcus asked.

"Wave your hand so you can feel the water."

"All right," Jamarcus said, and as he did, he could see and feel reality ripple in front of him where his hands moved.

"Now put your hand in the water," Sneeze said.

When Jamarcus did, he felt his fingers dip into the ripples and disappear. When reality went back to normal, he felt the water hug his fingertips, wanting to go back to its natural state.

"So make a line of light," Sneeze said.

Jamarcus brought a bit of energy into his soul, which made it brighter. He then moved some of that light out of his index finger and into reality. A bright line stretched from his finger and began to spool around into a loose roll. Once he felt he had enough, he pulled his finger back, and space-time snapped back into place. The spool of light floated by Jamarcus, and he was able to manipulate it however he wanted.

"Make it you," Sneeze said, desperately wanting to play.

Jamarcus concentrated a bit and was able to put his consciousness into the lines of light. He moved about, making arms and legs and turning his head around. He even clothed it how he usually liked to dress, with combat boots, blue jeans, a tight-fitting T-shirt, and a leather motorcycle jacket.

"Okay," Jamarcus said as he made his figure land and walk up to Sneeze's. "What should we play?"

"Tag!" Sneeze yelled, and her figure flew toward and slapped Jamarcus on its chest. She then zipped up into the air, flying around in a circle.

With a smile and contagious joy from Sneeze, Jamarcus made his figure jump up and chase after her, and they both zigzagged throughout his apartment. At one point, Jamarcus was about to tag her, but Sneeze turned her figure and made her zap him with a blast of light.

"Hey," Jamarcus said with a laugh as his figure ricocheted backward, which made Sneeze giggle mightily. Jamarcus continued his chase, zapping at Sneeze's figure until they made it back into his bedroom. Jamarcus noticed Sneeze was reading his mind, anticipating his attacks. With a bit of strategy, Jamarcus made his figure zap Sneeze's, and when she dodged, Jamarcus zapped her again, this time making contact.

"Oh no," Sneeze moaned as she made her figure slowly fall to the floor, and her hair and dress fluttered as she dropped like a leaf into a dramatic heap.

"All right," Jamarcus said as he landed his avatar next to Sneeze's. "What should we play now?"

"I don't know," Sneeze said as she pondered, and they both were surprised when a plume of fire exploded between the figures on the floor.

Bernini appeared out of the smoke, dressed in wickedly spiked black armor. With a blazing sword, he swooped in and grabbed Sneeze's figure off the ground.

"Aha," Bernini bellowed in a menacing voice. "I've captured your princess. If you want her back, you'll have to face me in my castle if you dare."

"Oh no!" Sneezed cried as her figure swooned in Bernini's arms with her arms covering her face. Both she and Bernini disappeared in another puff of fire, and a dark and misty forest sprang up around Jamarcus on the floor.

For a few seconds, Jamarcus sat watching his figure, not doing anything.

"What?" both Sneeze and Bernini asked.

"Really? We're doing this?" Jamarcus moaned.

"Come get me," Sneeze said as she bounced up and down before Jamarcus.

"Fine," Jamarcus groaned as his figure began his journey through the forest.

It wasn't long before he heard growling in the woods around him. Soon large wolves made of smoke and flames leaped out of the mist, ready to attack.

"All right, wolves," Jamarcus said approvingly. "I haven't seen that done in a while."

"Play!" Sneeze said.

Jamarcus made his figure leap upon the wolves. He was able to fight them off pretty well, but he felt Sneeze and Bernini teaming up on him to make them stronger. He flung a wolf into a group to create some separation and conjured up nunchucks for his figure. With a flurry, he swung them around, making the wolf closest to his figure dizzy as it tried to follow his movements. Jamarcus then made his avatar stop, fitting one end of his weapon under his arms and holding out his other hand, beckoning them to come. The wolves flung themselves at the figure, and with one mighty swing, Jamarcus made the first wolf disappear in a billow of smoke.

"Watah!" Jamarcus cried as he soon defeated the wolves.

He continued on his way through the forest and soon arrived at a stone bridge that lay before a decrepit castle. Flames burst from the chasm before Jamarcus's figure, and a dragon's head of darkness and glowing heat rose from the depths with fire flickering from its drooling mouth.

"And here's the dragon," Jamarcus said as he created a sword and shield to battle the beast.

Try as he might, he couldn't beat it. He felt Sneeze and Bernini put all their efforts into working together to beat him. Jamarcus thought for a moment, put his sword and shield down, and created a bucket of water. As the dragon sprang to attack, Jamarcus tossed the water into the creature's mouth, dousing its flame. As the dragon coughed, Jamarcus smugly made his avatar walk by it on the bridge.

"Move, bitch! Get out the way," Jamarcus sang as he made his way through the castle and into the throne room. He saw Sneeze's figure chained to a throne lit in the moonlight as she wiggled to get free.

"Save me!" Sneeze giggled, and Jamarcus felt pure joy building up inside her as he walked into the room. A final blast of fire appeared in front of the figure as Bernini finally appeared, challenging Jamarcus.

"Ha-ha!" Bernini laughed as he confronted Jamarcus. "I see you beat my minions. Now let's see how you stand—"

Bernini's figure was cut short as Jamarcus shot him in the face with a blast. Bernini tumbled backward and got up in a huff.

"We have to fight," Bernini told Jamarcus crossly as he pulled out his flame sword.

"Okay, sorry," Jamarcus said as he created a green lightsaber. The weapon screeched as it moved in the figure's hands.

Jamarcus's and Bernini's avatars clashed, and they performed all types of acrobatic maneuvers as their swords smashed against one another with large sparks. Finally, Jamarcus was able to pierce Bernini's chest, and he crumpled onto the floor.

"No!" Bernini croaked before he dissolved into fire and ash. The chains holding Sneeze's figure disappeared too, and she rushed over to Jamarcus and hugged him around his neck.

"You saved me!" Sneeze laughed as she clapped. "Do you want to play again?"

"Yeah!" Bernini yelped from within Jamarcus.

"I'm down," Jamarcus said, and they prepared to brainstorm another adventure.

Chapter 14
<1>
February 2010

It was in the early morning hours as Jamarcus began a foot patrol of the plant during a rainstorm. There was a lot of turnaround with the security guards at the site, partly from the attitudes of the truck drivers and partly due to demands from the plant's management. Some of them weren't that bad compared to what Jamarcus had experienced in service, but half the people his firm sent to that site were kids straight out of high school with no idea how to stand a watch. Most quit after a month, which had been the case that week. Half the manpower was gone, and Jamarcus had to do the patrol graveyard shift after his usual guard booth shift.

It was a brutal night since Jamarcus refused to drink any coffee. He'd quit because he got agitated when he drank it, and he wanted to avoid any scenario that made him mad. He was glad he had to walk the plant because it kept him awake. The cold air helped too, and he was surprised at how frigid it got in the Panhandle. The main reason he'd moved to that area was because he believed its weather was comparable to Hawaii's. The first winter in that area had felt worse than any he'd felt in Virginia. The humidity in the Panhandle was much higher than where Jamarcus had grown up, and even though Jamarcus was able to be in a heated security vehicle to do his patrol, the cold air still hit him hard. The cold used to feel good to him as a child. Now it hurt his knees and hands on nights like that when it wasn't cold enough for it to snow.

"Hey, security, how is it?" his radio squawked as he finished checking a patrol point.

"This is security," Jamarcus said into his mic as he got back into the warmth of the security car.

"We got a worker here who is having a hard time getting access to an area," the man said over the air. "Can you help him out?"

"On my way," Jamarcus said as he drove to the admin part of the plant.

After he parked the vehicle, he entered the building and went straight to the guard's office to see one of the workers waiting by the door.

"You're the one who called?" Jamarcus asked.

"Yeah, man," the man said, scratching his head. "I can't get access through a door. I usually can, but now it's locked."

"You have your badge on you?" Jamarcus asked as he followed the person to the locked room.

"Yeah, but I can't get to this area," the man said as they reached a door that separated the plant from the managers' offices.

"Are you management?" Jamarcus asked.

"No," the man said as he stood by the office entrance, still scratching his head.

"You do know that after certain hours, this door locks to keep guys out of the managers' offices without the right security clearance, right?"

"Yeah, that's probably why I can't get through. I don't work this shift. Can you let me through?"

"Are you management?" Jamarcus asked again.

"No," the guy said, turning his head away from Jamarcus. "You know me, man; we talk all the time when I come in."

"Yeah. Why do you need to get into this area?"

"Fucking hell, man, just let me through this door. Dereck lets me through all the time."

"You mean Dereck who used to work this shift?" Jamarcus asked.

"Yeah, that guy," the worker said. "He was here longer than you. He was cool. Where is he?"

"He got fired for not doing his job properly," Jamarcus told the man, who looked blankly at him. "Does your supervisor know you need to get into this area?"

"Yeah, I'll go ask him," the man said as he walked away from Jamarcus, frustrated.

The exchange left Jamarcus in a foul mood for the rest of the morning hours, but he was pleased he'd been able to keep himself from letting his anger get the better of him. His heart still had blocked up during the confrontation, but he hadn't clenched up his stomach that time. Once he'd realized he was still scared from his time in Iraq, just telling himself that he wasn't there helped him immensely to keep his nerves in control. Jamarcus walked back to the security office and waited there until his relief arrived within the hour.

"How was your night?" she asked as she entered the room, getting her uniform ready.

"All right, except for one instance," Jamarcus said as he clocked out. "I had a problem with one of the plant workers wanting to get access to the managers' area."

"Was it a tall, skinny white guy with scraggly hair?" the relief asked as she clocked in for her shift.

"Yeah."

"You know that's the guy Dereck got fired for? He would make Dereck let him into that area to go to sleep, knowing none of the night-shift supervisors could get to that area to check it."

"Jesus," Jamarcus said after getting his gear on for his ride home. "Guess I'm lucky I did my job."

"Damn straight. See you next week."

"Later," Jamarcus said as he left.

He was soon on his bike and riding home to change for his day at school. Jamarcus's body was cold and numb, and his knees and hands were in pain from the frigid humidity. They stayed like that as he arrived at the campus and trudged his way through his classes, which were filled with the occasional student whose mind was still stuck in high school. In a lot of ways, the kids still trying to be cool and the workers in the plant who never could get their act together were similar—just people who still believed they were eighteen years old and refused to grow up. Statistics class was particularly obnoxious to Jamarcus, with three students seated next to him who felt the need to comment on the clothes he wore.

"Look at his boots," the female said. "They are so raggedy. Like he's playing army."

"Like he's playing army like those idiots in JROTC back in high school," her friend said.

"My brother was in JROTC," the third one said. "He was so weird. They take that shit way too seriously."

"And look at his clothes," the female said. "He looks so ghetto. I can't date somebody poor. I've got to be with somebody who can take care of me."

"You a gold digger." One of her friends laughed.

"What? I can't be with some tacky-ass bitch."

"His leather jacket is aight, though," her friend said before reaching over to tap Jamarcus on the shoulder. "Where did you get that jacket, man?" the student asked after Jamarcus turned to him.

After the question, Jamarcus picked up his things and moved to a different area of the classroom to focus on the lesson. After class, when everyone was leaving, another female student approached him as he exited the classroom door.

"I heard those guys giving you a hard time," she said as she walked behind him. "They were so rude. They act so materialistic. I hate people who only think about money."

"Get away from me," Jamarcus snapped, releasing his frustration from his entire day at her. His heart sank when he saw her face flinch, and he walked as fast as he could away in shame.

That shame lingered throughout the rest of his classes, and he gladly retreated to his motorcycle at the end of his school day. He wanted to get home badly to either play a game or do more UFO research.

After he arrived at his apartment, he switched on the heater and changed clothes to get more comfortable. He plopped down on his gaming chair, turned on his console, and started playing the fantasy RPG he and Kathrine had played together. After a time, Jamarcus stopped, with an empty feeling diving into his soul. He went over to his laptop and searched the web for more information on any type of alien phenomena but soon quit that, still not feeling satisfied.

He opened up video files he'd downloaded onto his computer from his time on Oahu. He picked one showing his first outing in the mountains with Kathrine and her friends. Kathrine had recorded the majority of it, and it was mostly footage of Jamarcus. Jamarcus watched in sadness as Nathan and Tasi struggled on the red dirt path lined with trees up the mountain.

"Whose idea was this?" Nathan asked as he stopped to bend over with his hands on his knees.

"Yours!" the rest of the group shouted at him, which made Jamarcus chuckle an empty laugh.

"What are you watching?" Bernini asked inside his mind, and Jamarcus could feel his consciousness appear within him as if Bernini were seated in his lap.

"A video of me back in Hawaii," Jamarcus said as he tried to get more comfortable to accommodate Bernini.

"I want to watch too," Sneeze said, and a force pushed inside Jamarcus hard enough to make him bounce on his chair.

"You guys take it easy." Jamarcus scolded the two kids as they wiggled inside his soul. He felt the energy and innocent happiness coming from them, and the sadness in his heart lessened a bit.

"Sorry," Sneeze said as they came to a stop.

Jamarcus continued watching the video as it followed him, with Sam and Mary walking hand in hand just ahead. Sam pulled Mary along as Mary reluctantly followed.

"Who are they?" Sneeze asked.

Jamarcus felt her excitement, which began to mingle with his sorrow. "Those are my friends," he said with a smile.

"Are you still friends with them?"

"Yeah, but they're on another part of this planet, so I can't be with them."

"You can still talk to them," Bernini said in a "Don't you know?" manner that made Jamarcus laugh inside.

"I'm not that important," Jamarcus said, speaking more to himself than to the others. "Besides, I wouldn't know what to say to them." He continued watching as he saw himself walk through the group, not affected by the slope of their climb.

"Let's go, you bunch of Ranger Ricks!" Jamarcus ordered as he gently pushed Tasi from behind. "We've still got six more miles on this trail. Double time!"

"I hate you," Tasi snarled at Jamarcus, and Jamarcus felt giggles coming forth from Bernini and Sneeze. He began laughing as they did, and their joy mixed with his grief. It began to swirl around in his heart with his pain, forming a mixture of his cold misery and their warm, innocent bliss.

"Honey, wait for me," Kathrine pleaded from behind the camera, and he watched himself wait with his hand extended until her hand grabbed his. She then let go when she was close enough and slapped his rear end. "Look at this butt," she huffed, and Jamarcus watched himself wiggle his behind for the camera. Bernini and Sneeze erupted in laughter, and their contagious glee caused Jamarcus to snort out a few snickers.

"What are you doing?" Sneeze asked, and Jamarcus could feel her little belly buzz with butterflies. They laughed on and off together as the group finally reached the top of the mountain, which revealed a scenic tropical view of Waimea Bay and the Pacific Ocean. The party lumbered about, breathing in as much air as they could, with Jamarcus laughing beside them all the while.

"Someone hold the camera," Kathrine said. "I want to see me next to Jamarcus in the video."

"I got it, sista," Nathan said, and the view tumbled about until Kathrine and Jamarcus could be seen rocking in each other's arms.

"We did it, honey!" Kathrine cried as she looked up at Jamarcus.

"Yeah," Jamarcus said, and they kissed, with the group hooting in admiration.

"Blah," the two kids groaned in Jamarcus's mind, and the silliness of their discomfort made him laugh. All of their wonder and peace began to mix into Jamarcus's heart of pain and discomfort, and the swirling mixture twirled over and over. It felt wonderful to Jamarcus, with their happiness washing away his grief, and he began to cry as, in the video, Sam tried to break up Jamarcus and Kathrine for too long. The sight of that made Bernini and Sneeze giggle even more, and Jamarcus joined them.

"Are you sad?" Sneeze asked, and Jamarcus could see her soul looking straight at his.

"No, I feel good," he said.

"You know we love you, right?" Bernini asked in an innocent voice, and Jamarcus wiped the tears off his face, trying to keep himself from bawling again.

"Yeah, I know," he said before he watched his friends begin their slow, pathetic walk back down the mountain.

<2>

At night, Jamarcus's consciousness was able to leave his body at will as more energy was able to flow through him, and he would float over his bed and meditate, listening and watching as much as he could. It was a frightening feat at first because he didn't realize just how much activity there was in the dimensions humans couldn't perceive.

He first could feel figures around his apartment, moving swiftly here and there, as if trying to keep out of his sight. When he was brave enough to want to see the beings, he took a look inside a neighbor's apartment, following a dark patch slithering inside it. He saw his neighbor in her bed, and above her was a dark figure hunched over her with its hand in her chest. When Jamarcus looked closer, he could feel that the figure was actually human, or once had been and that it pushed against the dim light of the woman's soul inside her body. The woman was awake and was in a panic, not understanding what was going on, since she couldn't move. Each time she tried to move and failed, the light in her soul increased in her body as she got scared. Each time the figure absorbed the increased light, it reacted like a junkie getting a hit. The more light the shadow received, the more light it shone with.

When the shadow had gotten enough, it slipped out the window next to the woman and slowly floated away, not even caring if Jamarcus could see it. Its body changed, appearing like a faded ghost figure from a horror film.

As more nights went on, Jamarcus guessed there were probably less than a dozen of the beings in his area, feeding on the lights of people to maintain their own like drug addicts. And not all of the figures he felt were human.

When Jamarcus became braver, he decided to see how high he could fly into the sky, and one night, he went as far as he could and found himself above the planet. The first time he did so, he reached out and felt nothing. Absolutely nothing. The emptiness of it frightened Jamarcus. Later on, as he began to get used to space and expand his consciousness more, he found out he had been wrong. The space was full of things, and it was very busy.

He felt various crafts entering and leaving Earth's atmosphere like watching a multitude of freeways, and the beings on the crafts were amazingly diverse. The majority of the beings were reptilian, like humans but with reptilian features, including their eyes and skin. Some beings looked like the stereotypical alien creature, while others looked birdlike or similar to amphibians. There were ones filled with genuine humans. Some of the beings noticed Jamarcus and flew their craft next to him, and he could see the beings looking at him with curiosity.

"Is this a new god?" Jamarcus heard a child ask his parents once, and the parents said yes. They moved their ship as close as they could to Jamarcus without disturbing him so their child could get a better look. Jamarcus waved his hands at the boy, who giggled in and out of his soul as he waved back before they flew off.

The comings and goings of the craft weren't always peaceful. One night, Jamarcus saw orbs zipping around in a fierce battle. At one point, a white target cross-lit an area in front of what might have been the fleeing craft, and when the orb entered it, a blast from Earth hit it, and the orb exploded in flames and debris. When Jamarcus flew his consciousness over to that area, he heard the residual screams of the pilot as the ship faded away. Frightened by what he saw, Jamarcus retreated into his body that night.

Jamarcus wondered what would happen if he tried to fill his light body with as much light as it could take. One night, as he floated in his apartment, he absorbed as much light as he could, and while he did so, he saw his bedroom begin to expand and curve away from him. It continued until his room seemed to flow down below him into a curved pool in a bright white space. The pool looked like an old, curved television scene, and Jamarcus soon found that he could manipulate it just like a touch-screen phone. As he moved his point of view, he again felt the movements in his body's forehead. In that manner, Jamarcus could swiftly leave Earth and scroll on the screen to different parts of the solar system. He became curious and scrolled faster, and he zipped away from his home system far enough to see the stars surrounding the sun.

Jamarcus became concerned, as what he saw left him disoriented. He believed the only way back to his home was to retrace his movements, but he had gotten so far away he forgot which star was the sun. He floated in the white for a while, not knowing what to do, until he felt a presence appear next to him. When he turned to look, he saw a white man clothed in simple garments. He was broad, muscular, and much taller than Jamarcus. He had shoulder-length blond hair and pale blue eyes. From within him shone a strong white light that seemed solid, and love also shone from him—a fatherly love.

"Hello, Scar," the man said when he noticed Jamarcus's nervousness.

"Hello," Jamarcus said as he tried to calm down.

"I felt that you were a bit skittish, so I came to help you feel better."

"Who are you?" Jamarcus asked, and he felt a smile in the man's soul before he answered.

"Still so skeptical, are you? I'm your father, Ra."

"Okay," Jamarcus responded.

"You feel unsure of yourself," Ra said. "You feel unsure because of what I am."

"I'm sorry," Jamarcus said. "I'm still trying to comprehend

what's been happening to me."

"You are uncomfortable with me. With the color of my skin."

"Yes," Jamarcus grudgingly answered.

"I understand," Ra said with a smile as he floated close to Jamarcus. "I had the same problem when I first saw my parents when I was on Earth. My mother was patient with me. She taught me to look not at her body but at her light. It is the same light in me and you. Now you're wondering how to get back to your body."

"Yes."

"Can you still feel your body?"

When Ra spoke those words, Jamarcus remembered that everything he felt as he traveled was in his body in his room. He slapped his light head with his hand when he realized how easy it was to get back.

"Where are we?" Jamarcus asked as he looked around.

"We are in the White," Ra answered. "It is the plasma field that surrounds the waters of your reality. Your coming here means you've reached the fifth density. That's why you are on Earth—to ascend on your own through the densities."

"You went through the same things I'm going through?" Jamarcus asked. "What is happening?"

"You were born to your mother and me, and when you were asked to go through the ascension process, you agreed. You remember your mother told you this?"

"Yes, but why did I need to do this?"

"To put it simply, because there is only so much light we beings in the higher planes can produce on our own. At the most, we can ascend to the sixth density, with a few prestigious ones of us being able to ascend to the seventh. However, that is the most we can reach, due to the physics of our reality. The best way I can describe it is that there is only so much weight a person can find and lift in one universe.

"It's because, outside the waters of a universe, there is no resistance to the flow of Aten Ka in our bodies. We simply can't shine any brighter. But when light enters the body of a third-density being, that resistance is nigh infinite. Lower that resistance to the flow of Aten Ka while in your human body will allow you to push past the seventh density. In essence, you are now lifting the weight of many universes."

"Is that why Ixchel asked me to change my diet?"

"You know, your mother is always listening to you," Ra said. "You should call her Mother."

"Sorry." Jamarcus laughed. "Is that why Mom asked me to change my diet?"

"The minerals in the food you eat now lower your body's energy resistance. It will allow you to reach as high as the tenth density like myself or even higher."

"Does this have anything to do with Sneeze?" Jamarcus asked. "She told me we are going to get married."

"Yes," Ra said. "It was arranged by me and her father. Her people wanted to join the Federation but didn't want to be under the rule of a house like ours. We came up with a solution that you would be the source of Aten Ka for her world, and you agreed."

"So individuals go through the process of ascension if they want to be a light for a world?" Jamarcus said.

"A light can go through the process if that light chooses to," Ra said. "I want you to go through it to learn the life lessons you can only learn in a world in the third density. What parent would want any less?"

"It is a prearranged marriage then," Jamarcus said.

"You disapprove?" Ra asked.

"No. It's just that I'm not sure if any of this is real. I could be hallucinating. And I'm not sure how to handle a relationship with Sneeze. She said she's half human, but this is so … It's hard to explain. I don't know if I can love a being like that. And she's only a child now."

"Yes, you can," Ra said. "It's hard to explain now because the culture you live in is fixed on the material, while ours is focused on Aten Ka. Your marriage will work. The love you will have for one another will give birth to a new species."

"What are Sneeze's people like, if you don't mind me asking?" Jamarcus said. "Mom hated it when I asked about different species."

"Yes, your mother has her ways. Sneeze's people rule the galaxy you live in now. They were very science-based for thousands of cycles, and they have begun reaching out to the Federation to build a new relationship with us. Do you remember playing with Sneeze when you were young?"

"That was probably one of the few happy moments of my child-hood—running around and causing a ruckus in the chateau."

"Your mother would yell at you two so much when your light was with us." Ra laughed. "Aten Ka, she would be so mad at you."

"What is Aten Ka? The light?" Jamarcus asked.

"That is a convoluted question with a convoluted answer," Ra said as he held out his hand. A small light appeared above it and then began to cycle around in a loop. The light increased the speed of its rotation until the loop almost seemed solid. The loop then began to spin on its north and south axes. It then began to spin on its east and west axes, until it looked like the perfect example of the duality of a particle. Another light appeared inside the first loop and gradually created a loop half the circumference of the first one. Another light appeared, but the loop it formed was only half the distance from the second one that the second one was from the first. More loops were made until the inside of the light was a whirling white glow. Jamarcus noticed that no matter how he looked at the light, it appeared just like the description of the tunnel of light in near-death experiences.

"This is Aten Ka," Ra said. "It has many names in many cultures—the Source, the Creator, the Matrix, God. I believe there a people on your planet who call it the Akashic Record. No matter what name it is called, all beings who have observed it agree it's the same thing: consciousness. A universal presence that is the source of all things. It is also the same thing wherever we can observe it. The Aten Ka in you is the same as the Aten Ka in me and is the same as the Aten Ka at the center of the Omniverse. It is as far as I can travel, but do you want to see the Aten Ka at the center of our multiverse?"

"Yes," Jamarcus said, and the light around them flowed below them in the same manner as Jamarcus's bedroom had before. This time, they came to a place that was completely black except for the curved screen of the universe below their feet. They ascended away from the surface until Jamarcus saw other curved universe screens around them. Soon a sea of universes was below them, and Jamarcus began to perceive a light above the universal waters. It was a massive white ball of swirling looped lights. The loops buzzed around at incredible speeds, and strings of the white light connected to the surfaces of all the universes Jamarcus could see.

"This is the Aten Ka of this multiverse," Ra said. "It is here that we received the light that flows in our souls and the gateway to the universal Aten Ka. The greater the amount of Aten Ka we can channel in us the higher in density we can ascend. Each loop of light is a density, and each density we ascend to allows us more abilities. This is how we can manipulate reality, fuel worlds throughout galaxies, and allow travel between universes."

"So your bodies are made of a type of plasma field," Jamarcus said to understand what he was being told.

"Yes, but that is only one aspect of Aten Ka," Ra said. "Spiritually, it is explained differently."

Next to Jamarcus emerged a vision that showed him in a sunlit sky with clouds below and above him. Hands sprang forth from below the vision version of Jamarcus and held him while his figure raised his arms and held up a white baby boy with wild blond hair wrapped in a blanket. The child's hand reached up into the clouds above him.

"Our light passes through the clouds of forgetfulness every time we live a life in the lower densities. Some of the experiences we have from previous lives come along with us to the next one, still having a grip on us. If we learn to let go of all the trauma we have experienced and learn to develop our light, we can leave this cycle of forgetfulness and bring everything we learned as we ascend into a higher density."

"The little boy I'm holding on to," Jamarcus said. "Is he me?"

"Yes. Do you want to see your future body?"

"Sure," Jamarcus said hesitantly, and Ra's light in his body expanded until it swallowed Jamarcus up. He found himself once again in a realm of white light, but it was filled with evenly spaced silver spheres that went on infinitely. No matter where Jamarcus looked in the realm, all the lines of balls connected in the far-off distance. Before Jamarcus could comprehend where he was, he sped off, with the balls forming a tunnel around him as he plunged and rose in all directions.

He came to a sudden halt when he appeared in a room he believed he remembered seeing in his childhood dreams. It looked like a simple nursery made for a boy. Ra stood next to Jamarcus as Jamarcus searched the room. Alongside one wall was a large technological box with light shining from its clear glass cover. The box seemed not to fit the simple aesthetic of the room. As Jamarcus walked over to the device, he saw a chubby little boy lying asleep, with pale white skin with pink freckles, clothed in a white onesie, floating in a curved bubble of sunlight. He was the little boy from Jamarcus's dream long ago.

"That's the crib that holds you," Ra said as he walked next to Jamarcus.

"He was me the whole time?" Jamarcus asked. "This is who I am?"

"No," Ra said, perceiving his meaning. "Remember, you are not this child. You are not the human you are now. You are Aten Ka. The same Aten Ka that is in me. We are all one in the light."

"I don't think I'm ready for all of this," Jamarcus said as he turned to face Ra, who he now noticed towered over him. "I get the concept of reincarnation. At least that's what I think you're explaining. I don't know how to explain it. I just don't have any memory of being this child. God, I don't know how to say this without sounding like an asshole. I don't want to … Jesus."

"You went through the clouds of forgetfulness to be in your current form," Ra said. "And you were still very young when you decided to ascend—a toddler on your planet. You still are a toddler to us. Your light hadn't begun to attach its identity to a form yet. It was just as hard for me when I returned. I had the same complexion as you when I was on Earth. You can't decide what body you will be in when you move through life in Aten Ka. We had no idea you would be who and what you are. But that isn't what's important. Aten Ka is."

Jamarcus looked back at the little boy and placed his sunlit hand on the glass cover. "I have to admit, if anyone were to give me the offer to be a parent, especially one of an alien race, no matter how racist it sounds, I would leap at the opportunity. Maybe I can find some solace in that."

Chapter 15
<1>
April 2010

Jamarcus lay in bed early in the morning, trying to go back to sleep. It was his day off, and he didn't have any school, so he wanted to rest as much as possible. He had been unable to sleep the previous night, however. Jamarcus had bumped into a person he knew from the halfway home, who'd told him about a meeting at the VA center for veterans who were dealing with PTSD. He'd invited Jamarcus to come by that weekend if he had free time, and all that night, Jamarcus had been able to think only about going over to the place and reliving his tours.

Jamarcus's phone rang, giving his heart a sharp start. Believing that his supervisor was calling him in to cover a shift for someone who'd decided not to show up, he looked at his phone only to discover that it was a call from his sister. Dismissing the call, he sat on the edge of his bed, miserable that he was completely awake. He put earphones on and plugged them into his cell phone to watch videos and listen to music. Nothing he watched seemed to satisfy him, and the music he used to listen to as a teenager didn't lift his spirits as it once had.

Frustrated, he put his cell phone away and sat down in front of his television to play on his gaming console. He tried to play multiplayer with his friends from college, but none were on. He played for an hour or so on a first-person shooter, but the toxicity of the people he played with made him stop with disgust.

He began to play his favorite fantasy role-playing game, and while he had fun, it wasn't nearly as fun as when Bernini and Sneeze visited. Jamarcus had noticed a pattern of when they visited: at night just a few hours before he fell asleep. When they were with him, he would play his role-playing game so they could watch, and when he went to sleep and had his light leave his body, they would have him take them wherever they wanted to go on Earth. One night, Jamarcus had taken them to a small village somewhere in southern Africa, where a friend of Sneeze's was in communion with the indigenous people there, in the midst of a dance. It had been one of the most beautiful things Jamarcus ever had seen, with Sneeze's and her friend's light entwining with the villagers'.

The kids weren't with him that morning, and they likely wouldn't come. Ixchel had gotten mad at Jamarcus and Bernini recently because Bernini had used the excuse of playing with Jamarcus to keep from doing his chores and keeping up with his studies. He was grounded until further notice, as Ixchel had put it, and Jamarcus wasn't comfortable in being with Sneeze alone. He could tell Sneeze liked him, and he'd requested that she only visit when Bernini was there also. Sneeze had protested, saying that her father was always watching, but Jamarcus had insisted. Besides, when they both were around, it felt like having two younger siblings he goofed off with. So with no Bernini, there was no Sneeze.

Jamarcus turned off his console and went to his kitchen, where he chopped up a salad to eat for breakfast. As he sat in the kitchen area by himself, loneliness kicked in while he ate. When he looked at the clock, he saw that it was only a few hours before the VA group would meet. Just thinking about getting out of the apartment made Jamarcus's joints hurt, but he needed to do something. There wasn't anything in his apartment that could give him joy.

With a bit of pain, he got up, cleaned his bowl and utensils, got his keys and jacket, and went out to his bike. For a while, he just sat on it, feeling the warmth of the sun and the cool breeze blowing over him. It was too early to go to a movie, and there wasn't any movie in particular he wanted to see. He thought about going to the motorcycle shop to look at the bikes there but didn't want to have to deal with salesmen who wanted to get him on a new motorcycle.

With a sigh, Jamarcus made up his mind, got his bike started, and drove to one of Fort Walton's parks by the bay. It was a nice ride on his bike, with other bikers waving to him as they drove by. Once he got to a park, he strolled the trails, saying hi to some of the morning walkers he passed, until he reached the waters. Less than a mile out over the bay was a beach with hotels built on it. He could see tourists lying on lawn chairs or eating in outdoor restaurants. It wasn't too cool that day, but it wasn't hot either—just perfect.

It reminded Jamarcus of Chesapeake Bay, which he'd looked out at in the backyard of his parent's home in Virginia Beach. Nature always had made him happy—being in the trees and grass or going on marches through the forests while he was stationed on Oahu—but now it barely gave him any happiness.

He realized now that there wasn't anything on the planet that gave him joy. Companionship and true friendship brought joy, yes, but those had been clouded by pop culture, ethnicities, religions, and politics. Jamarcus could now see how humanity had divided itself after having visions of aliens who only cared about his light. To feel their love and friendship and to then talk among those who only cared about the color of one's skin or how much money one possessed had made Jamarcus distance himself from humanity. He didn't know if that was for good or for ill, but that was the truth in his soul. He didn't recognize himself as human anymore.

When he looked at the time, he noticed it was only half an hour before the VA meeting started. Gathering enough courage, he made his way back to his bike and headed to the VA center. When he got to the parking lot, he sat on his bike, hesitating to go inside. When he noticed people staring at him, he got up and went inside, where he read the public direction signs in the halls that led him to the discussion room.

There was already a group outside the door, talking among themselves. As Jamarcus greeted them, he walked in to see that it was a simple room with light teal tiles and beige-painted walls. There was a table at one end of the room with snacks and coffee, and there were chairs placed in a circle in the center. Jamarcus sat in one of the chairs and looked out the window as he waited for the meeting to begin.

"Hey, brother," a man said as he sat next to Jamarcus. "New face. Their name's Jake. First time here?"

"Jamarcus," he said as he shook the man's hand. "Yeah. Been to a couple of these meetings?"

"Just a few," Jake said as he scratched his beard. "I didn't want to come. But after the first time I came, I realized how much I needed to be here. To talk to people who've been through the same shit I've been through. It's hard to talk about."

"Yeah. I've just only been able to talk about it without feeling like I'm going to have a heart attack."

"What branch were you in?"

"Army," Jamarcus said.

"Infantry?" Jake asked.

"Rangers."

"Did you want to go airborne?"

"I had a lot of my commanding officers ask me that while I was in," Jamarcus said. "I got put through Special Forces training at Fort Benning and placed in an assignment where we assisted some Special Forces guys. I just never wanted to. Maybe I had had enough of war."

"I hear you, man," Jake said as they watched the group take their seats around them. "How many years did you serve?"

"Eleven years."

"Taking advantage of the GI Bill?" Jake asked.

"I'm in school right now. Frankly, if it wasn't for that and work, I wouldn't even get out of my apartment."

"You've got to get out, man. I know it's scary, but you can't have fear rule over you. The one thing you're going to learn from this is that there is nothing to be scared of."

"Okay," Jamarcus said as the last of the group sat down, and the person who appeared to be the mediator arrived.

<2>

"Hello, everyone," the man said as he grabbed an extra chair and fit himself into the circle. "My name is Henry. I'm the guy who's running this talk group for the VA. I want to thank you guys for showing up, and hopefully, for the new people here, we can start a process for you to cope with some of the stuff you dealt with in the war.

"First, let me tell you a little bit about myself, so you all can understand what the process will be like here. I rose to the rank of first sergeant in the Marines as I served for twenty years. I was stationed in Korea, San Diego, and Pensacola, where I ended up staying after I retired. I was part of the Allied forces that went into Iraq for the first time during Desert Storm. Say what you will about the politics of what was the true cause of the war, but when I went in, I thought the US was doing the right thing. Saddam took over Kuwait and threatened to take Saudi oil fields. It was a war to save the world's economy.

"We all know how the war went down. We decimated them. I was part of a battalion charged with seizing an oil field in northern Kuwait. The marines I was with didn't do much—just sat back while air and artillery strikes took out most of the opposition. I still remember seeing all the charred vehicles and bodies as we rode toward the derricks.

"There were casualties on our side, so let me not paint a picture that we came in kicking asses and taking names. It was an open desert when the battalion I was with encountered troops. The men we lost in my company were caught out in the open with motor strikes as we waited for air cover. Truthfully, we got cocky. We were blasting through any enemy forces we met, which were mostly running away. It never occurred to us that some Iraqi soldiers would stand and fight. That squared my ass away. I believed my marines were invincible, and in less than five minutes, I was corrected. I lost two kids, and five others were severely injured. I still have those two boys' names written on a piece of paper I keep in my wallet.

"The crazy thing was that all of the command wanted to keep pushing to take out Saddam's forces. Maybe the fighting was too easy, and with what I believe was a false sense of confidence, they thought we could go north and take out the rest. I wasn't going to disagree with any command to continue fighting. We had been on the field for less than a month, and combat had all but stopped in less than a week. But I still had lost men, and I was scared to keep going. I didn't want to lose anymore. I thought, *If I die, that's fine. Just not another kid.* I felt I couldn't tell that to any of my fellow senior NCOs. They would say, 'It's war; there're always casualties.' So, I kept my mouth shut. I didn't tell anyone that I was relieved when we were told to hold the territories we'd captured.

"Later on, we found out that Bush Senior's administration encouraged civilians to take on Saddam. They got massacred. Kurds and Shia were mowed down by the thousands. We set up a no-fly zone, but I still feel guilty about that. I was too scared to keep going, but I still believe those Iraqis' deaths were because of us. Because of me.

"At the time, there was no program in the military to deal with what we now know as post-traumatic stress disorder. Anyone who tried to speak out about it was, sadly, labeled a coward. And I'm ashamed to say that I disciplined men who I now know were suffering the same way I was. Many armed service personnel feel proud of what we accomplished, but I can't. My soul just won't let me.

"When I got out of the military, I began working with the VA, and that's when I began to hear about PTSD and of the soldiers who suffered from it. So, I volunteered to hold talk groups, and I have been doing it for the last seven years. I'm lucky to have met many wonderful servicemen and servicewomen and heard their stories. And everyone I hear and see helps me get better a little bit. I hope one day I don't need to have the names I have in my wallet anymore. Maybe one of you can do that for me.

"So that's my story. Basically, in this room, with no criticism, this is a safe place for you to tell everyone what you've experienced. No politics or religion. You can go on online forums and rant all you want for that. I just want to give you guys a place where you can freely talk about what is still keeping you up at night. First, let's introduce ourselves. We'll go around in a circle if someone wants to start."

"Jake here," Jake said as he sat up next to Jamarcus. "I was a corporal in the Marines. I served two tours in Iraq before I got out last year. I'm working in construction now. Nice to meet you guys."

"Jamarcus," Jamarcus said, raising his hand. "Served for eleven years in the army. I was a staff sergeant. I served two tours in Iraq and one in Afghanistan. I go to school now and work in security."

"James," the man to Jamarcus's right said. "I served in the army for five years. Corporal. Served in Iraq and Afghanistan. One tour each. Haven't found a job yet, but I'm trying."

"Martha. I was in the army. I was a private first class. I served three years and did one tour in Iraq. I work at a bakery now. My own business, so I'm happy about that."

"Terrance, air force sergeant. I served for six years. I did three tours in Afghanistan for Special Forces. I work for search and rescue for the state. I love my job now but not as much as I should have when I was in."

"Steven. Marines. I was a corporal, and I served three years. I did two tours in Afghanistan. I'm still trying to find a job, but I'm going to school."

"Phillip. Army. I served for six years. Sergeant. I did a tour in Iraq and Afghanistan. I'm not working, but I'm hoping to fix that soon."

"All right," Henry said. "Now that we've introduced ourselves, how about we have someone start us off? Any takers?"

"I'll go," Jake said after a pause of silence. "I know how hard it is for some guys to open up the first time. This is my fourth meeting, so it's easier now. I wanted to talk about the time my squad was ambushed while on patrol in Fallujah. It happened a few years back. I wasn't part of the battle, but none of the anti-American sentiment went away. Hell, from what I learned, that place never liked outsiders anyway. Some of Saddam's top generals came from that city. And when we would patrol that area, the Iraqis there made it clear that they did not like us.

"So, there was this time when we were on patrol during 2007 in July. There was this huge civil war going on in Iraq at that time, and everyone was bombing everybody else and their mother. The marines in Fallujah at the time were part of an operation where we split up the city into sections, which made it easier to patrol the city. Every section had a police station, and it was our job to get everyone in the section we were in to go to the police station to get an ID card. Nothing big. Every other person we asked to go in thought it was a big deal.

"There was this group of guys, right? They were chilling by their homes. They were my age, and I'm sure they didn't have jobs. Later on, I would find out that one of them used to serve in the Iraqi army before the war. We had the interpreter ask them if they had any IDs. They looked at us like we were full of shit. And since we had to make these guys get IDs, things got even more heated.

"One of the Iraqis—I'm pretty sure it was the former army dude—went up to our interpreter and began yelling at him. And you've got to understand, we are fucking protective of our interpreter guys. They're risking their lives more than we are. One slip and their families are gone. This guy was laying it in with our man. Now, I don't know Farsi, but I'd been listening to our interpreter for a while and picked up a few phrases. So, the army dude straight-up asked our interpreter for his name. I'm pretty sure that's what he asked. And I saw our man bug out. So, I was mad, and I mean hot.

"I got right up in that guy's face, nose to nose. And I swear if it wasn't for our squad leader, I would have beat the crap out of that guy. I was so mad. I took him asking for our interpreter's name as a threat to his life. I was ready to drop those guys right there. Fight or flight, and I was choosing fight. My squad leader was cooler but was just as mad when he found out what the guy had said. We forced them to come with us and made them get IDs. All the while, they were swearing at us. At least the one guy was. And he was looking at me. And I was talking shit back: 'I'm not afraid of you, punk.' He left the station, staring us down, and I knew he said he was going to kill us. Like I said, I don't speak Farsi, but I feel in my heart that's what he said.

"The next couple of days were quiet. Didn't have any problems. And then boom. There was this massive attack at our headquarters. And I mean massive."

"I heard about that attack," Steven said. "Guys I served with said that shit was real."

"It was a battle," Jake said. "It started right out of the blue too. We were on foot patrol, and all of a sudden, we saw people rushing inside. Which I still say is bullshit. Everyone somehow knew when we were going to get attacked and hid, but no one dared to warn us. So we were close to arriving back to base, and we saw the locals fleeing the area. And that was when the mortar strikes came in. My squad fell to the ground, figuring out what was happening. It was lucky we got down because that was when gunfire came at us from down the street behind us.

"We were returning fire, and we made it back to base just when we saw a truck coming right at us. We got in just in time to have that thing explode right in front of the headquarters. That noise was so loud. The word *bang* was all I could see in front of my eyes for a few seconds. We set up defensive positions, still returning fire when another truck came at us. We were ready that time, but when that truck exploded, chlorine gas came out of it. My chest is still burning to this day from that blast.

"So we were there, eyes and chests in pain, waiting for anything else to happen, when we saw Iraqis with vests on rushing the compound. We took those guys out with no problem. Then everything stopped just as fast as everything had started. We searched the IDs of some of the guys we dropped, and boom—the pissed-off dude from before was one of the suicide bombers.

"At that time, I believed he got what he deserved. Now I see the war completely differently. I wonder what would have happened if I hadn't gotten so mad at that guy. I feel like I caused the attack. I do. Yeah, I know I'm trying to make it all about me, but it still haunts me.

No matter what, if I would have acted differently, someone could have been alive now. That guilt just won't go away."

"It's not your fault," Henry said. "One contained incident is not the culmination of all the bad things that happened over there. And even if your altercation with that man incited him to throw his life away, it was still his choice to commit the attack. We are all individuals, and no matter what happens around us, we still have ultimate control over what happens in our lives. And we must face the consequences of our actions, good or bad. The hardest part is dealing with the consequences sometimes. But that will come with time. Anyone else?"

"I'll go," Martha said as she rearranged herself in her chair. "I'm not sure what to say, so I'll dive right in. I was part of the 507 Maintenance Company, which provides transportation and support for the artillery and tank convoys. I wasn't part of the convoy that got ambushed that everyone remembers on television, but I was part of the first convoys that got into Iraq.

"I'm pretty sure most of you guys see on the news how often our convoys come under attack. It's either by small arms or IEDs, and you are always in a state of readiness. I call it a constant state of near panic. It's something I still do today. I'm always ready for something to fail, something to go wrong. Something good could be happening to me, but my mind won't let me enjoy it. The only thing I can see is the bad now.

"I was only in two real firefights. The second one was over just as fast as it started, just like yours, Jake. We were escorting antiair missiles to Baghdad from Kuwait. Some insurgents opened fire at us while we were on the highway. Our gunner on the fifty opened fire at them, and my fire team leader told us to start shooting to the south.

I just got my rifle out and fired a few rounds before we were told to seize fire. I think it was only a couple of guys who only had a rifle and a magazine each and fired off a few shots at us. It was a completely useless attack. That made me permanently on edge every time I got in a Humvee.

"The first firefight was when I was part of a group that was moving a convoy through Baghdad to Mosul. We were going through the southeast part of Baghdad, and for whatever reason, that place was still hotly contested after we entered the city the first time. We entered the city and were heading north past the rotary there, and just as we were about to hit the main highway north, an IED went off. It exploded right before the lead Humvee got close enough. So that was luck. But we had these missiles on some of our vehicles and could not let the bad guys get their hands on them.

"Our fifty was laying down cover fire. We were told to get out of the vehicle and direct fire to the guys ambushing us. I got out of the vehicle and swung around to the back, and I saw this guy running at us with an AK in his hand. Completely in the open. I fired a few shots at him, and he dropped. That was the only attacker I could see; for the rest of the firefight, I was firing shots at half a body hiding behind buildings, until everything stopped.

"When we knew the attack was over, my squad went to the guy I'd shot. His head was blasted open. I still see that image right now. It's embedded in my brain, and I think it will never go away. My squad was congratulating me on a confirmed kill. One of them wanted to marry me, saying I'm the coolest person he knows. They were happy, but I was not. All I saw was this guy's head blown out. Every time I'm happy or congratulated for something, I see that Iraqi's head. Every time something bad happens, I'm expecting someone to attack me. I'm never at peace. I work at my bakery, and it feels like a war zone."

"I think you said it best, Jake," Henry said. "Fight or flight. We as humans evolved to respond to certain moments of high stress by either running or fighting back. We in the military have trained for years to react to those types of situations of fight or flight in a very specific way. Which usually includes shooting at the source of the stress. Unfortunately, times of excitement and joy can also be stressful, and some memories can come back at the worst times. Having a flashback during a birthday party is not a fun moment—let me tell you. We were trained, and well, to react to those times of stress, so we must now train ourselves to react differently to those same stimuli. It will take time, but it will get better."

"Can I go next?" Jamarcus asked, and everyone nodded in response. "I was part of a Ranger unit that was the first to push into Baghdad. That rotary you went through, Martha, was where our company holed up and patrolled."

"I'm sorry," Martha said. "I didn't mean to imply anything."

"It's okay. Really," Jamarcus replied. "The thing was, our company was the first one into the southeast part of Baghdad. My platoon was the one who cleared out that rotary that allowed all the other convoys to enter the city. We got our asses kicked coming into Baghdad, and my platoon watched everyone riding in, screaming like they'd won the Super Bowl. It's in my top five weirdest things I've ever seen in my life.

"The only problem was, just like you said, Henry, it was a little too easy going into the city. Now our company was the only one in charge of patrolling that part of Baghdad. That was only two hundred twenty men to patrol that entire area. And because we blew into Baghdad, command thought there wouldn't be that much of a problem. But my men knew the Iraqi army hadn't gone away; they were living next door. The first couple weeks were fine, but when the US decided to leave the Baath Party out of government talks, that was when shit hit the fan.

"There had to have been a bomb that went off at least once a week. We were patrolling and carrying out raids that whole time, Martha. We just didn't have the numbers to cover the whole area. There were days when my men and I patrolled for over twenty-four hours straight. I still feel the pain from those patrols. I have panic attacks now when I have to stay on for sixteen hours or more at work.

"We did get the bozos who started the first wave of bombs in that region. My platoon was back from patrol, and my LT and I got summoned to the company commander's office, who was getting his ass chewed out by the command about the bombings in that area. So after we had just done a night patrol, we had to go right back out and find an IED that was placed on the major highway west of the Rotary.

"I was tired; my men were tired. I put two doughnuts and a large cup of sugar mixed with coffee in my belly, so I was amped up. We had to stop traffic going westbound, and the locals there were pissed, so I was pissed. We eventually found the IED, and I told a squad to stop traffic going eastbound. Those guys were pissed, so then I was even angrier. We called it in and waited for EOD, and this kid came out of nowhere, trying to cross the street right by what we thought was the bomb. I tried to get to him before he got close to it, but I failed. Since it didn't blow up when I got close, I was thinking that maybe I was wrong. I was feeling better when the thing blew up right behind me. One of my men dragged me back to our Humvee just in time for me to see two bozos watching the blast. They were the only two people standing outside of the apartments after the bomb exploded, and they were recording the whole time.

"I told my LT to call it in, and I ran toward the apartment before I gave anyone a chance to let them know I was going to get those guys. I was mad, just like you, Jake. I didn't see the kid, so I thought he was dead. And I thought those guys had recorded the whole thing. Just when a squad caught up with me, I saw those two bozos coming out of an upper-floor apartment, trying to climb onto the balcony of the next building. Now, they were not armed, so there was no reason for me to shoot. But I was too amped up on sugar to listen to my better judgment. I heard a voice in my head say, 'Don't shoot,' but I fired anyway, killing one and injuring the other. We went up into the apartment, and I found out there was a mother and her child in the apartment with the two men. I'd killed them both."

Jamarcus stared down at the ground, his stomach clenching up in pain. He knew he was scared but didn't want to say why. However, the horror of that day crept back within him, and he slammed his fist onto his lap as tears streamed down his cheeks.

"I'm so scared." Jamarcus wept. "I killed that family. There was no reason for me to shoot. I should have waited, but I didn't. The only reason I wasn't court-martialed was because, out of sheer luck, I shot down the two bombers. But it still hangs over my head. I'm still waiting for some cosmic judgment to punish my soul for all eternity. And I would gladly accept it. But the fact that I'm alive and they're dead is the worst nightmare to live in. I'm so scared."

"Where are your dog tags?" Henry asked.

"My dog tags?" Jamarcus said.

"Yeah. Do you still have them?"

"I keep them in a box with all my things next to my game console. I don't wear them because I want to forget about the war."

"You need to wear them," Henry said. "I do to remind me of what I did. I'll give you a bit of advice. That fear you feel now of the person you were in the army? Imagine that person as your dog tags. But I also see that person as a kid. Just like your son. Now, if we all had kids, we would love our kids with all of our hearts, no matter what those kids did. You have that kid now, Jamarcus, and that kid made a mistake in Iraq. If I had a kid who made a mistake, I would hold that kid as hard as I could and shower him with as much love as I could.

"That's what you need to do with those dog tags. Love that person with all your heart. Love yourself. Those things in the past can rob us of our sense of self-assurance and make us think we don't deserve to be happy. But that misery will never let us be happy, and the ones we care about around us will suffer because of it. You have to accept the fact that this person is who you are. You can't escape that. So you must love that person. Wear your dog tags with pride and wisdom. Because if you can't learn to love yourself again, no one will be able to fill that emptiness. Would anyone else like to share?"

Chapter 16
<1>
July 2010

"Go to the castle," Sneeze said as Jamarcus played his fantasy RPG late one summer night.

"Which one?" Jamarcus asked as he moved his character around.

"The one with all those soldiers at the front gates," Bernini said, and Jamarcus moved his character toward a castle up a steep hill. At the top of the hill, he saw a fortification on a road where soldiers in armor held their ground against waves of demons that kept pouring out of a gate of flames. Jamarcus could feel the nervousness from Bernini and Sneeze as he approached the gate, which made the experience more enjoyable. He knew that without their lights, he wouldn't have bothered to play the game.

Jamarcus checked his character, a brown-skinned lizard woman he called Sneeze, to make sure her health and armor were ready for a fight. There were no bug people in the game, so a lizard woman was the closest to Sneeze's appearance he could make.

"Am I ready?" Sneeze asked after Jamarcus was done.

"Yep. What should I do now?"

"Go ask those guards if they need any help," Sneeze said, and as Jamarcus approached the gate, he felt the anticipation build in

Sneeze's and Bernini's chests.

Jamarcus talked to the head guard, who asked Jamarcus to help the king of the castle push back the demons into their world.

"What did he say?" Bernini asked.

"You didn't understand?" Jamarcus asked.

"We don't speak your language, remember? We can only hear your thoughts."

"I'm sorry. He wants us to help push back the demons attacking the castle."

"Let's go," Sneeze clicked excitedly.

Jamarcus moved his character behind a group of fighters as they rushed a fire-engulfed gate that appeared. As he got close, imps and giant lizards ran forth from the portal and attacked Jamarcus. He felt the two kids leap in fear as a lizard struck the character.

"Kill it!" Sneeze shouted as Jamarcus blocked attacks and slashed his way through the demon horde. Every time the character was hit, his controller would vibrate, causing Sneeze and Bernini to jump into Jamarcus's soul. Jamarcus giggled every time that happened, until the first skirmish was over, and the gate disappeared.

"Am I hurt?" Sneeze asked as Jamarcus healed the lizard woman with a spell.

"It's no big deal," Jamarcus said after repairing the character's armor. He searched the slain creatures for any loot, finding a few pieces of gold here and a weapon there, until he searched for a creature that had a fork.

"What is that?" Bernini asked as Jamarcus stared at the television screen.

"A fork."

"Why does it have a fork?"

"I have no idea," Jamarcus answered, and he felt a silly laugh burst from Bernini and Sneeze. After he was done looting, he moved the woman after the group of fighters as they rushed the castle. There was another flaming gate inside the throne room, and more demons popped out of it, this time with a large hominid dragon with flames pouring out of its mouth leading the charge. Jamarcus felt Bernini and Sneeze hide inside his soul as he faced off against the monster. It was a tough battle, and Jamarcus had to use both weapons and spells, but he eventually beat the monster, with the two kids cheering inside him when he won.

"What's going to happen now?" Sneeze asked after Jamarcus finished restoring the lizard woman's health and armor.

"The king just asked us to go into the portal and stop what is causing the attacks from the other side," Jamarcus said as he positioned the character in front of the gate.

"We have to go inside?" Bernini asked, and Jamarcus felt the trepidation in his soul.

"That's the only way we're going to beat the game," Jamarcus said.

"Go in, so we can save the world," Sneeze said eagerly, and Jamarcus made the character jump through the flaming gate and into a scorched wasteland, where there was nothing but charred earth surrounded by rivers and lakes of lava. Above the character was a sky wreathed in fire and smoke. Everywhere he looked, Jamarcus saw demons walking around. The majority of the demons stood guard before a large black tower with metal thorns covered with what appeared to be blood protruding from its sides.

"We have to go in there?" Sneeze asked, her soul tainted with a little fear.

"We have to save the world, right?" Jamarcus laughed as he felt Bernini and Sneeze hesitate.

"That place is scary," Bernini said.

"Will you guys hurry up and decide?" Jamarcus yawned. "I'm getting pretty tired, and I need to go to bed."

"You want to go to bed?" Sneeze chirped in excitement. "Go to sleep. I want to play with you more."

"All right," Jamarcus said as he turned off the console and television. "Don't you guys bother me, though, while I'm in bed. Every time you do, you keep me awake."

"Okay," Bernini and Sneeze said as they slipped out of Jamarcus's consciousness.

Jamarcus changed clothes and opened his window to keep himself cool as he lay down. He only put the fan on at night and not the air conditioner, not wanting to run up his electricity bill. Being able to go to sleep with a fan blowing in his face was one thing Jamarcus was glad about from his tours in Iraq and Afghanistan.

It didn't take long for the light to pour through Jamarcus, and his consciousness left his body. As it did so, he saw Aten Ka fluctuating in the darkness of his mind before him. He was able to see six loops spinning now, and as he allowed more of the light to flow through him, Aten Ka grew brighter, until he was in the White, with the universe below him. He had gotten better at doing that, and by allowing more of the light to enter him again, he easily entered the Matrix, the place where there was nothing but endless rows of silvery spheres. Jamarcus assumed the spheres in that dimension were consciousness because no matter how hard he tried, he was never able to produce a body in that dimension. Because he saw only the spheres, he assumed he was a sphere also, and that sphere was his consciousness.

Another neat trick in that realm was that all he had to do was think of the place or person he wanted to see, and he was transported to that place. But before Jamarcus could reach out to Sneeze and Bernini, a force tugged on him. Not wanting to fight the force, Jamarcus allowed it to pull him through the Matrix. Around he flew through the spheres until, with a flash, he appeared above what looked like a college campus. It was a large facility with red brick buildings surrounded by hills and fields of maintained grass. Far off over a large hill, he saw an athletic building that stood before an athletic area that was three times the size of a football field.

As Jamarcus floated down toward a hill below him, he saw a thin woman who appeared to be in her late teens or early twenties. She had black hair that flowed halfway down her back. She wore a red-and-black prep school uniform that appeared to be for boys. She carried a backpack slung over one of her shoulders, and as Jamarcus floated next to her, he saw that her skin glowed white like Ixchel's, and her eyes were gray.

"Come on, Jamarcus," she said, and Jamarcus noticed that she spoke in a language he'd never heard before. It flowed like Spanish, but it wasn't. The woman grabbed Jamarcus's arm and led him down a hill, and he felt a huge sense of pride shining from her as she held on to his arm.

"I was supposed to play with Scar," Bernini complained in his mind as Jamarcus followed the woman on the sidewalk paths through the school buildings.

"I want Jamarcus to be my guard today," the woman said in her language.

"I'm going to tell Mommy," Bernini said. His soul was furious at the woman. Jamarcus felt the woman twirl her eyes in annoyance.

"Do whatever. I don't care. You can be so annoying."

With that, Bernini left them, and the woman continued to guide Jamarcus along. He saw many types of beings walking by them in the same school uniform, all eyeing them as if they were celebrities. Many were Andeans and Pleiadeans, but some were grays, either with darker or brown skin or with white complexions. Some beings were amphibious, birdlike, feline, and reptilian. Jamarcus was shocked when two giants with red hair walked over them. Almost all of them gave Jamarcus and the woman a side glance, which made the woman immensely happy. Soon a group of Andean females the same age as the woman, with different-styled black hair, approached her on tiptoe, their minds filled with mild shock and mischievous schemes.

"What are you doing, Rhiannon?" one of the women asked in the woman's language as they walked along.

"I want to hang out with Jamarcus," Rhiannon said in a serious tone. "He's been able to travel through Aten Ka, so I brought him here."

"Do your parents know what you're doing?" another asked, and Jamarcus began to feel the wily nature coming from Rhiannon.

"I'm allowed to have a guard wherever I go, and I want Jamarcus to guard me," Rhiannon said, and it felt as if, since she'd said it, it had to be.

"Did you agree to it, Scar?" one of the women asked Jamarcus, and Jamarcus shrugged as Rhiannon hugged his arms.

"I have no idea what's happening," Jamarcus answered truthfully, which made all the women laugh.

"You're so bad, Rhiannon," one of them said as they entered one of the buildings and walked their way through the crowds.

Jamarcus could feel the joy the women felt as they walked next to him. He felt as if he were walking next to the mean girls' clique in high school. They moved with pep in their step and their heads held a bit higher until they entered their classroom. The women sat in chairs at the back of the room, with Jamarcus sitting right behind Rhiannon in an extra seat. They talked among themselves until their professor, a being who appeared to be a Zeta Reticuli, entered the classroom and began the class.

"Hey, man," an Andean called out to Jamarcus, and as Jamarcus looked at the being's light, he saw that the man previously had been a human.

"Hey, guy," Jamarcus said. "Your name is Courtney, right?

How's it going?"

"Cool. How about you?"

"I'm just trying to figure out what's going on right now," Jamarcus said.

"Yeah. Lady Rhiannon does what she wants sometimes. Hey, guess where I grew up?"

When Jamarcus searched his mind, he smiled in recognition of what he saw. "Virginia Beach. That's pretty cool. Right by where I live also."

"Yeah," Courtney said. "My light parents sent me through the ascension process. I left my human form about fifty years ago, and here I am. It's grueling, but I'm so happy I went through it. I never would have been able to live the life I have now back on Earth. It's worth it."

"I guess, man."

"Can I ask you a question without pissing you off?" Courtney asked.

"Shoot," Jamarcus said.

"No offense. What does it feel like to be a black man back on Earth and to know that you're going to be a white prince here?"

"I don't know," Jamarcus said as he sat stunned by the question. Thinking about that concept was the only time Jamarcus had pondered what would happen after he left his body in earnest since he'd talked to Ra. Even after he'd looked at the boy in the crib in the nursery, he never had thought of the boy as real, as someone he would truly become. Just thinking about it made his mind fill with dissonance.

"I never really thought about it," Jamarcus said as he looked back at Courtney.

"Lord Scar, are you going to continue to disturb my class?" the professor asked as it peered into his soul with its unforgiving, large black eyes. Jamarcus then saw the entire class turn and face him with smiles on their faces.

"Sorry, Professor Sphere Pyramid," Jamarcus said. "I'll keep my mouth shut."

The professor looked at Jamarcus, and he felt its soul give him a raised eyebrow look before going back to the lesson. Rhiannon turned and slyly smiled at Jamarcus, and he shrugged before she turned back.

Jamarcus sat quietly throughout the class and the rest of Rhiannon's school day. All the while, he thought about Courtney's question. *That's probably the reason everyone stared at us as we walked by*, Jamarcus concluded as he walked with Rhiannon and she held him tightly. He was already famous to them. Jamarcus did not feel good about that. He was used to people either ignoring him or thinking less of him for being a black nerd.

After the school day, Rhiannon and her friends decided to shift to a restaurant to eat a meal before going home. Jamarcus noticed that when they ordered food, her friends used a debit card-like device to pay for their meals, but Rhiannon didn't; her meal was given to her automatically. The items they asked for looked similar to Earth-based food, except the equivalent of Earth's chicken seemed to be dinosaur-like animals.

"Sit next to me, Jamarcus," Rhiannon said as she sat at a table. When he did, she slid next to him, and she stayed close the whole time as she ate and talked with her friends.

"You know, I was worried about you," she said as her friends were talking among themselves.

"You were?" Jamarcus asked.

"Yes. I know you're in a lot of pain. I wish I could be there for you, but Mom said I can't."

"I hear she said the same thing about Thor and Athena."

"She said that about them because she and Daddy didn't want them to use your status to get things for them," Rhiannon said.

"That makes sense," Jamarcus said.

"But she said you were ready to be with me now. She didn't want you to be near me when you were younger." Rhiannon took a sip from her drink and looked up at Jamarcus. "You know we're not brother and sister right now, right?" she said, and Jamarcus felt butterflies fluttering in her stomach. "We're not even family. Your light is in another species' body. And you're a male. And I'm a female. One who loves you."

"So …"

"So nothing," she said as she hugged Jamarcus's arm. "Just right now, let's be friends on a date, okay?"

"Right," Jamarcus said as he watched Rhiannon join her friends' conversation.

<2>

Jamarcus floated in the darkness between Aten Ka and the sur-

281

face of the universe, observing the nature of the screen below him. It looked like a television screen to him, curved like the old cathode-ray tube television sets he had grown up watching. Jamarcus found he could manipulate reality on the surface of the screen much as he had when in the craft Bernini had arrived in. He scrolled around Earth for a bit, looking at different cities and watching the comings and goings of the people he saw.

When that became a bit creepy for Jamarcus, he decided to look around in the darkness to see if anything else was out there. When he expanded his consciousness, he felt another screen floating by, and he was able to mentally grab it and pull it near, or perhaps he moved his light to it. As Jamarcus inspected that universe, he saw a large grassy plain that sat on top of a cliff overlooking a large surface of water at midday. On the plain was a large rectangular gray-and-white castle. There was a large open area in the center of the castle, where Jamarcus saw a beautiful garden with three large trees and stairs that climbed toward one of the sides of the castle.

A long gravel road stretched away from the castle for miles, and on that road, he saw what appeared to be a limousine-like vehicle driving toward the building. The vehicle stopped on the gravel roundabout in front of the castle's main entrance just as two tall dark-gray-skinned beings with slanted black eyes, wearing clothing reminiscent of Near Eastern culture, emerged from the castle. They reached the back door of the limousine, and when they opened it, he saw a black human male in a dark military dress uniform exit the vehicle. He appeared to Jamarcus to be a hybrid of the dark grays next to him and a human. He walked toward the entrance and then paused as he turned toward four large animals that came racing at him. The beasts appeared to be lions but were shaggier than Earth's, with long maws and necks. The lions pounced on the man, biting his arms and curling into a ball at his feet as he petted them.

After the man played with the lions, he entered the castle, and Jamarcus used his light to look into the building and follow the man as he made his way through the many fancy corridors. He arrived in a banquet hall lined with extravagant paintings on the walls and lit by crystal chandeliers hanging from the ceiling. In the hall was an older dark gray being the same height as the hybrid. He wore similar clothing, but it was less formal. The hybrid knelt before the elder and then hugged him as they began talking about his trip home. They were soon interrupted by a young girl who came rushing toward the man. She was a toddler to Jamarcus's eyes, wearing a small red-and-white dress. Her skin was dark brown except for the top of her head and her elbows and knees, which were gray- and green-scaled. As the man picked up the laughing child, Jamarcus could feel in the minds of the two men that the elder dark gray was the girl's adoptive father, but the hybrid was the child's biological one.

Fascinated by what he had just seen, Jamarcus searched out in the darkness until he found another universe, and he looked inside that screen. In it, he saw people who were avian-like and just as diverse, with ducks, hawks, and fowl of different origins. The people Jamarcus saw seemed to live in an area similar to the Blue Ridge Mountains in an era reminiscent of the early twentieth century. The avian people lived in a coal mining town that was under the strict rule of the mine's greedy owner. The company that owned the mine even used the old practice of paying the people in the town in scripts instead of actual currency, forcing the workers to buy food and goods from the company's convenience store.

There was a trio of workers who were interested in Jamarcus. One was a red robin, another was a bluebird, and the third was a chubby white duck with a yellow bill. The three had somehow managed to find a group of hills that had a gold vein, and they mined the gold in secret, trying to get enough to leave the town rich.

Enforcers for the mining company found out about the gold and harassed the trio for the vein's location, threatening them and their families and even threatening the girlfriend of the robin, a green-and-brown duck. They couldn't go to the police, because they knew the police had been bought off by the mining company. Yet the trio never gave up their gold, denying that they had found anything in the hills.

One night, the enforcers grabbed the chubby duck and brought him to an abandoned house. Jamarcus watched in silent horror as the goons beat the duck for hours, trying to get the duck to give up the gold's location. The duck refused to speak and died at the enforcers' hands, which terrified the enforcers dearly.

When the other two found out the next day what had happened, they marched straight to the mine's goods store and the adjacent buildings with guns and torches. They proceeded to burn all the buildings down. When the lead enforcer confronted the two, a fight broke out, and two goons ended up getting shot but not fatally. However, the red robin beat the lead enforcer to death with his gun, and the two friends fled into the forest to avoid capture by the law. Jamarcus was so enthralled by what he was watching that he was startled when Ixchel appeared behind him.

"Did I frighten you?" Ixchel asked.

When Jamarcus turned to face her, he saw that she was wearing more traditional Andean clothing. "Yes, actually," he said as he floated next to her. "I was just focused on looking at the universes I found. They're amazing."

"You need to be careful as you watch them. The fact that you are capable of finding universes on your own and traveling to them means you have reached the seventh density. You will find that you can manipulate reality in the universes you contact. I came to warn you about that."

"I'm sorry," Jamarcus said in shock. "I didn't realize I could harm anyone."

"It is possible you may influence a being's light by accident if you are not careful. But do not be worried. It is a great feat that you have achieved. Very few lights are capable of reaching the seventh density."

"Thanks," Jamarcus said with a shrug. "Not sure how I did it. Not even sure what I'm doing."

"It can be confusing," Ixchel said. "There are not many cultures on your planet who can explain what is happening to you. Of those who can, I see that their cultures have mostly been disenfranchised. So it is easy to understand your ignorance."

"Father explained most of it," Jamarcus said. "About Aten Ka and how you said I needed to go vegan to have more of the light flow through me."

"He did not explain all of it," Ixchel said in a sober voice. "One of the reasons that a light chooses to descend into the third density is to increase the flow of Aten Ka through it. But there is another important element that I've barely explained to you, one I hope you are ready to understand."

"We're about to find out," Jamarcus joked to lighten the mood.

"Those two beings down in this universe, hiding in the forest— why do you believe they are hiding?"

"Because they're scared," Jamarcus answered. "They killed the guy they believe is responsible for the death of their friend. So they're running from a justice they think is unfair to them."

"Justice is irrelevant," Ixchel said. "They knew well in advance that killing that person and burning those buildings would get them in trouble, but they did it anyway. They understood the consequences of their actions, yet they chose to carry out a specific set of actions that possibly could have ended multiple lives and ruined the well-being of everyone in this town. Yet they still ran. Why?"

"I can't answer that," Jamarcus said.

"It is simple," Ixchel said. "They acted without thinking. It may seem more complicated than that, but it is the explanation for these two beings' decisions. They simply did not think. They understood the law in this area and what could happen to those they acted upon, yet their anger clouded their decisions. Now, I am not going to pass judgment on these two lights. I am an independent individual from another universe who has no input on any of the social institutions of this world that created this situation. However, if these two believe that what they did was the right thing, they should have been prepared to gladly face the consequences of their actions. But because they ran, ethically, they are no different from the person they killed. A person

286

who acts out of passion instead of reason.”

“Is that what I’m on Earth to learn?” Jamarcus asked. “To think before I act?”

“That is the most important thing any light can learn,” Ixchel said as she turned toward Jamarcus. “You will be a god. Whether you believe that or not is irrelevant. But as parents, your father and I must do everything we can to prepare you for that state of being. It would be folly to give such power to a light who cannot learn the actions of his ways when there are no consequences for his actions.

“If you were in this universe and were on this world, you could kill the same person these two beings killed, and nothing could happen to you, because you are a god. Think of the trauma the family of this being must be going through now. You may tell them that it was justice for what this man did to their friend, yet the pain of their lost loved one will not go away.

“Let us imagine that you decide to bring everyone back to life and restore the body and light of everyone who was killed. Will that trauma go away? Did you learn anything from this experience—the morals of killing a life for whatever reason? Did these beings learn from what happened, and what will they learn if they now know that light can remove the consequences of killing a life? Will they kill again and without thought?

“There must be consequences to our actions, good and bad, so that we as lights may learn what consequences we are willing to face, for better or for worse.”

“Well, I can tell you one thing,” Jamarcus said. “I have made some choices on Earth that I regret. Not a moment goes by that I don’t think about them. But they happened. And I can't escape them. But these choices made me who I am now. I may not like it, but that's the way it is. I know now there are some things in my heart that I don't want to do unless push comes to shove. I can accept that. In a way, it may have been beneficial to have these things happen to me, as horrifying as that may sound."

"Would you say the same if you knew that some of those events were engineered?" Ixchel said as she stared right into Jamarcus's consciousness. "Would you say that if you knew that your father and I caused some of the events that happened to you throughout your life?"

Jamarcus floated in silence as he stared at Ixchel and into her heart. It was stern and unwavering, like a steel blade. But there was love too, a wise love that had experienced much and would not hesitate to do what she believed was right. The more Jamarcus studied her mind and her past experiences, of war and cunning politics, of peace and caring for her family, the more he truly understood her nature.

"You are not angry," Ixchel said. "Why?"

"If this was a year ago, I would probably try to kill you." Jamarcus laughed. "But if you are gods, then you must have a culture that is beyond what I have experienced. A culture that's similar to any in which parents raise children, but it must be more difficult if you're raising omnipotent beings. You would have to do things that I understand would seem terrible to most mortals like myself. But I understand. Hell, I can see that if you do half a decent job, a child could seem like a pampered brat."

"Which brings me to you and Rhiannon," Ixchel said, and Jamarcus could feel her tough love plunge into his mind.

"Walked right into that, didn't I?" Jamarcus chuckled.

"I know she dragged you around university a while back. I would advise you against doing that again. Or interacting with her in solitary."

"I would agree to that," Jamarcus said ruefully.

"Rhiannon does not have any memories of you as her little brother, as Thor or Athena do," Ixchel said. "Bernini sees you more as a big brother, so it is fine for you to play with him. But Rhiannon only knows you as a male from another world whose light is now very bright. And in our culture, a bright light is very desirable. More than who or what that being may be."

"I think I felt that from everyone who saw us," Jamarcus said. "Everybody looked at us like we were famous."

"You are. Everyone on Nima knows who you are. You both are gods to many nations. And you probably feel how that got into Rhiannon's head."

"She did seem to do as she pleased, even though she's well-centered."

"That is because she has lived for one hundred sixty-seven cycles with everyone she knows adoring her," Ixchel said. "She lives believing that who or what you are is important. You know that is not true."

"Damn right," Jamarcus grunted. "It's not who or what you are that's important. It's what you do. What you do can have a terrifying way of defining you." He looked back down at the universe they floated above. "Mama?" Jamarcus said, and he felt Ixchel's heart skip when he said that word.

“Yes, sweetheart?”

“I hope one day I can thank you for what you’ve done for me,” Jamarcus said.

“I hope so too, sweetheart.”

Chapter 17
<1>
September 2010

Jamarcus lazily walked around his bedroom, gathering his clothes and putting them into his laundry hamper. He searched the rest of his apartment for anything that needed cleaning as he slowly marched about, moaning like a zombie. He wanted to lie down and go to sleep, but that afternoon was his only free time outside of school and work to do the chores around his apartment. He already had gone to the grocery store and bought food for the next week, and he knew that while he still had the energy, he'd better get his laundry done, or it wouldn't get done.

He grabbed some quarters to feed the washing machine, gathered the detergent and hamper, and grudgingly left his apartment, sluggishly making his way to the apartment complex's laundry room. He watched a car drive into the parking area past him and mused to himself that he always seemed to step outside his apartment when a vehicle was driving by. It was almost uncanny.

When he walked into the building, he saw one of his neighbors: an older woman with large hips, wearing yoga pants and a sports top. She was taking her items out of a washer and putting them into a nearby dryer when Jamarcus walked up next to her.

"Hey, Bethany," Jamarcus said as he opened up a washer.

"Hello, Jamarcus," Bethany said as she gave him a big, tight hug. "I haven't seen you in a while. How's school?"

"Tiring. Going to school right after I get off of work is kicking my ass. But I'm getting a lot of homework done at work."

"Is that why I don't see you? You changed shifts?"

"Yeah," Jamarcus said as he put his darks into another washing machine. "I got moved to the third shift because a new hire complained that she couldn't be with her family. As if my life was less important because I'm single. But I didn't complain. Like I said, more time for homework."

"Well, that's looking at the glass half full," Bethany said. "How many credits do you have left?"

"Well, I just got my associate's degree, so I'm halfway through."

"Congratulations," Bethany said, beaming up at Jamarcus. "Just keep going, even when things get dark."

"Yeah." Jamarcus sighed as he put his whites into a different washer. "Crawling through that dark tunnel is hard, but I'm beginning to see the light."

"What are you going to do after you get your bachelor's?" Bethany asked as she began loading more of her things into a dryer.

"Well, a degree in anthropology is useless unless you have a PhD. So I'm hoping my grades stay high enough to get a scholastic scholarship when I get my bachelor's."

"You'll get it. I know you will."

"What about you?" Jamarcus asked after he put quarters into the machines and started them. "How have you been lately?"

"Oh God," Bethany said as she turned on her dryer. "My Saints lost last weekend. My team is going to give me a heart attack one day, I swear."

"They look pretty solid this year. They may go far into the play-offs."

"Don't patronize me, Jamarcus. Our defense is horrible. We got rolled over by the Browns, of all teams. That's not good."

"They did beat a couple of teams, right?" Jamarcus said. "Glass half full."

"Depends on what type of water we're talking about," Bethany said as she leaned against a machine. "Who's your team?"

"Redskins," Jamarcus said as he leaned on a machine next to her. "I'm just glad I saw them win two Super Bowls in my life."

"And they won one with that black quarterback too."

"Doug Williams. That was pretty awesome to see."

"What about that other black quarterback who's with the Eagles now?" Bethany asked.

"I know who you're talking about. Yeah, he's really good. I hope he does well on that team."

"Too bad what happened to him. But those poor animals. And I love dogs—you know that."

"I can't judge him myself," Jamarcus said. "I did some things

I regret back in Iraq, so I'm not going to pretend I'm a saint compared to him. But we all have to suffer the consequences of our actions. That's what this life on Earth is for. At least he's getting another chance."

"Oh, I just remembered," Bethany said as she patted Jamarcus's arm. "I wanted to ask you about President Obama going on that apology tour when he was elected. I was talking to a few friends of mine about you, and they wanted to know how you felt about that."

"Everyone seems to be talking about it on the news," Jamarcus said as he winced. "But then most news channels focus on things that will get the most ratings, not if they care about what they report."

"I don't think it's right. You went over there and risked your life to give Iraqis the same freedoms we have as Americans. Why do you have to apologize for that?"

"It's tough," Jamarcus said. "We're living in a world now that is culturally different from the one we lived in ten or twenty years ago. It'll take time for us to walk through the darkness and figure out the right way to handle a situation like that."

"I can't understand why he has to apologize to the world like that," Bethany said. "It makes Americans look weak. Is it the whole Muslim–Christian thing?"

"I think I may understand what's going on, but I may be an archaic dumbass," Jamarcus said. "But listen to this argument. We were raised in the US, being taught one narrative about the history of the United States. We're taught that the ones who framed the Constitution are the forefathers because you can't have a nation creation without a divine origin story. And we're taught that all the rights and liberties we have, our health care, and the economy are the best in the world and that we're the ones who did it first.

"These are misconceptions. The writers of the Constitution didn't write it out of thin air. They took a lot of parts from the British and French constitutions, almost word for word, and reframed them to fit their philosophy. The rights we have now didn't start in the US either. Many nations in Europe already had abolished slavery. France's highest general below Napoleon was a black man. Hell, I'd probably have been lynched back then for talking to you."

"There were interracial couples back then," Bethany said.

"They were few and far between," Jamarcus said. "But like I was saying, the first democracy in the West was Iceland, and they had the first female members of a congress and president. You wouldn't know this growing up in the US because that knowledge isn't needed in American culture. Plus, the currency and health care in other nations in Europe are arguably better than in the US.

"Now let's take the viewpoint of people who grow up in Iraq. They're taught that civilization itself was created in Iraq thousands of years ago. There literally wouldn't be a US, a Constitution, or rights if they hadn't been invented in Iraq first. To add to that, all of mankind originated from Iraq; the gods came down and created the first humans on Earth there. That's not me or them saying that if Adam and Eve were an ethnicity, they were Iraqi. Plus, equal rights and the ability to vote are guaranteed to women and minorities in Iraq.

"Yet women and minorities are treated like shit over there; some are outright killed in the streets. Since the US occupied Iraq, the Iraqi men who were taken out of power took their frustration out on the

Kurds. They killed a Kurdish woman protesting for women's rights—snuck right into her home and killed her in the middle of the night. The government and police aren't going to do anything about it. Some of them approve of the violence. I know—I've seen it. Why would they care about the rights of minorities and women if the cultures that allow that are ignored?

"The problem I think we have with the US presence in Iraq—and I'm pretty sure I'm 99.99 percent wrong about this—is that we live in a culture that only sees the machine and not the ghost. We keep thinking that our consciousness is found in our bodies, but no one has even come close to proving that. There may be studies that say that culture and ethnicity are caused by nature and the environment. That's great, but what are the body and environment affecting? What is the thing we identify with? If it was the body, then every black male and every white female should act the same and only have slight changes based on the environments they find themselves in. And we know that's bullshit. That still doesn't account for the unique individual who pops up every so often. Maybe what's being identified isn't in the machine.

"If we lived in a world where we could see the ghost, maybe a lot of these issues could be solved. But unfortunately, we live in one where only the machine matters. And in the case of the US and Iraq, I think we have a problem that we can't imagine ourselves in the other person's machine and realize that we would believe in the same things other people do if our ghost had been raised somewhere else. But I don't want to think that all I did over there was nothing but a tragedy for the Iraqi people. I know I did some good over there, or I hope I did. I'm already having a hard time sleeping at night because of thinking otherwise.

"Now, for me, I don't understand why the president can't say, 'Yes, we made mistakes in Iraq.' I made them. 'But the democracy being created there is for the benefit of the region and the world.' Or I could be full of shit."

"You've thought hard about this, haven't you?" Bethany asked.

"Well, I'm majoring in anthropology," Jamarcus responded. "All we teach ourselves in our cultures is based on what we find in the material. No one considers what the soul has to do with anything. But maybe that's too metaphysical."

"Oh, by the way," Bethany said as she pulled her cell phone out of her top, "my friends and I went to the flea market, and I found this sign. It is so funny." She flicked through the images on her phone as she pressed her hips against Jamarcus. When she found what she was looking for, she raised the phone so he could see it. It was a sign in fancy red, white, and blue lettering: "Beware. My dog bites Democrats." Jamarcus stared at the picture with no expression on his face.

"Oh, come on," Bethany said when she didn't get the response she wanted. "It's funny. It's all in good fun."

"I don't think it's funny," Jamarcus said.

"Don't tell me you're one of those politically correct people now."

"This doesn't have to do with anyone's politics. I don't think it's funny."

"Don't tell me you're a Democrat," Bethany said.

"No. I'm not a Republican either. I just have this innate ability to think for myself."

"People are just not allowed to speak freely now, I guess."

"No, that's not it, Beth. I don't think you heard me. Can I ask you something? Well, a bunch of things?"

"Okay."

"You're a Republican, I'm assuming?"

"Yes," Bethany answered.

"Why are you a Republican?"

"Because I believe in this country. I believe that the forefathers who created this nation made it in a way that would bring freedom to this world. As a Christian, that is something I deeply believe in."

"Do you truly believe that being a Republican is the best way to live?" Jamarcus asked.

"Wholeheartedly," Bethany said.

"Do you want Democrats to live this way?"

"Democrats will never change their ways," Bethany said. "These young kids get taught in school to hate their country. There's nothing but socialists in these colleges, and they are corrupting our youth. I hate Democrats."

"No, you don't," Jamarcus said, rubbing his forehead in frustration. "I don't care about colleges. Or socialists. I'm talking about you. Do you think the world would be a better place if we were all Republicans?"

"I truly believe that's what God wants," Bethany said.

"Then how would you convince a Democrat of that?"

"You'll have to beat them over the head with a baseball bat," Bethany joked.

"You're not getting what I'm saying." Jamarcus sighed. "Look, my rant about the president's apology and Iraq wasn't based on my political views that I'm trying to force down someone's throat. I say those things out of true empathy for the individuals I'm trying to understand. I do it out of love. If I made a mistake in my reasoning, then I'm open for someone to explain to me how I'm wrong in a civilized way. I went to war and killed people because politicians couldn't come together and talk with compassion and reason. Because nobody thinks about their actions. Everything I do now is out of love for my fellow person. And if I'm wrong, then I'm wrong. But I'd rather be wrong for trying to do the right thing than for doing something without thinking."

"Maybe you just think too much," Bethany said.

"There's nothing illegal about thinking too much." Jamarcus laughed.

<2>

"This is Nima, your mother's home world," Ra said as he and Jamarcus floated above an alien planet. It appeared to be a world composed of many island continents separated by large riverlike oceans. The climate on the planet was similar to Earth's, although Jamarcus didn't see any hurricane-like weather patterns on the surface he was watching. The weather in the world was rather peaceful. The small continents looked like massive versions of the Polynesian islands of the Pacific. Just by looking at the patterns of the continents, Jamarcus could imagine in his mind the many enormous magma chambers and lava vents that had created the landmasses under the ever-changing oceans.

"That's where we live," Ra said as he directed Jamarcus's attention to a continent in the northern hemisphere of the planet that appeared arrow-shaped. The head of the arrow was dented inward at the western edge as the flow of the ocean weathered its way to the center of the continent. The ocean river split above and below the land and converged again on the eastern side. The central part of the island had tall, rocky mountains covered in snow. Surrounding the mountains was dense forest. There were two cities on the continent: one at the mouth of the indent on the west side and one on one of the many islands that dotted the southern part of the landmass.

"That's the city." Jamarcus gasped as he recognized the islands he'd visited in his dreams. "Is that where we live? What is the name of this place?"

"The city to the west is New Scarborough. I named it after your grandmother. It's a major trade hub on this planet for ships on and off-world."

"I can see that," Jamarcus said as he watched spacecraft in the hundreds leaving and landing in that city, with dozens flying to and from the southern city. "What's the name of the city to the south?"

"We didn't name it," Ra said bashfully. "I thought it felt awkward too. That city to the south is our home, Scar."

"Oh," Jamarcus said as he finally understood. "And the people who live there?"

"The people to the west all work for the different magnates and nations on and off Nima. The ones where we live work for us—for the many businesses and entertainment services we own."

"How many live in this world?"

"On the continent we live on, just over one million," Ra answered. "On the planet at one time, most likely just over a billion, depending on how trade is doing."

"So how does the economy work in the Federation?" Jamarcus asked as he turned and faced Ra, who wore a gray blazer with a white button-down shirt and dark slacks.

"'Equivalent trade' is the motto of the Federation," Ra said in an official tone. "Or at least that's what we like to believe. In essence, we trade in resources. Many people in our civilization either mine or grow the resources that they in turn trade for resources that they desire. It can be either a simple trade of the same mass or if one person is a craftsman in a skill—for example, making cars—that person receives an extra percentage of resources decided by the Council. Or by you when you are the speaker for our house. Right now, your mother and I have it set at ten percent."

"How do we get our cut of the pie?"

"If anyone uses our light for energy or travel, we ask for a certain amount of resources per month. If anyone uses our light to mine minerals and ores or to grow crops and livestock, whatever they make, we take another flat ten percent."

"How do we provide energy to these nations?"

"When we lower our resistance to Aten Ka and allow its light to flow through us, we increase the amount of pure matter in us. The more pure matter we can create, the greater our density will be. The increase of pure matter allows us to create pure energy, which we use to manipulate and pierce the waters of this and other universes."

"I think I'm following you," Jamarcus said. "This pure energy—it has a powerful electromagnetic field, which can create an induction current to anything it contacts. No matter what universe and, I'm also guessing, living or mechanical. How many nations do we supply energy to?"

"Us? Two hundred thirty-five across three galaxies in this universe, and we also provide for nations in several other universes."

"Aten Ka," Jamarcus said as he placed his brightly lit hands on his head. "The amount of resources you must gather must be nigh infinite."

"Technically," Ra said in a matter-of-fact tone.

"I guess owning a city is modest in a trans-universal civilization."

"Yes," Ra said, and Jamarcus felt laughter in his soul. "Your fiancée's father owns a planet."

"Ha." Jamarcus snorted as he tried to understand the nature of owning a world. "So what is the purpose of the Federation in all of this?"

"You have to understand, Scar, that the houses in the Federation are ruled by powerful beings," Ra said. "We are gods in every sense of the word. And these rulers have families that could act as pantheons to less dense beings. The Federation acts as a check and balance for us.

We may say that it's a coming together of many species and nations under the light of Aten Ka, but that's just the public image the Federation wants to create.

"If a culture wishes to join the Federation, they must agree to the policies of the government and guarantee the liberties of their people. If the culture has beings who can provide light to their people, we insist they do this. If the culture does not have the means to provide light as we do, we allow them to receive ours. If they don't, they'll still receive the protection and services of being in the Federation in exchange for equal trade in resources. We also try to intermingle with any species that enter the Federation as best as we can so that we are all one people and one culture."

"That's why I'm to marry Sneeze?" Jamarcus asked.

"Yes," Ra said. "You are to be the speaker for our house, which is the same as the president of the United States in your nation you live in. Each nation in our house is like a state in your country. Most are ruled by royalty because of their densities, and some are governed by democratic societies. The other houses are centered on individuals who provide light for them.

"The majority of civilizations are based on those who can provide light for a planet. Fewer still are those that are centered on individuals who provide energy to star clusters. When we decided to have you be the speaker for our house, Thor and Athena decided to build nations on their own. Thor provides travel and trade for species across star clusters. Athena is providing light for a solar system.

"But the nations that don't have beings who can provide light as we do join houses like ours. Your job as speaker will be to make the decisions on how the nations and species will be governed. To deal with trade and handle military issues. Not to rule but to help facilitate the services the nations need. With that in mind, I want you to accompany me to a few diplomatic meetings so you can better understand what the speaker of our house does."

"All right," Jamarcus said. "I'm confused about something, however."

"What's that?" Ra asked.

"We only have two hundred thirty-five cultures in our house?" Jamarcus asked. "In this universe?"

"Yes."

"How many smaller nation groups are there?"

"Thousands."

"How many houses are there?"

"Seven," Ra said.

"If we have access to the multiverse, that should be hundreds of trillions of people. That's not that many beings," Jamarcus said.

"There are infinite sentient lights in the omniverse, but only a relative handful have ascended their light to Aten Ka."

"Yeah, that makes sense. And you say there are only seven houses?"

"Yes. Houses are usually centered on beings who have reached the ninth density, and that is a very rare thing. The amount of trauma a being must go through to get that high would drive any light insane. Of the seven houses, there are only ten beings in this multiverse who have reached the ninth density or higher. I see that you will be the eighth house. That's why it was important for you to earn the title of speaker for our house; it couldn't be given to you. And after your life ends on Earth, you still have hundreds of cycles to go until you can officially become the speaker. We needed you to learn how to be a leader, to love peace, and to have understanding for beings different from you. When needed you to become a proper light before you become a god."

"Mama explained that to me," Jamarcus said as he looked down at Nima. "I told her that a year ago I would have killed you guys for what you did to me. Now I completely understand. It reminds me of the story of the Buddha, a religious figure on Earth. He was a guy who had everything, but he still thirsted for something that material wealth and possessions couldn't give him. So he left the comfort of his little personal universe only to discover the horrors of the real world. After meeting an ascetic monk who looked at peace in that world, he gave up everything he had and decided to live that same lifestyle.

"He learned all he could from the monks who taught him, but he left them because he still desired more. So he spent years in self-induced suffering until coming to rest under a tree. He meditated for days until he had a terrible nightmare. He first saw a being that represented the fear of death. The spirit tried to dissuade the Buddha, but he wasn't scared of dying. Next, three more spirits came to him: one representing the body's need to consume, one representing the mind's apathy and discontentment, and one representing our desire for material things. Buddha pushed those spirits aside like the wind, and his consciousness floated up until he could see a star, his Aten Ka. He had reached enlightenment.

"I realize now that for someone to let go of the physical and to focus solely on Aten Ka, the most efficient way to do it is to cause that person to experience pain from everything the material can offer. And when nothing in this world can bring you joy, you either go insane or learn to love yourself—to find peace in your light and to develop it—until you become the person you want to be. It just so happens that when you do that, Aten Ka enters your soul."

"I was afraid to tell you this," Ra said, "because of all the things we caused in your life. Because of what I am."

"Don't worry about that," Jamarcus said as he waved his hand at Ra. "Like I said, I understand now. And the thing with me being uncomfortable with what you are and with what I'll become? That's just racism on my part. That's something I must overcome. The physical appearance of a light doesn't matter, no matter how much the world I live in tells me so. Now I understand. It's just as you said. Don't focus on your form; focus on your light."

"That's right," Ra said with a smile. "I'm so glad you understand."

"Except for the vegan part." Jamarcus laughed. "That's kicking my ass."

"You need to keep that up," Ra said. "It's important not to falter now. It would set you back months if you do. Even years."

"Yes, Papa," Jamarcus said, and his soul felt a little better when Ra's light grew brighter from hearing that word.

Chapter 18
<1>
December 2010

"Today we are going to talk about existentialism," Professor Green said as he leaned on his desk, "which is a form of philosophy coined by a bunch of dead white guys. It gained popularity in the nineteenth to twentieth century, but its roots go much further back. It traces its roots back to Plato, as we in this class seem to have figured out. Just to remind everyone, this is a class on Western philosophy. If you remember, Plato gave us the concept of critical thinking, although many still attribute that to Socrates. But since there is still no definitive proof that Socrates even existed, we're going to stick with what Plato wrote about him.

"It was said that an oracle told Socrates he was the wisest man in all of Athens. Since he was perplexed by this, he decided to go around the city, asking everyone he met what was the best way to run the city-state. When he asked a politician, that person said it should be ruled by laws and regulations. When he asked a merchant, that individual used normal business jargon: maintain a budget, and always seek a profit. When Socrates asked a soldier, that person said Athens needed secure borders and a well-kept and strong army. When Socrates contemplated these answers, there was one thing he noticed.

"While everyone he'd asked had given an answer based upon his own life experiences, Socrates was the first one to admit that he had no idea how to run Athens. His interpretation was that he was the only one to admit that there were some things he didn't know and that if he was to form an idea about something, he needed to base it on actual empirical facts and not on conjecture or beliefs, no matter how much easier it was to do so.

"Then we get to Descartes and his meditations. We just finished studying how one day, Descartes was chilling in his apartment, enjoying his white-male-privilege lifestyle—yes, I said it; let's move on. He realized that he wasn't sure of anything that was around him. He wasn't sure about the clothes he wore or the bed he lay on. He even got metaphysical about a honeycomb in his home. You have to be privileged to focus on that.

"So anyway, he began to question his very existence and hypothesized that perhaps an all-powerful evil genius had created the universe and even him, and perhaps he wasn't real. But he soon dispelled that notion by coming up with one of the most important phrases in Western civilization: 'Cogito, ergo sum,' or 'I think, therefore I am.' But just as Descartes came upon that eloquent notion, he quickly made a Socratic mistake and assumed that since he believed there was a God, there had to be a God and boom—he crapped all over his logic. Now, to all the religions out there, we are focusing on existentialism, so don't get in a tizzy.

"Now we are going on to our main man: Sartre. Not our boy Nietzsche, who everyone says influenced the Third Reich, although he had nothing to do with it. He was already dead for over twenty years before Hitler rose to power. Anyway, back to our homeboy Sartre. Now, Sartre grew up in a life that he called bourgeois, which he always denounced, although he wouldn't have gotten that education his without the bourgeois life. Go figure. So because of his lifestyle, he went to college and began to study philosophy, among other things. But then he had to go to war and fight the Naazees. And he got captured by the Naazees."

"Why do you have to say *Nazis* that way?" one of the students asked with a chuckle, and the rest of the class laughed.

"How else am I going to say *Naazees*?" Professor Green argued. "So Sartre got captured by the Naazees. And because of his health and no small part that he was a French bourgeois college student—I hope you get the gist of what I'm saying—he was released by the Naazees and got a cozy job at a university.

"At that time, the rest of the world was fighting the Naazees, and Sartre was incapable of fighting the Naazees traditionally, so he began to write his most important works. He wrote some anti-Naazee articles in some magazines, but they didn't care. He was a French bourgeois. Yet Sartre felt that the French's complacency, and even his own, was wrong in an obvious way that Sartre was trying to understand at the time.

"But he was affected by what he saw during the German occupation of France. Just after the war, he began to work in earnest. He wrote *Anti-Semite and Jew*, in which he tried to get to the bottom of what hatred was. Yet his best and most well-known work was *Being and Nothingness*, a book he wrote during the occupation. In it, he laid down some of the foundations of modern existentialism.

"One of his arguments is the concept of existence before essence, or that we are free-thinking people before we are our physical forms. We are not an ethnic group or culture. We are not rich or poor, left or right, religious or atheist. We are free-thinking individuals, and we can only be defined by our actions and the consequences of our actions. To base our lives on anything relating to the previous notions is to act in bad faith. To Sartre, it was better to act in life as a good person than to be a stereotype or have the world tell us what we must be."

"I'm sorry," Thelma said as she sat up in her chair. "I just can't accept that. I'm a black woman. There are so many bad stereotypes about black women out there. We're always angry. We're ugly. I embrace that I'm a black woman. I love who I am. It is my very essence that I derive my strength from. Why is it wrong to gain strength from?"

"Because to Sartre, that doesn't mean jack shit," Professor Green said.

"How is that jack shit? Being a black woman is the most important part of who I am."

"Because how would you be different from a rich, privileged white guy if all you received in life was from being a pretty black chick?"

"There's nothing wrong with being a pretty black chick," Thelma said as everyone in class erupted in laughter.

"But look at Sartre's life," Professor Green said. "This is a guy who got a good education, was captured and released by Naazees, and had a great job during occupied France while he criticized the country that occupied them, all because he was a rich white guy. He wasn't even all that good-looking. Sartre realized the fallacy behind that way of thinking and wrote to destroy that way of thinking. He realized that a Jew was just as capable of doing his job, frankly, because he replaced a Jew at the college he worked at. What will define you from other pretty black chicks are your actions and the consequences of your actions. To act just on you being black or being pretty is what Sartre called the absurd.

"Now, the absurd is a concept that there is nothing in life beyond what we know. Thelma, you are beautiful and black—"

"Thank you," Thelma said with a smile.

"You're welcome," Professor Green said.

"Hey, now, easy with the fraternizations!" a student called out.

"Don't hate on the player," Professor Green said. "So, Thelma, you live your life based only on the fact that you are female, beautiful, and black. So you go forth in life thinking and acting in a way that these virtues are important, and you derive a career from this. You become a model or an actress—"

"Heh," Thelma said with a twirl of her head.

"But something happens," Professor Green said. "You get into a car accident. You are burned on your face and a good portion of your body. Your face is disfigured, and the complexion of your skin is ruined. This all but ruins your job as a model. If your whole life was based only on the belief that you are a beautiful black woman, you may think your life is over. To believe this is absurd.

"Your existence is not based solely on what you are but on what you do. You can go to school like you are doing now. You could get a degree in philosophy. You could present a new idea of universal truth that makes every college professor pee their pants. Will you face obstacles in life because you're a black woman? Yes. Will being a black woman in and of itself stop you from reaching any goals you set? Not if you choose differently. To base our lives on any concept or belief system outside of the hard facts we know and the decisions we make on those hard facts is absurd. We must push aside any form of thinking that contradicts our authenticity, no matter if it's our political views or the commandments of God."

"I don't think you have to disregard the Word of God," Melanie said. "You can find meaning in his message, a source of morality."

"Sartre would disagree with you," Professor Green said. "To find meaning in anything other than your consciousness is to deny your authenticity. You're not truly thinking for yourself. You're allowing another to think for you."

"No, I'm not," Melanie said. "If you are going to tell me that the Ten Commandments are absurd concepts, I don't know what to tell you."

"Nobody disagrees with that to a point," Jamarcus said. "It's just wrong to believe that no one else on this planet could have come up with those ideas on their own. Hell, the Ten Commandments were practically taken from the Egyptian Book of the Dead."

"But God is real," Melanie said. "No matter what anyone can say in this room, there is overwhelming evidence that God exists, that he did things in the past, and that Jesus is real."

"I don't know that there is absolute evidence of God existing," another student said.

"What about Israel leaving Egypt?" Melanie said. "There is evidence that the plagues did happen, causing Ramses to let Israel go. We know that Hebrews did live in Egypt. We know that certain events of the Exodus happened. The parting of the Red Sea happened. There've been chariots found at the bottom of the Red Sea that date back to the time of Israel's departure from Egypt."

"Well, for one, we know that a volcano was erupting around the period when most scholars believe Israel left Egypt," Jamarcus said. "It's safe to say that a volcano can erupt without the intervention of God. Next, the Red Sea parts all the time. Just like the Bible said, if you go to the right part of the Red Sea with the right tide going out and the wind is blowing in a specific direction, the sea parts for you. Tourists walk it all the time. I'm pretty sure those who found the chariots found them during those exact conditions."

"What about the miracles in the Bible?" Melanie said. "Jesus healing the leper. Restoring sight. Feeding a large group of people with two loaves of bread and some fish. What about Moses seeing the burning bush? Moses was real—why would he lie about that?"

"I don't think the existence of God or Moses matters in this topic," Jamarcus said as other students grumbled about Melanie's statement. "The argument of what Moses saw in the burning bush is focused on the wrong subject, I think. We should focus not on the fire in the bush but on Moses.

"What is Moses's education—his understanding of the world? Does he know what God is? Do any of us have a definitive answer on what God is? And if that is the case, how is Moses to know what God is when he sees God? Let's say it wasn't Moses who saw a presence in a burning bush. Maybe it was a theoretical physicist who saw the burning bush. If this person saw the burning bush and heard it say, 'I am what I am,' that person would probably think Popeye was getting high back there.

"I can make the same argument about a physicist observing an experiment to try to understand the duality of an electron. He experiments, and after many repeated attempts, he can't seem to find the exact location of an electron. He comes up with a different experiment based on what he's learned. He tries again yet still can't separate the particle from the wavelength.

"Maybe it's not the experiment or the particle but the person who is observing the experiment that is the issue. It's A + B = C, wherein A is the person observing the phenomena, B is the experiment, and C is the result of the experiment. The physicist thinks that by redefining B, he will finally understand what C is, but he won't accept the fact that he hasn't defined what A is.

"What is observing the experiment? What is observing the burning bush? What is deciding to be recognized as a hot black chick? If we can conclude what that is, what consciousness is, maybe we can get some answers on what is going on in this universe or if there is a God.

"And even if there is a God, it still doesn't take away the importance of our consciousness. We fundamentally make decisions on what is real in this world, no matter how faulty our thinking is. What if it's not that we exist because God exists but rather that God exists because we think he exists? Who is more important in that relationship then—God or us?"

"May I get back to teaching this class, Jamarcus?" Professor Green asked.

"My bad, Professor Green," Jamarcus said sheepishly. "I didn't mean to get carried away."

"Yet you did, and you'll just have to live with that," Professor

Green said. "Which is a good segue into the next topic in existentialism, which is facticity, or coming to identify with what we did in the past."

<2>

After Jamarcus traveled through Aten Ka, his light settled in the living room of his father's house in Suburbia. It took a while for the light of Aten Ka to fade back and reveal a modernly decorated living room that seemed space age and classic at the same time, like a scene from a sci-fi movie from the 1970s. The most notable feature of the room was that many of the furniture pieces and structures were made of natural material but also were missing parts. For example, the large polished wooden table and the chairs pulled up to it were not standing on legs.

In the center of the room were different items on the floor, such as cups and spoons, toys of animals, and other knickknacks, all with what appeared to be Post-it slips with alien writing on them. The lettering was the same as that found in the majority of the books in the library, yet the words didn't imprint into Jamarcus's mind the way the books did. Ixchel had written the notes, wanting Jamarcus to learn some of their language without having the words inputted in his light. As Jamarcus sat down and picked up a cup, he had to laugh at how Ixchel seemed to still treat him like a child instead of a grown adult.

"God dammit, woman," Jamarcus mumbled as he put down the cup. "I'm a grown-ass man."

"I heard that," Ixchel said boldly in Jamarcus's soul, causing him to snort a quick chuckle.

Jamarcus looked around the living room at the white walls and wooden shelves. The wall in front of the backyard was missing, and he could see the dark grass and solitary tree beneath the night sky. In one corner of the room, Bernini sat in front of a floating holographic screen that was locked into a position, getting frustrated with a platform game he was playing. Jamarcus walked over and sat next to him, smiling at his attempts to pass the level he was on. He could feel Bernini's excitement and anger every time he played only to die at some point.

"Scar, help me!" Bernini gave the controller to Jamarcus.

As Jamarcus grabbed it with his light hands, he felt his consciousness meld with the device so that he could feel and control the squat Andean character on the screen. Jamarcus moved around a bit, trying to figure out what he could do. The character was able to kill creatures by jumping on top of them, but that took multiple tries, so it was better to avoid them. Once things got going, Jamarcus could see the problem Bernini was facing. Many of the enemies went into the fourth dimension, where they would disappear and reappear at set sequences or smack reality to make movement harder for the character.

There was a boss at the end of the level who kept thwarting Bernini's attempts to pass. It was a big cloud entity that floated above a moving circular platform that floated in space. The platform was a good distance from another platform that had the exit. The mean cloud would grab him with space-time, and depending on how far he stretched space out as it tried to pull him in, space would sling him in the opposite direction. He couldn't attack the cloud, as it would harm him if he touched it, and he only had a certain amount of time before space slung him back to the cloud once it was attached, and if he aimed wrong, he would fall off.

Jamarcus figured out that if he positioned himself in the center of the spinning platform and waited for the cloud to grab him, he had to pull as hard as he could in the direction opposite the exit platform. Once time expired, he was yanked back at the cloud and took damage, but he was also flung to the exit.

Bernini cheered as Jamarcus moved to the next level, and his pure, radiant joy shone into Jamarcus. But something was off. Jamarcus realized he felt Bernini's joy, but he felt no satisfaction as he figured out the level—and Jamarcus loved video games. It was the same emptiness that nagged at him every time he wanted to feel good about something. Whenever he hung out with his friends, played online, or even rode his motorcycle, he sensed an emotion build inside him that felt close to nostalgia, but a memory of his time at war would shove its way to the forefront of his mind, stealing whatever bliss he'd almost had. He just couldn't allow himself to be happy.

A knock came on the front door of the house, and Jamarcus naturally gave the controller back to Bernini and proceeded to open the door. He stopped in a hallway when he realized he had no idea where he was going; the notion that he had faded like a forgotten memory.

"Ra, can you answer the door?" Ixchel shouted from a room upstairs.

"Yeah," Ra said, and after a few footsteps, he appeared, climbing down stairs that weren't connected to anything behind Jamarcus in the hallway. He had on a suit that was red, green, and brown and looked rustic and fancy at the same time. Ra patted Jamarcus's face as he walked by on his way to the front door. As Jamarcus followed him to the entrance, they entered a small corridor, where Ra let in a tall biracial boy of Pleiadean and Andean descent, much like Rhiannon. Jamarcus felt that he was only a teenager in maturity as the boy smiled at him with white hair and gray eyes.

"Hi, Lord Scar," the boy said with enthusiasm as Ra led him into the house.

"Sup, Pwyll?" Jamarcus said as he shook his hand while they walked back into the living room. The boy, Ra, and Jamarcus stood in the middle of the living room, while Bernini still played his game. Jamarcus looked up the stairs when Rhiannon climbed midway down wearing a white blouse and black shorts. As Pwyll smiled at her, she gave him an indignant look that made Jamarcus almost burst out laughing.

"Scar, come here!" Ixchel shouted from upstairs in an anxious tone.

When Jamarcus climbed the stairs past Rhiannon, she reached over and kissed Jamarcus on his cheek. Once he got to the top of the stairs, he reached out with his light until he found Ixchel sitting in front of the mirror in her bedroom's bathroom. As he entered the room, he saw that Ixchel was sitting on a regular chair with no top on, wearing only undergarments, as she held a hair shaver in her hand. Although she didn't have breasts, Jamarcus immediately felt uncomfortable, not sure how or where to look at her.

"Shave my hair," she ordered as she handed Jamarcus the shaver. "I do not want to get hair on your father's clothes. We have to look good tonight for a prime minister from a world that is thinking about joining our house. So I need you to shave my hair."

"I think it's short enough," Jamarcus said as he rubbed his hand over the black grains on top of her head.

"I have to cut it," Ixchel said, and Jamarcus felt the military discipline in her plea, so he immediately turned the clippers on and began shaving.

"I need your help tonight," Ixchel said. "While your father and I meet with a few Sirian diplomats, I want you and Pwyll to look after Rhiannon and Bernini. Pwyll will look after the house, while you make sure your brother and sister do not do anything crazy."

"Can't Pwyll do that himself?" Jamarcus asked.

"If anyone came here on their own, Rhiannon would make them do whatever she wants. And it would be bad if you were here by yourself because you have a bad habit of not saying no to your siblings. Pwyll's job is to watch the house; yours is to keep an eye on your siblings. Do you understand?"

"Yes, Mama," Jamarcus said as he finished.

After brushing off her scalp, Ixchel rushed into the bedroom in a hurry and put on a dress that was lying on her bed. "I hate wearing these," she said as she zipped up a white dress that had sparkling lights flowing about it. "I do not understand why so many species have genders wearing different clothes. It is annoying trying to find out which one is appropriate for specific situations."

"That looks pretty." Jamarcus tried to reassure her.

"It does," Ixchel said hollowly, and Jamarcus could feel she derived no pleasure from it. After she adjusted the dress, she and Jamarcus quickly tiptoed out of the bedroom and to the living room. Ixchel gave Rhiannon a smart look as she climbed down the stairs.

"I do not want any funny business while we are gone," Ixchel said as she fixed Ra's tie while her light looked directly at Rhiannon. "While meeting with the prime minister, our light will mostly be focused on his world, so we cannot keep an eye on you. That is why Pwyll is here—to keep you from doing anything foolish."

"We don't need a babysitter, Mom," Rhiannon said as she stood on her stair step, refusing to come down.

"Why can't Scar babysit us?" Bernini asked absentmindedly as he played his game.

"We already discussed that," Ixchel said as she walked up and kissed Bernini on his head. "We are leaving now, so mind your manners with Pwyll."

"Don't let them intimidate you," Ra said to Pwyll as they walked to the front door.

"I won't, Lord Ra," Pwyll said.

"Behave," Ixchel said as they walked out the door and to their car.

As Jamarcus felt them drive off, he was perplexed that they were driving a car instead of shifting where they needed to go.

"So what do you want me to do?" Pwyll asked shyly as he and Jamarcus stood side by side.

"I don't care," Rhiannon said with a twirl of her eyes. "Jamarcus, come here." She held out her hand as Jamarcus walked up the stairs to her.

"I want to come too," Bernini said as he put down the game controller.

"Fine," Rhiannon said as she dragged Jamarcus into her bedroom.

"Pink," Jamarcus said as he entered, as almost all of the furniture and linens in the room were that color. She had a collection of plush alien animals on a shelf next to her window, and there was a bed couch with a fixed hologram television before it. The television was tuned to a news channel.

"Yeah, it's lame," Rhiannon said. "I got most of this stuff when I was younger. Daddy wants to keep it this way since I moved out for university. He said it reminded him of me when I was younger. Come sit with me while I watch the news."

"All right," Jamarcus said as he lay down on the couch with Rhiannon. She held on to him tightly as Bernini climbed up onto the bed and lay on top of their legs.

"Stop moving around, tadpole," Rhiannon told Bernini as he got comfortable.

"Shut up," Bernini said as laid his head down on her lap. As he rested there, Jamarcus could feel the infuriation that Bernini and Rhiannon gave each other. But beneath it, there was a deep love that seemed connected in their light. As Jamarcus saw that light connect to his, he could feel the warmth and peace in it. It physically felt good to be in that bond, with their souls entwined together. But that emptiness was still there, snatching away some of the happiness he might have had.

"What are you watching?" Jamarcus asked.

"I have to write a paper for my exopolitics class," Rhiannon said.

"There's a conflict going on in a nation in the world I'm going to. I'm just trying to get as much research material as I can."

"Cool," Jamarcus said. As he watched the broadcast, he noticed he could feel the thoughts and emotions of the individuals he saw in the hologram. There was a school that taught students about the nature of Aten Ka, which was the basis of the Federation's education. The school was in a nation that traditionally prevented females from learning about Aten Ka.

Jamarcus saw a group of blue-skinned female hominids in dresses and white headscarves trying to enter the school while adults stood before the doors, blocking anyone from doing the same. Teachers from the Federation were seen talking to the protesters, but Jamarcus could feel the blue hominids' resentment begin to boil over. Someone threw a punch, and a ruckus broke out. Soon law enforcement officers in tight-fitting black uniforms flew in to break up the crowd, and afterward, everyone was dispersed. Jamarcus felt the fear and shame the female students had for just trying to get an education their parents believed would give them a better life.

"Are you sad?" Rhiannon asked in a concerned voice. "Your light is dimming."

"It is?" Jamarcus said, and when he looked at himself, he saw that the light from his chest had dimmed in certain areas like gray clouds floating around inside his bright light.

"Do you want me to change the channel?" Rhiannon asked.

"No, I'm fine. I just felt the emotions of those students who tried to get into that school."

"It may be from the trauma your human body experienced," Rhiannon said. "We study that the pain lights experience in their past lives sometimes carries on with them." She sat quietly for a while, gazing into Jamarcus's soul. A spark of inspiration blossomed in her mind as a smile came across her face. "Do you want to go inside your body here?" she asked. "It hasn't felt any pain. You might feel better in here."

"What do you want me to do?" Jamarcus asked, but Rhiannon already had pushed Bernini aside and climbed out of bed, pulling Jamarcus alongside her.

"I need you to make a window to the nursery here," Rhiannon told him.

"I'm not sure how," Jamarcus said as he tried to imagine a way to do that.

"Extend your sight out," Rhiannon said, and feeling what she meant, Jamarcus closed his light eyes. He began to feel everything in the room around him. He then sent that viewpoint up out of the house through the roof and high into the night sky above the city. He saw the island where the chateau was and zipped his vision over there. He slipped into the chateau, passing through the ceiling and walls, until he got to the nursery.

"Now fill yourself with light, and reach out into the room," Rhiannon said.

Jamarcus's light increased inside him and became more solid. Once he stretched his hand out in front of him, reaching out with his light, the nursery appeared in front of them like a large puddle of mercury standing on its side. Rhiannon walked toward the crib once the window appeared and opened it. Jamarcus watched as she picked up the sunlit sleeping child and walked over to him.

"Wait a second," Rhiannon said as she carefully placed the boy down on top of her bed. "Now stand still."

"Okay," Jamarcus said as Rhiannon walked over to him and placed her hands on his head in a way that allowed her to put a finger on the center of his forehead.

"Relax," Rhiannon said, and when he did, Jamarcus felt his light body crunch up into a small ball that Rhiannon held in her hand. She then placed the ball in the child's head, and when Rhiannon released his light, Jamarcus opened the eyes of the baby. The light inside him was hot, and he felt the heat in his physical body in his apartment. When he tried to move, the arms and legs of the child just flailed around like those of a baby infant trying to get his mother's attention.

"Pluussh," Jamarcus spit out before he realized the baby's motor skills weren't developed yet. Bernini got a huge laugh out of that sound as he crawled over Jamarcus and played with the baby's feet.

"I can't move," Jamarcus said with his light voice, and Rhiannon picked him up and held him tightly in her arms. Jamarcus felt the joy that shone inside her as Rhiannon held him like a big sister holding her baby sibling. When Rhiannon kissed him on his cheeks, Jamarcus tried to push her head back but only ended up lightly slapping her face, which made her giggle in delight.

"I want to hold him," Bernini said, and Rhiannon reluctantly handed Jamarcus over to him.

"Hi, Scar," Bernini said as he bounced Jamarcus around in his arms. The glee from Bernini tickled Jamarcus a bit, which made him laugh awkwardly in the baby's body.

"He still isn't happy, though," Bernini said as he placed his face close against Jamarcus's. "He still feels sad in his heart."

"Well, it was an idea," Rhiannon said as she rubbed Jamarcus's head.

"Oh, I know what will make him happy!" Bernini said with a light flashing in his head. He placed Jamarcus on the bed, held on to the baby's head, and pulled his consciousness into his hands. "Stand up," he said, and Jamarcus expanded his soul back out until he stood back on his toes. The heat he felt from being inside the baby boy remained, still coursing through his human form.

"Be careful with his body," Rhiannon told Bernini as she picked up the little boy and placed him back in the crib.

"Let's go to a beach," Bernini said as he followed her. "He likes it when he looks at videos of when he was at a beach with his friends on Earth."

"Oh, that's a good idea," Rhiannon said with a sly smile as she closed the crib, and she and Bernini stepped out of the wormhole. "Close the window," she said, and when Jamarcus let go of the nursery, the window collapsed, and reality neatly snapped back into place.

"Go put on swim clothes, and Jamarcus will take us to one," Rhiannon told Bernini as she searched in a drawer for a swimsuit herself.

"All right," Bernini said as he rushed out her door and to his room.

"Let me change," Rhiannon said as she pushed Jamarcus out her door.

"Isn't it dark out?" Jamarcus asked.

"Not on the other side of the planet, dummy," Rhiannon said as she closed her door.

Jamarcus stood silently in the hallway as he waited for them to get ready. Bored, he reached out to Pwyll, who lay quietly on a couch downstairs, watching a sporting event. It appeared to be a fighting competition in which two individuals used dark-matter generators to duke it out in space. Just as Jamarcus got interested in the fight, Bernini came rushing to him in swimming trunks, his sky-blue skin shining with anticipation.

"Are you done?" Bernini asked while he knocked on Rhiannon's door.

"Wait, you prick," Rhiannon said as she let them in. She wore a small bikini with black bottoms that just barely covered her thin waist and a yellow tube top that covered her small bosom. Her stomach tingled a bit when she saw Jamarcus looking at her. She tied her hair into a ponytail as she walked back to her bed.

"What's the deal with Pwyll?" Jamarcus asked as he watched Bernini run around in a circle.

"He's the son of a business owner who's a friend of Dad. His father is trying to set us up."

"He seems like a pretty nice guy," Jamarcus said.

"Shut up, Jamarcus," Rhiannon said, staring at him with a look that could have killed him.

"I want to go," Bernini said as he sat on the floor in an impatient lump.

"All right," Rhiannon grunted as she placed her forehead against Jamarcus's. A vision appeared like a floating television screen in his mind of a group of small islands in crystal-clear ocean waters. Jamarcus once again created a wormhole in Rhiannon's room that opened up onto a midday-lit beach. The warm, salty air rushed in, and as soon as Jamarcus felt it, happiness blossomed inside his heart as his skin tingled from the sea breeze. Bernini ran onto the beach and right to the water as Rhiannon grabbed Jamarcus's hand and led him to the shoreline. Jamarcus felt prideful joy coming from Rhiannon again as she held on to Jamarcus and watched Bernini run right into the incoming waves.

"Come swim!" Bernini shouted at them before he disappeared under the water.

Rhiannon leaped into the air, flew above where Bernini had disappeared, and dove in without a splash. Jamarcus flew up the same way, and after taking a deep breath, he dived in. He noticed he could see clearly under the water. The surface above appeared to be a waving crystal window that revealed small dinosaur-like birds flying in the air.

"You don't have to hold your breath," Bernini said as he swam next to Jamarcus, who then released his breath and inhaled with his body in his bedroom. Bernini then shot out through the water and down to the sea floor, with Rhiannon and Jamarcus close behind.

The sea life there was so similar to that on Earth that Jamarcus felt as if he were back on the north shore of Oahu, spear-fishing with Nathan. Wonder appeared within Jamarcus's soul as colorful fish swam around them, and he soon found he was able to feel the fish and slightly communicate with them. The fish swam in patterns around Jamarcus that he created, with Rhiannon and Bernini floating next to him in amazement.

"I want to play on the beach," Bernini said as he got bored of watching the fish, and he dashed upward and out of the water.

"Aten Ka, he can be so bossy," Rhiannon said.

"You both look black to me," Jamarcus joked, and Rhiannon slapped him on the arm when she understood the joke.

After they flew out of the ocean, the two found Bernini, who was playing with the sand on one of the larger islands with his mind. He was getting frustrated at not being able to make whatever he wanted.

"Make a pool, Scar," Bernini said as he ran over to Jamarcus as they landed.

"Right," Jamarcus said, and he concentrated on how he was going to do that. He first absorbed a bit of Aten Ka into his light, which grew more solid. He then waved his arm ahead of him, making reality ripple before him. When that wave went through the beach, Jamarcus felt the beach ripple also, as if it were a liquid he could control. He made a huge bowl out of the sand, with one side next to grass that lay in front of large fern-like plants that looked similar to palm trees and the other side close to the crashing waves. Jamarcus made a tunnel that connected the bowl to the ocean, and after a few minutes, the pool was filled.

Bernini jumped right in and swam around in the warm water as

Rhiannon stood on the edge of the pool. Jamarcus couldn't help but laugh every time Bernini swam close to Rhiannon; as she tried to reach out to him, he would zig or zag just out of reach.

"I don't want to play with you if you keep doing that," Rhiannon said in a huff as she walked out and over to hug Jamarcus.

Bernini ran out of the pool and sprinted over to them, pushing them around, as happy as he could be. "Can you make a slide?" he asked as a new idea to play popped into his head.

"Yes, I think I can," Jamarcus said as he looked over the pool. He knew he shouldn't try to make one out of the sand, so he flew over to the green side of the pool and made a mound out of grass and dirt. He molded a trench going from the top of the mound to the pool and picked up some water to spray the trench until it became slick mud.

"I want to ride down!" Bernini said. He rushed up to the top and then gave out a scream as he slid down and splashed into the water.

Rhiannon ran up as well and gave out a quick shout as she crashed into the pool. Over and over again, they ran up the hill and rode down, sometimes together, their hearts beaming with thrilled pleasure. They splashed each other and Jamarcus when they needed to make the slide wet again, and peace slowly grew in Jamarcus's heart as he watched them play.

Feeling the ocean air swirling around him and hearing the sounds of the waves colliding on the shoreline and the calls of the bird-like creatures above, Jamarcus now knew why he wasn't happy. He couldn't find joy anymore in material things. He had come to the grim realization a while ago that everything he had done in the army had been not for the defense of the United States but to keep its economy going. Since then, he had been unable to find the desire to buy a car, buy fancy clothes, or even watch television or movies. He could see that everything was a huge advertisement. Nothing had a soul. But out there on that beach island, in nature, he was happy. He could almost see himself and Kathrine walking along the shoreline as she dipped into the sand, looking for seashells.

"Kids!" Ixchel shouted from the house, and panic exploded in all their lights at the same time. Jamarcus wasn't sure if he panicked because Rhiannon and Bernini did or because Ixchel just created that much parental dread in his mind.

"Hurry up. We've got to wash off," Rhiannon said as the three rushed back through the wormhole and into her bedroom. Jamarcus collapsed the wormhole just in time to see Ra and Ixchel standing in the doorway, looking at them, as Rhiannon and Bernini stood covered with mud and sand, and all three smiled guiltily.

"At least they didn't burn the house down," Ra said as he walked away and to their bedroom.

"First off, you need to go back to your apartment," Ixchel said as she walked to Jamarcus with a cunning smile. When she touched his forehead, he was enveloped in white light, and he felt gravity pulling on his back as his light landed in his body, which bounced up and down on his bed.

Jamarcus leaned upward, his body still radiating with heat and his chest numb, as he pulled air into his lungs. He'd noticed those symptoms lately whenever he woke up after having visions of the family. They gradually had gotten worse over time, but he didn't think anything of it. Once the pain subsided, Jamarcus laughed silently as he lay back down in bed. He hadn't been that happy in a long time. As he searched his memories, he realized he never had been that happy away from Kathrine before.

As the alarm went off on his cell phone, he slowly got up and got ready to go to school.

Chapter 19
<1>
February 2011

"We are going over a touchy subject today," Professor Callahan said as she walked by the desks of a few students in the classroom. "So I need everybody to understand that this a lesson on politics and not a battleground. We are going discuss the topic of illegal immigration, including why it's happening and what the US is actually supposed to do about it, and hopefully, by the end of the class, we can all agree on a bill that you in the class will make together.

"First, why is illegal immigration happening? That is a dumb question because many of our descendants came to our country in much the same way many from south of the border come, except ours arrived in boats and were made US citizens as soon as they came onto Ellis Island, or they were shipped here due to slavery.

"Those who immigrated here by choice still had to deal with inspection procedures that are now seen as bigoted and racist. A small percentage of these immigrants were rejected due to eugenic reasons, such as low moral standards or disability issues. If you came during the wrong period, you were most likely conscripted directly into military services, such as what happened with many Irish immigrants during the Civil War.

"And Latinos weren't the first racial demographic who faced

widespread discrimination. Many Polish, German, and Eastern European immigrants faced disenfranchisement as they arrived here since the birth of this nation. We can't gloss over those of African descent who were freed after the Emancipation Proclamation and the Fourteenth Amendment as they tried to fit in side by side with the population who previously had enslaved them, the effects of which can still be felt today. And let's not forget those of Jewish and Italian ancestry, who still deal with stereotypes that the media won't let them get out from under thanks to the shadow of the immigration practices of this nation.

"So it's safe to say that almost everybody who came to this country faced some type of discrimination, except for the good old WASPs. Yet the US still let many of these populations into the country simply for the sake of keeping the economy going. One-fourth of the GDP is consumer spending, and a large part of that spending comes just from families buying things to sustain themselves. As long as there are couples making babies and those babies keep making babies, there will be a steady supply of consumers in the US economy.

"That steady population growth hit a curb during the Great Depression when there were economic woes all over the world. The number of immigrants entering the United States dropped, and families weren't producing babies, due to fiscal uncertainties. There was a lot of uncertainty until World War II when the country unified to face the Axis powers. Government spending to support the war effort gave a boost to the private sector, but what helped the economy was when all the servicemen came back from Europe after the war. And we all know what soldiers do with their spouses when they get home after a war. That's where the baby boomers came from, and with that much of a population boom came an increase in consumer spending.

"But a peculiar thing happened. The civil rights movement gained popularity, and with it, rights were guaranteed to people no matter race, sex, religion, gender, or disability. With the rise of women's rights came access to contraception which women had been denied before. The population decreased as women began to have fewer babies. Wages also decreased, especially for women, because there was twice the potential number of people in the workforce due to women entering it. After all, corporations still wanted to make a profit."

"That's not women's fault," a student said. "Women have the right to the same jobs and pay as men."

"And I'm not saying it is women's fault," Professor Callahan said. "If we'd lived in a matriarchal culture in which women worked and men stayed at home and then men had entered the workforce of a free market, those corporations would probably have made the same decisions. But this is a class not on sociology or psychology but on politics, and we are about to get to the crux of today's topic.

"The US population growth was at its lowest since the Depression by the eighties and nineties. However, the drug wars in Central and South America created several refugees entering the US to escape the violence. Say what you will about us being half as responsible for our part in buying the drugs that are made, but the increase of Latino immigrants and their normal birth rates are the main sources of debate.

"Are these people entering the country illegally? Yes. But that's mostly because it is much harder to become a citizen now compared to a hundred years ago. Are their numbers helping the economy in terms of consumer spending? Yes. But the social services they use are stretching legal citizens' pockets with their already limited budgets.

"Now, it's the legislative branch's responsibility to regulate laws to control immigration due to their plenary powers. But Congress has had a history of not making laws to deal with illegal immigration, and the Supreme Court has always followed a strict policy of not interfering with states' rights to make their immigration laws."

"We shouldn't be persecuting Latinos anyway," Carol said in a huff. "It's hypocritical to bash them for coming to the US anyway or to make laws that are completely racist. We are all illegal immigrants in the eyes of American Indians."

"Laws aren't made to discriminate against Latinos because they're Latinos," Paul said. "We make laws against illegal immigrants because they are illegal. I have no problem if someone who is Mexican comes legally, pays his or her taxes, and becomes a US citizen the right way. But when people come into this country and don't pay their taxes, that's the problem. I can't afford every new tax that's made."

"But that doesn't mean Latinos aren't being targeted wrongfully," Carol said. "Arizona made a law that practically gives the police the right to pull over someone who is Latino and ask if they are illegal. That's completely against the Constitution."

"I'm not denying that's wrong," Paul said. "I agree that's a bullshit law. But if someone is arrested for an already established crime and that person is not native to the United States, law enforcement has the right to ask for that person's citizenship. They already have to give up their IDs to the cops."

"How do you know they're illegal, though?" Carol asked. "How do I know you are a legal citizen?"

"You don't," Paul answered. "The only way you can tell is to look at my identification. We all have the responsibility to have legal identification on us at all times. I do. Are there a bunch of good old boys who don't carry theirs, because they believe we're to assume they're American because they're white? Yeah, and if they get arrested without their IDs, that's their fault."

"But don't you think it's wrong not to help these people who are fleeing their homes because of the violence?" Carol said. "They have nowhere to go. And they're not bad people. To call them criminals is inhuman, when all they need is help."

"But if they enter this country illegally, they are criminals," Paul said.

"And why are we giving so much help to Latinos coming into this country anyway?" Jessica asked. "Black people are still struggling as far as I'm aware of. The unemployment rate for black men is still the highest in this country, and black women are right behind. Latino men have a better employment rate than black women, legal or illegal. Why can't black people get some of this aid the Latinos are getting when they come here?"

"Because most Latinos who enter this country come as slaves," Carol said. "Say a Mexican man comes to Georgia and works on a chicken farm. He's illegal, can't find a decent apartment, and doesn't have the rights we have as citizens for just being a human being. The farm that employs him pays him less than minimum wage and provides a home for him, but all his rights and his stay are based completely upon the whim of that farm. At any time, that farm can fire that man and give him up to an ICE agent who is filling up his yearly quota. How is that different from being an indentured servant? At least in getting state assistance, Latinos coming into this country aren't treated like second-class citizens. They should be treated just like refugees from a war zone, in fact, and given asylum status to protect their rights here."

"How are we going to afford this?" Paul asked. "There isn't enough tax revenue from honest working people to pay for all of it."

"We should tax the rich and the corporations," Carol said. "The one percent of the world has more money than a third of the population on the planet. And a lot of what's happening is because of them. We should make them pay for it."

"It's this type of socialist short-sightedness that's messing up this country," Paul said. "It's nice to say we can help everyone we can who needs it. I want to. But there isn't enough money. Yes, if you take the richest people in America and pool all their money together, there is enough to pay for these social programs—for one year. But if you tax their net worth, it won't even pay for half the social programs for illegal immigrants. And we won't tax their total net worth; we will only tax their annual income, and that's even far less. And we can't tax the corporations, because those are our retirement funds. That means the government has access to your pensions, CDs, IRAs, and savings accounts. Would you still help if that means you can't retire? There isn't enough money."

"But capitalism is the reason for all this inequality in the world because it's capitalist countries that are causing the problems," Carol said.

"It isn't capitalism that's the problem," Jamarcus said. "It isn't socialism either. The problem isn't based on the policies of those on the left or the right. The problem is us. US citizens not fully understanding how the Constitution works is the problem."

"President Obama has been trying to implement policies to help immigrants for the longest time," Carol said, "but Republicans have been blocking all his efforts. And they don't want to admit that they are doing it because they are racist against Obama and Latinos."

"It doesn't have anything to do with Obama being black or immigrants being mostly Latinos," Paul said. "It's about the Constitution. What it says is right or wrong. You can't call me racist just for not agreeing with you."

"You know what the problem is with calling someone racist all the time?" Jamarcus asked. "It's the whole boy-who-cried-wolf thing. If you cry wolf too many times, what's going to happen when there is a wolf in Congress or as the president? Would anyone even listen to you?

"That's what I'm talking about. Everyone still doesn't understand how the Constitution works. You say the president has been trying to implement policies on how to deal with immigrants coming into the country. He isn't supposed to do this. A president is not supposed to write legislation; he is only supposed to enforce the legislation that Congress puts into law. And those elected into Congress are not going to make laws to deal with the immigration policies, because they fear the repercussions of their voter base if they do. They would rather allow the states to deal with the problem.

"It is a misconception that the president of the United States is the most powerful person in the world. He isn't, and the Constitution was set up to keep that from happening. The president only enforces the law, and the Supreme Court interprets it. But Congress writes the laws that the president must enforce. And we are the ones who vote them in.

"We, the citizens of this country, are the most powerful people in the world. We are the ones who vote in people who create the laws that we want them to, and if they don't or if the president refuses to enforce those laws, then we vote them out. The vote is the most powerful tool in any democracy, and we just waste it. Protesting is not going to help because protesting should be used by those who can't vote. Those who can could change policies in a voting cycle if they organized themselves."

"I voted for Obama. I vote Democrat," Carol said. "If everyone voted Democrat, none of this discrimination would be happening."

"Yes, it would," Jamarcus said. "You know that if immigration wasn't an issue, politicians would find another issue to get their voter base riled up. The immigration policies aren't even the real issue. We're trying to deal with the symptoms of a problem and not the cause of it, and that's the foreign political and fiscal policies Congress passes that create inequalities in Central and South America in the first place. And Republicans and Democrats vote the same on those issues. And it's our fault for not knowing. We're causing this situation."

"What would you do then?" Paul asked.

"Well, the first thing we should do is take away the right to vote from everyone for just being a US citizen over the age of eighteen."

"Wait—how is that different from being in a totalitarian or Fascist state?" Jessica asked.

"It isn't. I'm not saying it's not," Jamarcus said. "But just let me explain. The concern is that when you have this many people who vote on things who aren't necessarily educated or experienced enough to know what they are voting on or don't even understand the importance of what the vote can do, then you have a base who will vote on anything a charismatic politician says to vote on."

"I didn't vote blindly," Paul said. "I know the Constitution; I know my rights and liberties. I'm a patriot to this country, so I know the importance of a vote."

"And I argue that you don't," Jamarcus said. "Now, let me finish explaining. If you can vote just by getting to a certain age without earning the right to vote, there is no sense of importance to it. A privilege is not the same as a right, and unfortunately, voting is more of a privilege than a right. That's why I think the right to vote should be reserved for those who fulfill certain criteria: all those who serve at least three years in the military, are released by honorable discharge and have at least an associate's degree earn the right to vote. While in service or college, you will get an education on the Constitution and the legal mechanics of the federal system and should be able to write a law that could be introduced on a legislative floor. If you put these criteria in, then we would see the importance of what voting is."

"Isn't that a little harsh?" another student said. "Not everyone can fulfill those requirements."

"There aren't many people in Congress now who can either," Jamarcus said. "And when I say these people will vote, I mean they will vote on everything. In this system, once you fulfill these requirements, then you are entered into a draft for congressional service at either the civil, district, state, or federal level. You can choose not to serve. Terms are limited to three cycles to prevent too much corruption from happening.

"People in Congress can write laws and vote on which laws will be brought to the floor, but the vote to pass these laws falls on all those who've earned the right to vote. So there aren't any unknown issues, like policies that abuse low standards of living in countries that trade with us. We the people have the power then to fix the problems around the world. To be voted president and vice president, you'd have to serve at least three terms in political office."

"But this isn't about who should vote," Professor Callahan said. "This is about creating a law that deals with the immigration issue."

"Oh, okay," Jamarcus said. "Well, a lot of the problems deal with the fact that NAFTA gives companies the ability to trade with each other with relatively low expense but doesn't raise the standard of living or address the rights and liberties of impoverished people, like in certain areas in Mexico. It's the same with our trade deals with Central and South America. Why should a farmer working in Chihuahua, Mexico, work for a dollar a day collecting eggs for a shipping plant in Illinois that pays its workers fifteen bucks an hour to ship them to the grocery stores? Every new trade deal we make in the Americas must guarantee at least minimum wage in American currency to all its workers, and I think they should also provide healthcare coverage, which American healthcare providers can get in on. And these trade deals must ask all countries in the agreement to guarantee the human rights of their citizens.

"To deal with the crime in Latin countries, we should join with all other nations in the Americas to form our own Interpol. If we know there are cocaine producers sending drugs into the US in Guatemala, then this would prevent jurisdictions of sovereign countries from stopping law enforcement from going after these criminals. It would give guys in the military-industrial complex a hard-on if they could now equip international paramilitary organizations that would legally take on these drug cartels wherever they are."

"That's asking a lot of the American people," Paul said. "Our economy would take a hit with these policies. Why should I go without to help other people?"

"If we are to make the world a better place, it requires change from everyone," Jamarcus said. "But these are ideas to deal with the cause of the illegal immigration. And the only way to do that is to give everyone a better standard of life."

"Where did you come up with these ideas?" Professor Callahan asked.

"My father," Jamarcus answered with a shrug.

<2>

Jamarcus lay half asleep in bed with his mind still reeling from the classes he'd had the previous days. The last few weeks had been a blur for him. It seemed that almost every other day, someone at work called in sick or had a family issue, which meant that right after classes, he had to get to work. He most likely had to work a minimum of twelve hours, and right after work, he would go home, shower, change, and start the process all over again. It was painful, but he didn't get as mad as he used to, and when he got a chance to sleep, he did, mostly passing out as soon as he lay down on his bed.

His schedule didn't leave much time for Bernini or Sneeze to come play with Jamarcus. He could never guess when they would show up, although when they did, they arrived around the same time at night, usually around ten o'clock. They didn't show up that night around their usual time, so while Jamarcus lay asleep, going in and out of dreams, he was surprised when a presence appeared above his apartment and a force easily pulled his light out of his body and into the sky. After orienting himself, he saw Ixchel standing in front of him in a tight-fitting black suit just like the one Aapo had worn when Jamarcus first met him. The sight of the black suit and the somber emotion Ixchel was exuding seemed ominous to Jamarcus.

"Am I in trouble?" he asked as Ixchel stared into his mind.

"Hello, Scar. I am doing fine," Ixchel responded with the worst courteous smile Jamarcus ever had seen on their face. "How are you doing tonight?"

"Hi, Mama," he said as he floated over to Ixchel and hugged her. He could feel motherly happiness shine within Ixchel as they held each other in their arms for a few moments.

"You seem to be able to manipulate the waters around you fairly well," Ixchel said as she held Jamarcus out at arm's length. "So your father and I decided it was time to teach you how to properly use the light. Working with the waters is no small thing. I hope you realize just how serious that is."

"I do now," Jamarcus said.

"We'll see," Ixchel said as she turned from Jamarcus and increased the light inside her. When she extended her arms, a window opened to a field of asteroids of all shapes and sizes floating in the same direction like leaves on a river. She led Jamarcus through the window, and its space-time snapped back into place when they were on the other side.

"We know you have a hard time saying no to your siblings, but we did not expect you to just mold the land for them," Ixchel said. "Especially when they should learn how to do that themselves. So by our teaching you how to properly manipulate the waters, you will see just how dangerous what you did can be."

"All right," Jamarcus said, trying to stifle a laugh.

"What is so funny, Scar?" Ixchel asked with a bit of annoyance.

"Nothing," he said as Ixchel stared him down. He felt the sternness of her words in his mind, but her love coated every one of them. It felt good to have a being show that much concern for him and act as a parental figure. It was something he never had experienced.

"Focus," Ixchel spoke in a harsher tone.

"Ma'am, yes, ma'am."

"Now, the first thing I want to properly train you on is how to mold the waters around you. How you do that produces different effects on the environment. Like so." Ixchel grew brighter as she reached out in front of her. Jamarcus could feel space-time extend upward as if a person were pulling on the surface of an elastic plane over the face of a nearby large asteroid. The more she did, the more dust and rock began to float from the surface or fall upward into the gravity well. Once she let go of the well, space-time slung back into place, throwing all the debris it had caught up back at the asteroid and knocking it out into space.

"I want you to pick up seven rocks by doing the same thing," Ixchel said. "And I want you to mold the water in a way that it only picks up the rock and the area immediately around it. I hope you understand."

"I do," Jamarcus said as he filled himself with light. Searching out to the asteroid, he found seven decent-sized rocks. He made a well above one of them and pulled it just enough so the rock floated a few feet above the surface of the asteroid. While holding on to that rock, he reached out over and over again until he had all the objects floating as Ixchel wanted.

"Now I want you to release the molded waters just enough so the rocks fall gently back into place."

"Okay," Jamarcus said as he gradually lessened his mental grip on the gravity wells he'd made until the rocks softly fell where they had come from.

"Very good," Ixchel said as she flew away from Jamarcus. "Another thing you can do by molding the waters is to slow or even stop time in an area around you, in case you are in danger." She traveled away from Jamarcus until she was a small white light a few miles from him. "Reach out as far as you can in all directions," she said as she telekinetically grabbed a rock and pulled it to her. "Don't do anything yet; just feel as far as you can."

"Yes, ma'am," Jamarcus said as he reached out in his mind until he had a mental view of the asteroids around them in a couple-hundred-mile radius. "Is this good?" he asked.

"Yes. Now I'm going to hurl this rock at you. Are you ready?"

"Yes?" Jamarcus responded, not sure what to expect, and then his heart skipped a beat when a large fireball of death appeared in front of him, ready to knock him into his next life. Jamarcus instinctively clenched up, and when he did, the fireball slowed almost to a standstill, gradually ebbing its way toward him. He floated over to the side and watched the rock debris slide past him. Once he was clear, he released space-time around him so the fireball disappeared into the darkness of space.

"That was amazing," Jamarcus said, but he barely had enough time to get the words out before he felt another fireball hurtling toward him. Once again, he slowed time down to dodge the object, and he did so again and again as Ixchel continued to grab debris. Ixchel then shifted in different areas around Jamarcus, making sure he was searching out in his mind three-dimensionally.

"Good," Ixchel said once she was satisfied that Jamarcus was able to stop time by pure reflex, and she ceased throwing rocks, which allowed Jamarcus to reach out mischievously for a large piece of debris and pull it toward him. He pointed it at Ixchel and was about to fling it when she softly grabbed the rock with her hand and smiled at Jamarcus with that courteous and simultaneously evil smile of hers.

"What were you going to do with this, sweetie?" she asked in a polite voice.

"Nothing," Jamarcus said slyly. "I was just looking at it. Ah, doesn't it look nice? I wonder how many rare minerals you can find in this."

"Mhmm," Ixchel grunted as Jamarcus let go of the debris. "There is a lot more you can do with the waters around when you manipulate them, even reversing the waters of objects and individuals. But I will not teach you that until you get an education on the ethics of time-shifting. For now, I will tell you this: do not reverse time for anyone. Even for your brothers and sisters. Do you understand?"

"Ma'am, yes, ma'am," Jamarcus answered. "Are you mad at me for what I did with Rhiannon and Bernini?"

"Scar, listen," Ixchel said as she floated close to Jamarcus's face. "You need to pay attention to what I'm trying to teach you. Molding the waters can have a disastrous effect on everyone and everything around you. Beings at our density can even affect the water subconsciously. And there is no excuse, such as 'I did not mean to do it,' after all is said and done. And I do not do things in half measures. You served in the military, so you know what I am saying."

"Yes, ma'am," Jamarcus said.

"You were able to slide over to those islands Rhiannon wanted you to take them to fairly easily, but it still took a bit of concentration to do it. So I want you to practice that now. Slip over to that asteroid there."

As commanded, Jamarcus filled himself with light and reached out to the object Ixchel pointed out. He opened a window over the surface of the asteroid and floated into it.

"You do not have to do that," Ixchel said as she followed Jamarcus through the window. "When you try to slip to that asteroid there, pull the hole to you after you reach out to it."

"All right," Jamarcus said as he released his last window. As he reached out again to the next asteroid and opened a new window, he pulled it over himself and Ixchel with little effort.

"Very nice," Ixchel said. "Do it again."

Jamarcus did. He did it again and again until he didn't even need to create a large window as he and Ixchel shifted to each new destination he picked.

"Well done," Ixchel said. "Now I want to go over how to mold the waters of matter, which you did back on Nima. Pick up a piece of debris over there."

Once Jamarcus did, Ixchel floated in front of him and the rock.

"All matter that you see around you, even yourself, is composed of water that sings at different vibrations. By hearing this music, we can do practically anything with the water. First, I want you to feel the elasticity of this debris."

"Yes, ma'am," Jamarcus said as he waved his hand and sent a ripple of space-time through the floating rock.

"Can you feel how the debris ebbs back and forth as the waters wash through it?" Ixchel asked, and Jamarcus could see the rock expand and contract slightly as it was hit with wave after wave.

"I can feel it," he said.

"Once you feel the water of any object, you can manipulate it just like the waters around us. Try it."

"Okay," Jamarcus said, and he mentally warped the rock into all different shapes and sizes. He made it first into a ball and then into a cube, a cylinder, and a pyramid. When he got comfortable with that, he warped it into a cutlass, a shield, and, lastly, a spear.

"Now I want you to listen to the song it sings," Ixchel said. "Do not listen with your ears. Listen with your light."

Jamarcus held on to the spear with his mind and tried to imagine it inside his soul. When he did, he could hear the bright sounds of ringing, vibrating notes, like crystal cups being rubbed on their edges. "I can hear it," he said in wonder.

"Stop the song by holding the spear still in your light," Ixchel said, and when Jamarcus figured out how to do so, the spear shone with the same light his light body produced. "The spear is now made of the same pure matter that your light is made of," she explained. "That is why it shines the way it does. And more importantly, when you play a different song into this light, it becomes whatever material you sing. Try to find the material on Earth that you want to sing with."

Jamarcus reached back to his body and then shifted his vision to above his apartment. He reached out until he felt the copper wires of the power lines near his apartment. Once he heard the ringing of the wires, he connected the spear with the same vibration, and it transmuted into dully colored copper. Jamarcus was speechless.

"Try again," she said, and Jamarcus reached out again until he felt the chrome of the exhaust pipes on his motorcycle. Once he heard the song from them, he transmuted the spear into a brightly polished metallic material. Once he felt he'd gotten the hang of what he was doing, he decided to be bold and reached out further until he felt the material he was looking for on the nearby military base, and when he did, he transmuted the spear into hardened titanium.

"There is one more thing I want to show you," Ixchel said as she reached out and made the spear disappear in a small puff of smoke. "Not only can you turn any material into another by listening to and playing its song into it, but you can also create anything by singing a song into the water itself. Now I want you to reach out and find any object you want to create, and when you do, play its song into the waters."

After a little bit of thought, Jamarcus searched out into the college campus where he went to school and found the Zulu spear displayed in the African studies class. After listening to the song of the spear, Jamarcus dipped his hands into space-time and played the spear's song, and a replica of the weapon appeared in a puff of smoke. It floated before Jamarcus as he carefully inspected it before grasping it. It had the same iron-forged blade, the same wooden shaft, and the same cheetah fur covering with eagle feathers around its midsection. Ixchel floated silently next to Jamarcus as he began to fully comprehend, in horror and amazement, what he had just done.

"Aten Ka," Jamarcus whispered. "You are gods."

"A bit of advice," Ixchel said to bring Jamarcus back to his senses. "Whenever you create something out of the waters, make sure you disperse it. A lot of problems can come from creating things around beings that aren't capable of doing so. Now feel the waters of the spear, and blow it away."

After a few moments of feeling out with his mind, he did just that and then paused in deep thought.

"Do you fully understand now the significance of molding the waters around you?" Ixchel asked. "It is not something trivial to play with, like on a nice day at the beach. There are real consequences when you do it."

"I understand," Jamarcus said somberly.

"Try to make something else," she said, and Jamarcus reached with his mind to duplicate his motorcycle, but he grew concerned when the gasoline froze in the tank and deformed it.

"That wasn't smart," Jamarcus said before he dispersed it. "Can I ask you something, Mama?"

"Yes, sweetie?"

"My chest has begun hurting each time I have experiences with you and the rest of the family. Why is that?"

"Your Aten Ka leaves your body every time you do so," she said as she watched him create a small car without gasoline in the tank. "That is the source of life, the light. The more you have your light leave your body, the more that life is seeped away from it. You die a little every time you do so."

"Oh," Jamarcus said as he dispersed the car and thought of something else to create. "Okay."

Chapter 20
<1>
May 2011

"Hold still," Sneeze said in Jamarcus's mind as he stood in his bedroom late at night.

"What are you going to do?" Jamarcus said as he complied.

"I want to walk in your body again," Sneeze said anxiously as Jamarcus felt her light squirm around inside him.

"I want to do it too!" Bernini shouted in the center of Jamarcus's head, making him wince.

"Take it easy, you two," Jamarcus said. "One at a time. And be careful. The last time you guys did this, you banged my foot against the wall."

"That's because you have strange feet," Bernini said.

"I have strange feet?" Jamarcus grumbled. "Do you want to do this or not?" he asked, and he felt both Sneeze and Bernini become still from his irritation.

"Sneeze, you go first," Jamarcus said, and he felt glee burst in Sneeze's soul. He stood patiently as Sneeze seemed to push Jamarcus's consciousness back, making him see the world as if he were riding in the backseat of a car. Then a force took control of his body and made it stand still as it looked around the bedroom. Sneeze made the body take a couple of clumsy steps, but when she got too careless, Jamarcus took control to maintain his balance.

"Why are your feet so weird?" Sneeze asked as she looked at them.

"I have human feet. I don't stand up like you or Bernini."

"Why can't you stand on your toes?"

"Because my feet hurt, and I'm not a kid anymore," Jamarcus answered in an annoyed tone. "Are you going to do anything?"

"Yes," Sneeze said as she made Jamarcus's body walk out of his bedroom and into the kitchen. She stopped in front of the sink and looked at the cabinets above it, contemplating what to do next.

"What are you going to do?" Jamarcus asked in bemused dread.

"I want to fix you something to eat," Sneeze replied.

"You're not going to fix me something to eat," Jamarcus told her.

"But I want to make something for you."

"I already ate something earlier, and I don't want you to use the stove. I don't want either of you using the stove."

"Please?" Sneeze said, and Jamarcus felt her desire to eat something with a mouth that felt alien to her, especially his teeth—Sneeze was fixated on his teeth.

"Your turn is up," Jamarcus said as he forced his way to the front of his mind, which made Sneeze mad, and her light grumbled in the corner of his head.

"Your turn, Bernini," Jamarcus said, and once again, his perspective shifted as Bernini took control.

Bernini slowly turned the body around and headed back into the bedroom, but this time, he directed it into the bathroom. Bernini stared at the mirror and began to talk, looking at Jamarcus's mouth as he tried to pronounce the words.

"H-h-h-hiiii. Hiiii."

"Are you trying to say hi?" Jamarcus asked.

"Let me do it," Bernini said. "I'm learning Earth's languages in Seminary, and I want to try it in your voice."

"Okay," Jamarcus said as Bernini took back control of his mouth.

"J-j-juuu … Juuumm … Juuummp-p-p-p. Jummmp."

"That's right." Jamarcus laughed. "Good job."

"I want to try," Sneeze said, and Bernini slipped back so Sneeze could attempt.

"H-h-h-h … H-h-h-heee … Heee."

"What are you trying to say?" Jamarcus asked.

"How do you say my name?" Sneeze asked.

"Hold my teeth together, and blow through them," Jamarcus said.

"S-s-s-s … S-s-s-seee … Seee."

"Now tap the top of my mouth with my tongue while you do that."

"S-s-sneeez-z-z-e. Sneeeeze."

"And there you go," Jamarcus said with a smile.

"I did it!" Sneeze cheered, and then all three went quiet as a force splashed into Jamarcus, knocking the wind out of his chest. He felt Sneeze reach out with her mind above Jamarcus's apartment before her soul leaped, startled.

"My father is here," Sneeze said. "He wants to talk to you."

"He does?" Jamarcus asked, bewildered.

"You have to go to sleep so you can talk to him, he says," Sneeze said.

"All right," Jamarcus said, a bit hesitant. He had met many types of beings in his visions before, but the only ones who had visited him were the family and Sneeze. He didn't know why he was scared. He shouldn't have been, and he assessed it to be a fear of facing something unknown. But he was also excited. The chance to meet another alien species was something he didn't want to pass up.

Jamarcus lay down in bed and put himself in a meditative state, and it wasn't long before he felt energy coursing through him. Once he knew his body was asleep, he popped out of it and floated above his bed. He reached out into the night sky and felt three pyramid-shaped craft a few miles up. He shifted right beside one of them and was startled by the size of it and how it effortlessly hovered above Earth. It had the feel of aircraft carriers, like the ones that had taken his battalion to Iraq before the invasion but much bigger. The surface was the same gray as a naval ship, and a language was imprinted on the side of it in one section, different from the Andeans' language. It looked more like hieroglyphics, with symbols and figures of beings or objects.

Jamarcus felt three beings shift next to him, and when he turned, he was face-to-face with three tall Kaggen, mantis-like people. The one in the front appeared to be fifteen feet tall, his insect-like skin was obsidian, and his black eyes wiggled a bit as they focused on him. The other two beings behind were shorter; the one on Jamarcus's right was brown, while the female one on the left, who had a large abdomen, was green. Jamarcus stayed calm upon seeing them because the emotion he felt when they first appeared was immense fatherly and prideful love from the obsidian being.

"Hello, Scar," the tall being clicked. "I'm Sneeze's father. My name is Psssh."

Jamarcus paused and thought about the pronunciation of his name before he responded. "It's 'to make a soft noise to get someone's attention,' right?"

"Something like that," Psssh said with his light smile. "Are you okay?"

"Yes," Jamarcus said, his mind still racing.

"Is there something wrong?"

"No!" Jamarcus said before he moved over to Psssh and held his head in his hand. "This is just amazing. It's just that when I think of seeing extraterrestrials, well, I picture something like you guys."

"Oh," Psssh said as Jamarcus examined his body closely. His face seemed almost like that of a mantis on Earth. His mouth opened and closed sideways. His body was more hominid in shape, but the surface was like that of any insect. It was hard on the outside, with small thornlike structures scattered about like freckles. At the connections of his joints, from his hands and fingers to his arms and shoulders, Jamarcus could see his flesh underneath, which was dark gray and leathery in texture. When Jamarcus examined his hip, Psssh's light became uncomfortable, and Jamarcus flitted back away from him in a panic.

"I'm sorry about that," Jamarcus said with nervous laughter.

"That's okay," Psssh clicked. "There is an urgent reason I came to see you. Sneeze's mother is dying, and I wanted her to see you before she goes into the Source. Would you like to meet her?"

"Sure," Jamarcus said, and Psssh pulled him close with his mind as he shifted all of them into the helm of one of the ships. It was a half-circular room with a window arched before them, and control consoles beneath it were manned by Kaggen of different colors: green, brown, red, blue, white, black, and mixtures of all of them. A handful of them were hybrids like Sneeze, with the same variations of colors.

"Take us to Sarah," Psssh chirped, and two operators turned dials and flicked some switches, and the craft bounced up at incredible speed above Earth's atmosphere. When another Kaggen turned off a dial, the craft flew over to the mid-eastern section of the United States and then shot back down just as fast over a small, quiet suburb.

"Come, Scar," Psssh said, and when Jamarcus walked next to him, he shifted both of them into a dark bedroom, where Jamarcus saw the light of an old woman standing next to her body with a peaceful expression. When she saw their light, she turned and faced them, and a large smile spread over her lips as she walked over and hugged Psssh.

"Oh, I thought I would never see you again," Sarah said as she shook with happiness as Psssh held her.

"I brought someone to see you," Psssh said as they stopped hugging.

"Sneeze is not here?" Sarah asked with concern.

"She is back in my world, but I brought her fiancé with me."

"You did?" Sarah asked, her light brightening as Psssh showed her to Jamarcus.

"Hello, Sarah," Jamarcus said, and he watched as Sarah stood awestruck as she stared at him.

"Oh my God, you are an angel," Sarah said as she walked to Jamarcus and held his hand.

"No, ma'am, I don't think so," Jamarcus said as Sarah looked into his eyes. "I'm just like you. A human."

"But your soul is as bright as the sun at noon," she whispered. "You're so beautiful."

"Yeah, I'm pretty sure you are the only one who thinks that."

"You are, Scar," Psssh said. "I believe you are."

"Your name is Scar?" Sarah asked as wonder filled her soul with delight. "That's Nordic. Are you a Pleiadean?"

"My father is," Jamarcus answered. "Well, I think he is."

"Oh, I want to see you and Sneeze together," Sarah said, holding Jamarcus's hands to her chest.

"Yes," Psssh said, and he shifted all three of them back onto his flagship. Psssh left Sarah where she was as he motioned for Jamarcus to follow him to one of the helm's controls. "My home world, Roi Son, is close to your planet, but it will take too long to get there," he said as they stopped by a console with a slick black cover. "She may pass on into the Source soon, so I need you to place your light into my ships to get there faster."

"No problem," Jamarcus said, and he placed his hand on the black surface. He felt the field of the ship and absorbed it into his light, until, in his mind, his perspective was above all three ships. He drew in enough light to take the ships into the White and then turned back to Psssh. "Where do you want me to go?" he asked.

"The ship's navigation will take care of that," Psssh said with a bit of pride, and as he pointed to one of his crew, the ship slid over the surface of the universe.

The energy flowing in Jamarcus's body back in the apartment felt like a cool stream, almost soothing to him. After a few moments, the ships stopped, and Jamarcus saw a small red star with nine planets orbiting close to it. They were above one that had a large supercontinent covering the majority of the world, with oceans at the poles and in an area separating the eastern and western hemispheres. The massive landmass was covered with forest alongside mountain ranges, with a huge grassland in the open valley area of the central part of the continent.

Jamarcus lowered his light to bring them back into space-time, and the ships' operators shot the ships downward to a mile above the surface of a subcontinent that was shaped much like South America on Earth. The ships rested above the coastal edge of a city that was one part stone metropolis and one part jungle. A large black pyramid with four black obelisks at the corners stood at the edge of the city. There were large rectangle-shaped corridors cut into the pyramid on different levels, and Jamarcus could see lights inside it from stone structures. The red sun was high above at noon, but the land shimmered as if it were a few hours before dusk or after dawn.

Psssh shifted Jamarcus and Sarah into the pyramid, and they saw thousands of Kaggen walking about like folks in a business or shopping district. Many of them gave the three curious looks as they walked by.

"This is my castle," Psssh told Jamarcus, and he led them inside past the hustle and bustle of the citizens. There were no vehicles in that world; everyone either walked or shifted where he or she needed to go. Almost all were naked, with a small number of them clothed, the majority of which were hybrids like Sneeze and had humanlike anatomy to cover up—or partly cover-up, as Jamarcus noticed upon closer inspection. When they got to the central section of the floor they were on, Jamarcus saw Sneeze running toward them. The light of the three mounds on her head shone like car headlights as she ran into Sarah's open arms.

"Mommy!" Sneeze shouted as she jumped up and down in her grasp.

"My girl," Sarah moaned with happiness. "Oh, I wanted to see you so much. I missed you."

"I'm right here, Mommy," Sneeze said as she dangled in her arms. "I was always with you. You know that."

"But I wanted to see you," Sarah said, and then she pushed Sneeze over to Jamarcus. "And I wanted to see you with your fiancé."

"Like this?" Sneeze said as she held on tightly to Jamarcus's hip, bouncing on her toes.

"Yes, just like that," Sarah said in a monotone voice as she looked intently at them, her lips trembling, as tears rolled down her cheeks. As Sneeze held on to Jamarcus, her light twinkled and smiled innocently as Sneeze looked up at him.

"She is so happy," Jamarcus whispered as he looked down at Sneeze's beautiful smile, and then he looked with concern at Sarah as he felt her light begin to fade away.

"I'm so happy," Sarah said over and over again as her light faded away until she was a hovering Aten Ka of three loops, with each loop slowing from the innermost one to the outside loop, which stopped and disappeared.

"Bye, Mommy," Sneeze said as she danced in the area where Sarah had disappeared, and Jamarcus watched her quietly, thinking of Kathrine, as his light cried bittersweet tears.

<2>

May 2011

It was early in the morning as Jamarcus rode his motorcycle down a rural road, gazing at the trees and houses along the way. Summer seemed to come all at once in Florida; there was no such thing as fall or spring. The humidity made the long summers and short winters that much more unbearable. However, there was one short period at the tail end of winter when the weather was perfect. Jamarcus couldn't help but have a smile in his heart, feeling the warm breeze over his face and arms. He only recently had begun to enjoy his motorcycle

361

rides. Or perhaps he enjoyed them because the weather happened to be nice.

Jamarcus finally arrived at his clinic and parked as close as he could to the front entrance. It was partly empty, with only a handful of cars in the handicapped parking spaces. As he entered the clinic, he saw a sparse number of elderly individuals waiting for their appointments with their doctors. He approached the appointment counter and waited for the nurse behind the glass to roll over in her chair and give him a clipboard.

"Do you have an appointment?" she asked as Jamarcus took the clipboard from her.

"Yes, at ten o'clock."

"Let me see," she said as she turned to a computer. "What is your name?"

"Jamarcus Bridge."

"Okay, I see it," she said as she turned back to him. "Do you have any medical insurance?"

"Yes," Jamarcus said as he handed her his medical cards.

"Have a seat in the waiting room," the nurse said as she took the cards. "Fill out the form, and the doctor will be with you in just a few minutes."

"Thanks," Jamarcus said, and he walked over to a chair and sat near an older woman in a wheelchair. He noticed she eyed his bike as he filled out his form.

"Is that your motorcycle?" the woman asked, still looking out the window at it.

"Yes, it is," Jamarcus answered.

"What kind of bike is it?"

"It's a Harley. A Sportster."

"Oh, my husband had a Harley a while ago," the woman said as she turned to face him.

"He did?"

"Yes, and I hated it when I first saw him on it. He was the only boy in the neighborhood I knew, and he used to annoy the living hell out of me. And he annoyed me even more when he rode around on that thing. But he asked me to ride with him on it once, and—stupid me—I said yes. I guess I was his girl then. He got one of those touring models so we could both ride in comfort. God, I miss that bike."

"You didn't want to ride?" Jamarcus asked.

"No, I was fine riding in the back. You know they call that the bitch seat?"

"Yeah, I do." Jamarcus laughed.

"Of course you do—you're a man," the woman said. "I loved riding with him, but when he died, I just never had a chance to ride again."

"Are you saying you want to ride with me?" Jamarcus asked with a sly smile.

"If I was thirty years younger, yes," she said with conviction. "But I would still be married. Do you have someone to take on a ride?"

"No," Jamarcus said as he finished filling out the medical form. "Haven't convinced anyone to put up with me."

"Well, you can't take anyone for a ride on that small bike. You need one of Harley's larger models."

"Ha, I wish," Jamarcus grumbled. "Their bikes cost as much as cars now. I'm trying to make ends meet with work and going to school."

"Well, maybe one day you'll get one," the woman said. "Maybe you'll get one with the job you get after you graduate college."

"I hope so," Jamarcus said as he spotted the registration nurse walking over to him.

"Mr. Bridge, I'm going to take you back to the doctor's office now," the nurse said, leading him to the door to the back part of the clinic.

"Have a nice day," Jamarcus said to the elderly woman with a wave.

"You too," the woman replied just before Jamarcus entered a hallway with doors on each side and an examination area with medical equipment.

The nurse opened a door to a room with a patient bed, a stool, and a chair next to one of the corners of the room. "Wait here, and Dr. Lloyd will be here soon," she said before she closed the door.

Jamarcus sat in the corner and looked at a few charts on the wall. One was of the male urinary system and listed things every man should look for to test for certain diseases. Just the thought of having to be in that room at his age confounded Jamarcus a bit. It felt wrong for him to be in there.

"Are you okay?" Ixchel asked in Jamarcus's mind as a drop of concern popped into his soul.

"I'm okay," Jamarcus mumbled softly as he pulled out his phone to watch videos on an app.

A while later, a man with unkempt gray hair entered the room with his nose in a medical folder. The doctor sat on the stool and flipped through a few pages before he decided to look in Jamarcus's direction. "Mr. Bridge, how are you?" Dr. Lloyd asked in a cordial voice.

"Fine, Doc," Jamarcus responded.

"I see that you served in Iraq and Afghanistan. Did you have any medical issues while you were in?"

"None."

"Do you have a hard time sleeping? Joint or back pain?"

"Yeah, a bit."

"What brings you in, Mr. Bridge?" Dr. Lloyd asked.

"I've been having issues with waking up and my chest being numb, or at least my lungs are. It's with a cold sensation too. I'm also tired a lot. I have a hard time breathing too when that happens."

"Well, the first thing we should do is take some x-rays of your chest to see if we can find anything causing your difficult breathing. I'll also have some blood work and an MRI done just to cover all the bases, all right?”

“Sure, Doc,” Jamarcus said, and the doctor left the room with his nose still in the medical file.

After a few more minutes, another nurse arrived and led Jamarcus through different rooms to take his tests. He received a laugh from one of the nurses as his blood was being drawn.

“I guess it happens sometimes,” the nurse said as he filled up different vials.

“What’s that?” Jamarcus asked.

“Almost everyone who gets their blood taken freaks out when it gets drawn. You did absolutely nothing when I poked you with the needle.”

“It’s not that bad,” Jamarcus said. “I’ve been through worse.”

“If you say so, man,” the nurse said with a smile.

After all the tests were done, Jamarcus returned to the waiting room and sat until Dr. Lloyd arrived, this time with his attention focused on Jamarcus.

“All right, Mr. Bridge, I have a few questions, okay?” he said as he sat back down on the stool.

“All right, Doc.”

“How long have you had a hard time sleeping?”

“Well, my job has me working weird hours. And long shifts. Plus, I go to school, so I don’t get that much rest. I would say a couple years.”

"Have you had any episodes of sleep paralysis?"

"Yes."

"You look to be in shape, so I don't think you have any muscle loss. Have you had any instances of hallucinations?"

"Yes."

"How often?"

"A few times," Jamarcus said.

"I think you have narcolepsy, Mr. Bridge," Dr. Lloyd said. "There are reports of war veterans who suffer from the same symptoms you have. There are some options for you to help you cope with it. Are you open to taking stimulants or antidepressants?"

"No."

"You should consider it, Jamarcus. It can help—"

"No," Jamarcus said more boldly.

"Well, Jamarcus, there isn't much we can do. This is something that is a lifetime condition. You can live with it, and drugs can help. But outside of that, there isn't much we can do."

"All right," Jamarcus said as he stood up from the chair. "Is there anything else?"

"No, Mr. Bridge," Dr. Lloyd said as he stood and shook Jamarcus's hand. "Sorry, we couldn't do anymore. Have you considered going to a psychiatrist?"

"I'll think about it, Doc," Jamarcus said as he left the room. After returning to the appointment counter to check out and pay for his visit, he left the clinic, waving goodbye to the elderly woman in the wheel-chair.

"Are you concerned with your health?" Ixchel asked as Jamarcus headed to his motorcycle.

"No."

"Are you trying to prolong it?"

"Just trying to do the ethical thing," Jamarcus said as he started the bike and rode to the parking lot exit.

"Do you wish us to continue the process?"

"Yes, Mama, don't worry about it," he said as he made his way back to his apartment. "I'm still going through the process, regardless of the outcome. Well, because of the outcome. But I had to do my part to make sure if there was anything wrong with me, I fixed it. If not, then it may look like I knew I was sick and just succumbed to it with-out trying to live."

"Is it because you still do not believe we exist?" Ixchel asked.

"Partly because of that," he said as he looked at the sun through the trees. "I'm just a person who always tries to do what I'm supposed to do. That's all. Besides, if it wasn't for you guys, I would have killed myself a long time ago."

"I see," Ixchel said with a bit of worry.

"Don't worry, Mama. No matter what, I'm still going through the ascension. It's the one thing that's given me peace. And I'm meeting aliens, I think. It's my dream come true."

"If you say so, sweetie."

Chapter 21
July 2011
<1>

"Follow me, Lord Scar," an Andean in a black uniform told Jamarcus as she led him through a brightly lit white hallway. Metal archways divided the corridor into sections and open doorways. There were other Andeans in black and blue uniforms walking through also, and some wore a khaki-based uniform with shorts instead of pants. The blues didn't feel like traditional soldiers to Jamarcus, so he guessed they were the naval personnel, while the blacks were the marine forces.

There were other species also, and Jamarcus was a bit startled when he saw a red hybrid Kaggen walk by in a blue uniform. It was the first time he had seen any of Sneeze's people with the Federation. The Kaggen was just as startled to see Jamarcus and smiled broadly with his light and reached out to Jamarcus as he walked by. Jamarcus returned the gesture to the Kaggen just as he and his escort arrived at a large council room.

It was dimly lit and busy with what appeared to be highly-ranked military and political figures discussing policies. The groups of leaders all held their discussions in front of round floating tabletops that emitted light that curved reality about them. The escort led Jamarcus to a table where he saw Ra and Aapo talking to two other blue-clothed military officers, one a brown-haired Pleiadean and the other an Andean with a shaved head. There was a tan Andean in civilian clothing also, who felt more like an academic than a politician.

"Hello, Scar," Aapo said as Jamarcus and the escort approached them, squeezing his light arm.

"Is there anything else you need, Admiral?" the escort asked.

"No, Lieutenant, that's all," Aapo said, and the escort gave Jamarcus a small nod before she left the room.

"We need your help with a couple of exogenous issues," Aapo said as Ra and the group turned to them.

"I'll help if I can," Jamarcus said as one of the officers approached him to shake his hand.

"Hello, Lord Scar," the officer said in Andean as they grasped hands. "I assume this is how lights on Earth greet each other?"

"Yes, that's it."

"My name is Admiral Itza. This tall lady is Admiral Morrigan, and this is Director Sachi, who is part of a colony expedition. We want to hear your input on two issues of importance that recently came up. Because you live on Earth, you were the first one we thought might shed light on things."

"What happened?" Jamarcus asked.

"The first dilemma we have is that an independent exploration and research craft crashed on Earth, on the continent you live on," Admiral Itza said. He placed his hand on the table, which was divided into many panels. When he touched the panel, their environment changed so it appeared they were floating above a lonely dirt road in a secluded forest. The road led to a gate guarded by two well-armed human men. They had the appearance of being in the military, but Jamarcus was used to seeing contract security firms dress their personnel in such apparel to confuse the less experienced. Groups like those usually worked for private black-project companies.

"The researchers were looking at fauna near a bay in the northern part of this continent," Itza said. "But they encountered a high-intensity microwave pulse that knocked out their navigator, and they crashed in a wooded area by a small town. A military group appeared with an almost-too-coincidental quick response time, apprehended the researchers and their ship, and took them to this facility. Have you heard anything about places like these?"

"Yeah, but not much," Jamarcus answered. "They are civilian-run, not military. They specifically look military so that whenever they do things like that and civilians ask the military what's going on, the military will truthfully answer that they have no idea what happened. And because they are civilian-run, probably by a government-contract corporation, the government can't do anything if it's someone's private property. If those researchers and craft are there, they've all but disappeared."

"What do you think the company wants with them?" Admiral Morrigan asked, and Jamarcus was slightly startled when she spoke in a language that sounded almost Gaelic. He somehow knew what she said without feeling it in her light.

"I don't know, but what I've heard—" Jamarcus closed his mouth so quickly his light teeth clicked. He was somehow speaking in the same language as Morrigan, although he had no idea what he had said.

"You speak Pleiadean," Admiral Morrigan said with a smile.

"No, I don't think so," Jamarcus said, focusing on what he wanted to say. "What I wanted to say is that I don't know what that company wants. If you want a basic idea of how we do things, we humans do everything based on fear. You guys seem to do everything based on love and acceptance. You see a new species, you inquire if they want to join us in Aten Ka, and if they say yes, then you integrate and intermingle with them so we are one species."

"Don't forget the three cornerstones of the Federation," Aapo said. "Discipline, education, and the light."

"The bedrock of the righteous Fascist state," Jamarcus joked.

"It has worked for over two million cycles," Aapo said scoldingly.

"I see that. Humans do everything opposite the way the Federation does. They probably—and I'm not sure about this—think that even if the crew are researchers, they may have technology that will be a quantum jump for military or medical uses. This means more currency for this corporation, which they can use to distinguish themselves from and control other humans. All concepts are based on fear."

"That's troubling," Admiral Itza said.

"Do we know if they are okay?" Jamarcus asked.

"We can communicate with them, but they can't communicate with us," Ra said. "The humans seem to be giving them a diet that is blocking their ability to broadcast their light to communicate with us."

"Meat-based," Jamarcus said. "We humans are very empirical, which is another way of saying we refuse to think outside the box unless there is overwhelming evidence to do so. They are most likely thinking that what's good for us is good for you guys. Or they could know what they are doing and are feeding them that food to keep them from communicating."

"What should we do?" Ra said.

"What is standard operating procedure on this?" Jamarcus asked.

"That depends," Aapo said. "Usually, whenever there's a situation like this when a craft crashes in a civilization composed of third-density beings, we don't interact with them at all, because it may ruin their ascension into the light. All those who choose to go on expeditions like this accept the fact that if they get captured, they're at the mercy of such culture, and there is not much we can do. Your mother wants to send in a rescue team to slip in, retrieve our people and craft, and slip out of there."

"But that would cause alarm with the people there," Jamarcus said. "If we believe there is a species with the technology to come in and out of any secure facility at will and take whatever that species wants, the next encounter we have may be worse."

"It is a sticky situation," Admiral Morrigan said.

"Do we have any assets there?" Jamarcus asked.

"We have a squad of marines watching over the facility now, ready for us to make a course of action," Ra said.

"If you ask me, I'd have the Marines observe and report what is going on," Jamarcus said. "Get an idea of how the security and operating procedures are done there. Perhaps in a cargo movement while they are moving the prisoners, they may slip up, and the marines can take advantage of that. We have to let the craft go, though. No use risking lives over a broken piece of equipment."

"Lady Ixchel won't like that," Admiral Morrigan said in a troubled tone.

"What else can we do?" Admiral Itza said. "We have strict guidelines on how to deal with this scenario."

"I think we need to be a bit more patient with this matter," Ra said to calm the mood.

While they talked, Jamarcus leaned in on Aapo to talk to him. An instinct from within him came out from all his years in the army, compelling him to act. "Grandpa, you know we can't leave our men behind," Jamarcus whispered aloud into Aapo's ear, closing his mind out from everyone. When he did, he felt the light from everyone in the room jump a little bit. Jamarcus guessed it was a rare occurrence for someone to speak physically and not mentally. "Some bad shit may happen to them in that facility. We've got to do something."

"What do you propose?" Aapo whispered back in English.

"There is another matter we want to talk to you about, Scar," Ra said, bringing everyone's attention back to him. "If you are wondering, Director Sachi has asked for our guidance on an emergency that has occurred on their expedition vessel."

"It's not an emergency—more like a very unfortunate chain of events," Director Sachi said as he shook Jamarcus's hand.

"Any way I can help, I'll be happy to," Jamarcus said.

"We have an issue with the ship we are using to transport a colony to a new habitable world," Sachi said. "There was a navigation error, and we arrived at a different planet, and because of this predicament, a division has risen in our populous."

"Why is this colony going to this planet?" Jamarcus asked.

"Our culture is not based on the light as much as you are," Sachi said. "We are a more science-based society. As such, we feel that being in a federation that still stratifies itself based on one's density will leave us discriminated against. So a number of us have decided to migrate to a world where we can live by our principles."

"How many are traveling to this world?" Jamarcus asked.

"Just over six million."

"Is there any chance I can see this ship?" Jamarcus asked, hoping he could see a new planet.

"I will take us there," Ra said. "I'll talk to you later, admirals."

"Don't have too much fun," Aapo said as Ra increased his light and shifted Jamarcus, Sachi, and himself into a massive craft.

They stood on a sidewalk against a balcony overlooking the spacious interior of the ship. The large, cylindrical interior stretched for miles. The craft's inner hull had corridors and walkways cut into the sides of the ship but not on the top or bottom. Three large, circular microwave warp engines were in the center of the craft, connected to the inner wall of the vessel by several long metallic spokes. The three engines shone with a soft light that illuminated the interior of the ship.

"This way, please," Sachi said as he led Ra and Jamarcus into a set of corridors.

"Were you going to have your grandfather run an operation without anyone's knowledge?" Ra asked as they walked behind Sachi.

"Plausible deniability," Jamarcus answered.

"You are just like your mother." Ra sighed, and he and Jamarcus continued to follow Sachi through several doors and pathways. After a bit of time, they arrived at the helm of a ship manned by Andeans dressed like Sachi. The dark room was equipped with a set of sensory equipment lined on one wall, while two navigation stations were placed before a window that showed the dark side of a green world. Jamarcus's heart was elated when he saw the planet, and he was barely able to keep himself from smiling. He could see two continents on the hemisphere he was looking at: one was shaped like a large crescent moon with its dark part missing, and the other was a smaller continent that made up the missing part of the moon, floating away from the larger continent on the oceans surrounding them.

"This is beautiful," Jamarcus whispered to himself.

"It is, but this is not the world we originally wanted to arrive at," Sachi said as he guided them to one of the sensory stations. After he pressed a few buttons on a touch screen, a holographic image of a solar system appeared in front of them. "We hoped to arrive near the fourth planet closest to the star in this system," Sachi said. "Its weather is warm and stable enough to build a few cities and begin mining this system in less than its solar cycle. But we had a glitch in the navigation."

Sachi hit another button, and the hologram showed a red trajectory path aimed at a section of the solar system. "We had hoped that based on our coordinates, our ship would arrive at this part of the system. However, our math was wrong, and our ship locked onto the third planet closest to the star, which ended up being closer to the targeted trajectory because of its orbit. Now that we are here, a large number of colonists want to go down and set up on this planet."

"What seems to be the problem with this world?" Jamarcus asked.

"You can see here," Sachi said as he led Jamarcus and Ra to the window. "Can you see those storm systems?" He pointed, directing Jamarcus's sight to the crescent of the larger continent, where a series of hurricanes cycled through the coastline.

"Those look like category-three hurricanes," Jamarcus said.

"You can see how these storms may cause a significant threat to life," Sachi said.

"Yeah, and a meteorite can fall out of the sky and kill my human form at any time," Jamarcus said.

"You cannot make light of this," Sachi said. "I know you are used to this type of weather, but we are not."

"I'm not trying to, but I can't believe that if you have the ingenuity to get to this planet, you can't come up with a way to deal with these storms."

"We don't practice *geoengineering like the people on Earth," Sachi said in a huff. "We live in balance with the environment."*

"And you should," Jamarcus said. "That's not the point I'm trying to make here. I still don't understand. Why can't you go to the

planet you originally wanted to go to?"

"We don't have the fuel," Sachi said. "Our gold-encased urani-um blocks are almost depleted from the trip, and it will take time to go out into the system and find more resources to make more. Some of us want to ask the Federation to use your light to help us get to the planet we want, but a large number refuse to do that, wanting to settle here."

"And I agree," Jamarcus said. "Do you have people in the world you originally targeted?"

"Yes."

"And you have the means to go to that planet and the rest of this system?"

"Yes."

"Let them out," Jamarcus said.

"But the cost of life," Sachi said.

Jamarcus reached out and grabbed his arm, barely able to keep the anticipation inside him from shining through his light. "Trust me on this," he said. "Don't keep people on a ship if they don't want to be on it. Besides, the origin stories your people will tell thousands of years from now will be the stuff of legends."

"I see," Sachi said, consenting to Jamarcus's words.

"Do you have a name for this world yet?" Jamarcus asked.

"Etal," one of the crew members said, and when Jamarcus looked at her, he felt a determination shining from her light.

"Etal then," Sachi said. "All we have to do now is pick a location.”

“We have a location already chosen,” another crew member said. “It’s by the mouth of a river that empties into that large ocean.”

“Is it not in the middle of that storm?” Sachi said.

“The land there is stable,” the crew member said. “And there is a mineral deposit close by. We can begin mining there in a month.”

“It looks like everyone here is ready to go down,” Sachi mumbled softly.

“Is there a chance we can see the surface?” Jamarcus asked, his light shining with eagerness.

“If you have coordinates, take us down,” Sachi said. The crew hustled about in quiet optimism, preparing the craft to descend. After one of the crew declared their plummet, he pushed a series of buttons and the craft dipped downward and was almost instantaneously above a low green mountain range that overlooked the mouth of a river that was at least a mile wide.

“Begin colonization,” Sachi said after a moment of hesitation, and the crew cheered as they made announcements and began processes in the ship that made the entire craft vibrate.

“Do you want to go outside and watch?” Ra asked.

“Yes!” Jamarcus said, almost yelping.

Ra shifted them on top of a low peak of one of the mountains. The wind and rain fiercely blew past them, but Jamarcus didn’t feel the effects of the storm. He and Ra looked up at the cylindrical craft, which seemed to fill up the entire horizon, and saw a half-mile-long portion at the end closest to them phase out yet remain barely visible. Dozens of craft poured out and flew either to a patch of land alongside the river or off in every direction.

The ones that landed below them quickly settled in and began to create makeshift structures that could house families in mere minutes. The efficiency with which they worked amazed Jamarcus.

Suddenly, Jamarcus heard singing coming from the colony below. The voices were in the thousands, or perhaps the hundreds of thousands—Jamarcus wasn't sure—but the sound was loud, slow, and spiritually moving. Jamarcus couldn't understand the words, but he felt the meaning of the song. He closed his eyes as Ra grasped his neck in pride, and Jamarcus soaked in the emotion the colony was singing in. He could feel their hope.

<2>

October 2011

Jamarcus floated about in the Space Between, the area of darkness between the Aten Ka of the multiverse and the Sea of Universes. He had gone there to reach out with his mind to find whatever he could. He was amazed there were consciousnesses in the Space Between, albeit alien ones that didn't think the way he did or ones that a human hardly would have defined as consciousness. But ever since he'd begun his trek out of the cave, he'd learned to stop defining what consciousness was and just witness what he could find.

Last month, when he'd reached out with his mind, he'd felt a large blob of colorless mass connected to countless universes below it by tendrils of light, just as Aten Ka was connected. Jamarcus felt that the form was aware and called out to it multiple times to see if it responded. When the form didn't respond, he reached into it and felt that it wasn't much of a consciousness but was a theme.

Inside it were images of flora that light from different worlds and universes believed existed. There were trees with blue leaves, grasses in green and gold, and flowers of all shapes and colors. Some trees produced large apple-like purple fruits and vines that grew berries that were pink and red with slightly sweet red flesh inside. All the plant life in each universe connected to the form had mostly the same characteristics. Jamarcus assumed the form was part of a group consciousness of people who shared many parallel universes.

When Jamarcus reached out this time, he ended up finding a figure clothed in black. The figure was surrounded by a mist or cloud of emptiness that somehow was darker and more solid than the darkness surrounding them. Jamarcus wasn't sure if he should call out to the figure, but it noticed him as Jamarcus inspected it.

"Hello," Jamarcus said when he knew the figure was looking intently at him. He wasn't sure if the figure was going to do anything, but when he decided to turn his attention away from it, the black figure sprang at him from a distance across a length of universes at impossible speed. Before he could respond, Jamarcus's environment changed, and he found himself at a railroad station on Earth in the early morning hours, with people walking past him in clothing that appeared to be from the mid-nineteenth century and speaking in an English dialect that was from the United States.

Jamarcus felt inside his pocket, somehow knowing that his identification and his ticket were in it. After closely examining his paperwork, he heard the rumble of a loud engine and the shrill pitch of the train whistle as the train arrived on the track before him and slowed down in a mixed cloud of steam and smoke. Just as it came to a stop, a steward stepped off the train in a smart blue uniform and white gloves and stood in a professional pose as he raised his hands to his face.

"All aboard!" he roared, not caring if anyone heard him, and he pulled out his watch and looked closely at the time.

Jamarcus intuitively got in line to board the train. He didn't think anything was amiss and did not even question what was causing the vision he saw. He was simply curious to see where the train would take him.

Another steward looked at the tickets of all the passengers and announced out loud where they were going before he directed them to their seats. When Jamarcus approached him and the man read his ticket, the steward looked at him with suspicious eyes.

"You are going to Chicago?" the steward asked.

"Yes, sir," Jamarcus answered.

"I need to see your identification," the man said, and Jamarcus handed it to him with no hesitation. After inspecting his identification, the steward looked at Jamarcus with contempt in his eyes and tilted his head in the direction Jamarcus needed to go.

Jamarcus silently took back his paperwork and ticket receipt and walked that way, slipping past all the passengers who were still trying to get settled in their seats. When he found his seat, he sat down quietly and waited for the train to start moving, looking out his window at the friends and relatives of passengers saying their goodbyes.

Jamarcus suddenly lurched forward and back as the train began to head toward its next destination while the passengers and the people outside waved at each other. Soon the train was rolling along in a forest that cast darting shadows across the people in the car with him, who talked merrily among themselves. Jamarcus wondered what was happening when he saw the steward enter the car with his eyes fixed on Jamarcus in an intense, angry gaze.

To be cautious, Jamarcus checked his pockets again, and he froze in terror, as his pockets were empty. He calmly looked through all his pockets, but there was nothing—no identification, no train receipt. He looked on the floor about him, hoping to see that he'd dropped them, but he found nothing. He thought of an excuse to tell the steward when he approached, but his terror rose when he looked back at the man's black eyes. As Jamarcus looked closer, he saw that the eyes weren't just black; they were portals to an empty darkness that appeared endless.

Jamarcus got up from his seat and walked to the other end of the train car, and when he exited it, he saw that the steward slowly walked after him. Jamarcus gradually made his way from car to car, and all the while, the steward followed him, staring Jamarcus down with his empty black eyes. Jamarcus next arrived in a storage carriage with luggage, food, coal, and other train equipment on shelves to his sides.

Jamarcus came to the last car, the end of the line, and when he looked back at the door, he saw the steward slowly walk through it and toward him. The man's clothes began to deteriorate, burning from some unknown source. The flesh under his clothing scarred, and black tendrils flowed out of his eyes and across his skin. His dark hair fell from his awful scalp, and he finally stopped a step away from Jamarcus, standing still, not even moving to breathe.

"Where is your ticket?" the man asked, his voice echoing as if in a large empty room.

"I don't know," Jamarcus said, and his heart skipped a beat when the attendant produced a knife out of nowhere and raised it at him.

"I'm going to kill you," the man said, and then he stopped suddenly, looking at Jamarcus with a confused expression.

"Are you all right?" Jamarcus asked, and suddenly, the train disappeared, and Jamarcus found himself back in the Space Between. The man turned back into an empty black figure and retreated into the misty shadow he had come from.

Jamarcus floated where he was, just as confused as the man had been when he'd looked at Jamarcus. He reached out again to the black figure, but when he did, he couldn't feel any thoughts from him.

Jamarcus thought about what had happened for a while and slowly concluded what the figure was. Just as the blob he'd felt was a theme of nature, the man was a theme of death or perhaps the fear of death. The man placed himself in one's mind to make it seem like he was going to kill him or her in the most terrifying way possible to that individual. When the man had realized Jamarcus wasn't afraid of dying, Jamarcus hypothesized, the figure hadn't known what else to do and had gone back to where he'd come from. Jamarcus was so caught up in his study of the dark figure that he hardly noticed Ra and Ixchel appear behind him.

"Hi, guys," Jamarcus said as he continued to study the black man.

"I see you met the Darkness," Ixchel said as she listed next to

Jamarcus.

"Is that what you call it?" Jamarcus asked as he turned to face them.

"I am surprised you were able to face him and stay as calm as you did," Ixchel said.

"Which means you were watching me," Jamarcus said with a smile.

"Everyone has to face their fear of dying sometime," Ra said.

"What do you know about him?" Jamarcus asked, still fascinated by what had happened.

"Besides the fact that it is male and feeds on the fear of dying, nothing," Ixchel said.

"I have no idea why I think what just happened was so cool," Jamarcus said.

"Humans are very weird," Ixchel said.

"There is something we want to ask you," Ra said. "It's the main reason we wanted to talk to you."

"I'm all ears," Jamarcus said.

"You have reached the seventh density, which is a great accomplishment, and you are slowly making your way to fully be in the eighth. That is why you can see so many universes now. However, that path can take hundreds of cycles after your current life ends. We want to make you an offer. It is your choice to accept it, and we fully understand if you say no."

"What's the offer?" Jamarcus asked.

"The reason you are slowing down in your ascension process is because you've reached the limit that a light can reach if it's trying to surpass the barriers of a single universe. There isn't much more you can do without external assistance. I want to offer you the chance to go higher in density."

"What's the drawback?"

"Well, you know that as long as you train in your light form and stay out of your living body on Earth, you die a little each time. If we do this, it will drastically speed up the process of ascension but will drain your life even more."

"All right," Jamarcus answered plainly.

"Are you sure?" Ixchel said as she moved closer to Jamarcus. "We noticed how much you care about your life on Earth—how you are preparing for your education after you graduate from your school."

"But that's normal," Jamarcus said. "Besides, there is an Islamic proverb: 'Prepare to die tomorrow, and also prepare to live forever,' or something like that."

"So you are prepared to do this?" Ra asked.

"Can't stop near the end of the tunnel. I've got to go all the way out," Jamarcus said. "What do I have to do?"

"It's what I will do," Ra said. "I'm going to link the light that flows through me and have it flow through yours. You will have to lower your resistance to this energy even more and learn how to main-tain it yourself. That means nearly all live food and regular fasting.

And you will have to meditate in almost all your free time."

"I can do that," Jamarcus said. "Besides, I've kind of gotten tired of television and video games lately. Everything is just based on violence. I'd rather spend my time with you guys."

"If it's settled then, I'll link us," Ra said as he bobbed next to Jamarcus. "Now, stand still, and stay calm."

"Yes, Papa," Jamarcus said, and Ra placed a hand on Jamarcus's light head. Energy burst into him, and he saw what looked like light fireworks spark from the top of his head. The energy continued to grow until it felt as if it spilled out from the skin of his light body, and his vision was filled with white. The heat in Jamarcus's body welled up, and he was drenched in sweat. But he remained calm in the light—until everything suddenly went black.

<3>

Scar woke up in his bed and reached out to see if Sneeze was next to him, but she was gone. He reached out with his mind and found her downstairs in the kitchen, making a breakfast of unleavened bread and jelly made from berries from Sneeze's world.

"Sonlig!" Sneeze called out to Scar. "Time to get up. You have a meeting with the trade dignitaries from the Federation capital this morning."

"All right," Scar responded in a deep voice that startled him for a moment. He slowly slipped over and sat on the edge of the bed, placing his hands on his thick, muscular thighs, and flexing his strong, muscular arms before placing his chin on his large chest.

He sat there for a while, looking at the gray sheets beneath him, and then he slowly looked up at the dresser in front of him and at his alien appearance in the mirror. Scar was wearing a tight-fitting gray T-shirt and boxers that showed his toned frame. He didn't want to look at the white light that shone from within his body, because it forced him to wake up. It illuminated his pale white pink-freckled skin, which was enveloped in a close bubble of space-time curvature. When he slowly breathed in and out, the curvature expanded and retracted in the same pattern. He looked at his big, glowing blue eyes and thought he looked miserable, especially with his blond hair unkempt and blocking most of his face. Scar sat there a bit longer before he heard the small footsteps and laughter of children running toward the door of his bedroom.

"Guys, stop running around, or you're going to wake the triplets," Scar said, but the kids didn't listen to him, and soon he could see the light of his children at his door before they burst through and rushed toward him on their toes. The one in front was a skinny girl with pale white skin, white hair, and black eyes with a tinge of green covering them. She looked to be about seven years old and was wearing one of Scar's T-shirts, which covered most of her body, and she was being chased by her older brother. He was just as pale white, yet his eyes were different; they were normal, with dark pupils. The older boy, who looked eight, was dressed in a red shirt and black shorts, and he chased his sister onto the bed. They crawled their way around their father as the sister tried to keep Scar between them.

"Why are you guys making so much noise?" Scar grumbled as the girl plopped into his lap and used Scar's arms to block her brother from tickling her.

"Horus, stop messing with your sister," Scar said as he watched his kids play, and he couldn't help but get caught up in the light of their emotions. Their bodies were full of youthful energy. He gave up and reached out with his mind and pinned them both on the bed, tickling their bellies with his hands. His daughter squealed with laughter, and her cries echoed throughout the house.

"Hathor, you're going to wake up the triplets," Scar told his daughter.

"We're already awake!" one of them called out with his mind.

Scar reached out with his mind again to the nursery and saw his three toddlers lying in their crib. All wore onesies that matched their skin color: one brown, one green, and one white. The sister, wearing the green onesie, still slept, lying in the middle.

"Sneeze, can you get the triplets?" Scar asked as he tried to keep Horus and Hathor still, but Hathor slipped from his hands, and when he tried to grab her, Horus escaped, and they rushed out of the room to escape their father.

"I'm going to get you!" Scar called out after them, and he chased them using clairvoyance, following his children as they ran into each room to escape his sight. They ran through their bedrooms and the nursery, and the two little boys stood on their tiptoes at the side of their crib to grab onto their older siblings with their small, thin hands. When Hathor and Horus got to the stairs, they had to slow down, laughing even harder as they felt their father's presence hovering right over their shoulders. Scar grabbed Hathor telekinetically, and she easily surrendered, wanting her father to tickle her.

"You're supposed to run," Scar told her, and Horus rushed over and picked up his sister, and they rushed between their mother's tall, thin legs as Sneeze walked toward the stairs. They ran into the living room and hid behind couches and chairs, and Horus came up with the idea to run out to the field behind the house. They shifted through the glass barrier and ran through the grass toward the rising red sun, which made everything it touched glow in a fiery color. They were about to reach the tree line that separated the field from the beach, when Scar shifted out, grabbed them in his strong arms, and picked them up, with both kids wiggling in his grasp.

"No swimming in the morning, you two," Scar told his kids as they came to a limp rest in his arms.

"Okay, Daddy," Horus said as he climbed down from his father's hands and ran back inside the house.

Hathor grabbed onto Scar's neck and rested there as he carried his daughter back to the house, which stood at the foot of Psssh's large black pyramid castle, whose side glowed red from the incoming dawn. Hathor reached up and kissed her father on his lips and looked into Scar's eyes.

"Love you, Daddy," she said, and Scar's heart was flooded with love from his daughter. It was so deep that he began to feel weak, and soon his vision went dark.

With a bounce, Jamarcus landed in a bed and woke up. Hathor's eyes and love were still present in his soul. His chest was burning hot, and the energy Ra had sent rushing through him was still present. His breathing was hard and painful, but that didn't stop the joy he had in his soul. Jamarcus lay in his bed with tears falling from his eyes as he fell back to sleep, still hearing his children's joyful laughter.

Chapter 22
March 2012
<1>

Jamarcus looked at the four Andeans who waited with him in a hallway as they looked over their uniforms. They wore elegant, classic red military uniforms with many brass buttons golden breeches, and white socks that covered their calves and their feet except for their toes. Their hair was shaven to military standards. They fidgeted with the puffy parts of their white shirts, trying to make sure they were perfect.

As Jamarcus watched them, he could feel their happiness and excitement as they waited for their departure through the exit at the end of the hallway. The overwhelming emotion shining from them was the pride they felt that they were with Jamarcus in the coming event. Although they never looked at him, Jamarcus could feel the love they had for him, which made him uncomfortable.

Jamarcus was about to speak and strike up a conversation with the four to ease his tension when they all turned to see Kukulkan walking toward them in the opposite direction down the hallway. He was dressed in a rural dress suit that was green and dark gray. His attitude was serious and casual at the same time, with a mindset that it wasn't the first time he had done this.

"Scar Amun," Kukulkan said as he walked up to Jamarcus and

inspected the four guards who stood at attention. "I hope you are ready for your soul viewing?"

"Yes," Jamarcus answered nervously. "What's going to happen? What will I do?"

"You?" Kukulkan said as strictness bored into Jamarcus's soul. "You don't do anything. Just follow the guards, and everyone will do the rest. And smile to the people outside. There are millions of lights out there that have come across galaxies and universes to see your viewing. They care about you, so attempt to show the same compassion back."

"Why does everyone think I'm special?" Jamarcus said grimly to himself.

"Because what you did was special, Your Highness," Kukulkan said. "Very few beings in the multiverse have reached the tenth density, let alone the eighth. It is a once-in-a-thousand-cycle event. And to have two lights in the house of Xkit reach that status is a great accomplishment. They care because they know your success is their success. It shows that if you can achieve the tenth density, they can. Because we are all Aten Ka."

"Sure," Jamarcus said, feeling reassured after having Kukulkan scold him. "Are you going to come with me?"

"Me? Oh no," Kukulkan said with a chuckle. "I'm like you. I hate public events. Besides, this is all about you."

"That's kind of hypocritical of you," Jamarcus said.

"It is, isn't it?" Kukulkan said, ignoring Jamarcus, which made him laugh. "If you are laughing, then it means you're ready to get this spectacle over with."

"Yes, sir," Jamarcus said, and Kukulkan walked to the exit door, which slid up into the ceiling. Before him was a bridge that led to a craft docked within it. When the door opened, a roar of cheering erupted, echoing in the hallway. Jamarcus felt a rush fill the guards' lights, although they didn't show it.

"Let the networks know that Scar Amun is ready to move," Kukulkan mentally told someone at the edge of the corridor. He then breathed in and out deeply and turned to face Jamarcus. "Move out."

"Sir, yes, sir," Jamarcus said as he walked toward the exit. The guards took positions at his four corners, staying an arm's length away from him and staying in step.

"Don't panic," Kukulkan said as they walked by.

"Thanks," Jamarcus replied sarcastically, but he wasn't sure Kukulkan heard him amid the crash of adulation from a massive crowd of people. They were standing on the barrier edge of the second-level highway on the upper part of the Metropolis. The crowd spread for miles to Jamarcus's left and right. In the sky, he could see other citizens flying in designated areas, trying to get a better look at him. Higher still were thousands of ships of different makes and models dotting the sky. One golden sphere was large enough to block out the late morning sun in the sky.

The crowd, amazed, looked at Jamarcus's Aten Ka. His light blazed from inside him in a solid mass, with small windows of universes slipping about him like oil in water. The loops from his Aten Ka spun about him, with the outer one outside the reach of his light body. The crowd could see ten loops as they looked at Jamarcus, with many more buzzing in his forehead.

Jamarcus and the guards made their way to the craft that hovered in the air at the end of the bridge. It was shaped like a large vertical chevron. There was a large disk fuselage at the center point of the chevron, with another disk-shaped open deck halfway up the top half of the ship. Cameras fluttered back and forth, and Jamarcus could hear and feel the conversations analysts were having about him, discussing the events in his early childhood, his service in the military, and his ascension through the densities. The news folks, the crowd, and even the guards were showering him with love and admiration. It all felt weird to Jamarcus. For the first twenty years of his life, Jamarcus had been bluntly taught that who and what he was wasn't special, and for the last ten years, he'd learned that what he did was important. Now he stood before millions of lights who loved him, and he wished he wasn't there.

Just before he got to the open door of the ship, he remembered what Kukulkan had said. He stopped, turned to the crowd, and waved to everyone, which he soon regretted, as they grew even louder in response. Jamarcus gladly retreated into the ship, and the guards escorted him through a curved corridor to the right until they reached the helm of the ship. The helm was less utilitarian than the ones he previously had been in. It was more luxurious, with polished wooden floors and control consoles that floated in the air. All of the crew wore the same uniform as the guards. Two of the guards led Jamarcus to the pilot's chair, which was a rich leather seat in a polished wood frame, with a golden entanglement ball at the end of one of the arms.

"Please, Lord Scar, entangle with the ship," the guard said.

Jamarcus placed a hand on the globe, and once he felt the warp field, he drew it into his light. When he had done that previously, he'd felt the energy fill him up like a waterfall, but now it felt like a water faucet being turned on in his spine.

"Follow us, Lord Scar," the guard said, and they escorted Jamarcus to the open upper-level deck so he could stay given the massive crowd. The deck, made of polished wood, had a curved leather couch at the edge so one could sit and look out at the environment.

"Take us to the civic center," the guard said, and an individual by a console pressed a series of touch-screen buttons.

The craft slowly left the dock and flew through the city. It took long roads at a slow pace through the central part of the Metropolis, where millions more citizens stood by on both the lower and upper roads, all trying to catch a glimpse of the ship. The flight took more than an hour to accommodate everyone's wish to see Jamarcus. He stood on the upper deck, waving at the crowd while patiently waiting for the tour to be over.

The craft finally arrived at a large dome-shaped building on the upper part of Metropolis. More camera drones floated by the entrance to the building, but thankfully, Jamarcus noticed there was no crowd there. After the craft docked by the bridge to the building, the guards led Jamarcus off the ship and to the entrance. While the cameras flew by him, taking pictures of his every step, Jamarcus waved to them, feeling more at ease when there weren't any adoring fans who showered him with love.

The guards led Jamarcus to a large circular room with red carpet and brown wooden walls, where dignitaries from different houses and nations stood waiting for him. There were kings and queens, presidents and prime ministers, admirals, generals, and politicians. The guards guided him to the center of the room and turned to leave after they reached their destination. Through the crowd, Ra and Ixchel, in an elegant black-and-red tuxedo and dress, approached to direct everyone's attention to him.

"This is our son, Scar Amun, and he is here for his soul viewing," Ra announced, and then he and Ixchel stepped back.

"Is he truly at the tenth density?" a politician asked from the crowd.

Ixchel nodded at Jamarcus, and he felt what his mother wanted him to do. With a thought, he entangled the room with the Space Between. Everyone was able to see the Sea of Universes and could also see the universes curving under Aten Ka that Jamarcus was passively linked to. When Jamarcus felt that everyone in the room was satisfied, he returned the room to its original state.

A large reptilian general dressed in a black uniform approached Jamarcus with his mind focused on military discipline. He placed a hand on Jamarcus's head and poured energy into his light, just as Ra had done to him months before. The energy flowed through him like a high-powered hose as the general tried to pump as much as he could. When he saw that Jamarcus wasn't fazed, he nodded in approval and walked back into the crowd.

"Yes indeed," Jamarcus whispered to himself, trying to keep from laughing. A group of Zetas moved toward Jamarcus next. They stood and examined him, noting his height, body dimensions, and mental state. One also pushed energy through Jamarcus to see how much energy he could channel. They stopped as quickly as the general and went back with the other dignitaries, discussing their observations.

One after another, each person in the room greeted Jamarcus. Many congratulated him on his achievement of reaching the tenth density. Others told him about their relationships with his parents.

"Hello, Scar," a Lyran, a feline species, said as she approached Jamarcus. She wore a dark green dress that contrasted nicely against her red- and black-spotted fur. "My name is Hecate. My husband, Shou, is the speaker of his house. He used to be in the service with your mother."

"Did he?" Jamarcus asked to be nice.

"Yes. They used to be close friends, but he said your mother can be a bit too focused. Viciously focused. He thought he was in love with her at some point, but that hardness in her kept driving him away. I'm happy, or I wouldn't have met my husband."

"She can be like that, but there is love behind her strictness," Jamarcus said. "I love when she's like that with me. Maybe it's because I served in the military back on Earth."

"Maybe. Shou wasn't cut out for the service. He only served his mandatory ten cycles. But all things happen for a reason, as they say. It was nice to meet you, Scar Amun. I wish you much success in the future."

As she walked away, Jamarcus's soul eased when he saw Psssh walking toward him, shouldered by two other Kaggen. Jamarcus felt the unease that Psssh and his people gave the rest of the group, which made him feel more comforted as Psssh stepped up to him and placed his black hands on his shoulders. Jamarcus soaked in the pride and fatherly love shining from him.

"I, Psssh, hereby declare that Scar Amun, when in union with my daughter, Achoo, shall be our new god-king, and through their union, he will be our king father to give birth to a new race. Henceforth, your name shall be Sonlig. May we be blessed by your light."

Jamarcus stood silently during Psssh's short speech, feeling the pride pouring out of his light. When Push was done, Jamarcus waved for him to bend down so he could grab his head and place his forehead against his.

"Can you stay like this for a moment?" Jamarcus asked.

"Sure," Psssh said. As they stood with foreheads touching, Jamarcus could feel that the crowd was unsure what Psssh would do to him. Oddly, the prejudice he felt from the dignitaries toward Psssh somehow made everything feel normal to Jamarcus. He stood there holding on to Push, soaking in the emotion of family that shone from inside his light.

<2>

June 2012

"I'm dumbfounded that you still don't believe we exist," Ra told Jamarcus.

"That's the only thing that has kept me sane throughout this ordeal," Jamarcus said. "I would have killed myself years ago if I hadn't stayed a little skeptical."

"Yet you believe in Thor and Athena."

"I don't believe in them. I hope I can meet them someday."

"But here we are in the Space Between," Ra said. "We are looking at Aten Ka as it molds and creates universes as others fade away. You've met your mother, Bernini, Rhiannon, and me. You've been to Sneeze's home world and seen her father. You've seen dozens of worlds and multiple universes so far. None of that has convinced you that we are real?"

"It could be real," Jamarcus said. "Or it could be severe schizophrenic visions that a war veteran is using to cope with his PTSD."

"Then why go through all of this?" Ra asked.

"Just to find my paradise," Jamarcus answered.

"I have to say, you not believing in us is insulting," Ra said with a roll of his eyes.

"It shouldn't be," Jamarcus said. "Any person who thinks only of himself would believe he's the most important person in the universe after meeting you and being told what you've told me. And he would use what you told him for his gain, with no regard or love for you. I stay grounded, relying only on what I feel, and throw away anything I can't explain.

"Yet I still don't know that you are real. I don't know if you are a tenth-dimensional being. Everything I've seen, touched, heard, tasted, and smelled could have been made up. But I felt your love for me. The love that all of you have for me. I feel how you all treat me as a child or sibling. I adore Sneeze like a little sister. And that could still be an illusion. I just don't have any hard evidence that what is happening is real."

"Isn't that enough?" Ra asked with anger brewing in his light. "Isn't our love for you enough to believe in us?"

"It is," Jamarcus said. "It's the only thing that is important. But I don't believe in you; I know you. I know Mama, Bernini, and Rhiannon. I remember Thor and Athena. I know Posh and Sneeze. I know where I'm going to go after I die. I know the houses I will live in, who my family will be, and who I will marry and have kids with. I know—or I hope I know. It isn't any better than belief, but I hope you can feel in my light the difference."

"I do," Ra said. "It still discomforts me. Much like how you were during your soul viewing."

"That was different. I felt like a piece of meat in their eyes. Only a handful of them showed any inclination of treating me as a means instead of an end."

"They see you as a god. They all showed love for you in their way."

"I saw that," Jamarcus said. "My time on Earth has jaded me to the concept of God. I have come to my selfish conclusion that God only serves the purpose of placing whatever culture worships that specifically defines God at the center of the universe. Everyone else has to kiss their ass for any kind of grace from such a God."

"You know that Aten Ka is not like that," Ra said. "Yes, Aten Ka may be defined differently in different cultures. Yet that light is in every sentient being. With the sacrifice of the material, we all can have Aten Ka shining brightly in us."

"That is the core of the problem on Earth," Jamarcus said. "The overarching culture in the Federation is that we are all Aten Ka. Kuku-lkan told me something right before I went through the soul viewing. He said the people loved me because they saw the potential that was in them. That what I did was something they could do. They can see the light that could be inside them. It just requires change and sacrifice, like you said.

"But on Earth, God is used as an excuse not to change. We be-lieve we are not equal to God. We believe God created man to use the earth however we want. That we are the only sentient beings in our singular universe. Even those who don't believe in God think that. God even sent a sacrifice for our sins. We created all these myths in our minds to support the illusion that we don't have to change."

"That is just a phase that any civilization goes through as they collectively become more in tune with Aten Ka," Ra said. "That para-digm will pass, and a new one will come when humanity will see their place in Aten Ka."

"I doubt that," Jamarcus said. "I don't mean to be pessimis-tic, but humans will do anything to keep themselves from changing. God is tied to the belief that he will save our souls from death. Be-lieve in him, change to fit in with the culture that believes in God, and everything is okay.

"Those who reject that notion reject the concept of God entire-ly. They say that the material, technology, and science will save us. Don't worry about souls or death. Just believe in us, change to fit in with the culture of people who understand science better than you, and everything is okay. They don't realize how much they sound like each other."

"Why don't you tell everyone what Aten Ka is?" Ra said. "They may listen to you. If you can change one person's opinion, that's all you can ever hope to accomplish."

"Yes, you're right," Jamarcus said. "I don't think I can do that. There are already other people in the world who are doing what you're telling me to do. They have found their niche, but it isn't enough. Either they are completely rejected, or they are used to justify someone's previous religion and the meaning of their words is changed to fit another person's purpose. I'm huge on change. And everyone must change, or we all don't."

"You doubt yourself," Ra said. "Your ability to change someone's life. That you can make a difference for a person's light."

"No, I just don't want to be some guru or teacher," Jamarcus said. "I've been in the military. Fought through war. It will always be a part of me. I can't change that. If I were to teach people, it would be like boot camp: fast, meditate, go vegan, astral travel, and meet aliens. Do it, buttercup—no excuses. Don't ask for help; suck it up, and do it. I'm not cut out for that."

"You just weren't shown how to show your love to others," Ra said. "You can tell everyone your story. How we love you."

"That's the real problem I have," Jamarcus said. "Let's take that step by step. The main plot of such a story is that a male black human meets aliens who tell him he will become a white prince after he dies. It doesn't matter that I will be an alien; that's all they'll choose to hear and see."

"It isn't about what you will become," Ra said. "It's about Aten Ka."

"But humanity won't see that. First, let's take the black part. Because we are focused on the material, many will believe you are contacting me because I'm black. They won't believe or choose to understand that it's my light that's important.

"Next is the changing-of-the-race part. Papa, you are an alien. I know you see yourself as Aten Ka, but others will only see you as a white man, not as an alien species. And because they see you as white, then you must be justification for white ethnic groups and their culture. Not to mention those who will attack me for the idea of changing from black to white."

"That's ridiculous," Ra scoffed. "When my light was on Earth, I was African. I was a slave to those whose skin color was white. Why would we justify those who are white?"

"They don't care, Papa," Jamarcus said. "Remember what I said: God is justification for someone not changing. If I tell people I will become a white male, even though I will be an alien, they will hear it as my saying everyone has to adopt white culture.

"And finally, we get to the death part. To put it plainly, you are asking me to commit suicide. I know you disagree on this, but to choose to go through a process that will shorten my life on Earth has major ethical issues, no matter what civilization we speak of. Regardless of what I say, the mass majority will be scared off by the fact that all I've done will only be reciprocated when I die. If I try to reorient the focus back to the life one will have after death in the third density, religious factions will hear that as an attack on them—and it is. Just as many will say it would be pointless to give up so much on Earth for something after you die. Where is the proof? Even if I try to explain that my situation is unique and will happen to hardly any other individuals, no one will care.

"We place value on the dumbest things on Earth—skin color, hair, facial features, how much money we have, what country we live in, what our religion is. We focus on believing we are all different instead of knowing we are all the same. The only way to know we are the same is to understand the light, and that requires change from all of us."

"Then explain to them what the light is," Ra said. "You are a tenth-density light. Few in the multiverse can explain it better than you."

"But it won't do me any good if I can't prove the light exists," Jamarcus said. "If I try to explain it using culture or spirituality, I will get backlash from the bullies with muscles. People will say, 'You're a sacrilegious hack; you're trying to make your cult.' That alone will keep me from getting my point across. If I try using science to explain what Aten Ka is, I run into the bullies with books. I'm nowhere near good enough in math to explain what I've seen with the light. Aten Ka is the ideal line, or infinity, from what I can guess. The math for the ideal line is already established, and they will say I'm only repeating something already told. And I don't have the education to describe the loops of light in us."

"The only thing I hear is excuses," Ra said. "It seems that for you to tell everyone about Aten Ka, you have to change."

Jamarcus took in a sharp breath and slowly let it out, shamefully agreeing with Ra in his heart. "I am human," he said.

"Still an excuse."

"Papa?"

"Yes, Scar?"

"You said you were a black slave on Earth. Do you remember that?"

"Vividly," Ra said. "I was born in a small village next to the ocean. It was a simple life, but I was happy. My father was a fisherman. He took me out to the ocean with him a handful of times to teach me how to fish. I don't remember his name. And it still hurts too much for me to look through Aten Ka to know it.

"Raiders from another country captured my family one night while we were sleeping. They killed my father by accident and just threw his body aside like it was garbage. They chained up my mom, my sister, and me and dragged us with others in our village for days until we got to a shipyard. It was there where I first saw a white person while on Earth.

"The raiders exchanged bottles of alcohol for us, and then I was taken from my mother and sister and brought onto a ship. My mother screamed so loud. I didn't think a human being could scream like that. I was on that ship for more days than I could count. I was sick all the time. People were dying around me, and the crew would throw the dead overboard.

"When we reached the end of the trip, I was yanked out of the ship and put on a block, where I saw a group of more white people trade us for some barrels. Then I was yanked again onto a cart and driven to a farm. Those next twelve years were a nightmare. I was beaten for days for not being able to speak English. Then I was made to work picking tobacco for hours. And because I didn't understand

English enough, I couldn't understand the instructions I was given sometimes, and I would get beaten more for messing up.

"It wasn't the white farmer who beat me. It was a black overseer. I now know that he took his frustration out on us, but I couldn't understand why he was so angry. And he focused his rage on me many times. I was young and skinny, and it seemed he would take his frustration out on us young boys when the farmer got mad at him or told him what to do.

"One day, out in the field, he struck me while I had a pitchfork in my hand, and I snapped. I plunged it into his chest. I can still feel it now, how it slowly went through him, and the air exploded out of him. I ran from the farm. I ran and ran through the forest for days, cold and hungry.

"I ended up coming across an Indian village one day and begged them for food. That's how I ended up being a slave for them. They treated me just as badly as the white people did. I dealt with so much abuse for food and shelter. Months later, I fought back against anyone who tried to make me do anything, and I was driven from their village.

"I lay on the forest floor that night and cried out in my soul for anyone who would love me like my father did. That's when my mother, Scar, and my father, Amun, took my soul up and told me who they were and who I was. I lashed out at them just as you lashed out at us. I just saw someone who looked like the people who'd hurt me. But for the next few years, they taught me slowly about Aten Ka and what I needed to do to make it shine in my light.

"I gained the trust of the village again. Maybe they thought it was wrong to have someone starving so close to them, inviting bad karma. I did my part to help them but without truly being part of them. But I was happy with my parents. I lived that way until my life burned out in my human form, and I joined them."

"You still feel that pain," Jamarcus said, seeing Ra's sorrow in his light. "Do you think it will ever go away?"

"*Bado naweza kuhisi minyororo Hadi mimi,*" Ra said, rubbing his wrists and shaking his head. "*Nadhani haytapita kamwe.*"

"Yeah, I thought not." Jamarcus sighed. "But your parents' love is what got you through. I feel that. Earth's culture says that God shows his love to you by blessing you with material gifts. I've learned that God shows he loves you by revealing himself to you and saying with his light that he loves you."

Ra smiled down at Jamarcus as he watched the flowing universes below them. "Love you, Scar," he said.

"Love you, Papa."

Chapter 23
<1>
December 21, 2012

"So let me get this straight," Jamie said after she took a sip from her beer. "You were friends with us this whole time we were going to school, and you waited until we graduated to tell us your sister is Vanessa?"

"It wasn't important," Jamarcus said with a shrug while playing with his dog tags.

"How is that not important?" Joe exclaimed.

"It's not." Jamarcus yawned, trying to shake his fatigue. "Besides, you guys are the ones who found out. I don't tell anyone that."

"That's because she told everyone on television who you are," Eric said as he slapped the bar. "It was on TV the other day."

"It was?"

"Yes!" Robert, Jamie, and Joe shouted.

"I don't watch television, so there you go," Jamarcus said as he drank from his water bottle.

"So you had no idea she was going to talk about you on TV?" Joe asked.

"She called me last week," Jamarcus said as he looked at the crowd in the bar, who were getting excited about a college football game.

"She said that in her interview," Joe said, rubbing his forehead. "All this time, I could have talked to Vanessa. I worship her. No wonder you look so hot."

"Yeah, that's the reason," Jamarcus joked. "Because I look like a chick. I'd rather have someone say I look like a plain-looking guy."

"You know what I mean," Joe said.

"And this whole time, you were busting your butt going to school and work," Jamie said. "Doing overtime and having no sleep. You could have asked your sister for help, and you didn't."

"Why should I?" Jamarcus asked.

"Because she's a multimillionaire—that's why," Jamie said, confounded.

"I had the GI Bill," Jamarcus said. "There's no need for help. Besides, I'm not that close to my family."

"She said that too," Robert said as he pulled out his cell phone. "I can pull up the interview right here."

"So tell me about your brother Jamarcus," the interviewer said to Vanessa on Robert's phone.

"I haven't talked with him in over ten years—since 1996, to be exact."

"That long?" the interviewer asked.

"Yeah, I know. We weren't that close growing up. Jamarcus was so smart. He was able to read my mom's college books on physics and quantum mechanics when he was eight years old. I was only focused on Madonna or Whitney Houston, and I made fun of him for it. I wish I hadn't."

"Why did you want to talk about him?"

"Because he's a war veteran. He served in Iraq and Afghanistan. I had some fans send me fan mail saying they'd served with him and how much they admired him. One fan wrote that in the middle of an ambush in Mosul, he stayed completely calm and got everyone out of it alive. He wrote that he lost his arm in that fight, but my brother dragged him out of there and kept telling him he was going to be fine."

"Wow," the interviewer said.

"I know. My brother's a hero. I believe he was awarded the Silver Star for that fight. That's what one of my fans wrote. So I wanted to dedicate my New Year's Eve concert to all the veterans out there, and I invited four hundred army soldiers to watch me perform. Just to say thanks to them and my brother."

"Does he know about the concert?" the interviewer asked.

"I don't know. I tried calling him with the number my parents gave me, but he never answered," Vanessa said.

"Do you think he's suffering from PTSD?"

"He could be. I wish I knew. That's why I wish I hadn't made fun of him while growing up. You know the whole ancient alien theory that's gotten popular lately? My brother came up with the same idea when he was a kid. He told me one day that UFOs must have visited Egypt and the Mayans. That's why they both built pyramids. I teased him so hard for that, and he didn't even talk to me. Now I hear he's this war hero, and I can't tell him I'm proud of him."

"Well, I hope this concert will tell him and the whole world how much you love him," the interviewer said.

"Me too, Cici," Vanessa said with a smile.

"Holy shit, dude," Robert said as he looked at Jamarcus. "You got a Silver Star?"

"Yeah, I don't talk about that," Jamarcus groaned. "It happened when I was attached with some Green Berets for a raid in Mosul. It was bad intel on our side. Goddamn setup."

"You're a hero," Jamie said in awe.

"Every war vet's a hero," Jamarcus told her.

"Sorry, dude," Jamie said.

"Don't sweat it. I didn't even think about that fight until now. I don't think about a lot that happened out there. Except for the really bad stuff. Can't get that shit out of my head—civilian casualties, kids used as suicide bombers. That shit stays with me."

"I can't imagine," Robert said.

"Don't," Jamarcus responded. "You're better off."

"Your sister said you used to study ancient alien theory," Joe said. "Is that why you're so into aliens?"

"Hell yeah!" Jamarcus yelped, ready to change the subject. "I was hardcore into that. I love science fiction. Watched everything. *Alien* was the movie that made me realize I liked girls. Sigourney Weaver in that wet wifebeater and panties—I went through puberty in thirty seconds after seeing that.”

“I think I saw a UFO when I was young,” Jamie said.

“When was that?” Jamarcus asked eagerly.

“It was when I was in elementary school. My dad used to take me and my sister fishing in the bay by here all the time. I loved doing that. I’ve got to ask my dad to take me next year when it gets warmer.

“So one late afternoon, me and my sister were trying to put some bait on the fishing hook. We wanted to see if we could catch anything with our sandwiches, and my dad was laughing his ass off as we cast it in. Then my sister saw an orange orb going across the bay. My dad said it must have been the reflection of the sun, but we were so wrong.

“The orb was going in one direction. Then it stopped for a minute and went back the way it had come. Then it went underwater without making any waves in the bay. It did that for a good amount of time, moving back and forth and in and out of the water. Then it went into the water and never came out. Never told anybody that until now.”

“Holy shit, that was awesome,” Jamarcus said.

“That’s got to be one of the most dope things someone has told me,” Robert said.

“I would have freaked out if I saw that,” Joe said.

“Yeah, me too,” Robert said.

“Did you take any pictures?” Jamarcus asked.

“You know, we tried to do that,” Jamie said. “It disappeared just as my sister thought of getting her camera out."

"Anyone else has a UFO story since we're talking about it?" Joe asked.

"I do," Jamarcus said. He paused when the bar crowd howled in disappointment at a play in the football game. "This happened on the night when I last talked to my sister."

"Holy shit, dude." Robert sighed.

"I know. What a coincidence. Anyway, my mom was getting up my ass about me wanting to go to my friend's house to play *Dungeons and Dragons* when my sister had a performance at Georgetown."

"You didn't want to go?" Joe asked in shock.

"Yeah, I did, but my mom didn't want me and my brothers to go," Jamarcus said. "She wanted me to stay home and show my support for her. My mom was crazy like that. So I was lying in my bed, pissed off at my mom, when I saw a light in the sky. I looked closer at it, and I saw other lights flying around. I went out into my back-yard, dragging my brothers and dad with me. They were freaking out and went back inside after a few minutes. Later on, when I asked them about the lights, they didn't even remember seeing them or being out-side the house."

"Nothing?" Jamie asked.

"Nope."

"Man, that's creepy," Joe said with a shudder.

"Wait—it gets even weirder," Jamarcus said after a yawn. "So while I was watching the lights, they started flying through the air at speeds past Mach One, I swear. And they flew in patterns you'd find on a graph in calculus. The lights moved in that way in precise patterns, and I was thinking, *I wish I had done better in math to write down what I'm seeing.*"

"Really? Math?" Jamie grumbled. "Don't talk to me about math. Graduating with an electrical engineering degree was a nightmare."

"My bad." Jamarcus laughed. "So anyway, it started getting cold, and I went back inside to watch the lights in my room. I thought I'd only been out there for about thirty minutes, but my dad and brothers told me I was out there for over two hours."

"I've heard of that," Robert said. "That's called missing time."

"Right," Jamarcus said. "I went back into my room to watch the lights, but they disappeared while I was looking at them."

"Wow, that's straight up a close encounter of the third kind," Joe muttered.

"First kind," Jamarcus said. "I study this shit. This is the first time I've told anyone this myself. I figured I'd never meet anyone who would be interested in it."

"I think it's fascinating," Joe said with a sigh. "There's no way we are alone in the universe. There has to be something else out there with us."

"I think so too," Jamie said. "I think about that light I saw and just know it was an alien craft spying on me and my family."

"Who knows?" Jamarcus said, rubbing his eyes to stay awake.

"What do you mean 'Who knows?'" Jamie said. "How can you

see those lights in the sky and not think they're aliens out there?"

"Because all I saw was lights," Jamarcus said. "I study this, and the worst thing that experiencers do is jump to the conclusion that what they saw was aliens. I saw lights in the sky. I lost track of time. The lights moved in specific patterns. If I am to report what I saw, I have to say exactly what I saw—nothing more. To do so is to put conjecture or belief into the equation, and I don't work in belief. Only in what I know."

"You didn't want to tell the news?" Robert asked.

"I almost forgot about what happened to me," Jamie said.

"It wouldn't have done any good to tell them either," Jamarcus said. "The media have a strict policy of denying that what a person saw was a UFO and ridiculing the person from coming forward. It's routine."

"That would be crazy if aliens did show up on Earth," Robert said. "Why would they come here anyway?"

"My friend talks about that," Joe said. "She said she's a Starseed. They're people whose souls were once aliens, and they came to Earth for their spiritual growth and to help the people on Earth through the ascension. She said she was a Lyran, a catlike alien species. She said her alien soul looks like a tiger."

"Wow," Jamie said, wide-eyed. "That is something else."

"That's what she said," Joe said. "I believe her. She is a spiritual person. She is so loving and bright. I admire her for having the guts to tell people about her life. You guys should do that."

"I don't think so," Jamie said. "I hardly know what I saw."

"What about you, Jamarcus?" Joe asked.

"I wrote a book," Jamarcus said as he tapped his chest to keep his mind off the numbness. "My father told me I should write down what I saw and my hypothesis on UFOs."

"You talk to your dad, but you don't want to talk to your sister," Robert said.

"Relationships should be based on experiences instead of blood. I have had good experiences with my father. Not so much with my family."

"You should try to," Joe said.

"Yeah, you're right," Jamarcus said with a yawn.

"Dude, you need to go home," Jamie said as she watched Jamarcus. "You're barely staying awake."

"I think that's a good idea," Jamarcus said as he got up and placed money on the bar. "I've got work tomorrow night anyway, so I should get as much sleep as I can."

"You're going to ride your bike in the cold like that?" Joe asked.

"Yeah," Jamarcus said as he got his gear and helmet from the bartender. "I've seen guys in Afghanistan carry their whole life on the back of a bike."

"That's because we can afford cars," Robert said.

"I can give you a ride home if you're tired," Joe said.

"That's okay. I wake right up when I'm on the road. Thanks anyway, Joe."

"Bye, Jamarcus," Jamie called out as he walked out of the bar and to his bike.

It didn't take long for Jamarcus to get his gear on and get on the road to his apartment. He took his time as he drove, wary of the drivers at that time of night. When he got home and into his apartment, he sat down in his chair in front of his television, waiting for the bike engine to cool off.

He remained quiet in the chair, breathing in and out slowly, embracing the numbness and cold in his chest. He was about to fall asleep right there, when one of his neighbors drove by, and the bass from the car rattled Jamarcus's walls. He slowly got up, his knees popping as he did, and went out to put a tarp on his bike. When he returned to his apartment, he took off his clothes, put his pajamas on, and crawled into bed. He easily fell asleep. Numbness spread through his body, easing his bodily pain. His breathing slowed, and he unconsciously snorted in the air when he didn't get enough breath. Then his body came to a peaceful rest as his breathing came to a stop.

<2>

The first thing Jamarcus saw in the darkness was a single loop of light. As it spun around, more light loops formed inside the first one. When Jamarcus could see ten loops over a small spool of light, his vision was swallowed up by that light, and he was in the Matrix. He sped uncontrollably through it, falling and rising, swinging forward, backward, and to his sides. A tunnel formed in the spheres, and he flowed through it until his vision was once again filled with light and then suddenly went dark.

After a while, Jamarcus tried to look around in the dark, and he noticed he was able to move his head. When he opened his eyes, he saw that he was inside a glass-encased bed. When he tried to reach up to touch the glass, he had a hard time moving his arm. As he turned to look at his arm, he saw a white sleeve that firmly covered a pudgy form, with only his pink-freckled pale white hand showing. Jamarcus filled up his body with light to move his arm and touched the glass, and the cover opened at the touch of his fingertips.

Jamarcus struggled to get out of bed, lifted himself out with his mind, and settled on the floor. He landed on his toes and stumbled about before he got used to standing on them. He looked about and saw that he was in the nursery. He looked at the crib. He remembered crawling under the crib when his parents first brought it home, and with that first memory, an ocean of others flooded inside his light.

He remembered playing with the toys in that room and his father getting mad at him for playing with them so hard. He remembered the first time he had seen Sneeze, who'd taken him to the tree hole, where they'd played with toys she'd brought with her. Jamarcus walked around the nursery, picking up other items he remembered: his favorite book about a boy and his portable wormhole that took him to different places, a ball he used to throw about the room, and a Federation scout craft that looked like a small winged plane with a long nose that he used to pretend he flew in as a marine.

After walking over and grabbing the scout plane, Jamarcus inspected the rest of his body. He looked at his pale arm. His legs were just as chubby, and he stood on the tiptoes of slender feet. He couldn't see a zipper or Velcro that indicated how to get out of his onesie, but he decided to worry about that later. He walked out of the nursery, wanting to look around the chateau. He began to fly when he decided to go to his parents' room.

"No flying in the house," Ixchel told Jamarcus in his light, and Jamarcus dropped back down onto the wooden floor. "Be careful, Scar. Your father and I will be there as quick as we can," she said, and with that, Jamarcus walked through the hallways until he found his parents' room.

It didn't look as if anyone slept in the room at all. The furniture looked more decorative than useful. Seeing an adult-sized mirror, he walked over to it to look at himself. He was the boy from the dark room, with wild blond hair covering his eyes. When he moved his hair, he saw that his eyes were the same blue as before, almost glowing in their intensity. They also looked larger than the rest of the features of his face.

Jamarcus turned to his father's chest in the corner of the room. Ra had told him about the items in the chest when he first mentioned the process of ascension. When Jamarcus opened it, he saw clothing made from brown leather and jewelry made of opals and strings. He saw a rusty chain with cuffs at the ends and a doll that looked as if it belonged to a little girl.

Satisfied with what he'd found, he left the room to explore more of the chateau. Just as he walked out the door, he heard footsteps running toward him. Bernini appeared, his sky-blue skin shining with delight that his little brother had come home. Feeling his joy made Jamarcus laugh, and the light inside shone from him like a high-intensity bulb. Happiness inside him poured out in a way he hadn't felt since he was a teenager playing *Dungeons and Dragons*. He danced on his toes, clapping his hands, when Bernini scooped him up and kissed him on the cheek. Jamarcus tried to push his face away, but Bernini kept pecking away at his face.

"Come on. I'm going to take you to the tree," Bernini said in Andean as he carried Jamarcus through the chateau. "I want you to stay there until Mommy and Daddy come home."

"I want to walk," Jamarcus said clumsily, not able to control his mouth properly.

"No, Mommy told me to take care of you," Bernini said with authority, and Jamarcus felt the sincerity in his light. Jamarcus grudgingly agreed and allowed Bernini to carry him until they came to the center of the house, where the tree stood in a circular open-air room. Jamarcus looked up to see the sky beginning to light up the white walls with the rising sun.

"Stay here, and read your book," Bernini told Jamarcus as he placed him in the hole under the tree, which was filled with soft grass and pillows. Bernini put a children's book in his hand and stepped out, giving him a final stern look. "I'm going to get you some cookies and something to drink. Stay right here, okay?"

"Okay," Jamarcus said, and Bernini walked off.

The cover of the book showed a green Kaggen child with black eyes in a disk-shaped craft with a glass canopy flying down toward a small moon where an Andean child stood waving at him. Jamarcus remembered that it was a book Sneeze had made for him. Opening it, he saw pages of pictures showing the Kaggen child and the Andean child having fun in different worlds. The text was written in the same language that appeared on Psssh's ships. The book was able to place the words in his mind so he could read it, which disappointed him a bit. Jamarcus wanted to be able to read the language without assistance.

Putting the book down and looking around in the tree, he decided he wanted to go out to the back of the chateau and walk along the beach. He waited patiently until Bernini came back with a bowl of oval-shaped dark cookies and an orange plastic cup that looked like it was made in the 1970s.

"I want to go out to the beach," Jamarcus said before biting into a cookie. Its taste was a mixture of chocolate and strawberry.

"No, Mommy wanted me to keep you safe," Bernini said as he sat next to him and took a cookie for himself. Jamarcus sipped from the cup, which was filled with a deep red liquid. The taste was tart but sweet enough that it was also refreshing. The taste and smell of the snack made Jamarcus's body tingle with joy. He couldn't help but be happy and wanted to run around.

"I'm not going to do anything wrong," Jamarcus said as he gobbled up the rest of the cookies.

"No," Bernini adamantly said.

"Let him go to the beach," Ra said in their minds. "Just watch over him."

"Fine." Bernini relented with a sigh.

After he got permission, Jamarcus slurped down the rest of his drink, placed the bowl and cup on the grass, and ran out of the tree and toward the rear door of the chateau.

"You can't leave your cup and bowl here!" Bernini said after Jamarcus. "Bugs will crawl all over the tree."

"Just place them in the kitchen sink," Ixchel said in their lights, but Jamarcus's mind was focused on going outside. He couldn't contain the energy bouncing around inside him; every thought he came up with was filled with boundless enthusiasm. He burst through the door and onto the forest path, dashing between the trees, imagining himself as a marine, as he had when he'd played with Sneeze long ago. He ran around so carefree that he tripped and fell on his face in a lump.

"Be careful," Ixchel told Jamarcus, but he wasn't paying any mind to her. He was free, with none of the pain of his human body. He could feel happiness again, like a bottomless pool that fueled everything he did. His laughter was like a drug, giving his body pleasure as he heard it bouncing around the trees.

"Scar, come to the beach," Bernini said, and Jamarcus ran as fast as he could toward him on the dirt path. Jamarcus couldn't stop himself and ran into him, making them both giggle. It didn't take long for Bernini to lead Jamarcus to the beach, which was spotted with large stones that protruded out of the sand. Jamarcus was about to climb up onto the large, slanted stone at the end of the path when he saw someone flying toward them out of the sky.

Rhiannon floated down wearing white slacks and a buttoned collared shirt with a red vest. When she landed in her red shoes, she ran straight to Jamarcus and yanked him up, squeezing him tightly in her arms. Jamarcus felt longing, joy, excitement, and a small bit of sorrow shine from her light, and he held on to her neck just as tightly, not wanting to let go.

"You're home! You're home," Rhiannon said into his ear, and

when she held him up in the air, Jamarcus saw tears falling from her eyes, which he tried to dry with his hands. She carried him over to the large stone, and they saw Ra and Ixchel standing at the end of the path. Ra held Ixchel in his large arms. Once seated, Jamarcus kicked at the water that washed over his feet. He couldn't feel the cold from it, but it was soothing to have the ocean slip over his skin. Bernini and Rhiannon splashed water over Jamarcus's legs, enjoying hearing him squeal with laughter each time.

It was then that Jamarcus felt two more people shift in close to them. Turning toward the other end of the beach, he saw Thor and Athena walking toward the family, wearing navy blue military-style uniforms. Jamarcus felt the aching sorrow and longing from them, and his happiness grew inside when he saw them, causing his light to become a solid bright white orb that covered his body. Jamarcus cried from the joy of seeing them, like a child seeing a loved friend he hadn't seen in a long time.

"It's okay," Rhiannon said as she picked him up, wiping his tears from his face.

Jamarcus stopped crying, realizing how silly he have must looked crying like a little boy—and then it sank in that he was a little boy. *For better or for worse*, Jamarcus told himself. Reaching out with his hand, he shifted the letter Kathrine had given him when he left Hawaii and his dog tags from the army out of his apartment and onto a shelf in the nursery. With a deep sigh of relief, Jamarcus finally made an important decision.

"I'm home," Scar said.